A Season for Tending

Amish Vines and Orchards Book 1

BOOKS BY CINDY WOODSMALL

ADA'S HOUSE series
The Hope of Refuge
The Bridge of Peace
The Harvest of Grace

SISTERS OF THE QUILT series
When the Heart Cries
When the Morning Comes
When the Soul Mends

NOVELLAS
The Sound of Sleigh Bells
The Christmas Singing
The Scent of Cherry Blossoms

NONFICTION
*Plain Wisdom: An Invitation into an Amish Home
and the Hearts of Two Women*

A Season for Tending

Amish Vines and Orchards Book 1

CINDY WOODSMALL

New York Times Best-Selling Author

WATERBROOK
PRESS

A SEASON FOR TENDING
PUBLISHED BY WATERBROOK PRESS
12265 Oracle Boulevard, Suite 200
Colorado Springs, Colorado 80921

The characters and events in this book are fictional, and any resemblance to actual persons or events is coincidental.

ISBN 978-0-307-73002-2
ISBN 978-0-307-73003-9 (electronic)

Copyright © 2012 by Cindy Woodsmall

Cover design by Kelly L. Howard; photography by Kelly L. Howard and Jutta Klee

All rights reserved. No part of this book may be reproduced or transmitted in any form or by any means, electronic or mechanical, including photocopying and recording, or by any information storage and retrieval system, without permission in writing from the publisher.

Published in the United States by WaterBrook Multnomah, an imprint of the Crown Publishing Group, a division of Random House Inc., New York.

WATERBROOK and its deer colophon are registered trademarks of Random House Inc.

Library of Congress Cataloging-in-Publication Data
Woodsmall, Cindy.
    A season for tending : a novel / Cindy Woodsmall.—1st ed.
        p. cm.
    ISBN 978-0-307-73002-2 (alk. paper)—ISBN 978-0-307-73003-9 (electronic)
    1. Amish—Fiction. I. Title.
    PS3623.O678S43 2012
    813'.6—dc23
                        2012021263

Printed in the United States of America
2012

10 9 8 7 6 5 4 3

In memory of Raymond Woodsmall Sr. (1897–1977)
and my father-in-law, Raymond Woodsmall Jr. (1922–2011)
and dedicated to Uncle Jack Woodsmall

These men are the original apple orchard overseers.

Apple orchards are a large part of the Woodsmall family history, and while writing the Amish Vines and Orchards series, I relied on the skilled experience and vivid recollections of a former apple farmer, Jack Woodsmall of Sterling, Massachusetts.

For nearly fifty years, Raymond Woodsmall Sr., my husband's grandfather, was an overseer of an apple orchard in Leominster, Massachusetts. My father-in-law and his younger brother Jack worked on that apple orchard from the time they were little boys until they left home to serve in the military.

That orchard is called Sholan Farms, and the original farmhouse was built in the 1730s. Although Raymond Woodsmall Sr. never owned the land or the house, he moved into the original farmhouse before the Depression as a young man in his prime and remained there as an overseer of the orchard until he was no longer capable of such hard work. He then made room for a younger overseer and moved from the original farmhouse to a smaller place on the land, but he continued helping with the orchard until a few years before he died.

My husband grew up making yearly visits with his family to that farmhouse where his grandparents lived, and he spent hours walking the orchard with his grandpa and sitting under apple trees, mesmerized by the stories his grandpa told. Our children sat around the dinner table listening to their dad share those same stories.

Grandpa Woodsmall saw the apple orchard through droughts, floods, blizzards, pestilence, and the worst tragedy of all, the Great Hurricane of 1938, which nearly destroyed the orchard. He and his two sons worked long, hard years to restore the apple trees.

Time passed, and his two sons joined the military. They never returned to work the orchard again.

In 1982 the house sustained damage from a fire, and what was left of the home was dismantled, sold, and shipped to unknown destinations. Later, the orchard was abandoned. It was during this time I first walked that land. While viewing the acres of dying trees, I longed for what had once existed.

Clearly others were stirred too. In 2001 the Sholan Farms Preservation Committee (SFPC) purchased the land. Soon afterward, a new group was formed, Friends of Sholan Farms (FOSF), and they took on the task of revitalizing as much of the orchard as possible. Today on twenty acres of the original sixty-acre farm is a thriving orchard where families from across the States can come and pick their own apples. The land now produces four thousand bushels of apples per year. I know Grandpa Woodsmall would be pleased.

Welcome to Amish Vines and Orchards.

Come with me into the Amish Country of Pennsylvania, into an apple orchard farmed in the same way Grandpa Woodsmall and his sons farmed all those years ago. Let's take a journey that will be a tapestry of what was, what is, and—perhaps—what will be.

ONE

It's time...

Emma's voice rose from the past, encircling Rhoda and bringing a wave of guilt. Unyielding, unforgiving guilt.

Rhoda plucked several large strawberries from the vine and dropped them into the bushelbasket. "Time for what?" she whispered.

The moment the words left her mouth, she glanced up, checking her surroundings. She quickly looked beyond the picket fence that enclosed her fruit and herb garden but saw no one. Her shoulders relaxed. When townsfolk or neighbors noticed Rhoda talking to herself, fresh rumors stirred. Even family members frowned upon it and asked her to stop.

It's time...

Emma's gentle voice echoed around her for a second time.

"Time for what?" Rhoda repeated, more a prayer to God than a question to her departed sister.

God was the One who spoke in whispers to the soul, not the dead. But whenever Rhoda heard a murmuring in her mind, it was Emma's voice. It had been that way since the day Emma died.

The sound of two people talking near the road caught Rhoda's attention. Surely *they* were real. She rose out of her crouch, pressing her bare feet into the rich soil, and went in the direction of the voices, passing the long rows of strawberries, blueberries, and blackberries and her trellises of raspberries and Concord grapes. Heady scents rode on the spring air, not just from the ripening fruits, but from her bountiful herb garden that yielded rosemary, sage, scarlet bergamot, and dozens of other plants she'd spent years cultivating. Dusting her palms together, she skirted the raised boxes that held the herbs and peered through a honeysuckle bush.

She was relieved to see actual people speaking to each other. Then she recognized them, and her fingertips tingled as her pulse raced. Her mother's eldest sister walked beside Rueben Glick, a man who wanted to make her life miserable.

"Surely her *Daed* will listen to me this time." Aunt Naomi clutched her fists tightly. "He indulges her. That's the real problem."

Rhoda had no doubt they were talking about her. Since Emma's death two years ago, the church leaders had avoided responding to all the trouble that Rhoda caused, however unintentional. They offered grace and mercy as her family tried to deal with their grief from the tragedy. But Rueben and Naomi made it their responsibility to keep Rhoda's family aware of how the Amish and non-Amish in Morgansville felt about her.

"I can bring a witness this time, more if need be." Rueben's tone was confident, with a familiar edge of bitterness.

More than anyone else in Morgansville, Rueben detested her. But unlike the others, he was only too happy to speak his mind directly to her and her family. And Rhoda knew why. He wanted to make her pay for turning his girlfriend against him. Rhoda had plenty of things to feel guilty for, but Rueben losing his girlfriend was not one of them.

Her aunt paused at the corner of the fence, studying Rhoda's house. "There should be no need for a witness, especially from those who are not Amish. The quieter we keep this matter, the better."

Rueben had found witnesses who weren't Amish? How? She tried her best to keep anyone from knowing her business. She never even shared with her family her comings and goings based on intuition. Dread pressed in on her, and she bit back her growing contempt for Rueben Glick.

"*Kumm.*" Her aunt crossed the driveway with Rueben right beside her. Naomi tapped on the screen door and waited. The fact that she didn't let herself in was a sign of the troubled feelings between her Daed and his sister-in-law.

Not counting Rhoda, six adults and five children were living in the house right now—her parents, two of her brothers, and their wives and children. Regardless which adult answered the door, Naomi and Rueben would take up matters concerning Rhoda with only her father.

Mamm came to the door and invited her sister and Rueben into the house.

Rhoda moved out from behind the honeysuckle bush, curiosity and anxiety mixing inside her. What accusation did Rueben have against her this time? Regardless of the new charge, this visit would put more tension inside an already overloaded household and would only isolate her more. No matter how many people lived with her or how deeply loyal they were, she stood on an island by herself, forbidden to acknowledge the largest part of who she was.

She meandered toward the gate, running her fingertips across the various herbs as she went. A few bloomed now, in May, but come July these plants would be bursting with vivid color. More important, they would provide people with natural relief from certain illnesses. She paused in front of the red clover, but despite its name, this particular clover was splashed with lovely purple blooms.

Many of these plants—the clover, dandelion, and thistle, to name a few— were considered nuisances. Like Rhoda herself. But each herb offered health benefits under the right circumstances. Maybe she was like them in that way too. Her people used to believe her, used to trust her with their health. If they would only give her a chance, perhaps she could help them again.

"Rhodes?"

She blinked, coming out of her thoughts and realizing that someone had been calling her name. She turned toward the road that ran along one side of her berry patch.

Landon was sitting in his old pickup on the main road, banging on the door. Officially, he worked for her, but he was also one of her few friends. "There she is, back from Oz again."

Although she hadn't seen the movie, he'd explained enough that she understood Oz was somehow connected to witches. And he was talking about it out loud, right here in the thick of busy Morgansville. She put her index finger to her lips.

Landon grinned. "Okay, I'm hushing—not that it'll do any good."

A short line of cars stacked up behind him, and someone honked. He drove forward twenty feet and pulled into her driveway. Once out of his truck, he walked toward her. "In my two years of working for you, I don't think I've ever seen you doing nothing while standing inside this garden." Before opening the gate, he grabbed one of the empty baskets stacked outside the picket fence. "What has you so distracted?"

She turned away and walked down the long path at the end of the rows. "Just wondering if I ordered enough canning supplies to last through the month." She kept her back to him so he couldn't read her face and know she was fibbing. She returned to her strawberry bush, crouched down, and began dumping more of the velvety fruit into her basket.

He went to the other side of the row and started picking. "You were studying the red clover. Rotating it out seems like it was a good idea. Looks like we'll get a bumper crop this year. That should give you lots for making that ointment."

"Ya," she mumbled, wishing she knew what was going on inside her house. Did Rueben have proof that she'd disobeyed the church authorities and her parents?

When the back door slammed, she jolted. But it was just one of her sisters-in-law taking another load of freshly cleaned diapers to the clothesline.

"First you're in la-la land, and then you jump at nothing. What gives, Rhodes?"

Landon knew her better than most. Emma had once known her best, but what good had that done Emma? If Rhoda had been half the sister Emma deserved, she would still be alive.

Rhoda moved the basket down the row. "How are things at the mail store today?" Maybe if she got him answering questions rather than asking them, she could avoid his probing. The tactic worked most days.

"Still slow. If the economy doesn't pick up soon, working for you may be the only job I have."

"I wish I could afford to pay you for more hours."

"Me too, although both of us in that tiny cellar working long hours week after week might cause one of us to disagree with the other, ya?" His grin lifted her spirits a little.

One of the things she enjoyed about Landon was his ability to speak his mind with total honesty. She loved truthfulness between people. Stark. Radiant. And powerful.

Unfortunately, it seemed to be in short supply—from her most of all.

"What's going on with you today?"

"Nothing."

"Don't lie to me, Rhoda."

His use of her real name caught her attention, and she turned to face him. He pointed at his eyes, demanding she look at him. "It's not your fault."

She stared at him. Would she ever be able to believe that? Since Emma's death, she hadn't found one moment when she could accept it as true. There was nothing she could do to free herself. And if he knew everything she did, he wouldn't say that to her.

Images flashed through her mind—fire trucks, policemen with guns strapped to their hips, groups of women whispering on the sidewalk. Even now, a crushing sense of guilt and panic rose within her again.

All her sister had wanted was for Rhoda to help her bake a cake for their Daed's birthday. And Rhoda had promised she would. Throughout the morning Emma kept asking Rhoda to stop weeding her garden and to go buy the items they needed. Even though she was seventeen years old, Emma hated going places by herself. Strangers frightened her. And Rhoda kept putting her off, assuring her they'd have a great time making the dessert when she was finished tending the garden.

Finally, fed up with waiting, in an unusual act of self-reliance, Emma stormed off to the store without Rhoda, her eyes filled with tears.

A strawberry flew through the air and hit Rhoda on the shoulder, followed in quick succession by a second and a third one. "Stay with me, Rhodes," Landon called to her.

She blinked. "Sorry."

"You tried to save her, almost broke your leg—"

"Rueben's here." Rhoda had no desire to listen to Landon's version of that day. She wasn't a hero. More like a murderer. And what she'd done had divided this town, making both Amish and *Englisch* distrust and fear her. "He's inside with my aunt Naomi."

Landon chuckled. "On a witch hunt again, I take it."

"That's not even a little bit funny, Landon."

"Come on, Rhodes. You know I tease because it's all so ridiculous. Gimme a smile. You can't change what they think. What's Rueben's problem now?"

"Remember when several Amish communities were at that regional function a couple of months ago?"

"Yeah. Your Mamm insisted you go, and you came back with your feathers ruffled at Rueben. But that's about all I know."

"He spent two days harassing me and making fun of me. On the second day he got bolder, saying things to me he shouldn't, in front of a large group of singles, including his girlfriend. He was being a bully, and I lashed out."

"What'd you say to him?"

She picked up her basket, ready to head toward the gate. "I looked into his eyes and knew a secret he wasn't telling anyone. His guilt was easy to see—if anyone had a mind to look. I called him on seeing another girl while he was out of state helping some Amish farmers. He denied it at first, but I knew when he was telling the truth and when he was lying by the guilt on his face. He thought that I'd spoken to the girl directly, that maybe she'd come to this area, and he owned up to his cheating. As I walked off, I let him know that I had no proof whatsoever, that he'd simply told on himself."

"Rhodes, you didn't."

At times she picked up on silly, nonsensical stuff without even realizing it—an aroma from someone's past or a distorted image in place of the person in front of her. But that didn't stop her from relying on a reasonable intuition when it came to her.

"He asked for it, taunting me, saying if I *knew* anything, Emma would still be alive. Daring me to tell his fortune. He was vicious, and I gave him what he deserved." She set the basket on the ground. "But ever since, I think he's been scheming ways to force me out of this garden. Biding his time and planning carefully. That's more wrong than anything I did to him. I make my living off these fruits."

Landon brushed a gnat away from his face. "You think he can do something to take away your business?"

She padded across the warm dirt to her raised beds of herbs, drawn to them like bees to pollen. This was her favorite part of the garden. The medicinal plants in particular. Each one had properties that could help people whose bodies hurt as much physically as her heart did emotionally. Whenever people were strengthened through the power of her herbs, she felt strengthened too.

Landon joined her.

"I followed my instincts again. And it sounds as if Rueben has proof."

Landon rolled his eyes. "Geez, Rhodes, why would you do that? You know you either have to do what your people expect or get out."

"And go where, Landon? To the Englisch? They fear me just as much as my people do."

"Then move somewhere else. Start new."

"And leave more holes in my parents' hearts? They've lost enough. I can't do something that selfish."

As she walked the row of herb beds, warm memories of her childhood, of laughter, and of fun-filled days rose within her. "I was seven when my Daed bought each of his daughters a blueberry bush and an herb plant. Did I ever tell you that?"

A slight grin lifted one side of his mouth. Nothing like being a paid employee who had to listen when the boss wanted to vent or reminisce. "You've only mentioned it a couple of times."

"He helped each of us plant his gifts. But as the days moved into weeks, my three teenage sisters were more interested in their friends or boys than gardening, and they neglected their gifts. Emma wasn't even four at the time, and she only cared about dolls and playing house. But I adored tending to those plants. And every birthday and Christmas since then, Daed has bought me at least one new bush, herb, or gardening tool." And every year that she proved faithful in what he'd given, he allowed her a little more land to expand her garden until she now had every spare inch of ground they owned.

"I understand why you don't want to leave your folks. But either keep a low profile and don't make waves in the community or be willing to leave. It's that simple."

She inhaled the sweet aroma of her apple mint plants. What a multipurpose herb. It repelled nuisance insects while attracting beneficial ones. Was flavorful in dozens of drinks. Aided indigestion and stomachaches. Eased the pain and swelling of insect bites. Relieved morning sickness in pregnant women. It was even alleged to calm the nerves and clear the head. She'd like to be in her cellar sipping a cup of mint tea right now.

"So what did you do this time, Rhodes?"

She thought back to the events that had probably led to this latest uprising. "Not long after I got back in town, I was on one of my long walks, and as I passed a home, I had a strong sensation to go up to the door. I stood on the sidewalk, trying to talk myself out of following that feeling. But I sensed the woman inside the house needed someone. So I rang the doorbell. We got to know each other a bit. She talked about feeling anxious and depressed, but I knew she'd been entertaining the idea of suicide. She's a young mom with three children and a husband who travels a lot. I took her some herbs. She's already doing better, and sometimes I wonder if it's the herbs or my regular visits that have helped her."

He rubbed his forehead. "As long as you don't tell people you helped her based on a premonition, it shouldn't be a problem."

"I've asked you before not to call it a premonition. I just have a little intuition, that's all. And at times it's clear enough for me to follow without botching up someone's life."

Landon peered at her over the rosemary. "Was she the only one recently?"

Rhoda pulled some leaves from the plant's thin stalk. "No."

He sighed.

She brought the leaves to her nose and drew a deep breath. "About six weeks ago I was at the grocery store in town, and the minute I saw this Englisch guy on the far end of an aisle, I knew in here"—she tapped her chest—"that he dealt with unbearable migraines."

"So you struck up a conversation and gave him some herbs too, didn't you?"

"What am I supposed to do? It's not something I choose to feel, but when I do, I act on it."

"You've been to see this man several times?"

"Ya, feverfew gives him some relief, and I purchased a bit of butterbur root. That seems to be helping too."

Landon's forehead crinkled. "And you think Rueben knows about all this?"

"I can't imagine how. I'm discreet."

"You're playing with fire, Rhodes. After exposing him as a cheater, damaging his reputation, and causing his girlfriend to break up with him, I'd say he'd plow your whole garden under if he could."

"Daed wouldn't let that happen to my garden."

"Yeah, well, maybe you should have thought about the possible consequences before you ruined Rueben's relationship with his girlfriend."

"Someone needed to tell her he was cheating on her." The faded blue geranium petals caught her attention. As an herb, geraniums were supposed to relieve anxiety, although no one could prove that by her. She did believe valerian to be potent, and maybe she should harvest some to fix a brew for herself.

Now that Landon knew what all she'd been up to the past two months, he could probably use a cup to settle his nerves too.

She heard men talking, and she turned to see her Daed, Rueben, and Naomi coming out of her home. If her Daed had been able to settle the matter, Rueben and Naomi would have left her house by themselves and gone home. Instead, the three of them were walking toward her, and now she would be pulled into the discussion too.

"It's time you head home, Landon." Her family appreciated Landon and his loyalty to her, but incidents among the Amish were not discussed in front of those who weren't Amish. Landon studied her for a moment before he pulled the keys out of his jeans pocket.

Her Daed, Naomi, and Rueben crossed the driveway toward her garden. Unwilling for Rueben Glick to set foot inside her sanctuary, she went toward the little white gate, Landon mere steps in front of her.

He held the gate for her. "Keep your head, Rhodes," he whispered. "You have to try to undo some of the damage."

TWO

Samuel put his forearms on the antique oak desk while he pored over the bills. The sweet scent of apple blossoms flowed in through his bedroom windows, riding on the May breeze, and the waning sunlight made shadows bob and dance across the paperwork. As he studied the numbers, he could hear his grandfather's voice rumbling aged wisdom: *Take care of the orchard, Samuel, and it'll take care of you. Never give up. Loyalty is the key.*

He missed his grandfather. It'd been eight years since he passed. But if he could see Kings' Orchard now, Samuel believed he'd be pleased. They'd suffered a few disappointing harvests in the last several years. That wasn't unusual for an orchard. But it'd been a good spring thus far, promising an excellent harvest. If Kings' Orchard could have a bountiful harvest this fall, he would ask Catherine to marry him.

Thunder rumbled in the distance, and the smell of rain mingled with the sweetness of apple blossoms. He tossed his pen onto the bills and walked to the window. He looked beyond the yard and the barns to the rolling hills filled with acres of apple trees, all of them lush with white and pink blossoms.

The image of his grandfather's rough, weathered hand reaching for the first ripe apple of the harvest was vivid. He always gave it to Samuel during his growing-up years. Always to him. Not to Samuel's grandmother or to his Daed or to Samuel's brothers. And *Daadi* would say, "A good man is loyal to what God has given him." Then he'd place the apple firmly in Samuel's palm as if bestowing on him the responsibility of the orchard and instilling in him the loyalty to see the job through.

These days Samuel gave the first apple of the harvest to Catherine. She was the one who understood him. What he thought often didn't line up with what actually left his mouth. But Catherine heard him when he spoke, and she knew what he meant before he did.

A banging on his door vibrated through the room. "Samuel." Leah knocked again.

"Kumm."

She walked in, carrying hangers with shirts on them. "I'll just put these in your closet."

Samuel held out his hand.

She huffed, but she stopped and passed him the ten hangers. He inspected the shirts that draped from them.

Leah put her hands on her hips. "I have plans for tonight. Can I get paid?"

There wasn't much way of telling where she'd go tonight, and if he asked, she'd lie. Nothing like the *rumschpringe* years to keep the family in the dark about where young people spent their evenings, so he was in no hurry to give her money. He consoled himself with the reminder of his own running-around years. Now twenty-four, he had left behind his time of extra freedoms quite awhile ago, but he'd learned some valuable lessons the hard way—like going to a theater cost a lot more than it was worth, and playing video games never won you anything. In fact, the opposite was true. He'd lost valuable time that he'd never regain.

He thumbed through the shirts. She'd done a half-decent job. The collars were clean, and his Sunday best were well pressed. He'd pay her for those. But his everyday shirts hadn't felt much heat from her iron.

Leah extended her palm toward him. "Anytime today would be really nice."

He held up three hangers with half-ironed shirts. "These need to be redone."

"No way." She huffed. "You only wear them to work in the orchard. I see no reason to heat a pressing iron and work up a sweat to make them crisp."

It didn't actually matter how his work shirts looked, but she hadn't done an acceptable job. He continued to hold out the hangers with the wrinkled shirts. "The principle is always the most important."

Leah took the three hangers. He gave a half nod to affirm that she'd made the right decision to redo the shirts. But instead she went to his closet and hung them up. "You've never washed or ironed anything in your life. If you ever do, we'll have this conversation again." She returned to him and got the rest of the hangers. "I'm not laboring one second longer on any of those. It's a complete waste of time."

Samuel went to his sock drawer. She deserved a reasonable fee for what she had done well. "If a job is worth doing, it's worth doing well."

"Ya, right. Like you'd spend any time on something as boring as doing laundry or dishes. Maybe if your work were as dull as mine, you'd do something with your money besides save every penny. You should use some of it and enjoy today, but we all know that's not going to happen."

He hadn't removed money from his savings account since he put the first twenty dollars in it at fourteen years old. Leah spent every penny she earned.

By offering to pay her to do his laundry, he'd hoped to encourage her to want to work. If she didn't develop a desire to do something other than read novels and go out with friends, he didn't know what her future held.

He placed seven dollars in her hand. "You'll get the other three when you redo the shirts that need it."

She tightened her fist around the money and walked back to his closet. After grabbing the hangers that held the wrinkled shirts, she went toward his door.

Samuel smiled. "I'm glad you know I'm right."

"Ha." Leah swung them over her shoulder. "You'll get these shirts back when you pay for the labor I've already poured into them."

The old wooden floor creaked as he followed her into the hallway. Where was she going to hang them? He'd need those before the end of the week.

She pulled them off the hangers and twisted them into a ball. Apparently her plan didn't include hanging them anywhere. "Let's see you wear them now, Samuel." She bent over and scrubbed the wooden floor with them and then took them into the bathroom, where she picked up a bottle of pine cleaner and squirted them.

"That was very mature of you, Leah. You should be proud."

She left them in the bathroom sink, went into her bedroom, and slammed the door.

Catherine was right. There was no way to get a point across to a fence post or to Leah.

Rhoda caught her father's eye while he, Naomi, and Rueben crossed the wide driveway toward her. He carried so much these days, more than any man should have to and more than her aunt or even the church leaders knew, but his shoulders remained broad and strong. He was determined to see his family through these dark days and into good ones again.

Did better times exist for them?

Daed stopped and studied her. "Fresh concerns have been raised." He moved next to her. She knew he longed to defend her. If she was innocent.

Rueben eased forward a bit, his gray eyes carrying more hardness than the last time she'd looked into them, the day she'd uncovered his deceit in front of his girlfriend. "I know what you've been doing." He said it quietly, and she knew he hoped to convince her to own up to her rebellion.

Out of the corner of her eye, she saw an image. A young Amish woman stood near the house. Rhoda turned to see if one of her sisters-in-law had come outside. But no one was there. Just her imagination conjuring up a vision of Emma—her dainty features, beautiful green eyes, and her gentle smile.

Was this what *"It's time"* meant? Did Emma want her to give up her garden? Rhoda couldn't do it. Not then. Not now.

At first Emma's death stole all of Rhoda's desire to set foot inside her garden ever again. The very idea turned her stomach. But she soon learned it was the only place she could hide from her family's watchful eyes. They wanted to comfort her and be comforted by her. She couldn't manage either, and she discovered that the harder she worked, the more her family accepted her pulling away from them. The distraction the garden offered became like a drug, and she was an addict. Her source of guilt became her place to escape.

Rueben studied the area near the house that had captured Rhoda's attention. Of course he didn't see what she had. He frowned, looking uneasy. "The Amish in this town take a black eye because of the rumors and nonsense that surround you. We've had enough."

Rhoda folded her arms. "What is your accusation this time?"

He shifted. "You make it sound as if I bring false claims. I have the truth."

Her aunt rubbed her hands down the front of her apron. "Rhoda, why don't you tell us what you've been up to the last few months?"

"I've been tending to my berry garden mostly, canning the early strawberries and getting ready for another abundant summer."

Fear crept into her aunt's face. She was one of many who thought Rhoda used unholy methods to produce such abundance.

But she'd defended herself before on this topic. "Whatever I have in the way of bounty is from God and His wisdom."

Naomi took several steps back, her eyes wide, her hands starting to tremble. "You…you read my mind."

Daed put his arm around Rhoda's shoulders. "We all knew what you were thinking, Naomi. You've expressed those same thoughts many times. My daughter's done nothing wrong."

Rueben removed his straw hat. "Why don't you tell your Daed about your contact with Mrs. Culpepper and Mr. Amerson?"

Daed removed his arm from her, and she knew he too wanted an answer to Rueben's question.

Rhoda's mouth went dry, and she found it hard to respond. "Have you been spying on me?"

"He's watching out for you," Naomi said. "He's taken it upon himself to be sure you don't cause any more problems among our Englisch neighbors or your own people."

That wasn't the least bit true, but if her aunt Naomi believed that and dared to come here and say so, she had to have the backing of at least two church leaders.

Rueben jumped in, explaining who Mrs. Culpepper and Mr. Amerson were and what Rhoda's contact with them had been. Her Daed looked disappointed.

"You need to stop dabbling in magic," Rueben said. "If you could find it in yourself to yield to a higher wisdom—"

"Higher?" She moved in closer. "As in your wisdom, Rueben? Be honest. Isn't that what you mean?"

"At least my good judgment would not give in to premonitions and the use of herbs with incantations."

"That's not what I do at all! I've told you that again and again. I've never used incantations."

He pulled a notebook out of his pants pocket. "There are more and more witnesses who say you do."

"Then they're lying."

Rueben passed the notebook to her Daed.

He flipped through it and handed it back. "That's full of nothing more than rumors."

"Rumors come from somewhere, Karl." Naomi turned her focus to Rhoda. "Why don't you tell us what you're doing to cause constant gossip about you and witchcraft?"

"I follow gut feelings. Gut feelings that turn out to be right once in a while, and I'm able to help someone. How can helping a person or saving a life be counted as wrong?"

"Rhoda," Naomi said, "giving and taking life does not belong in your hands. That is God's choice. Only His."

"But if He puts something in a person's hand, then it came from Him," she said.

"Karl." Naomi looked at her Daed. "The church leaders are on the brink of getting involved. They've waited this long only because of their sympathy for your loss. If you don't show some attempt to control the problem and stop the rumors, the entire Byler family will be disgraced, even those of us who are in-laws." Naomi motioned toward the raised beds beyond the gate behind Rhoda. "The herbs are the real problem. Every story of scandal goes back to her using them in some mystical, ungodly way. I think they give her a false sense of power."

Rhoda tightened her fists. "Nobody in all of Pennsylvania feels less power-ful than I do. I can't breathe without causing a scandal."

"Seems to me you deserve to have people watching over you," Rueben said.

Rhoda wanted to cram a handful of *Dryopteris* down Rueben's throat. The herb was good for killing tapeworm, but in the dose she imagined giving him, he'd land in the hospital too sick to stir up trouble for her.

"Rhodes." Her Daed's tone indicated his sympathy for what Rueben and Naomi were saying.

She bit back tears. "You too?"

Her father took her by the hand. "Perhaps it's time to uproot the herbs."

It's time? First Emma's voice in her mind, and now her Daed's words?

"I can't do it." Tears filled her eyes as she gazed over her shoulder at her herb garden. She couldn't rip it up. That'd give Rueben his way, and she'd be laughed at for being disciplined by the church.

She faced her Daed. "I've gone to a handful of people's houses over the last two years. I know I wasn't supposed to, but if you talk to them, they'll tell you that I helped them feel better. That isn't the trouble. The problem is the gossip Rueben is stirring."

"What?" Rueben exploded. "I'm not the problem."

"You spy like a fox waiting to raid the henhouse," she spat.

"Enough," Naomi snapped. "Karl, the church leaders have been very patient. It's been two years since Rhoda showed her true colors. You need to give the community and our church leaders a sure sign that you want to put an end to the ungodly image of Rhoda casting spells. Our Englisch neighbors need that from us too."

Daed stared into Rhoda's eyes. "If getting rid of the herbs will stop the lies among our people, it's the right thing to do. In time maybe it'll help ease the tension between us and our Englisch neighbors. And you'll still have your berry bushes and your canning business."

"No!" She turned away and looked over the four-foot fence, watching her herbs sway in the spring breeze. Even the drab ones, with their brownish green and soft gray tints, held a special kind of beauty.

A noise caused her to turn back in time to see Rueben and Naomi entering the shed where she housed her gardening tools. Her father stood at the doorway of the building, still talking to them. Rueben came out carrying a shovel, and her aunt followed behind him, pushing a wheelbarrow.

"No." She positioned herself in front of the gate.

"The herbs have to go," Naomi said. "It's best for the whole community." She took the shovel from Rueben and held it out to Rhoda. "You should do it yourself."

"Please, no." Tears blurred her vision as she shook her head. She could already envision Rueben destroying her herbs. It wouldn't take him any effort to scoop the herbs out of the raised beds with a shovel.

Daed's supportive hand cupped her elbow. "Kumm." He took several steps back, and she moved away from the gate.

She wanted to grab the shovel and uproot the plants herself just to keep Rueben out of her garden. But sorrow filled her like lead as she watched, unmoving, while he destroyed her plants. And she knew this was only the first victory he hoped to win against her.

THREE

The mid-July sun bore down heavy as Samuel swung the sickle to and fro, making his way through a section of the apple orchard. Eli and Jacob were heading toward him, each pushing a reel mower and probably as ready to stop for the day as he was.

But he kept working, and with every swing he prayed for a good crop this upcoming harvest. Tiny apples hung thick on all thirty acres of trees. That was a great sign. If he could keep the trees healthy for the next three months, Kings' Orchard could make up some of the financial loss from the disappointing harvests of the last few years.

His Daed handled the care and feeding of their fifteen milk cows and sold the raw, organic milk to a small Englisch company that made cheese products. But he'd given charge of the orchard to Samuel several years back.

Jacob stopped the reel mower a hundred feet from Samuel. "I'm starving." He grimaced, rubbing the back of his neck.

Eli came to a halt too, released the push mower, and stretched to work out the kinks. "Can't we head in?"

Samuel removed a handkerchief from his pocket and wiped the sweat off his face. He was sure his younger brothers' bodies ached as much as his did from a week of constantly cutting grass, but it'd be foolhardy to give the mice ample places to build their grassy tunnels straight to the tree trunks.

"Soon. I want to walk the back tierce first."

"What?" Eli frowned. "That's crazy. We've worked too hard, and it's too late in the day to do that."

Samuel shoved the handkerchief back into his pocket. "I keep promising myself that I'll get out that far. It's been too long since I've inspected it."

"It's my section, and I'm telling you it's fine," Eli said.

Jacob shrugged. "He's got a point, Samuel. You put it under his care. Trust him."

Samuel knew he should've gone out there earlier today without mentioning it. The thirty-acre orchard wasn't large compared to the corporate-owned ones, but it took the three of them from sunup to sundown daily to tend it. Every season required unique care to keep up with the front, middle, and back tierce, as they called them. The word *tierce* was Latin for "third," and even though they helped each other as needed, each man was responsible for a specific tierce.

Jacob eyed the three horses that stood grazing under a nearby tree. He moved closer to Samuel and nudged him with his elbow, clearly making plans for getting back to the house before their youngest brother. Samuel shook his head. He wasn't one to play, but Jacob was, and he often prodded his brothers into it.

"We have work to finish, Jacob."

"There's no such thing as finishing, just stopping, and I say it's time to call it a day." Jacob turned from looking at the horses, glanced at Eli, and winked at Samuel.

Each horse had on a harness but no bit in its mouth and no saddle to make mounting it easier. He and his brothers had ridden them that way to the orchard this morning, and sometimes, when they were working near one another, they'd use them to race each other home.

"Fine. I'll check on the back tierce another day. But let's get the mowers and tools under a tarp first."

Eli groaned, too distracted by his sore shoulder to realize Jacob was plotting against him.

The three of them laid the blue tarp over the tools and mousetraps and then placed a few broken tree limbs around the edges to keep the wind from snatching it. To retain their organic growers status, they avoided putting any kind of poison around the trees and instead used mousetraps that were small homemade cages.

Eli dropped a heavy log into place.

Samuel rolled his eyes. "Careful where you put the weight on the tarp, Eli. You could damage the mowers or the mousetraps."

Eli did what he did best—ignored Samuel.

Just as Samuel placed the last log, Jacob took off running for the horses.

"Hey!" Eli hollered. "He tricked us, Samuel. Kumm. We can't let him win." He bolted after Jacob.

Samuel moaned, positive there were better ways to use their remaining energy, but he took off and soon passed Eli. "I can't let you win either."

When he'd almost caught up with Jacob, Samuel reached for Jacob's shirt and had nearly grabbed it when Jacob bobbed to the left. Samuel took the opportunity to get ahead of Jacob, but he stepped into a hole and fell hard, scaring the horses and scattering them.

Jacob stopped short, laughing so hard he had to put his hands on his knees to catch his breath.

Samuel rolled onto his back, chuckling. "Guess we all lose this round."

"Not quite," Eli yelled.

Samuel leaned up on one elbow in time to see Eli mount a horse.

"You scared them right toward me." He raised both fists into the air. "Victory is mine!" He rode off, whistling.

"You'd better enjoy it!" Jacob hollered. "It's not going to happen again." He looked down at Samuel. "You're never going to get home lying down on the job."

"I'm no worse off than you are, Brother. We're both without horses."

Jacob frowned. "That's true." He held out his hand and helped Samuel up. "How did we let Little Bro beat us?"

Samuel removed his straw hat and used it to dust off his pants. "Don't know what your excuse is, but I'm getting old."

Jacob chortled. "Face it. You were born old."

Samuel looked up to see Jacob's horse standing twenty feet away. "But I still have a trick or two up my sleeve." He pulled a cube of sugar out of his pocket and held it toward the horse. She whinnied and trotted over to him.

"If you're so smart, why didn't you do that sooner?"

"Forgot I had it." He took hold of the mare's harness while she ate the sugar from his hand. "As I said, I'm getting old."

"I'll say." Jacob clutched the horse's mane and mounted her.

"Hey!" Samuel tightened his grasp on the harness.

"Sorry, Brother, but second place is better than last." The horse danced one way and then the other, and Samuel lost his grip.

Jacob clicked his tongue, making the horse head toward the barn.

"I'll get you for this, Jacob King," Samuel laughed.

"Not tonight you won't," he hollered over his shoulder.

"Could somebody please tell me what brothers are good for?" Of course, Jacob couldn't hear him over the thundering hoofbeats.

Samuel studied the remaining horse, a good thirty feet away. If he had an apple, he wouldn't need to walk the twenty-plus acres between here and the barn. He got a sickle from under the tarp, wondering how he could get one of those tiny apples down without damaging the branch or the surrounding apples. Since they weren't even close to ripe, they wouldn't fall easily. He went to a low-hanging branch, hooked it with the flat part of the sickle, and pulled the limb toward him. The bough slid off to the side, and the apple waved at him from its secure perch.

Giving up for the moment, he decided to do a better job of securing the tarp over the equipment. He removed the covering altogether and did some minimal upkeep on the two mowers—tightening the blade reel and rollers and wiping the metal handles with an oily rag so they wouldn't rust where the paint had chipped. After he finished taking care of things the way he'd wanted to earlier, he grabbed the sickle again, returned to an apple tree, and started trying to get another one down. Before he succeeded, he heard hoofbeats coming his way. He lowered the sickle and turned. Jacob was riding well ahead of a girl, both heading straight for him.

Samuel leaned the sickle against the trunk of a tree, grateful again that his brother had given up traveling a year and a half ago to help the family work the orchard. "Hey, what's up?"

"Catherine came to the house looking for you."

"Ah." He grinned, realizing she was the girl heading his way. He'd thought about her all day but hadn't expected her to come visit him. "Girlfriends tend to come over unannounced from time to time. If you ever had one, you'd know that," Samuel teased. "We'll have to work on getting you one."

Jacob chuckled. "If you ever find a woman who is one-fourth as interesting as my beloved ocean, I'll consider courting her."

"That's a tall order. Your scuba-diving adventures held your interests pretty captive for a while." Samuel tugged on his wet, smelly shirt. He'd planned to get a shower before he picked up Catherine tonight, for her sake.

Jacob glanced back, seriousness written on his face in spite of their joking. "She's upset about something. Wouldn't say what, only that she needed to see you right away."

Concern barely nibbled at Samuel. She was tender-hearted, and it didn't take much to upset her. That was especially true at the end of a workweek after she'd cleaned homes for numerous Englisch families. "I appreciate your bringing her out here."

Her sense of direction was good on a road, but in the midst of the orchard with no road or house in sight, she easily got turned around.

Catherine brought the horse to a stop, and he helped her down.

"You okay?"

She glanced at Jacob before turning her head the other way. "It's about Leah," she whispered.

Samuel's heart cinched tight with frustration. He pulled her into a hug and felt her trembling. "Take a breath, sweetheart." His seventeen-year-old sister listened to no one, and he feared for her future.

From his perch on the horse, Jacob pulled a small apple off a tree and tossed it on the ground near Samuel, giving him a way to easily catch the last horse. What they needed were better-trained horses, ones that came to them—or at least could be approached—just because their owners needed them, not because they were bribed.

"I'll go now." Jacob clicked his tongue, and the horse headed toward home.

"*Denki*, Jacob. I owe you." Samuel traced Catherine's cheek with his index finger. "What happened?"

"I was at Zip'n Mart less than an hour ago and saw Leah coming out of the girls' rest room. She didn't see me, and I didn't want to confront her there." Concern was reflected in her eyes. "Oh, Samuel, she was scantily dressed and got into a car with some other teenagers dressed the same way. I'm positive they were heading for a party. Someone said they were going to Morgansville. If you hire a driver and—"

Samuel pocketed the apple and held out his hand. "Let's walk."

She put her soft, petite hand in his. He took hold of one rein of her horse and looked it over. "Eli must have thrown a bridle and saddle on this horse pretty quick for you." Samuel held the rein, and the horse ambled behind them. He and Catherine were likely to walk the whole way home.

"Ya, and Jacob brought me out here without even taking time to dismount. They both must think I'm such a...girl."

He chuckled. "I'm sure they do. But don't mind that. Your being a girl is one of my favorite things about you."

She grinned. "You're awful."

"Horrible."

She grew serious again. "What are we going to do about your sister?"

He wanted to shake some sense into Leah. When he saw her next, he intended to lecture her until she finally understood the importance of living as she should. But right now he was more interested in putting his and Catherine's date night on a happier note. "I've considered locking her in a closet until she turns twenty. I think that'd fix the problem. How about you?"

She shoved her shoulder into him. "This is serious, Samuel."

"I know. And I'll do what I can to address her behavior once she gets home. But it's Friday night, and she's not the one I want on my mind right now."

Catherine stopped. "You really are horrible."

"Ghastly."

She moved in closer for a second. "Ach." She backed away, wrinkling her nose.

He chuckled. "So now you notice that I need a shower."

"Boy, do you."

"I need food too."

"Your Mamm was getting dinner on the table when I arrived at the house. The reason I stopped by Zip'n Mart in the first place was because I wanted to make your favorite dessert, but now I'm all off schedule."

"You were going to make me a blueberry pie?"

She nodded.

"And you let seeing Leah at the store stop you?"

"Not reason enough?"

He grabbed his chest. "You're killing me, Cat."

"Do not call me that."

"Please, Miss Catherine, if you'll make me a pie while I shower, I'll take you anywhere you want to go."

"Anywhere? How about to the Lapps' place?"

"We've talked about this enough. The answer remains no."

"But it's been months, and the Lapps still have puppies that need a good home, really cute ones."

"I don't want a dog."

She poked out her bottom lip. "You could at least go see them."

He sighed. "Why? Who goes to look at free dogs when they don't intend to get one?"

"Me for one. I've gone often since they were born. If Daed wasn't allergic,

I'd have two by now. And another person who'd go is a boyfriend who offered to take his girl wherever she wanted."

"Okay, if that's what you want, I'll take you."

"But no chance of getting a dog?"

"Kumm on, Catherine. Dogs ruin floors and tear up things. I want to keep saving for a future home, not spend money replacing stuff in my parents' house."

Catherine squeezed his hand. "That was a good answer."

"Ya, I figured you'd like it."

Now that Catherine seemed calm and content, Samuel could no longer keep at bay his disappointment in Leah. It angered him that Catherine had witnessed his sister's inappropriate behavior. His very tender-hearted girlfriend wouldn't get over this anytime soon. When he saw Leah, he'd have plenty to say to her.

But regardless of what he said, he had more power to change the weather than to stop his little sister from sowing her wild oats. The tradition of rumschpringe gave her the extra freedom. No one under the age of sixteen had that kind of freedom nor did any baptized member. It was meant as a bridge between the confines of childhood, when a person was always under a parent's watchful eye, and the independence of full adulthood. It was a time to relax and grow new bonds among the Amish community that would last throughout one's life. But his sister was using her running-around time to experience how the godless lived, and the results were surely bound to haunt her.

Catherine pointed overhead. "Wow, there's no shortage of apples this year."

"Isn't it a gorgeous sight?"

"You told me about it, but seeing it in person is eye-opening."

"I'm hopeful, but many things can go wrong between midsummer and harvesttime."

"Is one good season enough to get Kings' Orchard out of the hole from the last few seasons?"

"Afraid not. We're in more debt than a good year can fix, but it'd help a lot."

"Your Daed stopped by the house a few nights ago, and he said he's hoping to hire fifty pickers this year."

"It'd be nice to need that many. Of course, then the challenge is how best to get all the workers back and forth to wherever they're staying, since we don't have a place for them to live throughout the harvest. But the downside is, if we need that many workers and can't find them, the fruit will rot on the ground."

"You'd never let that happen even if you had to work night and day for the entire harvest."

He pondered the situation, enjoying the mental exercise of finding a solution. "If we were faced with that circumstance, I'd put tarps under the trees we couldn't pick and let the fruit fall on them. We'd only get cider apples that way, but at least it wouldn't be a complete loss."

She studied his face. "Could you sell that many Grade B apples?"

He wouldn't explain to her again that apple growers didn't refer to them as Grade A or Grade B. The inedible ones were cider apples, and she knew that, but she continued to refer to them as if they were eggs. "Ya, no problem. But we'd need to find a way to close the gap between the money we'd make off the eating apples and what we'd make off cider apples. Even with a good harvest, it'd be nice to make more income from the cider apples."

"May I offer a suggestion?"

"Of course."

"I recommend you figure out that problem."

He chuckled. "Denki, sweetheart. I'll work on that."

She squeezed his hand. "Anytime. So what happens if the crop is damaged or destroyed before the harvest?"

Another year of bad weather or any kind of calamity could mean the beginning of the end of Kings' Orchard. Large corporations owned most apple orchards, and they had the money and power to survive the lean years. A family-owned place didn't have that luxury.

"I need to think positive, but your question is valid. I have to look at the big picture, consider how we keep operating."

While they walked through the orchard toward home, his thoughts returned to his sister. He hoped she'd wise up before she got in over her head. He used to long for the day when she'd stop stealing away to the barn loft to read fiction. Since she was seven or eight years old, she'd disappear every chance she got, shirking her chores to read. Before long she was into murder mysteries, old classics, and legal thrillers. These days he wished that was all she did when she sneaked off.

FOUR

Catherine squeezed Samuel's hand as they walked from his rig to the Lapps' home. They'd shared a meal with his family, and now it was nearing eight o'clock. The sultry heat waned as the sun slid closer to the horizon. "The Lapps will be surprised that I'm not visiting the puppies by myself this time." She already felt calmer about Leah, thanks to Samuel. He always seemed to know what to do to ease her anxiety.

"They'll think you've brought me to help pick one out."

The Lapps' seventeen-year-old son, Christian, came out of the house, putting on his straw hat. "Hey, Samuel." He crossed the front lawn. "How's the orchard doing?"

"So far, so good. We've got a little problem with mice, but there's always something to contend with."

"I saw your Daed a few days back, and he said you'll probably get a bumper crop this year."

"That'd be nice."

Catherine gave Samuel a subtle nudge. She didn't want to interrupt the men, but if they were going to stand around and make small talk, why not do so in the barn where she could see the puppies?

"We dropped by to look at the pups. We don't want one. We're just out enjoying a Friday night."

"Sure." Christian headed toward the barn. "We have two litters. One of our dogs delivered a month or so ago. And we still have a few three-month-old pups from another mama. Negligence on our part, but both mama dogs have been spayed now."

"You could take the litters to the flea market and be rid of them all by the end of the day."

Catherine poked Samuel's side. "Just because you don't want a dog is no reason to give them ideas for how to get rid of them."

He raised his eyebrows. "You already have a favorite one picked out, don't you?"

She cleared her throat, hoping she didn't look as awkward or as guilty as she felt. "Maybe."

His lopsided grin, which spoke of his utter acceptance of her, made her want to kiss him. And after they were married, she was going to make a habit of that. But he hadn't proposed yet. He'd told her he wanted to wait until he could afford a house for them, which might not be for two years yet. That seemed forever, but no man was worth waiting for more than Samuel.

Catherine slipped her hand into the crook of his elbow, already dreaming of having his children.

Christian pulled open the barn door. The earthy aroma of animals over-powered the smell of hay. They followed him to the far end of the barn, and as he neared the last horse stall on the left, high-pitched yelps greeted them.

Catherine adored this sound. She knew Samuel, and they'd leave here without a puppy. Still she couldn't help but dream. Every girl she'd graduated eighth grade with was already married; most either had a baby or were expecting one. But here she was at twenty-one still waiting to be officially engaged. If she couldn't yet have a home of her own or start a family, it seemed a puppy would help the days, months, and years pass more easily.

Christian opened the top half of the stall door. In one corner was a mound of hay covered with sheepskin. Another area had bowls of food and water, and the far corner was filled with sawdust for the dogs to use to relieve themselves.

The mama dog lay on the sheepskin, watching her five buff-and-white puppies roll around and on top of each other, tussling over a colorful braided cord.

"Oh, Samuel, aren't they adorable?"

At the sound of her voice, her favorite pup stopped playing and looked up at her, barking.

"Did you see how she recognized my voice?" Catherine reached her hand across the stall door, talking to her. "Hello, you precious thing."

The puppy excitedly spun around in circles, barking, while her long, fluffy ears flopped about her head. She then put her front paws on the door, yapping at Catherine.

She reached in and scooped her up. The little pup licked her face, and the scratchy tongue against her cheek made her giggle.

"Seems like they'd shed a lot," Samuel mumbled.

"Most dogs do, but cocker spaniels aren't the worst." Christian rubbed the head of the pup Catherine held. "Would you like to see the other dogs?"

Catherine wasn't ready to put the cocker spaniel down yet. She held it while Samuel went with Christian to the opposite stall.

Christian grabbed a scoop of dry food and poured it into several bowls. "So, did Arlan finally get what he wanted from the music store?"

Catherine's throat constricted. "I heard your Daed paid him today for his weeks of hauling hay. But I didn't realize my brother was planning on taking the money to a music store." Her voice cracked.

Christian's eyes grew big, and he looked first to Samuel and then back to Catherine. "I assumed you knew. That's all he's talked about for a month." Christian tossed the scoop back into the bag of dog food. "He was hoping to meet up with Leah and—"

Catherine turned to Samuel. "He's with your *sister*?"

Christian laughed. "Wow, that's a growl to put these mama dogs to shame."

Catherine quickly backtracked. "That's not what I meant. I love Leah. But I had no idea she and my brother had plans to meet tonight."

"Maybe they didn't," Christian said. "She might've had a date. But if she was free, Arlan wanted her to go with him to the music store. He's been planning to buy another guitar."

Anxiety twisted inside Catherine's chest, threatening to steal her breath. Christian had said "buy another guitar" as if it were something to be proud of, something that was part of the Amish ways. Her brother's defiance in this area had caused their parents to be excluded from the last communion service. Arlan had regretted pushing the limits and causing the church leaders to discipline his parents, so as an outward show of repentance, he'd turned over his guitar to the bishop. When he'd brought the forbidden item under Daed's roof, he'd known that their parents would be held accountable to the church leaders…if the ministers found out, which they did. Arlan had agreed never to go that far again. So what was he thinking?

Christian sighed. "Sorry I brought it up." He rolled his eyes. "But it's not news that Arlan loves music or that he wants Leah's opinion about nearly everything. She even got him a gig in town next weekend."

"A gig?" Catherine asked. "What's that?"

Samuel shook his head, his facial expression saying it wasn't important.

"You don't know?" Christian all but gawked at her. "Did you do anything remotely against the *Ordnung* during your teen years?"

The Ordnung was the set of rules the Amish lived by. The word meant "order." Did Christian think it was fine to live the teen years in disorder? To do things they'd regret the rest of their days?

Samuel closed the top part of the stall where the golden retrievers were. "She's always accepted the Old Ways and honored God through sacrifice of self." He winked at her. "It's who she is."

Christian looked doubtful at Catherine, as if he disliked this revelation about her. "Getting a gig means Leah arranged for him to play his guitar somewhere specific and get paid for it."

Catherine grabbed Samuel's arm. "Tell me she wouldn't have done that. Surely. I thought he gave up music after—"

Christian scoffed. "What planet do you live on?"

"Christian," Samuel corrected, "you're not helping."

"Sorry."

Catherine bent down to put the cocker spaniel back in the stall, but the pup clung to her arm and whimpered. After she peeled her paws off and stood, the pup climbed the wooden slats, barking and jumping to get back to Catherine. "Samuel, you have to do something about Leah. It's bad enough that she's doing things she shouldn't, but to pull Arlan down too..."

"It's music, for Pete's sake." Christian propped the palm of his hand against a support beam. "A lot of it is about God and family."

Samuel slid his hand into hers. "You know Arlan. He's not going to do anything stupid, even if Leah is helping him play for money."

She gazed into his eyes, begging him to think of something. Unlike him and every other Amish family they knew, she had only one sibling. That pain still tore at her mother's heart, and it'd kill her parents if they knew Arlan was buying another musical instrument.

"He'll be fine, Catherine," Samuel said. "He's doing what young people do—trying new things and discovering they're not as fun or valuable as they first thought."

She took a cleansing breath, trusting his words. "Okay."

"Instead of focusing on things we have no power over,"—Samuel reached into the stall and picked up her favorite buff-colored pup, the one with her paws stretched up high on the stall door, still trying to get to Catherine, and placed the dog back in her arms—"how about we focus on our new dog?"

"What? Really?" she squealed, wanting to give him a great big hug—puppy and all. But she restrained herself for the sake of propriety. "This is the best way ever to redeem a difficult night, Samuel. Denki."

As they walked back to the rig, Catherine cradled her adorable cocker spaniel. Pink and orange hues striped the sky as the sun began to dip behind the mountains. "What should we name her?"

"Whatever you want, sweetheart."

She gazed at the pup, whose bright eyes were beginning to get a little droopy with sleep. "I don't want some generic name like Daisy or Ginger. I think it should mean something special to both of us."

After Samuel helped Catherine into the rig, she settled the puppy in her lap. The puppy looked as content as if she had been there all her life.

Samuel climbed onto the seat beside her. "How about Token?"

"What?"

"As in a token of comfort."

She giggled. "That's wonderfully romantic."

"Romantic? How about practical? I salvaged our evening, maybe our weekend or even our entire year, with a dog that cost me nothing."

"Puppies are never really free. You know that, right?"

"I know. But I'll swing it without dipping into savings, and it'll be worth it if she'll remind you that our siblings will grow up, and until then we can't take out our frustrations on each other, okay?"

"You mean me not taking my frustrations out on you. Your sister is the one always stirring up trouble, not Arlan."

He didn't respond. Did he disagree with her?

She slid across the seat and snuggled against him. "I don't think I could take life in stride if it weren't for you." She stared at the furry little face, which was looking more tired every minute.

Samuel flicked the reins to get the horse moving. "Arlan has a good head on his shoulders."

Catherine relaxed a bit. Samuel was wonderful at calming her too-easily-frazzled nerves. As she cuddled the new puppy, she raised her little head and looked up into Catherine's face, eyes gleaming with hope for a happy, carefree life with her, just as Catherine hoped for her future with Samuel.

"How about if we name her Hope?"

"That sounds like as good a name as any."

She snuggled deeper into Samuel's shoulder and listened to the puppy snoring in her lap. Hope. Ya, that suited their pup—and their life—just fine.

Something clanged and clattered, drawing Rhoda's attention from the raspberry vines sprawled on a trestle in front of her. Dusk had fallen, and she hadn't even noticed. After gently dropping the ripe berries into the bushelbasket, she straightened the kinks in her back and looked beyond the picket fence to her elderly neighbor's garden.

Sweat trickled down Rhoda's back as she searched the neat rows of half-grown cornstalks and struggling vegetable plants to see if the woman needed help. The mid-July air vibrated with the sounds of insects. A tin pail rolled to a stop, and the clanking noise ceased. A thin, shadowy figure stepped out from the cornrows, walked toward her, and picked up the bucket. Then Mrs. Walker did something she hadn't done in years: she lifted her face toward Rhoda. Perhaps in the twilight she was unsure who Rhoda was and thought Rhoda was Mamm, because Rhoda favored her mother a lot.

Rhoda remained in place, waiting, hoping Mrs. Walker would realize who she was and speak anyway. She knew better than to initiate a conversation. Her instructions were clear: keep doing her tasks and say nothing to Mrs. Walker.

But was it possible the old woman had changed her mind about Rhoda?

Rhoda had all but frightened the life out of Mrs. Walker two years ago, and although Rhoda was no people pleaser, she'd love to make up for scaring her so badly—if the woman would give her a chance. But despite Daed's hopes of making peace with their neighbors by removing her herb garden two months ago, Rhoda had seen no evidence of reconciliation.

A nighthawk cawed a nasal *peent, peent,* then flew inches from Rhoda's face, startling her. The air seemed to quiver with tension. "Easy." She spoke quietly, as if cooing to a skittish horse.

Even in the fading light, Rhoda saw the woman tense. Mrs. Walker threw the tin pail to the ground and hurried toward her home.

Disappointment wrapped itself around Rhoda. Biting back the sadness, she gently plucked more berries. She couldn't help how Mrs. Walker felt about her. She couldn't stop the rumors. The lies. The fear.

Strums of music, like someone practicing chords or tuning a guitar, broke through the sounds of nature. She guessed the neighbor down the block was gearing up for another Friday night party.

Ignoring the unfamiliar tune, she sang softly as she worked, stopping her songs only long enough to whisper work-related instructions to herself. With her basket full, she headed for the gate.

Children's voices filtered from inside the house, and she noticed a light moving from one window to another. Someone was wheeling the gas pole lamp from the kitchen to the living room, most likely her Mamm or Daed. Once the sun began to sink behind the hills, they tended to keep a light with them rather than rely on those sitting on a counter or table. But there was no shortage of people to move the lamp. The house already bulged with the three families living there, and her sister-in-law Lydia was expecting another baby in three months.

Landon pulled into her driveway and hopped out of his truck. He grabbed a roll of packing tape and several flat cardboard boxes from behind the seat of his truck. "It's almost dark, and you're just now finishing. I knew I was a genius to partner with Rhode Side Stands."

"Who'd have thought that a UPS Store clerk would become such a loyal assistant and friend?"

"Me." He followed her across the paved driveway.

Four years ago, when she was eighteen and started selling her produce to various stores, she'd taken her jars of canned goods to the UPS Store to have them packaged and delivered. Landon had offered all sorts of tips and ideas to save her money. He'd also suggested she let him drive some of the items to nearby stores and had volunteered to come to her place for a Saturday or two to teach her how to pack and ship as inexpensively as possible.

Until that time, Rhoda ran her business without much advice or help from others. Her brothers John and Steven were handymen, just like her Daed. They could do whatever people needed: build out unfinished rooms, like basements, or clean gutters or make repairs. Admirable work, but no one made a lot of money. They had some business knowledge, but none of them had known how to help Rhoda go from selling items at a roadside stand to selling them to stores.

Landon had. He'd even set up what he called a simple website for selling her product. She'd looked at it once at the UPS Store, but Landon handled all that, updating the site and bringing her the few orders that came in.

If she had room to grow more fruit and had a bigger workspace to can it, her business could easily grow. Even if she could use her mother's kitchen, she could accomplish a lot more in less time. But so many people sharing the same house meant little kitchen access.

Her brother Steven and his wife, Phoebe, had once owned a place of their own, but the economic downturn had caused him, her Daed, and John to make less money. When Steven could no longer afford their house payment, he had to sell the house for less than he'd paid for it.

John and Lydia had always lived in the Byler home. Even with their economic struggles, they had been saving for years and house hunting for several months. With three children now and another on the way, they needed their own place.

Rhoda didn't go with them to look at houses. Even if she had time, which she didn't, entering a place where other families had lived caused her senses to play tricks on her, making her pick up on echoes from the past.

Once she and Landon reached the narrow set of stairs that led to the cellar, he went ahead of her, entered the room, and held open the screen door. Two people could not stand side by side on the cellar steps. If she even wrapped her arms around a bushelbasket before taking the stairs, the cinder-block walls would scrape the skin off her arms.

She entered the dank room, poured the berries from the basket into a large sieve that sat in one of the two oversized mud sinks, and turned on cool water to soak them. Dark and confining as it was, this was the center of operations for Rhode Side Stands.

Landon unfolded a box. "I saw cars parking along the sidewalk on the other side of the street, and I heard a band or something when I turned onto the block."

"Woohoo." She raised her fists in the air, mocking enthusiasm. "Another party. I just hope they leave me and my gardens alone this time."

"I don't think it's the guys who live there that throw rocks and stuff. Seems more like something—"

She held up her hand. "I don't want to hear your suspicions. Just work."

She struck a match and lit a natural gas lantern that hung from the ceiling. Her workspace was more primitive than any Amish business she was familiar with, like carpenters' or quilters' shops or a dry-goods store. Although a lot of Amish women canned, she didn't know of any full-fledged Amish business that operated out of a cellar.

The cellar and her parents' home above it had been built in the seventeen hundreds. She thought of the Amish men, her ancestors, digging out dirt more than two hundred years ago to build this cellar, and here she was, past the new millennium, still using the compact space. It had the original dirt walls, but her Daed had constructed concrete walls and floors over the dirt and sealed it, making the place clean for her food preparation.

Rhoda walked to the firepit. She stirred the embers under the large black pot and added more wood. An oversized round hood was attached to the ceiling and hung over the firepit. The smoke went up it, through the hidden flues in the walls of the rooms above them, and out the roof of the two-story home.

Landon grabbed the pot off its crane. "How much water do you need in this thing?" He took the pot to the second mud sink. "A little less than half full?"

She raised her eyebrows. "You, my sorting and crating specialist, volunteering for something outside your job description? I don't like the sound of that. The last time you did that, you had bad news you didn't want to share."

He shrugged, and she knew he was hiding something.

She pointed at the galvanized bucket she used for measuring liquids. "Fill that with water three times and dump it into the pot."

He followed her orders. "This setup is positively medieval."

"One day when we've made enough profit, I'll invest in building a separate kitchen, maybe where the shed stands now, only we'll take up some of the driveway too. It'd be a dream to work in a spacious room above ground." She dumped mounds of sugar into the pot and stirred it with a specially designed, oversized wooden spoon that her eldest brother had made for her as a graduation present nine years ago. Life seemed simpler then. Straightforward. Uncomplicated. Life now was anything but simple.

Landon hurried to the storage room at the top of the steps and quickly returned with white packing paper. He wrapped pieces of paper around the jars of jelly and jam they'd canned last night. "I saw Mrs. Walker scurrying toward her house."

"It's too sad to talk about, so let's don't." Rhoda crushed raspberries with the back of a flat wooden spoon, preparing to make fresh jam. "To think Rueben had the pleasure of destroying my herbs for no good reason already makes it difficult to sleep at night."

"You know what I think the solution is?" Landon popped a raspberry into his mouth. "Maine."

He'd expressed this opinion several times since her troubles began. His granny lived there, and she kept him informed of all the best land deals.

"I'm not moving, Landon. My Daed needs me here. For reasons that defy all logic, my presence brings him comfort, and I'm not running from the likes of Rueben Glick and his tiny band of merry nitwits."

Fear was the real enemy. Without it, no one would believe the lies about her. Much of her reputation was her own fault. She'd been naive, thinking she could respond to her gut feelings without fueling others' misconceptions. She prayed she'd never have another urging, but if she did, she was determined not to respond to it.

Landon filled the box with jars of jelly. "It's getting worse. Everyone's gardens should be producing by now, and only yours is. More than half of the vines in the area have shriveled to nothing in the last few years. Even those that are producing don't do near what yours do."

"It's called husbandry. Nothing more."

"It's a gift, a good one, and there's nothing wrong with admitting that."

She put the clean raspberries into a colander and rinsed them one last time.

Landon folded the top of the box and set it next to the door. "How about you let me get the voice mail messages from the phone shanty for the next few days?"

She knew now what was going on. Landon had heard new rumors about her, and he wanted to shield her from a fresh round of prank calls. "Denki, but I can deal with the phone calls, same as I always do." Her voice sounded stronger than she felt.

A small group of Amish and Englisch youth, maybe four or five kids, had been harassing her for years. They had pulled stunts and damaged her plants, but she hated the phone calls the most. Eerie voices begging for help, declaring that she knew who they were and only she could save them.

She never returned those calls to give them a piece of her mind. She could have reported the numbers that showed up on her caller ID, but she wasn't interested in revenge, and she did *not* want to involve the police. She wanted peace. And a friend.

The phone outside rang. Landon reached to open the screen door.

"You stay here with me," Rhoda ordered. He stopped cold. "Good boy," she teased and swung the crane holding the kettle away from the heat. "We have work to do." She dried her hands on a clean towel. "I'll deal with the phone calls myself. Later."

Jacob saw no one as he went through the barn and into the small office at the back. He closed the door behind him. Old file cabinets, several ladder-backs, and a large desk that was too small to hold all the paperwork sat inside a room with a wooden ceiling and floor. Rustic was one thing. Messy was another, and this space stayed piled with files and paperwork.

Numbers, tons of them, danced through his head as he glanced at stacks of information: how many crops this plot of ground had yielded since 1840, how many land managers had tended this land, and how long each had lasted. Catching a glimpse of a year written on a folder made numbers buzz inside his head like yellow jackets on the attack: the number of days in a decade, the number of minutes in a year, the number of trees that produced fruit each harvest, the number of bushels from each tree—

"Okay." He sang the word as he closed a folder. "That's enough of that."

He took a seat in the captain's chair behind the desk, picked up the phone, and dialed the number etched deeper in his brain than any other. Should he leave well enough alone? He'd asked himself that question a hundred times since leaving her to return home eighteen months ago.

The ringing stopped. "Hi, you've reached Sandra and Casey. If this is a sales call or a creditor, please hang up and don't dial us again. All others, you know what to do."

Jacob could hear little Casey in the background, saying, "Mommy, look," over and over again.

After the beep he said, "Hey, it's me. Just checking in. Anyone home?" He waited, wondering if Sandra was there but unwilling to answer the phone. Was she at the beach, enjoying the rolling waves with Casey? Or was she curled up in a ball, trying to muster enough strength to face another day? "I hope everybody's okay." That was probably wanting too much, but what else could he say? He held on until he heard a long beep that ended his time.

Creditors? Was she being harassed by bill collectors? Or was that message meant to sting those who owed her?

Should he have stayed? He still didn't know.

He opened a drawer, pulled out an envelope and a piece of paper, and wrote "Call me" and his phone number, even though she already had it. Before he'd left, he'd stuck it on her refrigerator, taped it to the mirror in the bathroom, and pinned it on her pillow.

He licked a stamp and pressed it in place before pulling his billfold from his pocket. He counted out hundred dollar bills, allowing figures to run through his head: the difference between what Sandra earned and what she'd need to make ends meet.

He put the last of the money from his billfold onto the stack on the desk, shoved it into the envelope, and sealed it. When he heard his Daed whistling, he slid it into his pocket.

The office door swung open. "Jacob, I didn't realize you were here. Glad you are, though. I've been needing to talk to you."

Jacob pointed at the calculator as if he actually used one when working with figures. "I've run the numbers on the dairy side, like you asked." He picked up a beige folder. All the papers for the dairy side of the business were kept in beige folders. The apple-side documents were kept in red folders. "It's all in here."

"Good." Daed took the folder. "But what's on my mind is this year's Amish Benefit Mission." He opened it and glanced at the figures.

Daed had been head of the Amish mission outreach for years, and it consumed every bit as much of his time as running the dairy. He closed the folder. "Unless we do something drastic about contributions for the mission, we're not going to meet our goal. I've been talking with some of the men about a solution. I need volunteers, strong men who can build a house that we can sell. And I need a team leader."

"You asked me the same thing last spring and the one before. It's not happening, Daed. Sorry."

"But construction is your area of expertise."

"Not anymore."

Daed's eyes held concern. "What happened out there, Jacob? When you were away?"

Jacob got up and went around his Daed, offering him the chair behind the desk. "If you decide on a moneymaking venture for the mission that doesn't include my doing construction work, I'll do it. You name it, it's yours. But not this." He made a conscious effort to speak softly. "And I'm not answering any questions about it." He headed for the door. "See you later."

He left the office and stepped onto the hay-strewn dirt walkway of the barn. It agitated him how many people thought they had to know the *why* behind every *no*. He grabbed a blanket and saddle and put them on his chestnut Morgan before bridling her.

He mounted his horse, ready to make his routine Friday night ride into town to mail the envelope. He wanted to help people: his Daed, Sandra, Casey, his family, and even strangers. But his days—past and present—were not open to anyone. And he didn't do construction work anymore. Period. End of discussion.

SIX

Leah glanced up at the night sky, wondering what time it was. It'd been dark for five or six hours now, so maybe it was two, possibly three, in the morning? One thing for sure, all the butterflies that had fluttered in her stomach when she'd arrived at this party had vanished. But the ache in her heart hadn't yet dulled, not even a little.

Her head spun as she walked across Brad's backyard, winding her way around dozens of other young people. About half of the crowd was Amish, but not one was dressed in the traditional manner. The guys wore jeans and T-shirts instead of trousers and buttoned cotton shirts, and the girls wore short skirts and knit tops.

Leah's clothes hugged her curves just like the other girls' outfits, but with her larger figure, she didn't look nearly as good as they did. Still, on the way to the party, she'd stopped at a convenience store to change out of her brown dress and apron, take off her prayer *Kapp*, comb out her hair, and put on makeup. Her parents would be hurt if they could see her now. Why did they have to take the way people dressed so seriously, as if anything other than a long polyester dress was a sin against God?

As she walked toward one of the blankets on the ground, her inner voice reminded her that, unlike all the other girls here, she was neither pretty nor cool. But at least the constant chant wasn't as loud now that she'd had a few drinks. Holding a beer bottle that was no longer cold, she sat in the middle of the blanket, hoping she didn't look as out of place as she felt.

The party had been inside Brad's house until something caught fire and the rooms filled with smoke. The musicians had packed up and gone home about an hour ago. Arlan could've outplayed any of those guys.

These gatherings exposed her to live music. People brought various instruments and gathered around whoever was playing guitar or piano. They laughed at silly songs she was unfamiliar with, but she'd fallen in love with music and instruments. Until then her only love had been novels, which her parents frowned on but hadn't forbidden.

A few circles of people shifted, and Michael came into view. He stood some twenty feet away, talking to an unfamiliar girl—an Englisch one. Surely he'd walk away from that girl and look for her soon. She'd started coming to the parties about six months ago because Michael invited her. He'd given Leah her first beer, but being around Michael felt totally intoxicating even without the drink.

Earlier today she'd paid good money to have her hair styled in long layers so she would look as Englisch as possible. But Michael had barely noticed her tonight. Or last night. Or—

"Leah?" The deep male voice came from beside her.

She saw his boots first and tilted her head back until his face came into view, but the move made her dizzy. She blinked, trying to focus her eyes. The stars sparkled. The silvery moon glowed. She wished it were Michael calling her.

The young man crouched beside her blanket. He was nice looking, with brown hair and broad shoulders. She'd probably seen him before, but her sights had always been on Michael. The way this man looked at her made her feel pretty—and awkward.

He grinned. "Brad told me he gave you a ride here tonight."

"Yeah." She'd almost said *ya,* but she didn't want to sound Amish. *Englischers* often held strong opinions against the Plain sects. Her people had plenty of preconceived ideas about them too. "He brought as many people as he could fit in that van of his." She did her best to sound like an Englisch girl but was sure her accent gave her away.

"I'm Turner."

She looked Michael's way again. He smiled as he talked to the girl wearing the size 0 jeans. What was it about the superthin ones that always caught Michael's attention?

"It looks like you're about done with that beer. Can I get you another one?"

Leah tried to remember how many she'd already had. She ran her fingers through her sandy blond hair, enjoying how silky soft it felt. "I'd take a cold beer, thank you. And a cigarette."

He grinned, revealing a set of perfectly straight teeth. He pulled a pack of cigarettes out of his shirt pocket, tapped one out, and passed it to her. She put it between her lips and waited for him to strike a flame on his lighter. He held it, looking pleased with himself and comfortable with her.

If he were Amish, he'd never know what it felt like to be pleased with himself. She hated being Amish.

He lit a cigarette for himself and pointed at her with the fingers that held it. "I'll be right back with some beer. Don't go anywhere." He gave her a half smile before he walked off.

She appreciated his offer, but she might need something stronger than beer. All she wanted to do was become someone else. Could he drum up a potion for that? She had spent all her hard-earned money buying the right kind of clothes and getting makeup and haircuts, but it wasn't enough to make her feel self-assured. She took another drag on her cigarette, trying to appear more confident.

Folks in the Englisch world seemed to understand so much more than she did. She'd been out of school for four years, and every moment since, six days a week, had been filled with chores and rules. Even Sunday, the supposed day of rest, wasn't free of chores as the women provided food and childcare. What would it be like to have one moment when she didn't think or feel Amish?

Michael looked as if he fit in no matter where he went—whether sitting on a hard bench during an Amish church meeting or standing in someone's backyard with a drink in his hand. She'd never accomplish that.

Turner came back, carrying two bottles. He took the lid off one before passing it to her. The bottle was dripping with condensation. He wiped his hands on his jeans. "May I?" He gestured at the blanket.

"Sure." She moved over a bit, making room for him.

He sat beside her, opened his beer, and took a long swallow. "It's too hot to be outside in July—unless you're at a pool."

She wanted to say something witty or charming, or at least not stupid, but nothing came to mind. Despite having a cute guy sitting beside her, she couldn't stop watching Michael. Rather than losing interest in the new girl, he seemed to be wrapped around her finger.

Turner wiped sweat from his forehead. "I roof buildings for a living. Talk about hot work. But once I'm showered for the evening, I like to stay in the air conditioning. The house is almost totally aired out now. Some people have already gone back in. You want to go inside?"

"What is it about guys falling all over skinny girls?"

"What?" His brows tightened.

She pointed at the happy couple.

"Oh." He took a swig of his drink. "I think you should forget about Megan and what's-his-face and enjoy your evening."

"His name is Michael. You know the girl?"

"A little. We went to high school together back in the Dark Ages."

"Dark Ages?" Leah's world spun a little more. She took another gulp of her beer. "How old are you?"

"Twenty-three. You?"

"Oh, twenty-one. Most definitely."

He chuckled. "Of course. Where there's alcohol, everyone is at least that old, right?" He scratched his eyebrow with the back of his thumbnail. "Are you still in high school?"

Had he not picked up on her dead-giveaway accent? Or did he know so little about the Amish that he didn't realize they rarely attended school past the eighth grade? "No, I've graduated."

"When, last spring?"

"Nope, back in the Dark Ages."

He laughed. "Yeah, I bet." He leaned back on his elbows.

Michael laughed loudly, and when Leah looked up, he had that girl by the waist, swinging her around as she squealed and giggled. When he set her feet on the ground, he held out his hand. She put her hand in his, and slowly their lips met.

Leah jumped up, tossed her cigarette to the ground, and headed straight for him, ready to tell him what she thought.

"Leah, what's up…" Turner's voice faded as she stormed across the lawn.

"How dare you," she seethed at Michael.

He stopped kissing Megan and shot Leah a disgusted look. "What's your problem?"

"My problem?" She could barely breathe. "How can you even ask that?"

He gave Miss Size Zero's waist a squeeze. "Give me a minute, will you?" He winked. "This won't take long."

Leah's knees felt like a child's squishy ball.

After Megan wandered off, Michael glared at Leah. "You got something to say to me?"

She could think of plenty to say. But she didn't have time to analyze her words. In this moment she had the chance to win Michael back or lose him forever. Her entire future hung in the balance. "I love you," she whispered. At least she hoped it was a whisper. But for some reason the more people drank, the louder they got. "I thought you felt the same way about me."

His laugh said she was trying to reason with someone more drunk than she was. "Really? Because I'm pretty confident you decided that on your own."

How could he be so flippant? The tender way Michael had spoken to her, the romantic words he'd said, the things they'd done together—they had made her believe he was the man she'd spend the rest of her life loving, taking care of, and raising a family with. She'd given her heart to him. And she'd thought he loved her too.

"Look, we had some fun, but that's it. Don't make a big thing out of it. If you got the impression it was more, that's yours to deal with." He shrugged.

Leah's dizziness threatened to overpower her. "But…you…I thought we…"

Michael glanced toward Megan. "I'm not going to stay here and argue. I have other things I'd rather do, if you get my drift."

If? How stupid did he think she was? She feared her stomach would empty itself right onto his shoes. "Get away from me." She shoved him, but she bounced off him as though he were a wall and fell on her backside. Snickers and laughter filled the air, and she realized that people, a lot of them, had been watching their exchange. Tears stung her eyes. She had to get out of this place.

She rose and headed for the house, determined to grab her purse, find Brad, and tell him she had to leave. Oh, and she had to find Dorothy too. Her cousin was here somewhere, and the two of them were supposed to leave the party together and catch the usual ride with Brad. She didn't know what their plan was for the night, but they wouldn't go back to Harvest Mills. They'd told their parents they were camping out tonight, which meant neither of them had a curfew. But Leah hadn't spotted Dorothy in a couple of hours.

Halfway to the back porch, Turner stopped her. "Are you okay?"

What a dumb question. If she looked anywhere near as miserable as she felt, he'd have to be blind not to see it. "I'm great. And you?" She brushed past him.

He caught up with her. "You can't force someone to be with you."

"It's not supposed to be that way, not between Michael and me." She stumbled to the door, yanked it open, and went inside. With a pounding head and misty eyes, she searched for the people she'd come to the party with, but she couldn't find any of them. She climbed the stairs and looked into the first room on her right—an empty bedroom.

Unable to stand on her shaky legs any longer, she locked the door and sat on the edge of the bed. She stared at the brown carpet, scolding herself for her stupidity. Tears ran down her cheeks, and she broke into sobs.

When she finally calmed down enough to stop crying, she went to the adjoining bathroom. Her cheeks were streaked with tears, and her forehead and temples were blotchy with makeup. She washed her face but could do nothing about her puffy red eyes.

Returning to the party, she tried again to find Brad or her cousin or anyone else she'd ridden with, but few people were still hanging around. The wall clock indicated she'd been upstairs for more than an hour. Three thirty in the morning? No wonder almost everyone was gone.

Three people she didn't know were sitting on a couch, talking. "Anyone know where Brad is?"

A young man set his drink on the coffee table. "He left with a bunch of people."

Great. Her cousin and friends had abandoned her. They probably didn't want to be seen with someone who'd made such a fool of herself. But if she wasn't meeting up with Dorothy, Leah had to get home before her parents figured out she and her cousin weren't camping. So how was she supposed to do that? She grabbed another beer from a cooler and headed for the curb, hoping that when Brad returned, he'd agree to make a second trip to Harvest Mills.

As she sat under a tree near the sidewalk, sipping her beer, she heard giggling and Michael's voice. She peeked around the trunk and saw him and Megan going into the house, entwined in each other's arms. Probably on their way to find a quiet room where they could *talk*.

This couldn't be happening. How could the man she loved dump her and take up with another girl right in front of her?

Stifling the scream that threatened to come out and wake every neighbor within miles, Leah threw the beer bottle into the grass and ran down the sidewalk. She didn't know this area, so she had no idea where she was going. But she had to get away from here. Away from Michael and Megan.

Two houses down, the churning in her stomach started bubbling up. Any minute now she'd be on her knees, embarrassing herself. Michael and Megan might come outside again, see her, and make fun of her. Unable to stand the thought of further humiliation, she searched for a place to hide.

Relief surged when she saw a home without electric or phone lines attached—a sure sign it belonged to an Amish family. If she got caught hiding there, the property owners wouldn't likely notify the police. She could only hope they wouldn't call her parents.

She moved into the shadows around the side of the house and spotted rows of tall bushes behind a picket fence. That would keep her from anyone's view. Following the darkest areas, she crossed the distance between the home and garden area. She searched for a gate, found it unlocked, and hurried into the bushes, going deeper and deeper until she was near the back fence. Feeling safe here, she sat in the soft dirt, pulled her knees to her chest, and wept.

SEVEN

Dewy air enveloped Rhoda as she left her house with an empty bushelbasket and crossed the driveway. Sunlight peeked over the horizon, spreading its glory across the land as it greeted her. By noon the summer's heat would make her feel as if she were in a frying pan over a blazing fire. But right now, as hues of pink and orange painted the sky and crickets continued to sing their night song, it was a taste of heaven.

She entered her berry patch and shut the gate behind her. A familiar feeling crept over her, and the hairs on the back of her neck stood up. Something was different. Looking around, she decided her senses were playing tricks on her again, and she moved toward the blackberry bushes.

As she passed her grapevines, she saw a girl curled up in a ball in the dirt. *Emma?* Rhoda's breath caught in her throat.

Impossible, of course. But the sight reminded Rhoda so much of her little sister, who'd always slept curled up in her bed like that, she wondered for a moment if this was some kind of vision.

Rhoda eased toward the lump on the ground. As near as she could tell, the girl was about seventeen. Emma's age when she died. Kneeling beside her, Rhoda almost expected her little sister to wake up and give her a hug. Rhoda touched her shoulder. She was real.

The girl opened her eyes and gasped when she saw Rhoda. She sat upright and scrambled backward, away from Rhoda.

"I'm sorry. I didn't mean to startle you." Looking closer, Rhoda realized she didn't favor Emma at all. This young woman had blond hair and carried a fair amount of weight. Emma had dark hair and had been as thin as they come, a waif of a girl, really.

From the clothes the girl wore, Rhoda would have guessed her to be one of the Englisch who partied at the house down the street. But for some reason she couldn't put her finger on, that didn't seem right. "My name's Rhoda. Rhoda Byler."

The girl peered at her with large brown eyes as if trying to decide whether to trust her. Or maybe she was just hung over. "Leah King."

Rhoda picked up a whiff of cigarette smoke and alcohol on her breath as well as an Amish accent.

"Sorry to bother you." The girl stood slowly, wobbling. "I'll be off your property as soon as—" Crumbling to her knees, the poor girl retched.

Rhoda pulled a cloth out of her apron pocket, the one she kept handy for wiping her forehead when the day grew hot. When Leah finished emptying her stomach, Rhoda handed it to her.

"Thanks." She wiped her mouth. "I'm so sorry."

"No worry." Rhoda stood. "I add all kinds of odd things to the soil to help my plants grow. You may have provided a new kind of nourishment."

The girl's eyes widened with embarrassed horror, and she trembled with hurt that Rhoda could neither absorb nor understand. The girl seemed to be a torn soul—caught between pushing her boundaries and regretting her choices. "Kumm. I'm sure I have something cleaner that you can wear."

The girl looked at her immodest clothes. "Are you going to call my parents?"

"No." Rhoda started for her house.

Leah grabbed her arm. "Who's inside?"

"No one. Everyone went to Lancaster yesterday to visit relatives. My brothers and their wives are house hunting, and they'll be out with a real-estate agent until late this afternoon. Kumm." She led the way through the berry patch, across the driveway, and into the house.

It was probably a good thing for Leah that Rhoda's parents were gone. They would surely frown on an Amish girl who smelled of sin and puke coming into their home. And her brothers and sisters-in-law wouldn't appreciate

Leah's getup or the questions she'd cause their children to ask. But Rhoda wasn't a purist. "Pretty is as pretty does" was a stupid cliché in her estimation. Pretty is what God does in the hearts and minds of people who are a mess— whether outwardly or inwardly or both. Rhoda hadn't felt that beauty inside herself for two years now, but she believed she would again someday.

"Do you feel steady enough to take a shower?"

Leah stared at the ground. "I don't want to be more of a nuisance than I've already been."

"Gut." Rhoda lifted the girl's chin. "Then stop acting like you're a troll and I'm a saint. Ya?"

Leah's eyes welled with tears, and she shrugged.

Rhoda lowered her hand, wanting to engulf the girl in a warm embrace. How long had it been since Leah felt loved or worthy? "Do you live nearby?"

Leah shook her head. "I'll have to call someone to come get me."

"Do you want to be in those clothes when they arrive?"

"No."

"Then kumm." Rhoda led her to the bathroom. After getting a clean washcloth and towel from under the sink, she doused the rag with cold water and passed it to Leah. "Put this on your lips. It'll help you feel less nauseated, and I'll be right back." She went to her mother's bedroom and grabbed a set of clean clothes that would fit: a sage-colored dress, black apron, and a prayer Kapp. Once in the bathroom again, she put the items on the counter. "You need anything else?"

Leah shook her head.

Rhoda pulled the door closed behind her. While Leah took a shower, Rhoda washed the dishes from earlier and prepared Leah some breakfast.

The door to the bathroom creaked as it opened slowly. Leah's footfalls were light as she hesitantly entered the kitchen, carrying her dirty clothes inside a towel. Her wet hair was pulled back in a long ponytail. She looked like a different person from the one Rhoda had found near her grapevines.

"You must be hungry." Rhoda poured her somber guest a cup of hot tea before putting scrambled eggs and toast on a plate. "This should make you feel better." When she set the plate on the kitchen table, Leah hung back. "Well, come on."

Leah put her bundle in a corner. When she sat down at the table, Rhoda nudged the mug toward her. "There's nothing like a nice cup of licorice-root tea to calm an upset stomach." Leah scrunched her face, making Rhoda chuckle. "Try it. It's delicious and naturally sweet." Rhoda couldn't grow her own herbs anymore, but she could still purchase whatever she wanted. She'd found a wonderful herb place in the historic section of Mechanicsburg—an old home called the Thyme House and Gardens. Rhoda hired a driver to take her there the first time, but since then she'd placed her orders by phone.

Leah took a tentative sip, and her face relaxed. "Denki."

"Eat up. Those eggs will help remove the toxins from your body. And the natural fruit sugar in that blackberry jelly will give you back your energy."

Leah looked skeptical. "I thought dry toast was better for…upset stomachs."

Rhoda knew she meant hangovers but didn't want to admit it. "Trust me."

After Leah took a few tentative bites, her appetite appeared to kick in a little, and she ate half of what was on her plate. Her washed-out cheeks regained some color. "I do feel better. Do those foods really help, or did you make that up?"

Rhoda went to a bookshelf and waved her hand across three rows. "That kind of information and more is in here somewhere."

"But you didn't eat any of it."

"I had breakfast before I went outside to work."

Leah groaned and slouched. "Chores," she muttered. "The curse of being Amish."

Rhoda refilled Leah's cup from the pot on the stove. "Oh, I don't know. Work has plenty of benefits. And if you discover a job you're good at, it comes to mean a lot to you."

Leah lowered her eyes. "I'm not good at anything."

"Nonsense. You just haven't found what your specialty is yet."

Leah folded her arms, looking sullen. "I'll never live that long."

Rhoda heard the words *I hope* at the end of Leah's sentence as clearly as if the girl had said them.

EIGHT

Leah stared at the honey-colored liquid in her mug. Would the embarrassment of last night ever end?

Waking up in a stranger's garden was too humiliating. Did Michael have a clue she was missing? Did he care? And what about her cousin and friends? They'd left without her.

Rhoda reached for the plate. "You done?"

"Ya."

Rhoda removed it from the table and put it in the sink. "Where do you live, Leah?"

This woman had more questions than a parent. "Harvest Mills." She lifted her eyes to watch Rhoda, feeling like the troll she'd mentioned earlier. Rhoda was beautiful. Thin. Clear skin. The bluest eyes ever—almost hauntingly so. No. This girl had never had boy problems a day in her life. Never been disgraced in front of a crowd. Never been called fat.

Rhoda wiped off the kitchen table. "And where do your folks think you are?"

"Camping out with my cousin Dorothy in Lancaster. She went to the party, but she left without me." Leah looked at the clock on the wall. It was past seven already. "Maybe four hours ago."

"Don't you think you need to call your cousin and find out what's going on?"

Leah hated that idea, but she nodded. Feeling like a criminal going before a judge, she followed Rhoda to her phone shanty. The message light on the phone blinked.

Rhoda pulled out the chair for her. "Just ignore the flashing light. I have calls to tend to later today."

Rhoda left, and Leah called her cousin. She got an earful about how Dorothy suddenly felt sick during the party and had someone take her home. Leah had serious doubts about Dorothy's explanation. She'd probably gone off with one of the guys from the party, but Leah had no proof, so she didn't challenge her.

"Anyway," Dorothy said, "I woke up worried about you, so I called your place. Samuel answered."

"What?" Her cousin hadn't cared enough last night to let Leah know she was leaving, and then once the alcohol wore off, Dorothy had sobered up and realized she'd abandoned Leah. "Good grief, Dorothy. I hope you used your brain and didn't say anything stupid."

"I had no idea where you were."

Leah's stomach rolled, and she wished she hadn't eaten. "I can tell you exactly where I am—in trouble, thanks to you. Now Samuel knows we didn't camp out together, and he'll ask where I was."

"Well, forgive me for being worried about you."

"If you'd held off calling my place, we could be talking cover stories right now." Leah needed smarter friends, hopefully ones who had at least a few ounces of loyalty. "I gotta go." She had the phone halfway to its cradle when Dorothy said something else. Leah put the phone back to her ear. "What now?"

"Samuel thinks you're missing. He's calling every number he can think of to find you. If he doesn't locate you soon, he may call the police."

Leah hung up, mumbling to herself, "Do yourself a favor and never make plans with Dorothy again." She rubbed her aching stomach and then dialed the number for her family's barn office. Before the first ring finished, someone picked it up.

"Leah?" Samuel barked.

"Ya. And I'm fine."

Her brother spewed angry questions mingled with half lectures for a full minute before he drew a breath. She hadn't wanted to tell him that she woke up in someone's garden, but during his rant he insisted she tell him where she'd slept last night.

He sighed. "So where are you?"

That was a good question. She looked through the papers on the home-made counter where the phone sat.

"Leah?"

"I'm, uh…" She moved a thick phone book and flipped through it, finding nothing useful.

"You don't actually know where you are, do you?" Her brother's disgust was clear. What she wouldn't give to leave home and never return.

"Of course I do." She found a sheet of paper with a header and Rhoda's name and address on it. "You got a pencil and paper ready?"

She shared the address, and he growled his way through telling her his plan. It was never simple to get their uncle's driver to lend a hand in carting them around. Craig always managed to help, but it took him time to finagle it around his workday. "It could be hours, Leah. And when I arrive at this address, you'd better still be there." He hung up.

Leah wanted to punch out his lights, beg him to hold her, and curl into a ball and cry—all at the same time. Who had that many emotions colliding at once? Why was she such a mess? Fresh heartache pounded as she remembered Michael taking up with someone else last night.

She left the phone shanty and spotted Rhoda picking blackberries in her garden.

The *clippety-clop* of a horse and rig passing by grated on her nerves. If she could, she'd own a car and would never get into a carriage again.

She went to the white picket fence. "My eldest brother will come get me later on." Leah hated that her voice trembled, making her sound like a frightened child. Beyond Samuel's anger, he sounded disappointed in her.

Rhoda left her basket and came to the fence, her stark blue eyes studying Leah. "Are you afraid of him?"

"He's furious."

She nodded, but Leah detected genuine concern for her.

"Why don't you come into the garden?" Rhoda gestured toward the gate. "I'll show you around. It'd do you good to get some exercise helping me and then to rest for a bit."

Leah hoped to make herself at least sound appreciative. "Sure. What all do you grow?"

She went into the garden, and by the time the dew had dried off the ground, Leah had learned how to cut ripe strawberries from their stems and had managed to almost fill a bucket. Rhoda told her that strawberry season was supposed to be over several weeks earlier. Leah wished they were already gone for the season, but she pushed against the desire to move slowly. She needed Rhoda to give Samuel a good report. Her hands trembled as she wiped sweat from her forehead.

Rhoda glanced at her and straightened. She'd picked several buckets of blackberries and didn't seem bothered by the scorching heat. "Why don't you take your container of strawberries to the cellar and set it near the sink? Then go inside and lie down."

Although Leah wanted nothing more than to get out of the sun and lie down, she said, "But Samuel should be here soon—"

"It could be a while yet, and you need some rest. Besides, I'd like to talk to him for a bit before you go. My room is the second on the left at the top of the stairs."

Relief on both counts flooded her—to stop working and to have someone else face Samuel first when he arrived. "Denki, Rhoda." She carried the berries to the cellar and then walked to the door of the house. The moment she went inside, she appreciated being out of the sun.

What was Michael thinking about now? Leah went up the stairs and sprawled across Rhoda's bed. Maybe he regretted what he'd done last night.

Maybe he still loved her.

Rhoda continued working the berry patch. Leah's despair worried her. A great deal. But what could she do about her concerns—meddle in someone else's life? A rig pulled into her driveway. She wiped her brow and headed for the buggy.

A beardless man about her age was tying his horse to the hitching post as she approached. He turned toward her with a harsh look on his handsome face, but it faded. "You must be the woman Leah told me about on the phone."

"Rhoda Byler." She extended her hand. "And you must be Samuel."

He removed his hat, revealing silky, straight blond hair. "I apologize for my sister's behavior, Mrs. Byler."

Her heart jolted a bit. Amish men didn't use titles like Mr. or Mrs. when talking to other Amish, but she figured he was aiming to be especially polite. His assumption that she was married annoyed her a lot more than finding a rogue teenager in her berry patch. At twenty-two years old, she was starting to be considered an old maid by the Amish community. It was so absurd she could launch into an hour's sermon on the topic. The Amish who didn't know her assumed she was married; those who did know her speculated that her strange ways drove off suitors or that God was so angry with her He'd taken away the blessing of marriage.

"Please, call me Rhoda."

"I hope my sister hasn't caused you too much trouble." He spoke through gritted teeth, and she felt sorry for Leah.

"Not at all. I've enjoyed her company."

"Really?" The disbelief on his face said more than his lone word had.

"And she helped me with my work."

"My sister? Leah?" His effort to be polite didn't hide his agitation or his skepticism that his sister was a good worker.

"Ya."

He crumpled the brim of the hat in his hand. "Well, I'm glad you made her pay for her irresponsible behavior. I assure you, she'll receive the proper consequences at home as well."

Rhoda cringed. "I wasn't trying to punish her." She wasn't a parent—and probably never would be. Being the eighth of nine children, she'd seldom been in a position to instruct a sibling, but his viewpoint of chores and punishment going hand in hand was ridiculous.

"It doesn't matter. If she worked, she took it as discipline."

It didn't matter? His tone concerned her, and she didn't like the idea of Leah facing his anger once they were alone in the rig. Rhoda had to soften his irritation toward his sister. "We all do stupid things sometimes. Especially when we're young." She stepped under the shade of a nearby oak tree. "Whatever she did to land here will fade with time, but your reaction as her older sibling will remain with her forever." Rhoda turned on the spigot at the side of the house and rinsed her hands, hoping he didn't realize that she was speaking from personal experience.

"Good. I hope it does."

She turned off the water and stood up straight. "Do you? Even if that means it'll haunt you as well as her?"

"The only thing that will ever haunt me is my sister's ridiculous behavior. She knows better than to follow her wants and feelings."

"If everyone who knew better always made the right decisions, we'd all be saints, wouldn't we? And I'm not. Are you?"

Samuel frowned, looking less patient by the moment. "I'd like to take my sister home now."

"She's resting in my bedroom." An idea came to her, but it'd require inviting him to stay longer. She didn't want to spend more time with this gruff man, but if she could convince him not to be rough on Leah, she'd at least feel as if she'd done what she could for the girl. "Do you have any interest in horticulture?"

"Excuse me?" Samuel clearly bristled.

"Horticulture. Plant cultivation."

"I know what it is, but your question came out of nowhere."

"Sorry, I tend to do that. I thought if you had any interest in the topic, you might like to see my berry patch before you leave."

She thought she detected a little curiosity, so she went across the driveway, expecting him to follow her, which he did. She went to the white picket fence and opened the gate.

"How large a tract of land do you have?"

It was his first question void of frustration.

"A little over an acre. I take care of most everything myself, from planting all the way to canning and selling. I have a hired helper who comes a couple of evenings a week and on Saturdays. His specialty is getting the canned goods packaged and to the stores."

"When do you find time to tend to your family?" His brown eyes studied her, full of inquisitiveness. And honesty. He didn't have enough information yet to form a complete opinion, but that was his goal—to know, to decide who she was or wasn't. She could feel that and see it in his eyes.

"They take care of me. Not that I require much other than food on the table at mealtime."

He angled his head, looking confused. If her goal hadn't been to relieve the tension in him so he'd feel kinder toward Leah, she wouldn't answer his question. What right did he have to determine if she lined up with *his* ideals of being righteous?

"I live with my parents."

"Oh." He seemed relieved that her husband wasn't cooking while she spent her days working the berry patch. "My family has an apple orchard. We—"

"Really?" Finally neutral ground, a topic they could chat about. "My great-great-*Mammi* used to have ten or so apple trees about where the barn sits now, from what I can tell by her diaries. It wasn't an orchard, mind you, but she created some of the best recipes for apple goods you can imagine. She baked while her little ones slept, and she set up a roadside stand on her property to sell her goods while the children played outside."

"So it's in your blood."

"It is. Yours too, I imagine."

"Feels like it drives me rather than the other way around. But I love it."

She soaked in the sense of comradeship on this topic, surprised at how pleasant it was to speak to another fruit grower. "I'm sure your family has some great apple recipes."

"Ya." He looked a little unsure. "They're good, but it'd be interesting to see the ones your great-great-Mammi left behind." Without any doubt he meant what he said, and she realized that's who he was. He said too much at times, but when he spoke, it came from his heart. He had a lot less pretense than most, and she could see the value in it. She imagined his honest ways butted strongly against Leah's sneaking around.

"I'd show you the recipes now if I knew where to find them." Her brothers had boxed up a ton of things while trying to make room for Steven and his family to move in with them a few years ago. They'd stored all the items somewhere, and she'd yet to find Mammi Byler's recipes. She'd have to start looking again.

Samuel walked the rows, studying her plants. "Our orchard has had some good years and some not so good, but your plants are hanging thick with fruit."

"Denki. God's blessed this patch of ground so much that it almost keeps me too busy. Fourteen-hour days, six days a week."

"Every year?"

"Ya."

"What's your secret?"

Rhoda never discussed her methods with strangers. No one ever asked, and she didn't want to raise additional speculations if people found the idea of putting fish guts in the soil weird. Before she answered him, she wanted to know something. "Does Leah help with the work in the orchard?"

"No. We don't need that kind of help."

"What kind? A girl's?"

His eyes searched hers before he started down the row of raspberry trellises, gingerly touching the ripe fruit. Behind his bristly exterior she saw some-one who enjoyed working the land and bringing things to life as much as she did, and her heart murmured with excitement. Leah seemed fragmented and confused about life, but Samuel appeared whole and focused. Maybe a little misguided when it came to his sister, and he probably saw life as distinctly black and white, right and wrong, but she suspected he was dedicated and loyal. And painfully honest, the one trait she admired above all others.

"If you'll help me pick some berries, I'll let you in on some of my secrets."

His half grin told her she had his attention. "You've got a deal."

"Have you ever picked blueberries?"

"My fruit-picking experience is limited to apples."

She led him to the patch and handed him a small metal bucket. "Hold this under a bush with one hand, and with the other hand cup a ripe bunch and gently rub them with your fingers. The ripe berries will drop into your bucket, and the unripe ones will remain attached to the bush."

He tackled the task with the eagerness of a little boy learning to play catch.

She grabbed another bucket and worked alongside him. "I put some rather unusual things in my compost."

"Such as?"

"Well, fish for one thing."

"Real fish, not fertilizer with fish in it?"

"The real thing."

"Makes sense, I guess. Native Americans were doing that generations ago. Where do you get the fish?"

"I tried catching them in the local lakes, but I couldn't stand the thought of killing them myself. So I struck a deal with the local market that sells my canned goods. They give me fish that are past their sell date, and I bring them the first canned goods of the harvest. That has provided me a greater variety of fish, and with a little trial and error, I've figured out which fish work best."

He set down his bucket and stretched. "Interesting." His relaxed expression put her at ease. "What else?"

He was business minded for sure, but he talked to her as an equal. She hadn't expected that. "Herbs."

He frowned. "Herbs?"

"I used to grow beds of them for seasoning food and for their medicinal qualities. One year I had more than I needed for everyday uses, so rather than letting them go to waste, I put them in the mulch. The next year my crops did a lot better. So I began experimenting by adding other things."

"What other things?"

She nodded at his bucket, and he returned to picking blueberries. "I get hair clippings from the local barber shop. But animal hair works better."

"Seriously?"

"And bee droppings have proven quite effective."

He laughed. "How in the world do you get that?"

"By placing a mesh net below my uncle's beehives."

He scratched his jaw. "I bring at least twenty hives onto my property every pollination season, but I've never thought about using their droppings for anything."

Rhoda watched him work as he mulled this over. She'd not had the privilege of knowing how fun it was to discuss her horticultural ideas with someone who understood and appreciated them—and didn't consider them proof that she was off her rocker. "Animal urine does wonders as well."

He lifted an eyebrow. "I'm not sure I want to ask how you get that."

She tossed a shriveled blueberry at him. "Strapping a bucket under a horse for a few hours provides a lot."

He laughed, and she joined in. "So, animal urine, human hair, bee droppings… What, no eye of a lizard? Bat wings? Whiskers from a black cat?"

Her laughter stuck in her throat. How foolish she was to think that someone would see her as innovative rather than as simply odd. She dumped her half-full bucket into the basket and started to pick it up.

He stepped forward. "I'll get that. Where to?"

His eyes indicated that he hadn't meant to suggest she was doing anything unnatural, nor did he realize he had. She motioned toward her workshop. "The cellar."

They left the berry patch and were soon going down the steps to her underground room.

He set the basket on the counter. "Interesting place." He looked around. "Tight quarters, though."

"This is where I do most of my cleaning, packaging, and canning."

"I think it's admirable that you care so much about your harvest you're willing to try new things. If I don't have a better harvest this year than I did last year, I'll be looking for horses to strap buckets to."

His humor caught her off guard, and she broke into laughter while plucking stray stems off the berries. "Two springs ago it rained nearly every day during pollination season. I remember. My blackberries suffered the most."

"Kept the bees from being able to pollinate, and then the ground was sopping wet for nearly two months. But we have a lot of tiny apples hanging on the trees this year."

"That's gut."

"We don't use compost; there's too much ground to cover and no evidence it helps apple trees." He walked to a long shelf of her canned goods and studied them. "But if I had a smaller orchard and thought those types of ingredients would make that much difference, I would try it—no matter how weird it sounds."

"Not everyone would agree. Most folks are afraid of anything different."

He picked up a jar of strawberry preserves and turned it in various directions, reading the label, looking through the glass, and tapping on the lid. "Do you mind if I ask what percentage of profit you make per jar?"

"Fifty percent."

He whistled. "That's remarkable. But you must get some curious responses when you ask people for hair clippings and day-old fish and buckets of horse urine."

"'Curious' is putting it mildly." She tossed a handful of stems into a bucket of compost.

He gestured at her shelves of canned goods and containers of fresh fruit. "But how can they argue when your harvest is that plentiful?"

He seemed taken with her tiny operation, but it felt sinful to enjoy someone's admiration so much. Despite her initial impressions, maybe he wasn't as judgmental as a lot of people.

Rhoda's thoughts returned to the young girl who'd dropped into her life that morning. This might be her last chance to help her. "Leah hates herself."

"What?" Confusion covered his face as if the idea of self-hatred were foreign to him.

"I don't know for sure if that's how she feels—she didn't *tell* me—but it's pretty obvious. I hope you won't do or say anything that makes her feel worse about herself. I mean, that's not useful for her or anyone else."

"You want me to pat her on the back for this stunt she's pulled?" Part of him appeared baffled, and part seemed determined to straighten out his sister.

"No, of course not."

"Then you're suggesting I stay completely silent about it?" His brows were furrowed as he searched her eyes, giving her a brief window to clarify herself.

Feeling flustered, she shook her head. "That's not what I meant."

"Then what?" He shrugged his shoulders, teetering on the verge of frustration. "I don't understand what you're saying."

It was hard to believe that moments ago they were pleasantly chatting about orchards and vines. "Just show some compassion toward a young woman who has no sense of her value."

"If she'd behave, she'd like herself. And if I don't do something to make her settle down, she could regret that I didn't take a stand, that I didn't holler 'fire' when she needed me to. I have no choice but to speak harshly to her."

"There is no need for being mean. I did something once that was more stupid than Leah could ever imagine."

His eyes held concern. If she didn't explain quickly, he'd likely assume the worst. "I didn't drink or smoke or stay out partying all night. But if it weren't for the loving words and kindness of my family, my wrongdoing would've grown into something far worse."

He scoffed. "What could be worse—murder?"

Her heart shuddered as he tossed out the word so lightly. He couldn't possibly understand the ugliness of it. But he'd likely find it easy to judge whoever was to blame for such a horrid act. "You're missing the point." Her voice held an edge to it, and she drew a breath. "She needs to know that you see value in her and that you truly love her."

"My sister knows that. And she knows right from wrong. What she doesn't know is how to control her impulses, and I intend for her to figure that out. While I don't see that it's any of your business, if you think I'm not *valuing* her enough, perhaps you should stick to nurturing plants."

Rhoda's skin burned with indignation. Afraid that if she stayed another moment she'd say something she would later regret, she headed for the cellar door.

NINE

Samuel's head throbbed as Rhoda fled up the cellar stairs. He couldn't remember when he'd been so frustrated by a woman, unless it was Leah. At one point they talked like neighbors who had a common interest in an upcoming harvest. The next thing he knew he was trying to reason with someone as stubborn as Leah.

That was just what his rebellious sister didn't need, a sympathizer. It'd be like tossing a rock to a drowning man. His sister's lack of respect for others was infuriating, and it had put him in an overwhelmingly embarrassing situation.

He did value Leah. He valued who she could become if she ever stopped thinking like a worldly, self-centered teen.

Rhoda's inaccurate evaluation of Leah aside, her husbandry skills were fascinating. She was connected to her berry patch in an odd way that he'd like to understand better.

The sweetness of strawberry jam laced with the aroma of freshly picked blueberries washed over him. He caught hints of tart blackberries. He pulled a jar off a shelf and read its label—Rhode Side Stands. He caught the play on words, but did she sell her products to a lot of roadside stands? He set the jar back on the shelf, agitated with the jumble of thoughts she'd stirred.

His sister's voice disrupted his thoughts, and he went up the stairs. Rhoda stood beside the carriage, putting a basket of canned goods and fresh fruit on the floorboard. How was he supposed to discourage Leah's poor choices if Rhoda kept rewarding her for unacceptable behavior?

"You're ready, then?" he asked.

Leah jolted at the sound of his voice, and she nodded without even looking at him. He was sure that Leah's reaction made Rhoda think he beat his sister or something, but right now he didn't have it in him to put on a front and be gracious and polite. He just wanted to go home.

"I appreciate your hospitality." He pulled his billfold out of his pocket. "I'd like to pay for what she's eaten and—"

"Don't be silly. Your kindness to her is all I request."

She wanted a promise that he and his family would be gentle and encouraging with Leah? That was none of her business. He shoved his billfold back into his pants. "Would you like us to join hands while we sing her praises?" He untied the horse from the hitching post and got into his rig.

Leah got in on the other side.

The driveway was typical for the Amish, large enough to turn a rig around in.

"Leah." He sounded like a gruff old man, but his sister's actions gave him little choice. "Do you have any idea how many people you've inconvenienced?" He tapped the reins against the horse's back and pulled onto the road. "Rhoda, me, and even Craig. He's Uncle Mervin's carpenter and driver, not our personal chauffeur. I'm grateful he could leave his work to help us out and at least get me to Lancaster. But I shouldn't have to interrupt his day, period. It's ridiculous."

"It's not that big of a deal, but I'll apologize when I see him."

"And Rhoda. What were you thinking, pulling a stranger into your ridiculous behavior?"

"I'm sorry, Samuel. I really am. What else do you want from me?"

He came to a four-way stop and waited his turn. "For starters, I'd like to know why you would stay out all night and wind up sleeping in someone's garden."

"Don't you ever get tired of it all—the chores, the monotony?" She didn't sound curious about how he felt, only angry to have been born into an Amish home. He'd been born into the same home, same lifestyle, and he had no qualms with it. Actually, when he did think about it, he was grateful.

Samuel held both reins in one hand while he rubbed his forehead, wishing he had something for the throbbing pain. "Work is part of life. What do you want life to be, an endless party? Oh, that's right. That's exactly what you want."

"I want to have some fun, yes."

He jiggled the reins and clicked his tongue, causing the horse to go through the intersection. "And in order to get what you want, you're willing to behave in ways that will embarrass your family."

"Please don't tell on me."

"So you don't care that you've been out partying, but you do care whether our parents know? Does the word *hypocrisy* come to mind?"

"You don't understand! You've never understood! Life has always been easy for you. No matter what's going on, you fit right in. Me? I don't fit in our family or anywhere—not even with the Englisch!" She burst into sobs, and Samuel wished, not for the first time, that women didn't cry so easily.

If he could only figure out a way to get through to her, he'd be willing to drive the rig around and spar with her all day, all year. Maybe he was going about this wrong. "Leah," he said softly, hoping to calm her, "you do know that we love you, every one of us, right?"

She studied him. "What on earth would make you say that?" She wiped her tears. "You, Daed, Mamm—the whole family just tolerates me at best."

"That's not true. You're being ridiculous." But he wondered what she truly believed. "Did you go to that party with Michael?"

She rubbed at the berry stains on her fingertips. "No."

"Then who took you to Morgansville?"

"I rode with someone you don't know. His name is Brad, and the party was at his house."

He didn't know Brad, but he knew his kind well enough. "And what do you think his purpose is in picking up Amish girls to take to a party? Let me explain it. He and his buddies used up all the girls from their own pool—schools and colleges and churches—all the ones who didn't mind being used. And then he and his friends went looking for less used ones, and you raised your hand, saying, 'Pick me, pick me.'"

"So everything about me disgusts you," Leah whispered. "That's not surprising."

Samuel had lost this round. In fact, he couldn't remember when he'd won one. Was taking a hard stance the best way to help her see the path she was on? "I'll make a deal with you."

"About not telling our parents?"

"Ya. You're not to go to any more Englisch parties for at least four weeks." He hoped in that span of time something would get the desire out of her system. He wished he could insist on longer, but he didn't have that much leverage. If he pushed too hard, she would refuse his deal. After all, if she faced their parents' wrath, they'd only ground her for two or three weeks, giving her grace because of her rumschpringe. "In exchange for that, when Mamm and Daed ask why you didn't stay with our cousin last night like you were supposed to, I'll tell them you slept at Rhoda's and then helped her today, which, as I understand it, is true."

"It is."

He hated covering for her, but he'd hid some things during his own teen years—watching movies, playing video games, listening to music.

His words drew a hesitant smile from his little sister. "Deal."

"I think you owe it to Rhoda to return and spend a day helping her."

"No way. She works long, hot hours in the sun, bent over in her garden."

"Grow up, Leah. Work equals food, clothing, and shelter. Did you eat this morning?"

"Ya, just a tiny bit."

"Are those your clothes?"

She shook her head.

"Then you held out your hand for two things she had to work for. They didn't just float down to her from heaven like manna."

She crossed her arms, looking as sullen as a five-year-old and clearly unwilling to say anything else.

Rhoda wanted him to accept Leah's behavior and attitude, but he wanted to ask Rhoda the same question Christian had asked Catherine: What planet do you live on?

TEN

Catherine grabbed a couple of kitchen towels to protect her hands and pulled the hot pan out of the oven. The delicious aroma of sugar-sweetened blueberries wafted in the steam as she set the pie on the counter.

Creaking stairs signaled that Arlan was finally on his way down to breakfast, despite it being past noon. Mamm was in her vegetable garden, weeding, as she had been since around sunup. Daed had gone to a neighbor's house early that morning to help clear out furniture and set up the benches for church services to be held there tomorrow.

While baking this morning, Catherine had daydreamed of marching up the steps and banging on her brother's door, demanding he tell her what he was doing at the music store. But it wasn't like her to be confrontational, so she held on to her questions until she saw him.

He walked into the kitchen, freshly scrubbed and his well-combed hair almost dripping with water. He had on some shiny athletic shorts and an unbuttoned shirt with nothing under it. "Morning."

"Afternoon is more like it."

He glanced at the clock. "Afternoon." His tone was just as chipper as before. He understood nothing. Less than nothing.

"Where did you go last night?"

"Out. And you?"

"I've been worried sick."

He raised one eyebrow, a slight smile making him look wary. "If you're going to get all emotional, take it elsewhere."

"You think this is funny?" She fought to stay calm. "Mamm and Daed were humiliated once because of you. I thought you'd changed."

"I did, and then I changed back again." He opened the refrigerator and grabbed a jug of juice. "Look, I don't want to hurt anyone, but I've decided I'm not giving up music."

"Did you buy another instrument?"

"No." He opened the cabinet and took down a glass.

"Good. That's a start, because—"

"Not so fast, Sis." He poured some juice. "The store didn't have anything in the price range I was looking for, but they're getting a shipment in a few weeks. Besides, I couldn't make myself plunk down money on a guitar Leah hadn't listened to first. She can tell a cheap-sounding one with a few strums, even in a store with lousy acoustics. I can't. It's like a gift of hers."

Arlan and Leah were friends, nothing more. That used to give Catherine a good measure of relief, but when she realized that he hung on every word Leah said, it pretty much canceled all comfort of their being *only friends.*

He gulped down some juice. "Did you know she has an ear for music like that, able to hear the right key?"

"No, and if you were walking according to the Ordnung, you wouldn't know it either."

"I know just what you mean." His sarcasm rang out clearly as he wiped his mouth with the back of his hand. "Because it's totally immoral to play an instrument. Reports have it that God never did like anyone strumming chords, not even in the Old Testament."

Her heart pounded as he heaped his casual disrespect onto her. The church's stance on musical instruments was one of those really difficult topics. She didn't understand why the Old Order Amish took the view they did, but she accepted the church's position. It made sense to avoid being the center of attention when the whole congregation couldn't participate. Also, it seemed reasonable to accept what she'd been told: outside of a church setting, music easily became filled with ungodly lyrics and devilish beats that appealed to the sensual side. But apparently Arlan thought the whole topic was some kind of joke.

She bet Samuel could have a helpful conversation with Arlan.

The screen door popped open, and Mamm walked into the house. "The morning was beautiful and cool, but the temps are soaring now." She held her dirt-covered hands away from her as she went to the sink. "I put off weeding that garden for far too long. They'd threatened to take over." She flicked on the faucet and scrubbed her hands. "Going to Samuel's, are you?"

Catherine glanced at Arlan, wondering how he could do something that might cause his parents grief. "Definitely."

Mamm pulled a carton of eggs out of the refrigerator. "And if you take him the pie you made, you'll be able to play with little Hope instead of simply talking about her nonstop." She got a bowl out of the cupboard and glanced at Arlan. "Your sister finally has a dog. Did you know that?"

"Cool." Arlan set his glass on the counter. "Where is it?"

"*It* is a she." Catherine got an insulated carrier from the cabinet and set it on the counter. "Her name's Hope, and she's staying at Samuel's. She's the most adorable thing I've ever laid eyes on."

Mamm pinched her cheek. "That's how I felt about you the first time I held you in my arms."

Mamm would have loved having a large brood of children, but after Arlan was born in a home delivery, she had complications and was rushed by ambulance to a hospital. Whether right or wrong, the doctors felt it necessary to remove her uterus. She was unconscious, and Daed gave them permission.

Mamm kissed Catherine's forehead.

"Well." Arlan dusted off his clean hands, a motion that meant he was brushing them off or at least this conversation. "I'm outta here. That's all the gushy stuff I can take for the day, the month, the year."

Mamm held up an egg. "I was going to make you something to eat."

"No thanks." He ran up the steps. "I'm jumping into some real clothes, and I'll be gone in less than a minute."

"Where's he going?" Catherine moved the pie to the cooling shelf just inside the open window.

Mamm put the egg back into the carton and slid it away from her. "Not sure."

"He sleeps half the day and then just leaves?"

"He's been hauling hay for weeks in this heat, and it's his day off. He's earned it and however he wants to spend it."

Catherine plunged her hands into the sink of lukewarm, sudsy water and began washing a few more dishes.

"Don't go worrying about him." Mamm wiped sweat from her forehead. "He's fine. Both of you grew up way too fast, but I can't treat him like a child just because I want him to be that way. He'll be a legal adult in a little more than a year."

Catherine envied her friends who had many little brothers and sisters that they helped and nurtured as they grew up. Arlan was never one to be babied. Now many of those same friends were married and starting their own families. Samuel didn't understand how hard it was to be in her position. But all she could do was remain patient with him and look forward to the day when they started having children. Her mother would love it. "Mamm, did you have to wait for Daed to be ready to get married?"

Arlan bounded down the stairs, dressed in jeans and a T-shirt. "Bye." He ran out the door while they both said good-bye.

Mamm put the carton of eggs in the refrigerator. "Now, where were we?"

"I asked if you wanted to get married long before Daed did."

"No. But everyone's story is different. You know your father. He isn't afraid to make a decision based on feeling. The minute he fell in love with me, at nineteen years old, he asked me to marry him. Of course we ended up living with his parents for about five years. But Samuel's not like your father. It'd kill him to follow his emotions ahead of what's logical."

"He agreed to get a puppy. That wasn't based on purely rational thought."

Mamm grinned. "Oh, I'd say he has plenty of give in him concerning what others need or want, especially you. But you are not a puppy that can be put in a crate or in the barn while he carries on with work. You are his life, and he wants to carefully plan for your future, knowing you will be with child soon after you're wed."

"That's what I needed to hear." She finished washing the baking utensils she'd used earlier, dried them, and put them away. Then she eased the pie into the insulated carrier and went to the barn. After hitching up her rig, she set the pie on the floor of the carriage and headed for Samuel's place.

Fifteen minutes later she pulled up at the Kings' house. His Mamm was in the backyard, using a broom to whack a braided rug hanging from the clothesline. Billows of dust filled the air with each hit.

Catherine parked the rig at the hitching post and took the pie carrier with her.

"Hi, Catherine." Her future mother-in-law stopped beating the rug. "Samuel's not here." Elizabeth worked the kinks out of her back. "He got a call from Leah early this morning, asking him to come get her at her cousin's house. She and Dorothy went camping last night."

Camping? Catherine knew better. Leah's cousin had probably gone to the same party that Leah got all dressed up for last night. Dorothy's father was a preacher in Lancaster, one of the church leaders meant to uphold the Old Ways. How difficult it'd be on him if he knew what his daughter had been up to.

"How'd he get there on a Saturday morning?"

Elizabeth handpicked tiny clumps of lint off the rug. "His uncle's driver, Craig, came from Lancaster and got him. Good thing someone in this family has a business with a full-time driver."

"I guess so." Catherine appreciated that Craig never failed to stop what he was doing to drive any of the Kings to Lancaster when they needed it. But once Samuel arrived at his uncle's, Craig would return to his carpentry work, leaving Samuel to hitch a horse to a buggy to get around. "You haven't heard from him since he left this morning?"

"Not yet." Elizabeth brushed the balls of lint from her hands.

Catherine imagined that neither of Samuel's parents knew the real story behind his picking up Leah. No matter. She'd find out soon enough.

"Is that your special blueberry pie?"

"Ya."

"He'll love it. You'll stay for dinner, right?"

Catherine had hoped she'd ask. "I will now."

"Good. Go ahead and put the pie in the kitchen. Then I suspect you'll be wanting to go see that new pup of yours."

"I hope you don't mind her being around."

Elizabeth grinned. "Not at all. She's a cute little thing, and the girls are thrilled."

Catherine took the pie to the kitchen, where Samuel's youngest sisters were making biscuits. "Hello."

Thirteen-year-old Katie looked up from kneading a lump of dough. "Hey, Catherine." She raised flour-covered hands and wiggled her messy fingers. "Want a big hug?"

She laughed. "Maybe later."

"How about from me then?" Eleven-year-old Betsy left the round cookie cutter in a square of rolled-out dough and wrapped her arms around Catherine's waist.

After returning the hug, Catherine took her pie out of the carrier and put it in the icebox, disappointed that Samuel wouldn't be able to eat it while it was still warm. "How do you like the puppy?"

"Are you kidding?" Katie sprinkled more flour on the cutting board. "We go out to the barn every chance we get."

Betsy pressed the cookie cutter into another section of dough. "Which has been ever so much fun." She lifted the circle and set it on a baking sheet.

Catherine wouldn't ask them to join her now. They had a chore to finish. "I'll go see her, and you two come when you're done."

"We'll be there later. But we're likely to have to bake and throw out a few batches before we get it right. Mamm's determined we get the hang of making biscuits...*today*."

"Sounds good." Catherine left the house and went to the barn.

Hope was in a stall, but it wasn't like the solid wooden stable at Christian's place, so Samuel had lined it with chicken wire. The cocker spaniel ran around in circles when she saw Catherine, barking as she had at the Lapps' place. Hope jumped up on her hind legs, her front paws resting on the fencing.

Catherine picked her up and stroked her soft fur. Despite the turmoil she felt over Arlan and Leah, Catherine found solace in the puppy. Samuel had known that when he put the pup in her arms. If only he were as eager to marry her as she was him.

She found an old towel to play tug of war with Hope. The puppy rough-housed for a while, and then Catherine sat on a bale of hay, and Hope snuggled into her lap and took a nap.

It seemed as if only minutes had passed before Katie and Betsy joined her. They chatted and played with the puppy, and when the dinner bell rang, Catherine turned to the girls. "It can't possibly be that late already."

Katie giggled. "That's how we were this morning. There's just something about a new puppy that makes the hours fly by."

"Apparently so." Catherine put the puppy into the pen. Why wasn't Samuel back yet? He'd have come to the barn to let her know if he was home.

Elizabeth was punctual about mealtimes, so Catherine hurried the girls to the house, and they washed up before sitting down at the table. Samuel's Daed, Benjamin, was there, but none of the other King men were. Although Catherine enjoyed Elizabeth's delicious apple-glazed chicken and stuffing and the girls' biscuits, she couldn't stop wondering what was keeping Samuel. It wasn't unusual for him to sit and chat with his family in Lancaster over coffee or something, but surely he would've planned to be back in time for dinner.

Jacob and Eli finally came in from the field, saying the day's work load had taken longer without Samuel. As the men started filling their plates, Catherine heard a car drive up outside. She excused herself and went out the front door, straightening the folds in her apron. Samuel and Leah got out of the car.

Neither looked happy.

Samuel had been at the dinner table for ten minutes, and he couldn't take much more of listening to Leah tell half-truths. He rubbed his aching head, and Mamm got up from the supper table. She passed Samuel two Advil.

"Denki, Mamm." He picked up his glass of water and swallowed the pills.

"Gern gschehne." Mamm took a seat again. "Leah, I can't believe you and your cousin pitched a tent in someone's berry patch."

"What tent?" Leah asked. "I slept under the stars. It was warm enough."

"I doubt the person who planted those berries intended for a couple of teenage girls to simply set up camp and help themselves." Samuel's Daed crossed his arms over his chest.

"I didn't help myself." Leah swallowed a mouthful of stuffing. "And the woman who owns the patch is Rhoda. She didn't mind me being there."

Samuel picked at his food. Their parents didn't question her story, and Samuel intended to add nothing. He simply sat there.

Samuel glanced at Catherine. How well was she holding up?

Daed picked up the saltshaker. "Samuel, what's your take on all this?"

"Leah slept in the patch. Rhoda found her and fed her, and then Leah helped pick berries, so I'm hoping she paid the woman for any inconvenience she caused."

Leah nodded. "I did. Trust me."

Samuel stiffened at Leah's "trust me." The meal continued with very little else said.

When everyone was finished, Catherine put her fork on her plate. "Anyone ready for dessert?"

Samuel appreciated her effort, but he'd eaten enough to assure his family he was fine. That's all he could stomach right now.

Katie's face glowed. "Catherine brought one of her blueberry pies."

"Maybe later." Samuel set his napkin on the table. "I wouldn't do it justice right now." With a brief glance at Leah, he rose and left the room.

Although Catherine usually stayed in the kitchen to help clean up after a meal, he was glad when she excused herself and followed him outside.

She took his hand. "Want to go see Hope?"

"What?"

"Our puppy, silly."

He'd forgotten about the dog. "Oh. Ya, sure." He tightened his fingers around hers. The moment they stepped into the barn, Hope started barking. Samuel had to do something useful and mindless, so he brushed the horses.

Catherine grabbed the towel again and tussled with Hope. While he spread a scoop of oats into the horses' troughs, she dropped the towel and came to the short wall of a stall. "You calm enough yet to talk?"

The puppy shook the towel and continued playing.

Samuel left the stall and put two milking stools side by side near Hope. "Sorry I wasn't here when you arrived."

Catherine sat and patted the other stool. "You know that's not a problem, right?"

He took a seat and exhaled before telling her all that had taken place since early that morning.

Her brown eyes flickered with offense for all he'd been through, but the tension in his shoulders began to ease. "Samuel, getting that call from Dorothy had to be awful."

"To say the least."

"Where was Leah when she called you?"

"About thirty miles away in Morgansville, but it's mostly highway between here and there. Once the driver got me to Lancaster, it took me about twenty minutes by horse and carriage to get from my uncle's place to Rhoda's. By the time I got there, I was so irate I took it out on the woman who helped Leah. But she didn't make matters any better, spouting a crazy idea about how our family needs to love Leah and build up her self-esteem or some such nonsense."

Catherine nodded, looking sympathetic about his day. "Leah's problem isn't a need for love. She needs self-control and self-discipline."

"That Rhoda woman had a very different impression." She was completely wrong, wasn't she?

"Morgansville?" Catherine put the whimpering pup in her lap. "They must be under a different bishop than Lancaster, because I don't remember meeting many Morgansville Amish at regional gatherings."

"Ya, they're off by themselves in lots of ways. Town living. A few Amish homes with large lots and small barns. Some houses have shops beside them. It's a pretty place, now that I think about it."

Catherine smiled. "You mean now that you can see straight."

He rubbed the top of Hope's head. "Leah and Dorothy have told so many lies to cover their tracks I doubt our families will ever know all that's going on. Unless the girls mature enough to confess. Until then, I'm stuck in the middle, trying to do the best I can."

"Maybe you're trying too hard to shield her from your parents' anger."

"Leah fears our parents and the church leaders discovering what she's been up to. I don't know why. She gives off a vibe that she doesn't care what others think. But I believe if that one obstacle were removed, if all the adults in her life knew the truth, she'd probably walk away from the church."

Catherine jolted, eyes wide. "If Leah left, she'd likely take a friend with her, and Arlan would be first in line."

"I know, and I intend to do what I can to keep that from happening."

"She's only seventeen. She can't legally run off, and she has no skills to support herself, does she?"

Samuel took her soft hand into his. There was so much Catherine couldn't understand about someone like Leah. "She doesn't care what's legal. And she may be lazy, but she's far from stupid. She could figure out a way to take care of herself. If I'm right about what's motivating her to stay, we need to keep her secrets and hope she grows up before people find out what she's up to."

"I'll keep her secrets to the bitter end. My parents couldn't stand losing one of their only two children."

"All we can do is our best."

"And pray."

He nodded. "And pray."

Leah came into the barn. "Is it true that you got a puppy?"

Samuel took the dog from Catherine and held Hope out to his sister. "Go on."

Leah reluctantly moved in closer and took her.

Catherine stroked the puppy's head. "Her name is Hope."

"Thanks for covering for me." Leah's eyes didn't quite meet his.

"You need to stop doing things that would hurt the people you care about. And stop mooning over Michael. He's not worth it."

Leah seemed like a child in some ways, as innocent as Katie and Betsy, who'd been so excited about Hope. But the excitement he'd seen in her moments earlier had disappeared. She looked as if she'd like to melt into the floorboards and disappear.

Leah pulled the furry little pup closer before she passed Hope back to Samuel and left without saying another word.

Catherine put her hand on Samuel's back and scratched it lightly. "I see the guilt on your face, Samuel. But she needs to know you don't approve of her behavior."

He felt the weight of Leah's actions more than he should. If messing up her own life wasn't hurtful enough, and it was, he knew Catherine would never be the same if Leah left and Arlan followed. "I'm doing my best. You know that, right?"

"I know, and you'll get us beyond our current problems with our siblings, and our days will become peaceful as we focus on our life together and having a family."

Catherine's viewpoints tended to be oversimplified, but she often said what he needed to hear.

He propped his forearms on his knees. "I hope you're right."

ELEVEN

Leah sat on a hard bench in her neighbor's barn, trying not to think about God while the minister preached on and on about being faithful to His perfect, divine plan. She and Arlan had talked a lot about her feelings toward God, but he never felt exhausted by the topic the way she did. He embraced every thought about God, and then he either accepted what was said as accurate or filed it away as skewed. It'd be nice to have that kind of peace.

But this was a church Sunday, and every other week she had to sit with the single girls in her age group, each of them wearing a white organdy apron to signify her purity. She hated pretending to worship a God who, at best, didn't like her any more than she liked herself.

When the sermon finally ended, everyone moved from the benches onto their knees for silent prayer. Leah stole glances at her girlfriends, whose heads were all bowed reverently. Elsie, Anna, and Nancy had gone to the same party she had on Friday night, but here they were, heads bowed, eyes closed, wearing the pious clothing of a people who'd separated themselves from the world. Maybe Samuel had a point about her being a hypocrite. But the only way she could stop being a hypocrite was to leave the order. Being seventeen and jobless, she had no way of doing that.

"Amen." The preacher's voice echoed through the old barn, and the congregation stood.

Leah looked past the preacher's stand at the hundred or so men with their hats in their hands. She couldn't see Michael among them, but she knew he was there toward the back with the rest of the single men his age. Did he know she'd left the party by herself? Did he even care?

She filed out of the barn behind the girls who'd left her at the party. Her mind burned with choice words she'd never say to them.

A group of little children, free from their parents' restraints after the three-hour service, fled into the yard to run off their energy. Leah wished she could so easily escape the restrictions that bound her.

She needed to talk to Michael so they could patch things up. Ever since he started his rumschpringe, he'd been flirting with other girls, had even dated a few, but he always came back to her. Always.

Ignoring her so-called friends, she followed the older women toward the house. Tables needed to be set and food served. Halfway between the barn and the house, Nancy and Anna came out of nowhere and grabbed her arms. Leah let them lead her to the middle of the yard before she jerked free of their grip.

Anna moved in close, whispering, "What happened to you Friday night?"

"You all left without me."

Elsie joined the group. "Shush." She glanced at the men who were moving benches from the barn into the house for the midday meal. "Either talk quieter or not at all. I'd rather not give my parents a heart attack on a Sunday."

"Ya." Leah rolled her eyes. "That'd be more ungodly than doing so on Monday through Saturday."

Elsie scoffed. "Fine, Leah. Let's all watch while you tell your parents what you've been doing with your Friday nights."

Her blood boiled. "You *should* watch—watch me tell them how you left me at some Englischer's house. How you didn't even check on me all day yesterday after you abandoned me!"

Anna raised her nose, looking down on Leah as if she were as unimportant as a bug on a sidewalk. "We didn't leave *you* Friday. We met at Brad's car at the same time we always do, just like we were supposed to, and we waited for twenty minutes. You never showed."

"Girls," Mamm called from the front porch. "Kumm help. Now."

"Ya. *In paar Minudde.*" Leah assured her Mamm she'd be there in a minute. "I always thought my *friends* cared about me, no matter what. But you really showed your true colors Friday night. I asked Mamm, and she said no one called or came by or anything yesterday." She walked off.

Nancy caught her by the arm. "You're right. And I'm sorry."

"Ya, me too," Elsie said.

They sounded sincere enough that Leah was tempted to believe them.

"We're all really sorry," Anna said. "We thought you got a ride home with that Englisch guy we saw you with at the party—Turner?"

Elsie touched Leah's shoulder. "Let's meet at the Zip'n Mart next Friday. And we won't let Brad leave without all of us. Okay?"

"Not me." Leah straightened her apron. "Samuel had to come get me, and I had to buy his silence. I won't be going much of anywhere for at least four weeks."

The girls looked horrified—whether out of concern for her or because they couldn't stomach the idea of not getting away on the weekend, she didn't know.

Leah hurried inside and began helping the other women put out place settings and move food from the icebox and kitchen counters to the individual tables. Since only four or five tables fit in a room, the church leaders and elders would eat first, then the other men. It'd be an hour or so before the women her age could eat. As she took a platter of freshly sliced homemade bread to one of the tables, her stomach rumbled.

Why did the Amish have to live in the Dark Ages? Honestly. The men had it made. Not only did they get to eat first, but they had almost no chores on Sundays. They got a weekly day of rest, but the women still had to serve meals, clean up, take care of the babies. *Join the twenty-first century, people. Or at least the twentieth.*

Her Mamm always said she should be glad the Sunday church meals were simple and prepared ahead of time—bread made the day before; ham, cheese, and peanut butter spreads; fresh fruits; pickles; red beets; raw vegetables; prebaked pies, with coffee, water, and lemonade.

After the first group had been served, Leah sneaked outside where the young people gathered in small groups on the lawn. Spotting her younger sister

Katie in a huddle of girls that included her so-called friends, Leah headed that
way. Surely none of them was so loose lipped as to tell her little sister about
Friday night.

When Leah arrived at the group, she pulled Katie aside. "Hey, why don't
you come inside and help me?"

"Mamm said I could stay out here."

Leah tucked her arm tighter around Katie's. "Kumm. Please?"

"Okay." They walked arm in arm. "I heard that all you teens got together
somewhere Friday night and that Michael was flirting with some other girl.
And right in front of you. Why would he do that?"

Leah wished she knew. "What else did you hear about Friday?"

"Nothing. Is there more to it?"

Leah figured way too many of the youth now knew about Michael's embarrassing behavior toward her—mere months after she'd told everyone they
were seeing each other. That's what Michael had told her, wasn't it? That they
were on their way to being married one day?

From the corner of her eye, she saw him laughing with a group of young
men. He seemed completely content without her. Maybe he didn't care about
her at all. Or maybe that girl at the party had just temporarily turned his head.

She couldn't talk to him right now. It wasn't the Amish way to get in
mixed groups and chat before everyone had been served their after-meeting
meal. But she'd catch up with him later in the week, and she held tight to the
hope of winning him back.

The buzz of casual conversations in Pennsylvania Dutch filled the Amish home,
reminding Jacob of all that was good inside his community. There were few
Amish traditions higher on his list of cherished moments than the after-church
mealtime.

He stood in line, about the thirtieth man back, waiting to enter the room
of tables and benches. Samuel was ahead of him by six or seven people, but

when they sat, they'd be at the same table—the one for single men in their age group.

Someone poked him on the shoulder, and he turned.

Mark grinned while stepping back into his spot with the four young men behind Jacob. "You comin' tonight?"

Jacob had missed the conversation that prompted this question, but he needed no lead-in. Every Sunday night youth singings were held for all the singles from their district and others nearby.

Jacob shoved his hands into his pockets, feeling the tug of his suspenders against his shoulders. "Sure. Where will it be this time?"

"Don't know yet." Mark's ruddy skin turned a darker shade of red as he answered. Being the same age, Jacob and Mark had begun and finished school together, but despite their proximity, Mark didn't know him, not even close. It seemed odd how little anyone—even those who'd grown up in the same home—knew about him, from his talents to the horrors he'd survived.

A sound of glass breaking caused everyone to turn in that direction. Leah stood in the kitchen, eyes wide. Shattered glass and water from a pitcher surrounded her feet, and the lower half of her dress was wet.

She scanned the onlookers, and her eyes met Jacob's. She hadn't been herself last night or today—pale, shaky, and quiet. And recently, incidents like these, where she felt insecure and clumsy, really rattled her.

He gave her a subtle nod, hoping she'd remember a conversation they'd had awhile back about handling public mishaps. The taut lines of embarrassment on her face eased. She held out her hands, palms up. "Well, let's hear it."

Immediate applause rose, along with a few *hoorays,* and like magic the tense, awkward moment began to fade.

"That's more like it," Leah quipped before grabbing a kitchen towel. Several of the women scurried to pick up the broken glass and ice cubes while others mopped the water from what had to have been a full container.

Leah had plenty of guts, but in the last year or so, that quality often hid under a massive boulder of insecurities, especially when she was in the same

room as Michael Yoder. Jacob glanced down the line behind him and saw
Michael studying her and then whispering something to the guy beside him.
Jacob didn't care for Michael, never had, and he certainly didn't like that his
impressionable teenage sister was under the spell of an insincere twenty-
year-old.

Whose spell were you under at seventeen? That thought hit Jacob, and he
didn't like the answer. Turning his head, his attention zeroed in on a newspaper
tucked inside the wooden mail center that hung on the wall some three feet
ahead of him. Even folded, he could see enough to know it was the *Washington
Post.* But how old was it? The half he could read revealed partial sentences, and
he could make out a few jarring words: *conviction, cover-up, construction.* His
heart beat faster.

If it weren't Sunday, he'd amble that way, start a conversation with whoever was nearby, and ease it out of its holder, hoping the onlooker never became
suspicious of such a move. But reading a paper was frowned on until church
was officially over, and in the eyes of the people in this room, church wouldn't
be over for hours yet.

The lines shifted, and Jacob moved past the paper without getting much
of a look, then headed with his group to their table.

He took a seat on the bench and was quickly flanked by other single men.
Did newspaper headlines ever worry any of them? He doubted it unless it con-
tained news of an accident in the Plain community.

Jacob absently put food on his plate as bowls and platters were passed. A
kick to his shin startled him, and he saw Mark grinning at him.

"You got that far-off look in your eyes again. What's up?"

Jacob pulled his attention back to those around him. But Samuel glanced
behind him to see what Jacob had been looking at.

Jacob stuck a dull knife into a bowl of peanut butter spread and put it on
a piece of homemade bread. "Just wondering why we still bother going to
singings."

Mark took a bite of the sandwich he'd made. "Didn't you hear me? I said there's a group of girls from Ohio visiting in the next district, and they're coming tonight."

Jacob hadn't heard him, but he wasn't interested in admitting it. "At least those girls don't know us."

The young men laughed, one of them slapping Mark on the back. "That fact still won't help you any."

Mark's cheeks flushed red as he chuckled. "Ya, but with Jacob going, that'll help."

"The Englisch call it being a wingman." Jacob took a drink of water.

Mark made a face. "As long as you don't let me crash, I don't care what it's called." He wiped his hands on a paper napkin. "The key at these things is breaking the ice, and Jacob can melt an arctic glacier with just a few words. I've seen him do it."

That wasn't true, but Jacob wouldn't argue. He usually ran girls off, tending to come on a little strong, but that let him know what a girl was made of. Why waste time? What was the point?

He glanced around the table. Most of the single men were seeing someone, not anyone who would interest Jacob, but at least his friends weren't alone. It'd be nice to have someone with him on weekend nights. Someone to think of when they weren't together. He actually longed for that. Sometimes, when isolation pressed in hard, Jacob wondered if he too easily wrote off the women he met because of his need to hide a part of himself. If one ever got close to his heart, she'd have questions that couldn't be brushed aside with witty remarks.

He glanced at the newspaper. He had so very much to hide.

TWELVE

A crying toddler woke Rhoda from her nap. She stretched, grateful for between-Sunday afternoons. Nonchurch days were the most restful, even if naps were often cut short due to the bustle of her nieces and nephews. A warm breeze flowed in through the open windows, making the sheet over her flutter.

Muffled voices of adults murmured from various places inside the old house, and the chatter of children bounced off the walls. But the cries had stopped.

Rhoda slid out from under the sheet and pulled her dress over her head. With temperatures outside nearing a hundred, she'd peeled out of everything except her undergarments hours ago.

She'd searched the attic again that morning, looking for her grandmother's recipes, but she hadn't found them. A new idea of where her brothers might have put them came to her, and she went to her closet, unlatched a small door to the attic, and peered inside. Normally she'd crawl into the small, dark space to look around, but it had a new box jammed in the entryway. She tugged on the box, dragging it out of her closet. She opened it and went through the books one by one, flipping the pages, but she didn't find what she was looking for. A stash of newspapers covered the bottom.

Someone tapped on her door.

"Kumm." Rhoda picked up a newspaper from a decade earlier and began looking through it.

"Rhoda?" Lydia sat on the edge of the bed.

She lowered the newspaper. "Sorry. I almost forgot someone had knocked."

Lydia put her hand on her protruding stomach. "I was hesitant to interrupt since it appeared you were praying about something in that old paper."

Rhoda caught a glimpse of herself through Lydia's eyes. She was on her knees with her mouth moving as she read the newspaper. "Ten years ago a drought destroyed nearly all the crops here in Morgansville."

"Oh." Lydia stretched her back. "Did your search turn up Mammi Byler's recipes?"

"Not yet." She'd begun to wonder if her brothers had thrown out the tattered cookbook that Mammi Byler had created. The last time Rhoda saw it, the yellow pages were slipping from the faded blue cover. It could've looked like trash to them, but her grandmother had handstitched the binding to hold the treasured pages together. The thought of never finding the recipes again weighed on Rhoda, but she wouldn't voice that to her sister-in-law.

Rhoda got up and sat beside Lydia. "Did you get a chance to rest?"

Her sister-in-law shook her head, her dark eyes holding a hint of worry. "I wanted to tell you something I found out a few days ago. I didn't say anything sooner because I needed some time to adjust to the news."

"Tell me what?" A nugget of anxiety formed in Rhoda's chest.

"The midwife says I'm having twins."

"Oh." Rhoda reached for her hand. "It's one of those good-news, scary-news things, isn't it?"

Lydia's smile quivered like a candle flame threatening to go out. "It's exciting, and it's overwhelming. We'll have five children under six, and we don't even have a good prospect for buying a home yet."

"Either you'll find a house, or you're meant to stay here a while longer."

Lydia played with the strings to her prayer Kapp. "Banks are being so strict. We found a place we could afford, but the underwriters turned us down for the loan—even after we were preapproved. The agent said the banks are fearful and the housing market is crazy right now."

Rhoda held her sister-in-law's hand and squeezed it. She had no words. Living in a home with three men and their families was trying on everyone, and with each new child who came along, the stress went up. She couldn't imagine how little sleep everyone would get with two newborns added to the mix. But they'd pull together. They always did.

"Two more Bylers in the family will be a blessing. And Mamm and Daed will embrace every blessing that comes their way. You know they will." Rhoda got up. "That chocolate cake Mamm made yesterday is calling my name. Care to join me?"

Lydia reached for her hand and held it gently. "Karl and Bertha never get any rest as it is. They've worked hard all their lives and don't even have their own house to themselves."

Rhoda made a *tsk* noise with her tongue. "Mamm and Daed welcomed you into their home seven years ago, and that won't change because you're expecting two babies at once."

"But they've been really interested in helping us find a place, even when they thought we were having only one."

"Don't take it personally, Lydia. It's a tight squeeze for everyone right now. But you and John and the children could not be more loved, regardless of where you live, ya?"

Lydia released Rhoda's hand. "You're right. I'm letting myself get too sensitive. It's just that I want us to get a home of our own so badly I can hardly sleep at night."

"If I knew something helpful to say, I would." Rhoda put her head covering over her messy hair, planning to comb her hair and repin it into place later. She took Lydia by the hand. "Kumm. Chocolate cake will make it better. I know it will."

The sound of a little one pounding on her door vibrated the room. "Mamm!" Linda Lou wailed. *"Du rei do?"*

Rhoda opened her door, and her two-year-old niece ran to her mother.

"Kumm!" Linda Lou grasped her mother's finger and pulled.

John stopped at Rhoda's doorway, carrying his four-year-old son, Enos, who looked as if he'd just gotten up. John smiled at his wife. "How about a lazy Sunday afternoon wading in the creek behind the Stoltzfus home? Steven, Phoebe, their children, and Mamm are already walking that way."

Lydia wiped sweat from her face. "Ya. Sounds gut."

"Rhoda?"

"*Nee,* denki," she declined, wanting a little time to talk to her Daed when no one else was around.

John held out his arm for Lydia. She took it and waddled slowly down the stairs, Rhoda close behind. They headed out the front door, and Rhoda waved.

Going through the living room on her way to the kitchen, she saw Daed dozing in his recliner. He opened one eye. "There she is." He sat more upright, smiling. "Have a good nap?"

"Ya."

He picked up the folded newspaper lying on an end table next to him. "And now you're on your way to get a piece of that chocolate cake, I'm sure."

"You know me too well. Care to join me?"

He got up. "Sure."

They went into the kitchen, and she pulled two dessert plates out of the cabinet.

Her Daed set his newspaper on the island and got the cake down from the top of the fridge. She removed the lid from the three-layer cake and cut them each a slice.

After he poured both of them a glass of cold milk, they sat at the island. "I walked through your berry patch earlier. Looks like you'll have a great crop of blackberries this year."

"I think so too."

"Strawberries appear picked clean."

"They are. They're usually gone by the end of June, but I was still gathering enough to make jam until a few days ago. Mid-July—can you believe it?"

"I'll believe almost anything when it comes to your berry patch."

He said little about most things, and it wasn't easy to know what he thought. It left her wondering how he felt after insisting she let Rueben and Naomi uproot her herb garden. Before Emma passed, she'd always known when her Daed was feeling stress, because whenever she got up during the night to get a glass of water or to go to the bathroom, he'd be up. But insomnia was a way of life for him now. He meandered through the house at night like a man who'd lost his way.

"So how's my girl holding up in this heat?"

"As long as there are Sunday afternoons when I can sleep and cake to eat when I wake, I'm fine."

She longed for a real conversation with him, the type they used to have, which was as soothing as herbal ointment on a painful wound.

After Emma died, Rhoda had wanted to tell him the whole truth, to unload all her selfish, ugly guilt, but she'd gotten out only a few words when he held up his hand, telling her to hush. Then he'd bolted from the house. Long after midnight he'd returned and come to her, looking broken and not at all like the father she'd always known. He'd moved to the side of her bed and sat. When he finally spoke, he apologized for cutting her off and leaving the way he had. "Rhodes…" She still remembered the warmth of his calloused hand on hers. "There are subjects people can't talk about, and for me this will always be one of them." His eyes had brimmed with tears as he tried to speak, and it broke something in her to see him that way. "We'll ask God to forgive us." He fell silent, and it was quite a while before he spoke again. "And He will…has already. Let that be it. Okay?"

She'd have agreed to anything right then. "Ya, Daed."

He'd given her hand a squeeze and left the room. They'd not spoken of that day since. In the two years that had passed, no one had made a cake on his birthday or dared wish him a happy birthday. They simply got through the day as best they could.

Time had moved unbearably slowly the year after Emma's death, each day lasting a week, each month feeling like six. And in that period she had walked in the midst of a dark cloud of grief as she continued building her business.

While she'd muddled through and tended her crops, people in the community and the church had nurtured seeds of fear and condemnation. She'd sown them herself.

After Emma had left for the store that day, Rhoda had continued working her garden until she sensed a warning of what was about to happen. She fought with herself for a couple of minutes, trying to discount the thoughts as nonsense, but she felt submerged in the foreboding, so she took off running for the store. She stumbled and fell in front of Mrs. Walker's house, smacking into the pavement and hitting her head. The elderly woman was working in her front lawn. When she came to see if Rhoda was okay, Rhoda stood, but then she stumbled and sank to the ground, too dizzy and addled to stay upright.

She told Mrs. Walker what she *knew* was about to happen and where. The woman thought Rhoda had knocked herself incoherent, and Rhoda began screaming for someone to save her sister, to get to the grocery store, to stop the man with the gun. People gathered. Everyone heard her cries. But no one listened. She finally got up and began hobbling there, her sprained ankle slowing her down.

And then a gun went off.

Again.

And again.

Rhoda never denied that she caused people to feel the way they did about her. But she wasn't a witch. She never sought to know *anything*. It just happened. And despite her Daed's warnings to keep that side of her hidden, everyone found out that day—and neither Rhoda's knowing nor her revealing the long-held secret had saved Emma.

Rueben and Naomi represented far more people than just themselves when they came against her. They acted as voices for those who were too respectful of her family's mourning, or were too polite or too cowardly, to speak up.

Landon had been on his way to her place when he saw the commotion at Mrs. Walker's. He'd stopped, carried her to his truck, and taken her to the store, to the scene of the crime. To his credit, through all the grief and turmoil, Landon had remained a steadfast friend and employee.

Her Daed's voice interrupted her thoughts. "Rhoda." He got up and put his empty plate and glass in the sink. "I need to ask you something."

"Sure. Go ahead."

"When we got home yesterday, there was a towel on the floor. I picked it up, and clothes fell out—non-Amish clothes. Do you know anything about them?"

She'd forgotten all about that. "They belong to a girl I met on Saturday—an Amish girl. She needed something clean to wear, so I gave her one of Mamm's dresses, and she must've left hers here."

He studied her, frowning and raising his eyebrows at the same time. Over the years she'd noticed that look—perhaps best described as surprised displeasure or maybe bewilderment—was most often reserved for her. Her unconventional ways confused him, but he always adjusted as much as he could without asking her to change.

One thing was sure, despite all they'd been through, she knew he loved her. At times she would have given up on herself, on life, if she hadn't been able to see herself through his eyes—a man who knew how to love unconditionally.

"You simply gave one of your mother's dresses away?"

"Ya."

"An older one?"

"That wouldn't be very nice of me for the girl's sake. Mamm will never miss it. If she does, I'll make her one when my canning season is over." She pushed her empty plate away. "That's really all I want to say on the matter if it's okay with you."

He took her plate to the sink and rinsed it. "You let a stranger stay here while all of us were gone?"

"No. Well, actually I guess I did. I let her take a shower, and I fed her. Then we worked the berry patch together before she took a nap."

"That's odd."

"A little." Her thoughts turned to Leah's brother. Her Daed's reservations about Leah being here didn't begin to compare with Samuel's. But she gave Samuel credit for speaking his mind—whether he was impressed with her garden or annoyed at her viewpoint. As crazy as it sounded, something about Samuel drew her. He was wound tight, at least he was the day she'd met him, but she'd bet two of her best-producing raspberry bushes that he was a man worthy of a girl's heart.

Daed grabbed a kitchen towel and dried his hands. "How old a girl?"

"Seventeen."

"You say she's Amish?"

"You know, you're not good at letting me drop a subject."

He sighed. "As often as you're in trouble with neighbors or with someone in our church, one would think you wouldn't get involved in someone else's scrapes."

"Then one would be wrong. There are many things I can't stop—like Mrs. Walker letting her fears rule her or the Rueben Glicks of the world making me their target. I can't even stop people in our church from being afraid of me and believing lies. But I can keep negativity from molding who I am and how I respond to others."

He put his hand on her shoulder. "You're an interesting child. Confusing, but you're definitely worthy of note."

"Denki...I think." She got up from the island, eager to change the subject. "Daed, Lydia's concerned that she and John aren't going to find a place they can afford."

"It's becoming a problem, ya."

"But what about building a house? He and Lydia talked about that for a while, saying it'd be affordable because our Amish friends could get the foundation in and put up the walls and a roof so they could live there."

Daed chuckled. "You mean dry it in."

"Ya. Then they could live in it and finish it as money allowed. But the next thing I knew, the subject was dropped, and nobody's mentioned it since."

"Buying land costs money too." Her Daed shrugged, but his manner and the look in his eyes indicated he was holding something back.

"What aren't you telling me?"

"Let it go, Rhodes."

"Daed?"

He stared at the newspaper as if he were interested in an article. When she said nothing else, he glanced at her. She'd seen that look in his eyes before—two months ago when he'd asked her to rip out her herbs.

"You need to do something with my berry patch."

"Don't *read* into this, young woman."

"Then talk to me."

"I don't want to. I don't want to admit the idea to myself, let alone to you."

"But?"

"But nothing. I've said all I care to on the matter. It's a topic I banned your brothers from talking about years ago, and I'm not changing my mind today."

Why would he ban anyone from talking about building a home? It wasn't like him to dictate what could or couldn't be spoken of, at least not inside the boundaries of their home—as long as the topic wasn't Emma's death.

He peered over the newspaper. "We're managing fine the way things are, and we'll keep doing what we've been doing until God opens a door."

In an instant she knew what she should have realized years ago: land was expensive because it was in short supply. And she had a little over an acre of Byler property. One of her brothers, maybe both, could build a house there. It'd cost them nothing for the land, and with the help of the Amish community, they could build affordable homes.

She quaked at the prospect of giving up her berry patch, wanting to slam her palms onto the island and reject all possibility of it. But she didn't need to get upset. Her Daed, the man who loved her in spite of all her oddities, had done everything in his power to keep the berry patch for her. It had hurt both of them too much when her herb garden was taken from her. Building a home wasn't worth giving up her fruit garden. Not for any of them.

THIRTEEN

Leah's stomach cramped as she helped her mother and younger sisters take laundry off the line. She'd spent all night throwing up, but chores still had to be done. Hope danced around them, barking. Katie grabbed an old washcloth and began playing tug of war with the puppy. Soon the younger girls were chasing the dog.

Mamm grabbed a sheet and nodded for Leah to take the other end. As she helped shake it out, another round of pains ran through her stomach.

"Are you not feeling any better yet?" Mamm asked as they brought the two ends together.

"No, and you're free at any time to say you don't need my help."

"Maybe you were out in the heat too much while working for that woman in Morgansville."

Or maybe Leah was just sick of herself, literally. Every moment, both awake and asleep, she saw the strangers from Brad's party watching her, and she remembered the awful way Michael had looked at her that night. If she'd been uncool before, she was minus a thousand points now. The whole mess had her stomach in knots. Even so, she continued to hope that Michael would keep the promises he'd whispered to her weeks ago, that he would realize he'd made a terrible mistake Friday night.

Mamm made the last fold in the sheet and took the bundle from Leah. "I'm proud of you for helping that woman. But if you'd been here Saturday to help with the canning, we wouldn't be doing laundry on a Tuesday."

"Ya, but we'd be doing some other exhausting chore right now." Another twinge ran through her upper stomach.

She picked up a basket of her brothers' clothes and headed toward the house, her body dripping with sweat in the humid midsummer air.

Before she reached the back door, she saw a rig turning onto the driveway. She'd forgotten that Catherine was coming for dinner. Leah's sisters raced past her and ran into the house, calling the puppy to follow them.

Catherine stopped the carriage near the hitching post and got out. "Leah, could you give me a hand?" She looped the reins of the horse around the post.

Leah didn't want to, but she would. Of all the people who didn't like her, Catherine was the most transparent. Leah put the basket of clean clothes inside the door. Her stomach gurgled, and she felt nauseated.

"Go help her, but don't dawdle." Mamm went into the house. "We need to get dinner on the table."

Leah nodded. When she arrived at the rig, Catherine passed her a baking dish of bread pudding.

"Denki." Catherine turned and grabbed a picnic basket out of the rig. "I'll be so glad when cool weather arrives." She closed the door to the carriage and peered at Leah with concern. "You look awful."

Leah rubbed her stomach. "I'm not feeling all that well."

Catherine studied her, looking suspicious. "As in too much to drink?"

"Don't be ridiculous."

"A virus then? Are you running a fever?"

"I wish I were. Then I could get out of chores and go read a book." Leah went toward the house.

"Leah."

She stopped.

"Are you… Have you been with someone?" Catherine clutched the handles of the picnic basket and stared at Leah with horror as she waited for an answer.

She couldn't be pregnant, although at the moment she didn't remember when she'd had her last period. She wasn't the type to be regular. She shook her head. "What? Just being at a party or two gives you no reason to jump to conclusions about me." Even as the lie left her mouth, Leah's worst fears crawled into the pit of her stomach. Surely she wasn't expecting. Michael had taken precautions. Each time they'd been together, he'd promised they'd have no chance of conceiving.

Like he promised to always love me and be true to me?

Had she played the fool for him?

"Gut." Catherine nodded. "I'm relieved to hear you say that. Kumm. Let's help get dinner on the table."

Leah went inside and set the dish on the island. Aiming to look calm, she leaned against the counter, ignoring those around her as they set the table and chatted. If she was pregnant, she'd have to tell Michael right away. Surely he would agree to marry her as soon as possible, wedding season or not. And everyone in the community would know her shame, even on her wedding day.

Mamm lifted Leah's chin, studying her. The concern in her eyes caught Leah off guard, and she again wondered if her family cared more than she thought. If they did, she'd like to find a way to spare them from the humiliation if she was pregnant. But that would be impossible.

She pulled away from her mother. "Would you stop?" she growled and left the room.

Once at the stairs she sat on the bottom step. What if she was pregnant and Michael didn't want to marry her? A shiver ran through her, and she couldn't bear to even think about it.

"Leah?" Mamm called. "Kumm break ice from the trays and fill the glasses."

Leah moved to obey, hoping she was as good at hiding her fears as she had been at covering her tracks.

※〜⋗

Samuel rode bareback in the direction of the back tierce, the sun still strong at three in the afternoon. Eli and Jacob were helping Daed with the dairy side today. Samuel went through Jacob's section of trees, inspecting them, and was pleased with the abundance of maturing apples he saw there. The trees were healthier than they'd been in years.

As his horse carried him into Eli's section, he noticed the leaves didn't look good, a first indicator that a tree was under stress. His heart seemed to stop as he directed the horse to move closer. He pulled the reins, slowing the horse, yet directing her to move to a tree trunk. Coming to a halt, he watched as tiny bugs the size of a dot moved up and down the tree.

Spider mites. Thousands of them.

No!

He dug his heels into the horse's side and went to the next tree. He moaned. "Please, no."

He went to the next. And on. And on.

All of them were infested.

"Eli!" he screamed, knowing no one could hear him. He turned the horse toward home and slapped the reins. His anger grew hotter the closer he got.

He should have checked on Eli's work long before now. Why hadn't he? He gave instructions every morning and followed up at the end of the day with questions about exactly what had been done. Eli gave his reports over dinner, but clearly he hadn't been following Samuel's instructions. Had he even sprayed his section of tree trunks with oil and water last spring?

If they used insecticide now to kill the spiders, they'd lose their organic status for the whole orchard. Besides, most of the damage had already been done.

Why hadn't he made the time to verify Eli's reports? Eli used to shirk his duties and run off with his friends the first chance he got. But last fall he'd asked for responsibilities in the orchard equal to his brothers'. They'd talked about it with Jacob and their Daed, and everyone had agreed Eli was up to the task and ready for the increase in pay that came with it. By springtime Samuel had stopped checking his work. He trusted him. What a huge mistake that was!

The July sun scorched the land as he crossed acre after acre. When he came near his home, he spotted his youngest sister in the yard, playing with the puppy. "Have you seen Eli?" he called out.

"Last I saw him, he was in the barn office with Daed and Jacob."

Samuel rode into the barn and got off his horse. "Eli!"

Jacob opened the door to the office. "We're in here. Something wrong?"

Samuel pushed past his brother.

Daed sat in a chair behind the desk, and Eli was in a smaller one in front of it.

"What have you done?" Samuel threw his straw hat onto the desk. "Get on your feet and answer me."

Eli stood. "Whatever you're hollering about, I'm sure it's because I didn't do something as great and fantastic as you would've."

Samuel pointed at the wall, imagining the orchard. "You mean do the job I was given? The trees on the back tierce are covered in spider mites. They'll be good for nothing but cider apples."

Eli doubled his fists. "Back off, Samuel."

"Are you kidding me?" Samuel asked. "You're going to challenge me? Because I'd love a fight right about now."

Jacob moved between them, facing Samuel. "I'm sure it's not as bad as it looks. Things rarely are."

"All ten acres, Eli," Samuel snapped. "You said you'd sprayed them in the spring when we were spraying our sections. Did you?"

Jacob blocked Samuel's view of Eli. "We'll find a solution." Jacob stared into his eyes. "Samuel, we'll find an answer. Now go cool off."

Samuel walked out of the office, slamming the door behind him. He paced the barn a few times, trying to calm himself, and then went back into the small room.

Daed was still in the chair behind the desk, absorbed in lecturing Eli.

Eli stared out the tiny, dirty window.

"The trees in every section but his are doing fine. Thriving, even." Samuel pulled a bandana out of his pocket and wiped the sweat from his face. "You want to explain that?"

"I did a lot of work, Samuel. Maybe I didn't do it as well as you, but I've worked hard on those ten acres."

"Nonsense!"

Eli stood face to face with him. "Are you calling me a liar?"

"Did you spray the trees with oil and water or not?" Samuel held up his hand. "And before you answer, I can find out by running an inventory. It'll take days to figure it out, but I will get the truth."

Eli stormed out.

"And there's our answer," Samuel called after him. "He knew how important it was to soak every trunk. He just didn't want to do the work."

Jacob rubbed the back of his neck. "I was depending on the cash from this year's crops to do more than just offset the financial struggles on the dairy side."

Samuel scoffed. "This affects all my plans."

If they couldn't find a way to halt the infestation, none of the apples in their brother's ten acres would reach their full color and size—not this year or next. And when produce was affected year after year, the family bills and taxes were in danger of going unpaid. Poor harvests the last three years had already depleted their savings. If the orchard again yielded more cider apples than eating ones, they'd have to sell off a good portion of the land just to pay the property taxes, and selling off land to make ends meet could eventually force them to lose the orchard altogether.

Samuel grabbed his hat off the desk and flung it across the room. "The back tierce is a sea of spotty leaves and damaged fruit. What am I going to tell Catherine? 'Sorry, honey, but my irresponsible brother wanted to make some extra money, so he agreed to more work than he was willing to do, and now we can't even think of getting married for another decade'?"

"It's not that bad," Daed said.

"Ya, it is. We're looking at ten acres of cider apples, and I can't imagine any solution. Not one."

Jacob leaned his chair back on two legs, probably already resigning himself to their future. "Somehow we have to find a way to make up the difference between the price of eating apples and cider apples for ten acres of trees."

"That's not possible. If it were, we'd have been doing that for years. And what's Eli's punishment going to be? Paying back some of the money he took for work he didn't do?"

"Leave it alone, Samuel," Daed said. "Watching us struggle to make ends meet or seeing us sell portions of land to pay the taxes will be punishment enough."

"He won't get it, not at eighteen."

Daed pointed at Samuel. "Just avoid Eli for a few weeks. He can increase his work with me on the dairy side until you cool off."

Samuel walked out, too furious to respond. He strode into the orchard, unable to see anything but red. His mind screamed and railed, and at least an hour passed before he returned to the office. Daed and Jacob were still there with the papers and ledgers pulled out, reviewing information from the dairy side, probably trying to figure out a new plan.

Sunlight streamed through the dusty windows as Samuel took a seat in one of the rickety ladder-backs. No one spoke. The smell of the blackberry jam on his father's half-eaten sandwich caught his attention. The thought of shelves of freshly canned jams and jellies in a Morgansville cellar came to mind.

Samuel watched dust particles float through the air, stirred into a frenzy each time someone moved. "The spider mites are so bad it could take three or four years before the trees are healthy again."

Daed slumped and put his head in his hands. "That's thirty-five hundred bushels of cider apples per year from that section alone. We won't be able to find buyers for that quantity. If we pick them, they'll rot in the storage house."

Samuel tried to focus his thoughts, and soon his mind churned with ideas. All of them useless. His thoughts moved to Rhoda Byler and her business again. He wondered if some of her crazy mulch additives might help restore the trees to health sooner than usual.

"I may have a new buyer for some of the cider apples." Jacob raked a hand through his hair. "He won't pay as much as the folks we already sell to. But he might be able to take some off our hands."

"It's better than nothing, I suppose." Daed sounded defeated.

Eli eased into the room. "I…I have an idea."

Samuel figured he'd been somewhere out of sight but within hearing range. Daed motioned Eli in. "Let's hear it."

Eli stayed near the doorway. "Maybe we should try to find someone who can make things from the overabundance of cider apples—like pies. That'd be more profitable than selling the apples themselves, wouldn't it?"

"We already sell apples to everyone around here who makes pies," Daed said. "Besides, Samuel ran the numbers on that a few years ago. There's too much overhead. We wouldn't come out ahead."

Samuel thought of the rows of labeled jars in Rhoda's cellar. Maybe Eli was onto something. "I have an idea, but it'll sound crazy."

Daed tossed his pencil onto the desk. "I'll consider anything at this point."

His brothers stared at him, their attention fully his.

"What if we found someone who's already set up to do canning in large quantities? Someone who could make apple butter, jelly, jam, applesauce, maybe even pie filling."

Jacob put the chair on all four legs. "So we get somebody to do the canning for us, then sell it as a Kings' Orchard product. If we shipped some of it to the touristy places, I bet we could turn a decent profit, at least enough to keep our heads above water until we get back to having really good harvests again."

Daed took a bite of his sandwich. "You got somebody in mind, Samuel?"

He shrugged. "It's a long shot. And the person I'm thinking of isn't from around here."

"Amish, though, right?" Eli asked. "Because all our branding and reputation is built on being Amish and organic."

Samuel didn't want to answer Eli, didn't even want him in the room, but he steadied himself and answered. "Ya, she's Amish."

His father choked. "Did you say *she?*"

"Ya. The owner of the canning business is a woman." Samuel went to the far corner of the room and retrieved his hat. "But if she can help us out of this fix, I see no reason not to look into it."

"You've at least met her husband and family?"

"She's single."

"Oh, this just keeps getting better and better."

Daed's tone bothered Samuel. He seemed ready to discount Rhoda's worth based solely on her gender and marital status.

"Do you want a man, Daed? Because if that's the answer, this room is full of answers, and you can see where that's gotten us."

Shock removed all other emotion from Daed's face. "Go on."

"You should see her setup. She's got a little more than an acre in Morgansville, and she cans all kinds of berry products in her cellar. As far as business goes, it left an impression, and I found myself looking for her goods in a few stores while running errands this week. The ones I went into carried Rhode Side Stands products. I even saw an ad in that magazine for Amish women, and it said her products are sold at stores in Ohio and Indiana. But none of it is made from apples."

"Morgansville, you say?" Daed picked up the pencil and put it behind his ear. "Is this the woman Leah worked for a couple of Saturdays ago?"

"Ya."

Daed took a sip of water. "You think this woman would make a good business partner?"

"I think it's a possibility that we have no choice but to investigate. Who knows if it'd be a good partnership, but it's all we've got right now. Jacob, she makes fifty percent profit from every jar. Can we make the offer worth her consideration?"

Jacob stared into the distance, thinking, and then he popped his knuckles. "It'd be safe to offer her twenty-five percent profit per jar, and that's a better deal than it sounds at first."

Eli scratched his head. "But a bushel of fruit is a bushel of fruit, right? So why would she be willing to take twenty-five percent less per jar of goods?"

Jacob interlaced his fingers and cupped the back of his neck. "The actual weight difference between a bushel of apples and a bushel of blueberries isn't all that different—not that blueberries are sold by the bushel. The real difference is found in other areas: how long it takes to fill a bushelbasket with blueberries compared to apples, and how many bushels one acre of apple trees can produce compared to one acre of berry bushes."

"So she'd make more money overall?" Eli asked.

Jacob tilted back his chair again. "It's possible, but we can't be sure right now. We don't know what the overhead would be or her productivity per day, but we know she wouldn't have to spend any time in the field tending to the crops, and we could keep her in as much produce as she could process for months at a time."

Samuel was now armed with plenty of information to take to Rhoda. "Gut. That's what I'll present to her." He made a sweeping gesture at all three of them. "Listen, let's keep the orchard situation within the family for now. I'd rather have a solution in hand before I have to explain about the back tierce to Catherine."

Everyone nodded as the dinner bell rang out.

Daed tossed his sandwich crusts into the trash. "I can't think of anyone else to consider, but tomorrow I'll do some digging to see if I can find other options." He put his hand on Samuel's back. "In the meantime you should go see this woman to find out if she's interested. Go alone. If she runs her own business, she's not going to respond well if she feels intimidated or thinks we're trying to drive her rig, so to speak."

"I'll go tomorrow."

FOURTEEN

Rhoda's knees ached. She'd been on them for hours, slowly making her way from one blackberry bush to another. Reaching deep into the thick of the plant, past several first- and second-year shoots with their awful thorns—"sharp teeth," as Emma used to call them—Rhoda plucked four more blackberries from the bush.

The gloves and her father's long-sleeved shirt, which she wore over her dress, helped protect her from the sharp prickles, but nothing stopped her from getting poked and scratched. "Ouch." She jerked her hand back, noticing a dot of blood on the end of her finger where the gloves' fingertips had been cut off.

"Are you giving blood, sweat, and tears, Rhoda?" Her little sister's innocent voice washed over her, and the familiar ache inside stirred again.

Emma. Sweet, sweet Emma.

"Will you marry one day?" Emma had once asked. "Will I? You can see so many things that are going to happen. Surely you can see this too."

Emma had always believed that Rhoda's ability—her gift, as Emma called it—was from God. Rhoda believed that too. How disappointed was God that she never handled the gift in the right way and always made situations worse?

Emma's question about marrying rang inside her.

"Of course we'll marry." At sixteen Rhoda had imagined only a smooth path ahead. "All Amish women marry, at least the good ones. We'll follow in their footsteps."

"Will we share a home, Rhoda? Your husband and mine could be great friends, maybe even brothers."

Rhoda remembered closing her eyes, trying to know what the future held, but all she'd seen was a black hole, like a starless night surrounding her.

Now two years later, Rhoda knew what she hadn't known back then. For all her so-called ability to see what would happen, she understood very little.

If a scene did come to her, it was nothing more than a snapshot image. And truth to tell, that's all life was. Pieces. Images. Hints at a whole that had yet to happen. She had no way to alter that future, even if she visualized it, any more than she could change the day Emma was killed.

If Rhoda had put gardening aside and gone to the store that morning when Emma asked, her sister would still be alive. There were so many ways Rhoda could've handled her day so that Emma would be here.

She stayed on her knees, whispering the lyrics to Emma's favorite song while moving from one bush to the next.

"Hallo." A man's voice startled her.

She let out a yelp, losing her balance and knocking over the bushelbasket. She peeled herself off the side of the overturned basket and stood, peering through the raspberry vines hanging on the trellis. Samuel King stood outside the gate, looking in.

Suddenly feeling undone, she raised her gloved hand above the trellises and motioned for him to come in. "Over here."

"Ah, I thought you'd be out here, but I couldn't see you. Still can't."

She brushed dirt off her palms and straightened her odd outfit while doing so.

"Wie bischt du Heit?" he called out while coming toward her, asking how she was today. He rounded the last bush, carrying a pot of healthy lavender. When he caught a full view of her, his eyes grew wide.

"Oh, I forgot." She jerked her Daed's straw hat off her head. The thought of peeling off her work shirt ran through her mind, but that'd be more improper than wearing it in the first place, and she was fairly sure Samuel wasn't a fan of anything improper.

He righted the basket she'd knocked over, set the pot beside him, and knelt as he began picking up dirt-covered berries and putting them back in the basket. "No worries. I suppose it's normal for some women to need a warning, and you weren't expecting company."

Did this man hear himself? She put her Daed's hat on her head again. "Some women? As in those of us who don't make ourselves look all Amish all the time?"

He gazed up at her, clearly caught off guard by her question. "I...I don't know." He picked up the pot of lavender and held it out to her. "But I came to apologize for last time, not to add blunders to it."

The earnestness in his eyes soothed her a bit. "It's gorgeous." She took the pot from him. "Lavender is in the mint family, but it's a great antiseptic and can soothe insect bites, burns, and headaches."

"I thought it was a flower."

"God's design is remarkable, isn't it? Attractive blossoms that are good for us in many ways. Many plants, the really fascinating ones, are beautiful, fragrant, flavorful, and medicine for the body." She closed her eyes and took a deep whiff, feeling almost intoxicated by it. "And good for the soul." When she opened her eyes, Samuel looked totally bewildered.

She couldn't help but laugh even as her cheeks burned with embarrassment. "Denki. Apology accepted." She wished she'd found Mammi Byler's apple recipes to show him. That might have melted some of the awkwardness between them. "Lavender happens to be a favorite of mine, among many others."

"You should plant some, then."

"Ya, I should." But she wouldn't. She pulled off her gloves.

"Neat gloves. Protective, while letting your fingers be nimble."

"They're the best solution I've found yet."

"Better for the hands than horse urine is for compost?"

"I didn't say they were *that* good."

He grinned. "You're a bit overzealous about plants, aren't you, Miss Byler?"

"It seems so, Mr. King, despite my best efforts to temper myself." She tucked the pot between the crook of her arm and her body. "But is that what you came for, to point out the obvious while bringing me an apology gift?"

"Actually, I had another reason. You see, we're having a problem with our orchard."

She bent to grab the basket, but he picked it up first. "What sort of problem?"

"A third of our trees are infested with spider mites, and we're an organic grower, so we can't use chemicals."

Pondering what little she knew about killing spider mites, she headed for the gate. If she had that problem in her garden, the solution wouldn't be too difficult. With the short plants on her small plot of ground, she could easily attach an oil-based mixture to the hose and douse the plants as needed. That would hardly work for an orchard of tall trees, however.

She opened the gate for him and led the way across the driveway and down the cellar steps. "Put the basket beside the sink, please."

He did so and then stepped away. She put a stopper in the sink and added a huge strainer before filling it with water and slowly pouring in the berries. "I've heard some people extract oils from neem trees."

When she glanced behind her, Samuel was walking around the small room, studying it thoroughly.

"I'm not familiar with that."

"From what I've read, it's supposed to be a good insecticide. Since it comes from a tree, it's organic. But it's very expensive, even for a garden my size. I can't imagine what it'd cost for an orchard."

"Even if it worked, that wouldn't help us this year. The damage is already done. Still, I'd like to hear your thoughts on the topic for next year." He stopped reading the labels on her canned goods and turned to face her. "You should be finished harvesting your garden, or close to it, by the time apples are harvested."

"You're interested in talking to me about canning apple products for you."

He blinked a few times. "Your mind moves fast, but, ya, we're pondering the possibility."

An unfamiliar sensation ran through her, and she took a moment to enjoy it. So this was what it felt like for someone outside her family to respect her. But it wouldn't end well. It couldn't. She'd do something weird. He'd hear about it and pull away, be sorry he ever got involved with her. "Look, I appreciate that you'd consider me, but I can't."

"You haven't even heard our ideas yet. Come see the orchard, talk to my Daed and brothers, and share a meal with us. Then I'll accept your answer, whatever it is."

"Then?" All feeling of being flattered faded, and she wrestled with offense. He should have accepted her refusal and thanked her for her time. She swallowed, unwavering in her desire to decline politely but firmly. "Look, Samuel, I appreciate the offer, but I don't need to think about it. I'm sorry you came all this way and brought me a plant only to receive a disappointing answer, but I won't change my—"

"Rhoda?" Daed called, interrupting her as he came down the steps. "Lydia said—" His eyes landed on Samuel, and he stopped in midsentence.

"Daed, this is Samuel King. He's the older brother of the young woman I met while you and the family were gone."

"Hmm, Samuel King," Daed repeated, looking thoughtful. "I'm Karl." He knew communities of Amish in every state and learned about a lot of families he'd never met through the two main Amish newspapers, *The Budget* and *Die Botschaft*. "Where are you from?"

"Harvest Mills."

"Of the Kings' Orchard?"

"Ya."

"No one told me that," Rhoda said.

Samuel focused on her for a moment, looking as if he had much more he'd like to say. Her heart beat a little faster. When he'd mentioned the orchard, he hadn't hinted that it was Kings' Orchard or that he was a descendent of Apple Sam, a man well known for his success with his apple orchard.

Her Daed shook his hand. "I met your Daadi many years ago. When he died, my wife and I attended his funeral. About five years ago?"

"Eight, actually."

"Time has a way of slipping by. Are you the grandson he told me about, the one he was grooming to take over the orchard?"

"Ya, but I wasn't nearly as prepared for that task as he'd hoped."

"Well, he wasn't expecting to die as young as he did, and I'm sure losing him was difficult."

"It was. And we work hard to carry on what he established even half as well."

"I have a lot of respect for that attitude." Daed pulled a box of matches from his pocket and put them on the counter. "Rhodes, I picked these up last time I was at the store. Thought you might need more. And Lydia sent me to let you know dinner will be on the table in twenty minutes, and she'd like you to bring some fresh raspberries to go with her cheesecake."

"I'll drain them and bring them up right away."

Daed kissed her cheek. "Will you join us for dinner, Samuel? My wife would be so pleased to meet you. She'll talk about it for a month."

Rhoda wished her Daed hadn't asked. Samuel had an agenda, and she'd answered him. Her Daed's invite would only make it easier for Samuel to find new angles to ask the same question. "Daed, he only stopped by for a minute. I'm sure he can't st—"

"Actually, Rhoda,"—Samuel glanced at a row of her canned goods—"I accept the invite."

~

Jacob pulled three one-hundred-dollar bills out of his stash. In all the hubbub about the back tierce yesterday, he'd missed sending an envelope to Sandra. At least he had money to send, for now. He hoped this woman in Morgansville could help Kings' Orchard. Hoped Samuel could convince her to partner with them.

Samuel was upset about what the damage on the back tierce would do to his and Catherine's plans, and rightly so, but the income from this year's crop supported far more than one man's dreams.

"It was an accident!" Betsy's scream caught his attention, and the next thing he heard was a door slamming.

He closed the chest at the foot of his bed and locked it. No doubt the youngest child in the family was in a heated argument with one of her sisters. Even though the younger girls didn't know the issues with the finances and the back tierce, it was possible they were reacting to the unspoken stress in the men.

"You were careless!" Katie screamed.

He shoved the money into an envelope and left his room. Katie sat on the top step of the stairway, holding a doll with a torn dress.

Jacob sat beside her. "Having trouble?"

"Look what she did." Katie showed him the rip, and then she leaned her head against him. "What's wrong with me? I feel like playing with dolls one minute, and the next I wish I had a beau coming to court me."

He put his arm around her. "You're growing up, and that's a lot like a spring day with showers. It's bright and clear one minute and cloudy with rain the next. But it's all necessary for the crops"—he squeezed her shoulders—"and little girls to mature."

"I'll grow out of this then?"

"The worst of it." He remembered being her age and finding the idea of growing up exciting and scary. He suspected she was feeling some of that too. But with a little searching, she'd find her own way to cope…or escape. But for the most part, he'd found that escaping fell short of its promises.

After seeing that newspaper last Sunday, he'd gone to the library on Monday and had found the same paper. The construction fiasco in the headlines had nothing to do with Jones' Construction—not this time.

Thoughts of Sandra's heartache pounded him like a rough surf during a storm, and he knew he had to mail the letter and find a distraction before the memories stole what little peace he'd found in returning home. "How about you and Betsy ride to town with me? After I mail a letter and pick up a few newspapers, we could go by the creamery."

"Jacob, why'd you leave us when you did?"

"Sometimes a person needs a change of scenery." That sounded reasonable enough, and he hoped it satisfied her. That made getting away seem simple, and life was many things, but rarely was it simple. "And right now I think a trip into town would be a perfect change of scenery." He nudged her shoulder. "Now go make up with Betsy while I hitch a horse to a rig."

She straightened the doll's dress, pulling the torn pieces together and probably thinking of ways to repair it. "I'm glad you came home. You won't leave us again, will you?"

The question gnawed at him. He stood. "Not today. Now go."

FIFTEEN

Rhoda ran her fingers through the soaking raspberries, torn between frustration and curiosity. She'd declined Samuel's work offer, so he should be leaving, not staying for dinner. "Why'd you accept the invite?"

Samuel shoved his hands into his pockets. "I'm not ready to leave."

She lifted two handfuls of dripping raspberries, shook off a little bit of water, and dumped them into a plastic container. "Why?"

He didn't answer, and she waited. He shifted from one foot to the other, seeming uncomfortable. She much preferred his blunt candor to his stoicism, but maybe his interest wasn't purely business. Although she didn't believe a working relationship with Samuel would land either of them in the right place, what about a personal one? Didn't seem likely—despite how hard her heart thumped at the very idea. And although she felt an undeniable tug of attraction, he also grated on her nerves.

"Kumm." She took the container of raspberries and went up the stairs.

The house was buzzing with activity when they entered: women setting the table, men getting little ones settled and trying to distract them until time to eat. She introduced Samuel to everyone and then showed him to a half bath to wash up.

Before long they were all seated at the table with their heads bowed. When she opened her eyes, she saw Samuel staring at her from across the table.

"Samuel," Daed said.

Samuel faced her father and tugged the cloth napkin into his lap.

Daed lifted the platter of roasted chicken and passed it to him. "What brings you to Morgansville?"

Samuel forked a piece of meat and put it on his plate. "I came with a business proposition to discuss with your daughter."

Pleasure radiated from her father's face. "My Rhodes working with Kings' Orchard?"

Samuel passed the platter back to Daed. "It's preliminary talk at this point, just trying to see if we could work something out that might be equitable for everyone."

After putting chicken on his plate, Daed passed the platter to her mother. "That sounds interesting, doesn't it, Rhodes?"

Her brothers and sisters-in-law watched with anticipation while filling their plates and passing bowls of food.

Rhoda scooped out some peas. "It's very good of Samuel to think of me, but I'm not considering it. I have more than I can keep up with for Rhode Side Stands."

A mixture of disappointment and frustration appeared on Samuel's face. "I know you're used to running a small business, so maybe you don't understand the benefit in seriously considering opportunities that are presented to you. Perhaps it sounds intimidating, but if you'd come look at the orchard, we can talk about it. At least then you'd be handling this offer with the kind of business savvy it deserves."

Rhoda's blood ran hot. "Are you good at math, Samuel?"

"Am I what?" He seemed confused for a moment and took a sip of his water. "Ya, reasonably so. Why?"

"Can you give me a rough estimate of how many insulting, condescending things you just said in your account of this small business owner?"

He stared at her, not looking angry or even dismayed but curious.

"Rhoda, sweetheart," her Daed said quietly. "He's our guest."

She wanted to say that he should behave like one, but she wouldn't be disrespectful to her Daed.

"I didn't mean it that way." Samuel wiped his mouth with the napkin. "I was making observations. Nothing more."

"Oh, I see." She bit her tongue to keep from challenging his *observations.*

Steven shook a little salt onto his potatoes and passed the shaker to his wife. "What did you have in mind for Rhoda to do?"

"Every year we sell our cider apples for mere pennies. But if those same apples were canned and sold using a label people already trusted, like Rhode Side Stands, we could make a better profit. We wouldn't be able to pay her much up-front, but we'd cover her costs and then give her twenty-five percent of what we made from each jar sold. Because all her time could be spent canning instead of tending crops and because of the amount of fruit we harvest compared to her garden, we believe she'd earn a much healthier profit than she gets from a summer of harvesting berries."

More profit from a fall of canning apples than a summer of harvesting berries? The idea suddenly held some strong appeal, not that she'd share that with him. But if he was right, she might be able to put away some serious money toward building a kitchen where the shed now stood. Still, none of that changed her impression of how a business deal with Samuel would end.

"Have you done this with other people?" John asked.

"No. We've considered a lot of ideas over the years, but this particular one came up after I saw Rhoda's setup and after I realized that we have a particularly large crop of cider apples this year. Eventually we hope to have more eating apples, as the profit is much better."

If Rhoda wasn't certain how poorly this business deal would end, she might consider it or at least enjoy a Saturday afternoon visiting an apple orchard. But she didn't appreciate Samuel's backhanded compliments or how he had a big role, with a lot of labor, envisioned for her without her input.

She cut up a piece of chicken. "After a summer of harvesting and canning, I'm more than ready by fall for life to slow down and to take a break. That's the beginning of your busy season."

"True. But think of how you could expand your fruit garden if you made extra money by working through the fall. You might earn enough to hire more help next year." He tore a roll in half. "We're honest in our dealings, and we'd do our best to make sure your efforts were worth it."

Did this man hear himself? "I believe you're honest. I can see that about you. But the problem I'm having right now is that you seem to think your ideas of what I should do outweigh mine."

"Rhodes,"—Daed tapped her leg with his foot under the table—"I think you should at least go to the orchard, look it over, and think about it."

So this was why Samuel had accepted the invitation to dinner—to run around her decision and convince her Daed. If Samuel wanted to dash any interest in his orchard by making himself an enemy, he was doing a fine job.

"Denki, Karl." Samuel forked a piece of chicken.

"Daed, I like the work schedule I have. Besides, I couldn't keep up with that much produce without hiring someone new, and Landon is the only person I want to work with under that kind of pressure."

"Landon?" Samuel paused, holding the fork of meat in midair. "You have an Englisch man working for you?"

A name like Landon was a complete giveaway that he wasn't Amish. Samuel's judgmental tone indicated far more than he realized.

"You're kidding me." Rhoda glanced at her Daed. "You also have an opinion about who works for me?"

Samuel studied her as if he was trying to understand her and to figure out what to say or do next.

Daed set his fork on his plate. "Rhodes, it was a simple question."

"He's never met Landon, and he already doesn't like him. That's prejudice talking." She pointed her butter knife at him. "I'll go one step further, Mr. King. Landon is my friend, and no one—not you or a dozen of the best Amish people—could ever replace who he is to me. If he's not welcome, I'm not the least bit interested in anything else you have to say."

Her family fidgeted, each one clearly uncomfortable with the exchange taking place.

Daed looked from her to Samuel with empathy reflected on his face. "Landon's a good man, and he helped Rhoda through the loss of her younger sister. I'm indebted to him."

Samuel nodded. "I shouldn't have expressed my opinion so quickly."

"You shouldn't have had one. Period."

A faint smile crossed Samuel's lips. "Now, Miss Byler, you'd find it easier to grow apples on your raspberry bushes than for me to be without an opinion. It's how my mind works, and it does so without my permission. Surely you have some area where you're not in control of how you think or feel."

Of all the people he could have said that to, no one would understand it better than she did. "Of course I have those areas. But to evaluate situations and people with rash judgments or prejudice is simply wrong."

"Yet in less than a minute, you judged my work proposition to be of no value to you."

"That's true," John said. "He's got you on that one."

Rhoda put her hands in her lap and wrung her napkin, quietly tearing some of the threads. "It's not a hasty judgment of others to know what I do and don't want concerning *my* business. And getting back to the point of your insulting view of Landon, it seems to me you tend to sum up people too quickly, including your sister."

Samuel sighed. "Okay, I'll admit my attitude was wrong where Landon was concerned, but Leah is an entirely different situation. She's earned the heat of my frustrations the old-fashioned way."

"Which came first, Samuel—her disappointing ways or your lack of valuing her?"

"Whoa." Samuel put his napkin on the table and scooted his chair back. "I'd like us to seriously consider a working venture. I think you and Kings' Orchard could profit from it, but there are areas where I will not be open to your opinion, and my sister is one of them."

She'd hit a raw nerve where Leah was concerned, and Rhoda knew he was at a loss concerning what to do about his sister. But despite Rhoda's earlier views, she now believed he loved Leah deeply. "I'll yield to that." Rhoda smiled, a faint, wobbly smile at best. "I feel the same way about Landon."

Samuel replaced the napkin on his lap. "How did you word it?" He realigned his chair closer to the table. "I'll yield to that."

"This"—Steven propped his elbows on the table and interlaced his fingers—"is the most interesting conversation we've had around here in a long time. Samuel, I doubt you've dealt with anyone like our Rhoda. She'd fight to the end to give people room to be themselves, to make mistakes and grow. But she has no tolerance for any hint that one person is making a quick, and therefore unfair, judgment about another."

"Ya." Samuel rubbed the back of his hand against his jaw. "I picked up on that the first time we met. It caused a rather heated discussion then too. Unfortunately, I think she and I are at opposite ends of a large field. My guess is that she is too open minded when a judgment needs to be made, and I'm too quick to form an opinion and make a ruling."

"Opposites." Lydia scooped up a few more peas from the bowl and put them on her daughter's plate. "Interesting."

Rhoda sighed. Lydia made statements regularly about opposites attracting each other—like the opposite ends of two magnets pulling together. Or like bees, which fly freely, being drawn to and sustained by plants that are rooted. But the word *opposite* did seem to describe how she felt about Samuel. One minute she found him fascinating, and he drew her in. The next she was appalled by him and wanted to bean him with something.

Samuel took her in, and she could feel the power of his stare. "It seems I'm really botching this. All I can do is hope that in your open-mindedness you'll reconsider visiting Kings' Orchard."

"Is Landon welcome too?" she asked, willing to be told no so she could put his invite out of her mind.

Wariness showed in his eyes, but he nodded. "Of course. Does this mean you'll come?"

She looked to Daed.

Samuel leisurely pointed back and forth between her Daed and her. "I should've thought about this sooner. Perhaps, as the head of Rhode Side Stands, you'd like to come too, Karl."

Rhoda rolled her eyes. Clearly Samuel was old school, thinking a successful Amish business had to have a man as a partner. "He's my Daed. Rhode Side Stands is mine. But I value his opinion, not because I'm required to, but because he's earned my trust."

"Then trust this, Rhodes." Daed grinned. "I think you should go. Spend an entire day if you can spare the time, and get a feel for what you should do."

He was giving her permission to put out her radar, to use her gut instinct before committing to a decision. "Okay, I'll make a trip there. But I'm not optimistic."

"And you can believe that I'll try to change your mind. Now, when's a good time?"

Samuel was an intriguing man for sure, even with a mind that assessed every little thing and brought the gavel down too quickly. His love of his family business and his respect for her work made her heart pound. But he also managed to cause the same reaction in her through opposite emotions, like irritation.

Rhoda pushed her plate back. "I don't know. This is my busy season, so I'll have to think about it."

SIXTEEN

Between Sundays used to be Leah's favorite day of the week. No church and minimal chores. She could sleep late and then go to the hayloft to read for hours without anyone demanding much from her. But today she'd never been more miserable.

Her family sat around the breakfast table, chatting about everything, but she couldn't hear any of them.

Mamm reached over and laid her hand on Leah's arm. "I fixed your favorite breakfast, and you've hardly touched it. What is going on with you?"

"Nothing." Leah pulled away from her Mamm. Like everything else in her life right now, her response was a lie. How could she tell anyone, especially her Mamm, that she might be pregnant, that with every passing day the increased possibility made her so nervous she couldn't eat or sleep?

"I don't believe you." Mamm placed the back of her fingers on Leah's forehead. "Are you still feeling poorly?"

"Only a little."

"That's not true, Mamm," Katie said. "I needed to go to the bathroom in the middle of the night, and she was in there again, throwing up. I think she's scared of going to a doctor, but she needs to."

"No, I don't. It's just a bug of some sort." Leah's heart raced with fear. "It's only been a week."

"You're sure that's all it is?" Concern filled Mamm's eyes.

"I'm positive." Leah fought to keep tears from her eyes and a tremble from her voice. "May I be excused now?"

Jacob studied her as if he were able to read her thoughts. But even if he could, he had no room to question her. He had his own secrets, a past that was open to no one.

Daed stopped talking to Samuel long enough to give a nod.

Leah stood. "I'm going to my reading spot, and since I'm not feeling well, it'd be really nice if no one needed me for the rest of the day." She took her plate to the garbage can and dumped the contents.

"Leah," Mamm called.

Leah put her plate in the sink and turned.

"If you're not better by Tuesday, I'm calling the doctor."

Leah's stomach twisted with anxiety, but she nodded and left the house. Biting back tears, she stormed across the yard to the barn. The idea of being pregnant had her so nervous that her stomach ached. Maybe that's all it was. Maybe.

She pulled her skirt out of the way and climbed up to the haymow, where she kept her stash of books. She needed to talk to Michael, to tell him what was happening. The only time she'd caught a glimpse of him since the party was at church last Sunday.

Her mind too cluttered to read, she moved to the open hayloft door and sat.

For months Michael had been kind, inviting her to go everywhere with him. When she attended her first party, it'd been more fun than she'd ever imagined. They laughed and talked and drank but felt intoxicated with each other.

How had she landed here: fearing pregnancy and not talking to Michael in weeks? Images of his holding her, being so gentle and sweet, tore at her heart. Memories she'd once cherished—of their first time to their last time—now cut deep. She'd believed he loved her, and she'd trusted him. But as suddenly as his attention came her way, it had disappeared.

Had he only pretended to love her?

Maybe he was a little like Samuel. During apple-picking season, her brother went weeks without seeing Catherine, sometimes even longer. It didn't bother

Samuel to have those spells, even though he cared deeply for Catherine. Still, Samuel would never treat Catherine with a hint of disrespect, let alone do what Michael had done to Leah. Miss Thin Hips had caught Michael's eye nine days ago, so he should be over her by now. Perhaps he was simply shy about coming to apologize for being so mean.

Leah had to see him. He had to know about her fears. Her stomach churned, aching with nausea and discomfort.

If she was pregnant, surely he'd marry her—after he got over the shock. They couldn't leave the Amish. They'd need their financial support. Since they weren't members of the faith, they'd both have to join the church before they could be wed. And that would be embarrassing, because the church leaders would have to hold special sessions just for them. They'd cover only enough so they could get married right away and then finish the sessions afterward.

They'd probably be shunned for six weeks as a discipline for their ungodly behavior. Rumors of the rushed marriage would spread far and wide, and the weight of it would hover over her head for years. But aside from that, after they were married, life would go on pretty much as it did for all newlywed couples, except she'd always dreamed of being free of the Amish life.

What a mess. Another pain shot through her stomach, and she gagged.

She could hear her sisters playing somewhere outside, chasing the dog, but Leah couldn't see them. Part of her wished she could go back to that innocent, playful time.

After her graduation from eighth grade, she'd spent all day at home with Mamm while her younger sisters attended school and the men worked. She couldn't date or drive a rig or do anything fun, and she began to feel restless and trapped.

When her rumschpringe began, she'd bolted out the door, sick of being bored and living under her parents' watchful eye. They counted everything as sin, from reading fiction to listening to music to girls wearing their hair down. It was impossible to please them, so why even try to do what was right?

She placed her hand over her stomach, wondering if a living being was growing inside her. Clearly there were some behaviors she'd have been wise to avoid.

"Leah?" Samuel called from the barn below.

She was supposed to be reading and didn't even have a book in hand. She scurried to her stash of books, some in cardboard boxes, some stacked side by side in an old wooden feeding trough, the spines of the books facing her. She grabbed one and hurried back to her spot.

His hatless head came into view. He climbed into the hayloft and walked to her. "Can we talk for a minute?"

She put the book in front of her face, realizing she'd picked up an ancient math textbook. "I've got no interest in being lectured."

He moved a bale of hay to a spot across from her and sat. "I want your opinion."

"Mine? What for?" She pretended to be reading and turned a page. "You've never cared one whit about what I think." She peered at him over her book.

Distress crossed his face, and he ran his fingers through his blond hair. "That's not true." His eyes held an apology. "But I sort of see why you'd think so. I share too many opinions too quickly."

She returned to staring at the pages and flipped another one. She didn't know why he'd come up here, but she wished he'd leave. He made her stomach hurt even worse. "Anyone who's ever come within hearing distance of your voice knows that."

"Is it really that bad?"

Surprised by his humble response, she lowered the book. "No, but it sounded good, and if you're going to open yourself up to insults, I have to warn you that I've been saving them up for years."

A faint smile crossed his lips, then he grew serious again. "The apple crop won't be near what we'd hoped. We'll yield a lot of cider apples, maybe more than ever. Daed needs all of the land on the dairy side, and if we have to sell some acreage, it'll come from the apple orchard."

He'd never shared anything about the business with her before. What little she learned, she heard at mealtimes while the men talked among themselves. "No one's said a word about that at the table."

"We want to keep it from the younger ones so they won't worry. I'm not even telling Catherine yet. I'm trusting you'll say nothing."

Leah cupped a few stray hairs behind her ear. "I didn't know you kept secrets. I thought that was left up to the likes of me and Jacob."

"Ya, about that. I may have been harsher than you deserved the other day." She dropped her book.

He picked it up and held it in both hands. "I spoke with Rhoda yesterday. Went there to discuss solutions for the orchard, and, well, she's convinced that I don't value you as I should."

Leah fidgeted with a piece of hay. One day, for just a moment, it'd be nice to see herself differently, maybe as Rhoda had.

"I think she's dead wrong." Samuel kept his eyes on his hands as he held the book between his palms, turning it a full circle, never once glancing at her. "But if that's how I come across to you,"—he held out the book to her—"I'm sorry."

"Wow." The hushed word fell from her lips before she could stop it. She took the book. "Not a problem." He seemed so vulnerable, and it had her curious. Since taking over the orchard, he'd become harder—more determined and less tolerant. She'd forgotten he could talk to her without being angry or disgusted, and this reminder took away some of the sting from the past few years. "Did Rhoda have any answers?"

A familiar look of frustration tightened his face. "We aren't that far along yet. And truthfully, I hope we can get to that place. She's not easy to deal with, and I can't afford to insult or offend her. But I managed to do both before realizing it." He propped his forearms on his legs. "You're the only other person around who knows her even a little. She's agreed to come here, and I'm desperate to not stick my foot in my mouth. Did you and she argue at all?"

"No."

"She says I'm opinionated. But I've got news for her. It's not just me."

"Oh, stars from above. I got it." Leah stood and went to her stack of books. "Your real problem is you don't walk gently. You trample like a horse in a tomato patch." She put back the math book and pulled out a well-worn favorite. *"Pride and Prejudice."* She dusted off the tattered cover. "It will drive you mad with how careful everyone is with their words, but if you can begin to see the value in having an opinion without sharing it—the beauty and strength it can hold—it might help you." She held out the book to him.

He made a face. "You and your books. No one should spend…" He dropped his usual speech about wasting the time God gave her on fictional nonsense. "Sorry." He took the book from her. "Maybe you're right about my needing a different perspective. But a girly book?"

"You want to get along with a girl you don't understand. This could help."

He flipped through the pages, still looking as if he'd tasted something awful. "Denki, Leah. I'm desperate enough to give it a try."

A desire to tell him her greatest fears pushed at her.

"I guess I'd better get started reading." He went toward the ladder.

"Samuel…" Leah's palms began to sweat.

"Ya?" He waited.

They'd just ended the best conversation they'd had in years, maybe ever. She didn't want to spoil that. "There's no hurry in returning the book."

"Denki." He left.

Her throat and mouth were dry as her heart raced. If she was pregnant, would her brother ever talk to her again the way he just had—as if she mattered?

SEVENTEEN

Catherine paced her bedroom floor, looking out the window at every sound, hoping it'd be Arlan returning home. He'd left after breakfast, saying he was going to church with some friends. Her parents didn't even question him. She'd asked for some details, but he'd ignored her.

She wasn't fooled by his lies. A teenager who said he didn't have a girlfriend had no reason to visit someone else's church. Once he'd walked out of the house, she'd hurried up the stairs to her room, the perfect place to watch him. A few minutes later she'd seen a car pull up at the end of their short driveway, and he got into it. Were the people inside the vehicle Plain? With the sunlight reflecting off the car windows, she couldn't tell.

She glanced at the clock. It was going on one in the afternoon.

A car door slammed, and she hurried to the window. Arlan waved good-bye to the people in the vehicle and then walked toward the house.

She ran down the steps, flew out the door, and met him in the yard. "Where've you really been?"

Arlan sidestepped her. "I was just checking out some things."

She grabbed his arm. "What did you need to explore on a Sunday?"

"You know, Sis, I have a news flash for you: I'm not your problem."

"What is wrong with you? We're supposed to honor our father and mother, not break their hearts."

"Give it a rest, Catherine." He tried again to go around her.

She got in front of him. "No. Not until you do what you should be doing."

"Who made you judge? Our first loyalty is to God, not man. And maybe it honors Him to use my free will during my rumschpringe to see God from a different viewpoint than the one I've grown up with. It proves our parents have raised a son who isn't content with easy answers. If you see my behavior as out of line, take it up with God, and leave me alone."

Her skin crawled with anxiety. "You went to church?"

He nodded.

"An Englisch church?" She looked heavenward before turning back to him. "What's wrong with you?"

"I don't expect you to get it. You question nothing about being Amish, but I do. And I'm searching for answers."

"You're opening the door for doubt and confusion."

"One of many differences between us, Catherine. I'm not afraid to wrestle with those things, not if it means I have a chance to be sure of what I believe."

"But, Arlan, you know those who go down that path are the most likely to leave our ways."

"So? You believe that leaving the Amish church is the same as turning your back on God. Christ has been around a lot longer than the Amish."

She choked back tears. "But we have to join with other dedicated believers, those who will help us navigate this wicked world without becoming ensnared. The Amish know how to do that."

"They can help you do that. But I'm not convinced it's the answer for me."

"There is only one answer—Christ."

"I agree with you, Catherine. But it seems to me that we Amish live the way we do out of fear."

"That's ridiculous. I refuse the world's ways out of faith, not fear."

"Then maybe, for me, grabbing on to the modern ways *is* walking by faith."

"You're talking nonsense."

"It's possible. But that's what I'm trying to sort through, so butt out." He headed toward the door.

"Ya? Well, while you're trying to figure it all out, do yourself a favor, and don't ask Leah. She understands even less about how life works than you do."

He turned. "Does Samuel have any idea how much you detest his sister?"

"I love Leah, but she's a troublemaker who thinks nothing of disobeying God."

"What has she ever done to you?"

"Nothing to me personally, not yet. But she stirs it up, and you have no idea."

"Wow, it must be nice to always be the one who lives right."

"There are moral lines to be kept, Arlan. I'm sorry it sickens you that I keep them."

"You seem to think I cross them all the time—whether I'm under Leah's influence or not. I like Leah, and I hope she'll attend this Englisch church with me sometime soon. One of the best things about her is that she's every bit as confused as I am, and she's not afraid to admit it or stumble and fall while trying to figure out life."

"You think that's so great? And what if she's pregnant? What will you think then?"

The lines of anger on his face vanished, and he all but gaped at her. Her own words began to dawn on her, and she wished she could take them back.

Arlan stared at her, a jumble of emotions showing on his face—fear and anger being the most prominent. "Why would you say that? That's a pretty big thing to accuse someone of."

"I shouldn't have said it."

"But you have reasons for thinking it's true."

She swallowed hard. "I was angry with you and said the first thing that came to mind."

He continued studying her, trying to distinguish truth from exaggeration. "So you, the one who is always preaching about honesty and morality, just lied to me?"

"I...I—"

"Which is it, Catherine?" His confusion yielded to anger. "You lied, or Leah is pregnant?"

Leah said she wasn't pregnant, but she lied about everything all the time. Still, Catherine should've kept her mouth shut.

He waited, and then he tilted his head. "What you said about Leah is true." When she didn't respond, he turned and strode toward the back field.

"Arlan." Catherine hurried after him.

He pointed at her. "Don't repeat what you said to anybody."

She nodded, hoping he'd do the same. "Let's keep it between us, okay?"

He shoved his hands into his pockets and walked off, probably going for one of his long walks to the pond. He'd likely stay there most of the day, tossing rocks and thinking. She wanted to beg him not to say anything to Leah. Or, heaven forbid, to Samuel. But asking that of Arlan would more likely cause him to tell both of them straightaway. All she could do was hope he'd use more discretion than she had.

She went to the steps and sat down. What had she done? And why? She'd promised Samuel she'd keep quiet about Leah's secrets so she'd have no excuse to leave the Amish.

Sometimes she didn't understand herself. As much as she admired Samuel, she felt the opposite about Leah. The girl got under her skin, but it wouldn't bother her so much if Arlan saw her for who she was.

Catherine had to talk to Samuel. She hurried to the barn and hitched a rig. As she drove to Samuel's, the tears flowed so freely that the front of her dress was wet by the time she pulled into his driveway.

If anyone could fix this, Samuel could. She tied the horse to the hitching post, knocked on the door, and went inside. Samuel was alone in the living room, his feet propped up on an ottoman and a thick book open in his hand.

"Samuel."

"Hey." He glanced at the clock while closing the book, looking as if he might be in trouble. "Did I get our plans for today mixed up?"

She shook her head. "I couldn't wait until tonight."

He stood and smiled at her. "I like the sound of that—" But the smile quickly faded. "Something's wrong, isn't it?"

She nodded, and he wrapped his arms around her. No place on earth felt as warm and secure as being in his arms. "I got into an argument with Arlan. He's wrong about everything, and he has no respect for me, but he hangs on Leah's every word. We have to keep those two apart."

"I don't think they've seen each other in at least a week or two."

"But he wants to take her to some Englisch church next Sunday or the one after."

Samuel propped his chin on the top of her head. "Oh."

"Oh?" Catherine backed up. "You've got to stop that from happening. If she goes and likes it, I think that's all it will take for him to break ties with us and join them."

His brown eyes flashed with disbelief. "What do you want me to do? Ground her?"

"Ya, that'd be a start."

He closed his eyes, shaking his head. "She's my sister, not my child, and that's only one problem with your plan."

"But you managed to ground her once."

"Not exactly. We struck a deal and only because I wanted to keep her from parties, alcohol, and Michael. She's been pretty low-key since then." Samuel rubbed her back. "What happened between you and Arlan?" His quiet voice washed over her.

"I didn't mean to get into an argument with him. I only wanted to find out where he'd gone this morning, and he got all rude about it." She wished she could ask her Daed to talk to Arlan, and she'd tried that a few times. But either he treated her concerns as if they were nothing more than sibling rivalry, or he got so angry with Arlan that the two didn't speak for days.

Samuel hugged her tight. "Men," he mocked disgustedly. "We've lost our ability to speak in a careful, genteel manner when addressing young women."

She pulled back, raising both eyebrows. "Genteel? You've never used that word before."

He rolled his eyes, a grin on his face. "I'm reading all about the more gen-teel ways."

She moved to the couch and picked up the book. "Why?"

"I'm hoping to learn a better way to get along with someone who's a little difficult. It's important for the orchard."

"Why haven't I heard about this plan?"

"It's new. Leah's idea, actually." He brushed his jaw line with the back of his fingers.

Catherine didn't pretend to understand what it took to run Kings' Orchard, but this made no sense. "If you're having trouble with someone, why not walk away from whatever business you have with them?"

"It's not that easy. Some relationships are necessary, even if we do own the land and crops."

"People are just difficult, aren't they?"

He chuckled. "Ya, *they* are." He took the book from her and ran his hands over the tattered hardback. "Unfortunately, it's beginning to dawn on me that we're people too."

Catherine sat on the couch. "Are you saying that I'm as annoying to others as they are to me?"

"I can't possibly see how." He kissed the back of her hand.

"Me either," she giggled.

EIGHTEEN

Rhoda stepped into the tiny phone shanty at the edge of her property. The display on her phone flashed a red twelve. She groaned. The dozen messages couldn't all be business. She'd checked the machine on Saturday, a few hours before Samuel arrived. Now it was Tuesday, and she had so many more messages? Just like last time, and the time before that, most would undoubtedly be crank calls—the same handful of Amish teens calling numerous times.

Bracing herself, she took a pencil and notepad from the top drawer of the small desk under the phone, sat in the vinyl chair, and pushed the green button to listen.

"I need your help," a distressed young female whispered on the other end of the line. "I'm lost, and I don't know how to find my way home. Wolves are howling all around me. I know you can *see* me. You're the only one who can save me. Find me, Rhoda. Find me!" A burst of raucous laughter preceded the beep that ended the message.

Rhoda pressed the green button to pause the machine. She closed her eyes, trying to convince herself she wasn't as alone, as friendless, as vulnerable as she felt. She wished her sister were here.

She knew not everyone was against her and only a handful made the crank calls. They'd stop for a while. But whenever she thought the nonsense had died down for good, they came again, like weeds in a garden. She guessed they were bored.

Rhoda pressed the button to delete the eerie message and waited for the next one to begin. "My boyfriend broke up with me," the caller whined, "and I don't know why. I'm sure you know. You can help—" She heard laughter in the background and a muffled sound before she clicked Delete. The notion that she had any insight into romantic relationships was almost funny to her.

The next message was a real business call—a request for several cases of strawberry preserves, the no-sugar-added kind. She didn't have enough white grape juice concentrate on hand, and this was a rush order. She added it to her shopping list.

Out of the dozen messages, five were for legitimate business. She left the shanty and went to the shed. Everything inside the building had been rearranged to make room for a set of old bookcases. Her brothers' work, no doubt. They had quite a knack for either rearranging or throwing out items, much as they'd apparently done with her grandmother's recipes. The need for space inside the house had them constantly moving items into the attic, barn, and shed.

While shifting some things around, she found the little red wagon her Daed had given her to carry items from the store. She heard a rig pull into her driveway. A quick glance confirmed that Daed had returned from one of his handyman jobs—maybe for lunch or maybe for supplies. Either way, her brothers weren't with him.

With the wagon in hand, she left the shed. Her Daed had already gone into the house. She pulled the wagon behind her, enjoying the idea of a good walk. Perhaps it would help her sort through her jumbled thoughts and emotions concerning Samuel.

The idea of getting to know him better, of maybe even going out with him, intrigued her, even as frustrating as he was. He was muleheaded, but she wasn't an easy person to get along with either. She and Landon had spats all the time, and no one was closer to her than he was. They enjoyed sparring, but her frustrations with Samuel hadn't been so amusing.

While she didn't really want to be put on the spot again about canning for Kings' Orchard, she looked forward to seeing Samuel. Her Daed had warmed up to him right away, as had everyone else in the family. Something about him was magnetic. She couldn't deny that.

She wondered if he might have a tiny spark of interest in her. She sighed, needing to free her mind of him.

As she passed Mrs. Walker's house, her skin suddenly crawled with goose bumps. She paused, studying the older home. Nothing looked out of place. Rhoda ignored the odd sensation and kept walking.

She placed one foot in front of the other without even glancing back. But the sense of eeriness remained in the air. Rhoda stopped.

Her intuition caused more problems than it ever solved. Still, she turned to face Mrs. Walker's home and closed her eyes, hoping the strange feeling would form a specific thought or image. It didn't. But she couldn't shake the idea that something inside Mrs. Walker's home was wrong, possibly with the old woman herself.

She moved the wagon off the sidewalk and hurried back toward her own house. Thankfully, Daed's rig was still in the driveway. She ran into the house and found her sisters-in-law in the kitchen. A large mixing bowl sat on the table, half filled with flour. Lydia cracked an egg and dumped it in.

Phoebe looked up from the recipe card in her hand. "Hey, Rhoda. I'm glad you're here. Do you think we could have a cup of your fresh—"

"Where's Daed?"

"Not sure. Maybe the vegetable garden." Lydia tossed the eggshells into Rhoda's compost bucket and peered at her.

Phoebe wiped her hands on her apron. "You're shaking."

"I…I think Mrs. Walker may need help."

"You think?" Phoebe glanced at Lydia. "I'll get your Daed. You get a drink of water and take a breath."

Rhoda got a glass out of the cupboard and filled it with tap water.

What if she was wrong about Mrs. Walker? She never knew if her instincts were right until she pursued them, and she often embarrassed herself and her family in the process.

Daed came into the kitchen, Phoebe close behind. "What's going on?"

"I have a feeling about Mrs. Walker."

He plunked down into a chair in front of her. "Rhodes..."

"I know, Daed. Trust me, I understand why you'd rather sweep this under the rug. I'd like that plan too, but we can't."

Her father gazed into her eyes. "You're absolutely positive?"

"I'm sure we have to at least check on her."

"There's something I haven't told you." He shifted in his chair. "Her grown children were in town for the holidays a couple of years back, and they came over here to ask me to make sure you left her alone. I told them we'd all stay away. If we go over there, how am I supposed to explain that to them?"

"Would you rather take the chance of letting her die?"

She didn't allow herself to say the rest of what she was thinking—*Like I let Emma die?*

His expression told her he read the desperation in her eyes and voice. "All right. I'll go over there. But you stay at the corner while I talk to her. I don't want her to see you."

She hurried out the door, and Daed followed her. He moved far too slowly as they went down the block. Rhoda stood at the corner while her Daed went up to Mrs. Walker's front porch.

With each knock Rhoda's heart beat faster. Unable to take it any longer, she ran across the woman's yard and joined her Daed on the porch.

"Maybe she's not home." He glanced at the sidewalk as if he was ready to leave.

"Maybe she can't answer the door." Rhoda peeked in the window, but drawn curtains prevented her from seeing inside.

"Rhoda." Daed frowned, cautioning her.

"Something could be wrong. We can't leave until we know for sure." She checked more windows. Shades or drapes blocked every one. "Maybe we should call the police or an ambulance."

"We can't call for help because a neighbor isn't answering her door, especially when that neighbor has asked us to leave her alone."

"What if I'm right and she needs help?" She tried to open the door, but it was locked. She knew the back door was probably locked too. Whenever she was in the berry patch, she would hear Mrs. Walker latch it every time, whether going in or out.

Daed went to the far end of the porch, looking into the side yard.

Rhoda spotted a small plant in a clay pot sitting on the railing. She picked it up and slammed it against the window. The glass broke in countless pieces that tinkled to the ground.

"Rhoda!" Daed hurried back to her. "How am I supposed to explain to the Walker family that you broke into their house?"

Without answering, Rhoda set down the pot, reached inside, and unlocked the window. She raised it and crawled inside. "Mrs. Walker?"

No answer.

She unlocked the front door.

Her Daed stared at her. "Kumm out of there now!"

She retreated deeper into the house. "Mrs. Walker?" When she entered the sunroom, she found the woman lying motionless on the brown carpet. She knelt beside the body. The old woman was still breathing.

Relief coursed through her. "Daed! She's in here!" Rhoda cleared her throat, trying to keep tears from falling. She hadn't let fear stop her, and even though it was hard to believe, she'd been right to break in. "Call for an ambulance."

The minutes ticked by, and Rhoda's heart raced. As thrilled as she was to have found Mrs. Walker alive, she couldn't stop asking herself why she hadn't managed to save her own sister.

It didn't make sense. And God seemed silent on it.

⬦

Leah stood in the bathroom before sunrise, fully dressed for the day but unable to leave this tiny, dimly lit space. She held a cool, wet washcloth to her lips, staring at herself in the mirror and realizing how unfamiliar she looked. Who was she?

Apparently someone whose boyfriend no longer cared about her. It was midweek, twelve days since the party, and he'd yet to come by or even call.

The flame from a kerosene light flickered in the soft glow of dawn. Her sisters slept, and she imagined Eli and Daed were still asleep too. She heard faint sounds of Mamm starting breakfast downstairs. Today was Jacob's birthday, so she might already be working on making him a cake.

Mamm had called the doctor's office yesterday, just as she'd said. She'd explained Leah's symptoms, and since the Kings didn't have health insurance, the general practitioner said Leah didn't have to come in for a referral. He wanted her to go to a specialist, a gastroenterologist. The doctor's office made the appointment for Leah and called Mamm to let her know the appointment was in a few weeks. The nightmare facing Leah grew more menacing by the day.

She longed for the time before she started chasing Michael, wanting him to love her, and then thinking he did. She wished to go back before her rumschpringe—the time she so detested until recently. One thing she knew for sure: she was never again messing around outside of marriage.

Sick of staring into her own eyes, she picked up the lantern and left the room. She tiptoed into the upstairs sitting room, grabbed a book, and sat in an armchair. Maybe if she got absorbed in an old Stephen King novel, she could forget for a while. It seemed so unfair. All she'd wanted to do was have a little fun—enjoy music, good conversations, and a world outside of Amish rules. Now she was stuck doing the only thing she'd been allowed to do before her rumschpringe: read.

"Leah," a man's whispery voice called from somewhere outside. *Michael?* Hope clutched her by the throat. She hurried to the window and pulled back the curtain. Pink and orange hues painted the clouds along the horizon, but the sun had yet to rise. She looked down toward the lilac bushes, a place where Michael had once stood while tossing pebbles at the window to get her attention.

"Down here," he whispered. She looked directly below and saw Jacob

sitting bareback on his Morgan. He had a second horse by the reins and held
them up to her.

He had to be kidding. Go for a ride now? She felt as weak as a kitten.

"Kumm on," he whispered. "It'll be your birthday present to me."

Tears pooled in her eyes. She used to love taking predawn rides with Jacob,
and like so many things she'd come to realize lately, she'd taken them for
granted. Why was it so easy to discount what you had until you no longer
had it?

He shifted, his brows knitting slightly, and she felt as if he were reading her
life story. "If you'll ride with me, I'll let you ask me a question about my past,
anything you wish, and I'll answer." He again lifted the reins to her.

Her heart fluttered. He stayed so closed about his rumschpringe days, and
she longed to hear what he thought of the Englisch world. What made him
come back home? Did he regret leaving? Or returning? Had he sinned as she
had, and did the fear of it catching up with him eat at him day and night?

But his offer to open up made her uneasy. Was he hoping she would talk
about her secrets as well? Regardless, she'd not refuse to go for a ride on his
birthday.

"Okay." She released the lightweight curtain and hurried down the stairs.
She'd almost made it out the door when Mamm spotted her.

"Where are you going?"

"Riding with Jacob."

Mamm put her hands on her hips. "Breakfast is almost ready." She sighed.
"It's been a long time since you two have done that. I'll keep your breakfast
warm on the back of the stove."

"Denki." Leah went outside and got on the horse. They went across the
main road and down the winding dirt path.

It wasn't like her mother to let her off the hook so easily for missing a meal.
Jacob, however, could get away with a lot. Because Mamm was so grateful to
have him back home, she was easier on him than the others, including Samuel.

Noticing that she'd fallen back a bit, Leah tapped her heels against the horse's ribs. It picked up its pace until she and Jacob rode side by side. "We haven't done this in a long time."

"I know. Think you can keep up?" He gestured, giving her a head start on the challenge to race.

She spurred her horse to a canter, but Jacob soon passed her. He still wasn't going nearly as fast as he could. If he were, he'd now be out of sight with only a cloud of dust surrounding her. She clicked her tongue and pressed her feet in, urging her horse to gallop. The cool morning air felt good against her skin as they raced down the hill and toward the willow tree near the creek.

He arrived first, brought his horse to a stop, and removed his hat, acting as if he'd been waiting there for a really long time. Bringing her horse to a halt, Leah pointed at him. "You win again." She swallowed back her nausea.

He chuckled. "You had doubts?" He clicked his tongue, and they rode slowly, watching the sun lift off the horizon like a hot-air balloon.

She knew if she didn't ask him a question, he wouldn't volunteer anything. "Do you regret coming home?"

"Not a bit."

"But you had complete freedom. No Old Ways bogging you down, no religious rituals. You could do anything you want. Don't you miss that?"

"I miss scuba diving." He grinned as if remembering the pleasure of it. "The beauty of being underwater can't be matched. I've never experienced anything like it, not before or since."

"I don't even know how far the ocean is from here."

"About two hundred miles, which by horse and carriage is way too far." He gazed out over the fields. "The sea is a world all its own. The blue water, sunlight making its way through the surface, the ocean life. Every minute I was diving, my heart raced, and no matter how much time I spent in the water, I always wanted more. When I wasn't doing it, I was dreaming about it. Constantly making plans and saving money to go again. As stupid as it probably sounds, I imagine what I felt was similar to being in love."

Leah could relate. Whenever she wasn't with Michael, she was thinking about him, making plans to see him, wanting more time with him. "Then why did you come back?"

"Oh, this and that. One reason is I realized something about the ocean."

"What?"

"That no matter how much I loved everything about the sea, it didn't care one iota about me. I could go every day and give it all my money, my thoughts, my dreams, and it felt nothing. The ocean was unchanging whether I was there or not." He put on his hat and faced her. "What a waste."

Was that how it was between Michael and her? Would his life go on the same whether she was in it or not? "But it meant something powerful to you. Wasn't that enough?"

"Maybe it should've been, but it wasn't."

"It does make sense, sort of." She shifted in her saddle. "So were you scuba diving when this new way of thinking emerged?"

He tugged on the left rein of his horse, turning around to go back home.

She did the same. "Jacob?"

"I offered you one question, Leah, and I've answered more than that."

"You know, you could hire a driver to take you to the ocean. You might get a few frowns from the church leaders and certain folks in the community, but there's no rule against scuba diving."

"Ya. And maybe I will someday, but right now I've lost my stomach for it."

They rode home in silence, and Leah wondered why he'd shared that bit of his past. Was he telling her that he cared? That he was here for her, that he would dive deep into her life and pour money and effort into her?

"Jacob, stop."

"Whoa." He waited.

She brought her horse to a halt beside his. "I…I might be…pregnant."

He showed no emotion, much as he'd done when they had played board games. "But you're not sure?"

She shook her head.

"Are you…late?"

This was a miserable topic to discuss with a brother, but at least he wasn't overreacting. "I've always had times of missing…" She shrugged. "Mamm says it's 'cause I carry extra weight."

"I'll get a pregnancy test for you later today. If you want to talk after that, I'll be around. Otherwise, it's your business, not mine."

He was so matter of fact, so calm. How was he going to get a test without causing suspicion? How embarrassing would it be for him to take such a thing to a cashier? But none of that seemed to bother him.

"Anything else?" he asked.

She should've known he wouldn't bother her with any questions, certainly nothing prying or accusatory. "No."

He waited, giving her time to change her mind.

"Denki, Jacob." Tears blurred her vision.

He leaned toward her in his saddle, reaching out to her. She put her hand in his, feeling the strength and calluses. He squeezed gently, neither condoning nor condemning what she'd done, and once again it seemed she'd been wrong about how her family felt toward her. If she'd been seeing them wrong for years, what else was twisted in her thinking?

As if a strong wind had kicked up unexpectedly, she felt stirred by the love and understanding he expressed, and she longed not to be pregnant—to get a chance to start over.

NINETEEN

The smell of leather, old wood, hay, and horses surrounded Samuel as he stared at the ledger in front of him. The barn had housed the Kings' business office since long before Samuel was born, but how much longer? The chair under him creaked as he shifted to pull another book from a nearby shelf.

He'd gone to see Rhoda on Saturday, and it was now Thursday. It'd been difficult not to pick up the phone and call her, but he'd exercised patience. How much longer should he give her to cool off and have a refreshed view of his offer?

His father leaned forward in his chair beside the desk, looking at the figures Samuel had been working on. "If we get our usual six bushels of cider apples from each tree in your and Jacob's sections, plus fifteen bushels of cider apples from each of Eli's trees, that's what? Around six thousand bushels of cider apples?" He whistled. "If we don't work out something with Rhoda, we'll be stuck with a lot of apples, because there's no way we can sell that many in one season."

"Actually, it'll be closer to seven thousand four hundred and forty-seven bushels of cider apples. And I doubt she could keep up with a tenth of that. But we'll figure out what she can do, and whatever that is, it'll cut our losses some. If she'll agree to work for us."

"I'm really surprised you're willing to do this with a one-woman operation."

"Me too. And surprised you're letting me."

"Your grandfather always intended for you to run this orchard, and when the time came, I was more than glad to turn it over to you. Before that, I was bone weary of keeping up with the orchard and our small herd. It's sort of like retiring to having only one full-time job." He grinned. "I'm relieved that Jacob returned to help and that Eli is showing a good interest in it too. I figure all that help in the orchard is why God gave me sons."

Samuel tapped his pencil on his ledger. "You don't have just sons, Daed."

"True. Maybe in time I'll have sons-in-law too." Daed's chuckle raised Samuel's hackles.

"We're talking about bringing a woman into our business, and I have to wonder if she'd be where she is today if her Daed and brothers treated her the way we treat Leah, Katie, and Betsy—as if they're too girly to be any real help."

"Oh, good grief. You sound like Jacob. I'll tell you the same thing I told him. Not one of the girls has shown any interest in the dairy or the orchard."

"Ya, I know. And I always thought the same thing. But maybe it's because we haven't spoken their language. What did you do to get us interested?"

"Started young. You boys loved coming to the orchard before you could walk. Then, when you were older, I paid you for your time, made your efforts worth it to you."

"Exactly. There was always a payoff for us. I'm hoping by bringing Rhoda in, Leah will feel there's a payoff for her."

"Leah has no interest in any kind of work. Have you forgotten that?"

"Maybe she's not as lazy as she is disinterested. And if she learned to enjoy the work, she might start feeling good about her abilities and make some money too."

"Seems to me all any girl wants to do is stay at home and make new dresses until she catches the eye of a worthy man."

"Really? Or is that all we've expected from them, so it's all we've gotten?"

Daed stroked his beard, quietly thinking for several minutes. "Do you really believe Rhoda's capable of keeping up with a good portion of the cider apples we'll send her way?"

Samuel let him switch the subject. He'd planted enough seeds of change for now. "I don't know the answer to that yet. She has no need of us. She likes her business the way it is, and it'd be easy for her to walk away. I should call her soon, though, let her know we're still interested."

Daed turned the desk phone toward him. "Speaking of making calls, I'm ready to do a little of that myself. I think I'll find out what's up by dialing the news line."

Samuel grinned. "Maybe you should call the Amish chat line instead. Neighborhood gossip would probably help your disposition more than breaking news."

The good old Amish chat lines—dozens and dozens, at times hundreds, of Amish people across the states on the phone at the same time, some taking turns talking, others listening silently for hours at a time. If one person mentioned an event on a chat line, it spread like wildfire.

Daed pointed a finger at him, his eyes dancing with humor. "Thanks for the reminder. After I call the news line, I'll check the chat line. Business before pleasure, after all."

His father picked up the receiver of the phone, and Samuel returned to looking at the ledgers. He couldn't shake the feeling that going with Rhode Side Stands was the right plan, the only plan.

If she'd let him look at her overhead and profits, he could get a better sense of what kind of offer would make this venture worth her time. But she had to be willing to entertain the idea of partnering with them before he could ask to see her records.

Daed snapped his fingers to get Samuel's attention. He covered the receiver with his hand. "That woman with the canning business," he whispered. "Did you say her name is Rhoda Byler and she's from Morgansville?"

Samuel nodded.

Daed returned his attention to the phone, listened for a few more minutes, and then hung up.

"Well?" Samuel asked. "Was there news about Rhoda?"

Daed stood and paced the small room. "Folks on the chat line are absolutely buzzing about her. Seems she broke into an elderly neighbor's home."

"Why on earth would she do that?"

"Rumor is she had some kind of feeling this woman needed help. Folks are calling it a premonition."

"And did the neighbor need help?"

"Apparently so. They say she was passed out in her sunroom. She has two grown children who don't live close by, and when some official contacted them, they said they have some suspicions where Rhoda is concerned. One of Mrs. Walker's children thinks Rhoda may have caused their Mamm to fall when she broke the woman's window and barged in."

What a tangled mess. Based on the conversations he'd had with Rhoda and her family over dinner and the compassionate way she'd treated Leah, he couldn't imagine her doing anything malicious.

"Her children aren't pressing charges, at least not yet. But the police have been questioning everyone, including Rhoda."

"Sounds ridiculous to me. Rhoda must've had a good reason for breaking into the woman's house besides a—what'd you call it?—a premonition."

Daed tugged on the phone cord. "It wouldn't be the first time."

"What are you talking about?"

"This is the same girl whose sister was shot at that market about two years ago. The one who 'saw' the incident before it happened. Or so the rumors said."

That was Rhoda? Some vague pieces from last Saturday's conversation finally took shape. When Samuel first heard about the incident years ago, with all the confusing reports about the girl being killed and her sister predicting it, he'd been intrigued. Some said she had a sixth sense and practiced witchcraft. He'd never imagined that he would one day consider going into business with her.

"People get spooked way too easily. Everybody gets 'inner feelings' from time to time." Samuel's feeling about Rhode Side Stands was like that. It made little logical sense. "Daadi Sam planted apple trees on this land because he had a dream about it." Samuel and his siblings had heard the story since they were old enough to sit in a lap and listen.

"That's true." Daed held up his hands. "She sounds flaky to me, but the decisions concerning her are up to you and Jacob." He left the barn.

Samuel picked up the phone and called Rhoda. He wouldn't mention the gossip he'd just heard, but he wanted to get a feel for how she was faring. He chuckled. Since he was looking for a gut feeling, maybe the gossipers should label *him* a seer.

After waiting through several rings, he assumed he'd get an answering machine. *What would Darcy of* Pride and Prejudice *say when leaving a voice mail?* he wondered.

Instead, someone picked up. "Look, I recognize your number. I don't appreciate being mocked. Stop calling me." Rhoda's tone was cool but even.

"Rhoda." He tried to grab her attention before she hung up. "It's Samuel. Samuel King."

"Samuel?" After a moment of silence, she cleared her throat. "But your number." He heard several beeps as if she was scrolling through the caller ID. "I…I'm so sorry. Your number is one digit different from… I thought you were someone else."

"I'm relieved to hear that." He tapped a pencil on his desk. He'd heard all he needed to. She was fine, and that's all he had to know to move forward. "I was wondering if you were ready to set a day and a time to come to the orchard."

"No, not yet. I have a lot to do around here."

"Ya, I know you're busy. But, well, the truth is, I need you to consider my proposal, and to do that you really should visit. Since it's a family operation, I'd like you to meet my family to get a real feel for who we are."

The silence on the line made Samuel wonder if he was pushing too hard too quickly.

"Actually, there are some things you should know about me."

"Okay. I'm listening."

She haltingly told him about the situation with her neighbor, explaining the break-in and her intuition about the elderly woman.

"None of that has any bearing on our discussion of a business relationship."

"I think we've found something we can agree on."

"Gut. I hope that's just the start. Is there any way you could fit in a visit tomorrow? I'm sure we could do it in about four hours, if necessary."

"Well,"—it sounded as if she was looking through papers, maybe a calendar—"I suppose I could."

Samuel grinned. "Perfect. And if you don't mind, I'd like to ask a personal question."

"Depends on the question."

"Are you seeing anyone?"

The line was silent, painfully so.

"I'm not sure that's a proper subject for a business conversation."

"It most certainly is." The men in *Pride and Prejudice* would have been slow and careful with their response, and he realized anew that he fell dismally short. If that's what Rhoda needed, would he be able to deliver? "What I mean is, there's no point in our discussing plans for this fall if you might abandon them to get married." He wished he could see Rhoda's face. Or better yet, read her thoughts.

"I'll see you tomorrow, Samuel. Around one?"

"Does that mean you don't have anyone serious in your life?"

"Good-bye, Samuel."

She wasn't going to answer him, not right now anyway. Or maybe she had and he didn't know it. "Bye." He hung up, hoping tomorrow went as smoothly as the future of Kings' Orchard needed it to.

TWENTY

Leah sat on her bed, staring at the pregnancy test. She'd spent most of the day right here, trying to absorb her new reality. Her Mamm had left her alone, probably because Jacob convinced her to give Leah some much-needed space today. She had used that time to cry until she felt numb.

She couldn't keep waiting for Michael to come over. She had to go see him. Surely he'd be home on a Thursday night.

"Leah?" Mamm called.

Guilt and fear pressed in, making her hesitant to face her Mamm. She hid the pregnancy test under her pillow and moved to the landing. "Ya?"

Her mother gave her the once-over. "We're going to my sister's. Do you want to get ready and go with us?"

"No."

"You're sure? She's making ice cream."

"I'm sure."

"Okay. Be good. We'll be home around ten."

Her mother stared at her for a long moment. *"Bischt allrecht?"*

Leah's mouth went dry. No, she wasn't well…not even close. She wanted to curl up in her mother's arms until all her fears faded into nothingness.

"Ya, Mamm, I'm fine." Her feet didn't want to move, but Leah went back into her bedroom. She meandered to the bed and pulled out the pregnancy test. One blue line stared back at her from inside the little window on the stick.

She slid it into her pillowcase and made her bed before she picked up a hairbrush off the nightstand. After she brushed her hair, she pinned it up and bundled it inside her organdy prayer Kapp. She put on her nicest Amish dress—the one that used to be Michael's favorite.

A light evening breeze stirred the humid air, and June bugs and tree frogs sang loudly as she walked to Michael's place. With each step she silently rehearsed what she'd say to him. She couldn't blurt out that she was pregnant. She'd have to lead into it. But by the time she stepped onto his gravel driveway forty minutes later, she still hadn't come up with a good way to share her news.

His house loomed large and uninviting, but she kept forcing herself to take one step after another. She was almost to the front porch when Michael barreled out the door, holding a set of keys. She'd been with him when he bought the old car he kept hidden behind the barn.

Once at the foot of the porch steps, he saw her and stopped short. "Leah. What are you doing here?"

"I… We need to talk."

His eyes moved down her. "You look good." He headed for the back of the barn. "Maybe next week sometime," he called over his shoulder.

She hurried to catch up with him. "Got plans with that girl from the party?"

"No." He opened his car door. "Just meetin' some of the guys."

"Michael," she said more forcefully, "could you manage to give me five minutes?"

He sighed and closed the door without getting inside. He leaned against his car, and for the first time in quite a while, he finally seemed to see her. "You still upset over what happened at the party?"

"It was very hurtful, but, no, that's not what this is about."

He paused, studying her. "What's wrong?"

This was the man she knew him to be, caring and gentle. Even though she dreaded telling him, she clung to the hope that he would step up and offer to marry her.

"I need you not to be in a hurry."

He stared off in the distance as if he was deciding what was most important. "Okay." He shrugged. "Forget the guys. Now I'm no longer in a hurry. What's up?"

Had he always been this wishy-washy? From the corner of her eye, she saw someone moving around in the barn, probably his Daed. "Can we go somewhere to talk?"

His lopsided grin worked its way into her heart again. "Maybe walk to our secret place?"

"That'd be nice."

He went to the trunk of his car and opened it. He pulled out a large rolled-up blanket. They walked in silence down a dirt lane toward the small pond on the edge of his land. Trees surrounded it, and a thin trail led through the four-feet-high underbrush. Once they were on the other side of that, no one could hear or see them. He'd brought her here before, and although she'd once loved this place and all that had happened here between them, she felt uneasy.

He stopped at the small clearing and spread out their picnic blanket. Leah sat.

Michael took a spot several inches from her, stretching out his long legs and leaning back on his hands. "I've been wanting to come by your place for a while now."

"Then why on earth haven't you?"

"Figured you were too angry." He plucked some dried grass from the ground beside him. "I don't remember a lot about that night, but I know I was a drunken jerk."

"The only thing worse than being a jerk is being one who doesn't apologize."

"Ya, I guess so." He leaned back on his elbows. "I've missed you. If I'd thought you might forgive me, I'd have come to see you."

"You always seem up for trying new things. Maybe you should've tried acting like a man and apologized."

"This is you not angry? I was supposed to come crawling to you with an apology so you could rake me over the coals? No thanks."

"I could've used some support."

"Support? What for?"

She tried to say the words, to tell him she was expecting, but she couldn't manage it.

"Leah?"

"I'm pregnant."

Jacob stood at a pay phone outside a gas station, waiting for Sandra's answering machine to pick up.

"Hello?"

She'd finally answered, and he couldn't manage to find his voice.

"You have to the count of zero to speak up."

"It's me."

"Oh."

That was it? That's all she had to say? Jacob gripped the phone tighter, reminding himself that he'd never know what it'd done to her to lose her husband as she had. He had to keep doing what he thought was right, but the fact was she'd only answered the phone because she didn't recognize the number. "I won't take long. I just needed to know if you're keeping your head above water." A couple of loud talkers walked from a gas pump toward the store, and he missed what Sandra said. He turned the other way, trying to block out the noise. "Could you repeat that?"

"I said that I...I don't blame you."

He swallowed hard, wishing he could believe her.

"I followed your advice, and I'm feeling better these days, even thinking about going back to school."

Her willingness to share a small part of herself again encouraged him. Maybe healing had begun. "That's great. Do they give degrees for being the queen of trivia?"

"I wish. If random, useless pieces of information had any value, I'd be rich."

"You're healthy and alive and have your daughter. You are rich."

"That and the money you send. You have to stop. Well, not yet, but soon."

He chuckled. "More double-talk, Sandra?"

"You want to hear confusing jabber? Wait until Casey wakes up from her nap."

Despite their best efforts to be encouraging and kind to each other, the conversation sounded hollow. But it was the best one they'd had in almost two years. He'd stay right here, standing in front of a gas station, and talk for as long as she was willing.

TWENTY-ONE

Leah's heart pounded as Michael paced back and forth in front of the small blanket.

He moaned and muttered to himself. His eyes met hers and were wide with fear. "You're sure?"

"I took the test today."

He sighed and sat down beside her. "I suppose this means we'll have to get married."

Not exactly the proposal she'd imagined, but at least he was leaning in the right direction. "It'll be rough on both of us for a while." She moved her hand across the blanket and closer to his, hoping he'd take the hint and hold it. He didn't. "Our families and the community will need some time to adjust." That was putting it mildly. But she had to present this in the best light possible, at least until he made a commitment to do right by her.

She wondered if she should mention the possibility of moving away.

"I do love you, you know." She moved her hand over his, slowly caressing it with her gentle touch.

Michael wrapped his arms around her, cocooning her in a warm embrace she wished would never end. He kissed the nape of her neck, and warmth spread throughout her.

He paused, gazing into her eyes with longing and desire. "Maybe we could make this work in our favor." He cupped her face in his hands and tenderly kissed her lips.

Leah never felt beautiful except in his embrace. Relief that he was willing to marry her ran through her veins. Everything was going to work out after all.

He loved her! She returned his kiss with passion and abandon. Tears of sweet release trickled down her cheeks.

His hand moved to bare skin near her ankle and eased up her leg. Leah's skin tingled. This was the father of her child. Her future husband. The man she'd spend the rest of her life with—having babies, raising children, building a life.

His fingers skimmed over her knee, slowly reaching higher.

"Michael," she whispered between kisses.

"Shhh. We're fine." His voice was husky as he gazed into her eyes with all the love she'd always imagined seeing in them.

"I don't think we should."

He patted the blanket. "It's all right, Leah. Just relax."

She pushed his hand away, lowering her skirt. "This doesn't feel right." She had made a vow to herself: no more messing around. She was already suffering the consequences. But how could she reject his affection?

He glanced around. "Don't worry. No one will see us."

If Michael was going to be her husband, she needed to trust him. Yet as he lowered his suspenders and began unbuttoning his pants, Leah went from feeling loved to feeling cheap. He pushed his hand under her dress again.

Leah ached to nestle against him, to feel him hold her in his strong arms and whisper words of love and desire for her. She wanted their intimate time handled in the right way now. "We need to wait"—her breath came in shallow gasps—"until we're married, please."

"It's not like we haven't already done it." He kissed her face while pulling her closer.

Done it? How could he refer to their time in such a crude manner?

"And since you're already pregnant," Michael mumbled around his kisses, "we don't have to use protection." His hand tugged at her to lie down. But she felt like a heifer he was trying to brand, property to be taken and possessed.

She pushed him away. "Michael, stop. If you love me, you'd at least try to understand how I feel." Her words caught her off guard. *If* he loved her?

She doubted how he felt?

He tugged at her again. "I can tell you want it as much as I do." He reached under her billowing skirt, putting his hand on her knee.

She recoiled and pulled away. "Do you even care about me at all?"

He looked hurt. "How can you ask that? Of course I care about you." He stroked her arm softly. "We've always had something special between us, Leah. You've been there for me, no matter what."

That was true, at least. She had been faithful to him for as long as she'd known him, even when he chased other girls, treated her poorly, or cast her aside after he got his way. And she always came back to him when he finally looked her way again, accepting any crumb of attention he was willing to give.

What a fool she was.

She scrambled a few feet from him to the edge of the blanket, determined to avoid being lured into his snare again. She could be any girl right now and he'd want to sleep with her.

"Fine. If that's the way you're going to be." He pulled up his suspenders and buttoned his pants.

Leah stared at him from her side of the blanket. She had a decision to make—one that would determine the course of the rest of her life. If she gave in to what Michael wanted, there was a chance she could convince him to stay with her, marry her, and raise their child together. But odds were just as good that he'd simply use her again and toss her aside when someone prettier came along—before they became husband and wife. *If* they ever became husband and wife.

"Ya, Michael." Leah felt a sudden surge of inner strength. "That's the way I'm going to be." She stood and walked away from him, head held high. Feeling confident. And like the stupidest woman alive.

She strode down the path toward Michael's home, straightening the Kapp on her head and trying to get the rumpled look out of her clothes—and out of her mind. Before reaching his house, she veered off the path and headed toward the road.

Thousands of questions pounded her.

Was Michael watching her? Would reality sink in over time and cause him to feel sorry for the way he'd treated the mother of his child? When it did, how would he respond? Would he be relieved that he didn't have to rush into marrying a girl he never really loved?

Never really loved? Was that true?

Would she have to raise his child on her own?

As she turned onto the road toward home, the weight of what she'd done mocked her. What if Michael never came to his senses? How could she bear the shame of being pregnant and alone? Her eyes blurred with tears that she didn't bother trying to stop.

She figured Michael wouldn't tell anyone about her being pregnant—for his self-preservation. But she wouldn't be able to keep this a secret for too long. And then the news would spread throughout the community like a brush fire on a summer day. Once her family found out—

She heard the rhythmic *clippety-clop* of a horse's hoofs and the steady rumble of spoke wheels behind her. For a second she wondered if Michael had come after her. But he would've driven his car or at least ridden a horse rather than taking the time to hook up a rig.

She could tell by the sounds that the horse and carriage were slowing. She turned around to see who was driving.

Jacob brought the rig to a stop. She didn't wait for an invite before climbing in. After she shut the door, her brother tapped the reins on the horse's back and headed down the road.

She brushed at her damp cheeks. "I'm pregnant." The words made her break into sobs. "And Michael's a total jerk. I thought... I was so sure he loved me." She put her hand out the open window, feeling the muggy air zip past her—much like her life. "If I'm honest, I never actually believed that. I only hoped it was true, and I was willing to lie to myself on the outside chance I could do something to make him love me."

"It's his loss."

Leah rolled her eyes. "He used me. Would have again if I'd let him. How could I be so stupid?"

"You're not stupid."

"Well, naive then."

"Everybody's naive at least once. Me included. You'll survive."

She moaned. "I'm just so mad at myself."

"Michael's naive too, you know."

"How?"

"If he thinks his behavior won't catch up with him and haunt him day and night, that's pretty naive."

"Do you think there's any chance the pregnancy test was wrong?"

"Sorry, Leah. I'd like to give you good news, but those things are really accurate these days."

"Great."

"You read the instructions and followed them, right?"

"They're pretty straightforward. I peed on a stick and waited until a blue line showed up in the oval window."

Jacob faced her. "You mean two pink lines, right?"

"No, one. Why?"

He laughed loud and hard. "Leah, one blue line means you're *not* pregnant."

"What?" Hope shot through her.

He shook his head. "You devour every word of your novels, but you don't take the time to read the instructions on something so important?"

"Oh, Jacob, are you sure?"

"Positive. I mean negative. One blue line means negative, which means you're not pregnant."

"I always thought negative meant a bad thing was going to happen."

"Ya, having a baby at seventeen would be a definite negative."

She nodded. "But I've been so sick lately. I was sure how the test would turn out."

"Well, depending on timing, it's still possible you're pregnant."

"But you just said those tests are accurate."

"They are. Unless you take the test too soon for it to show up. When were you and Michael together last?"

She didn't need to think long about that. The memory was crystal clear. "Six weeks ago." That's when he'd started avoiding her and going to parties without her, and she'd chased him.

Jacob grinned. "Then you are definitely not pregnant. The type of test I bought would have shown a pregnancy within that time." He shoved her shoulder.

"You sure know a lot about pregnancy tests."

He pursed his lips, sadness flickering in his eyes, and she regretted her words.

She hugged his neck, but as she settled back into her seat, a new fear came out of hiding. "So what's wrong with me, then? Why have I felt so sick lately?"

He glanced at her. "No, little sister, you're not dying."

"How do you know?"

"Because I know numbers, and I know you. Odds are you've done all this to yourself through worry. Nerves would be my guess. Maybe you've given yourself an ulcer. Whatever is going on, we'll find a simple solution, and before long you'll feel well enough to go back to avoiding your chores for less complicated reasons." He grinned.

How could she have been so stupid? She should have read the directions on the box more carefully. She'd almost given in to Michael again. But she'd made the right decision, and she'd like to do more of that.

TWENTY-TWO

Samuel steered the team of workhorses dragging a small Amish hay cutter. He went down the green space between the rows, cutting all the grass that wasn't in the drip line of the trees. Jacob pushed a reel mower under the drip line, destroying the grassy mouse tunnels that led to the trunks of the trees. Routine maintenance—that's all it was. But he, Jacob, and Eli had been at it since sunrise, making the place look its best for Rhoda's visit this afternoon.

Something caught Samuel's attention, and he turned. Leah was driving a pony cart toward them with Hope perched beside her, watching and occasionally barking.

When Jacob spotted Leah, he left the mower and headed her way. Leah brought the horse to a stop, motioned for Samuel, and held up an oversized thermos before she and Jacob started talking.

Samuel preferred everyone to stay on task, but he drove the hay cutter closer to them and brought the horses to a halt. "What's this?"

Leah took Hope off the wooden seat beside her and set her on the ground. "Can't a girl do something nice for her brothers once in a blue moon?" She lowered the tailgate on the cart. Samuel and Jacob took a seat while Hope ran from one spot to another, sniffing all the new smells.

Leah poured them cups of cold water and took a lid off a container of cookies.

Jacob's eyes grew round. "You made my favorite?"

"Ya." Leah held the container up to him. "Oatmeal chocolate chip."

"Oatmeal." Samuel mumbled a mock complaint as he took one and scrutinized it. "So where's my favorite cookie, Leah?"

"I'll leave that to your girlfriend."

Samuel shifted, getting more comfortable. Leah's face was pale, and her hand moved to her upper stomach often, but she seemed more peaceful than he'd seen her in a long time. Mamm was counting the days until Leah saw the specialist. "You're looking chipper today."

Leah looked at Jacob, and they seemed to share a moment of some kind.

"Hey,"—Jacob interrupted his thoughts—"this woman…Rhoda something?"

"Byler."

"You've told Catherine she's coming here today?"

"No."

"You like to live dangerously."

"Appears that way, but it's not my aim." Samuel pulled the handkerchief from his pocket and poured cold water on it.

Jacob took another bite of his cookie. "What if your girlfriend shows up in the middle of Rhoda's visit?"

"I, uh, took care of that last night." Samuel wiped his face and the back of his neck with the cool cloth.

"What does that mean?" Leah asked.

Jacob picked up another cookie. "I'm not sure you need to hear this, Leah. Whatever he's done, it'll give you the wrong idea concerning male-female communication."

"Don't listen to him." Samuel shooed his brother away. "He's inexperienced in these matters. If upsetting a loved one can be avoided, it should be."

"Uh-huh." Jacob grinned around a mouthful of cookie. "So what'd you do?"

"After I talked to Rhoda yesterday, I called Catherine and asked if she and her Mamm would like to go shopping in Lancaster today. When she said yes, I told her I wanted to give her an early present for the anniversary of our first date, so I hired a driver and gave her some spending money. It should be a fun day for both of them."

"That's pretty sneaky," Leah said.

"It's a distraction while I get some business worked out. Rhoda will be long gone before the driver returns to Harvest Mills. If Rhoda agrees to work for us, I'll tell Catherine everything."

"And if Rhoda says no?" Leah's brows arched.

Samuel drew a heavy breath. "Then what'd be the point of telling Catherine anything?"

Jacob brushed crumbs off his shirt. "Don't ask me, but I always thought the perk of being tied down was having someone you could share your burdens with."

Did Jacob know he often used the term *tied down* when he talked about being in a relationship? He'd always been restless. When Jacob graduated from the local Amish school at fourteen, he'd asked to leave the farm and to apprentice as a carpenter under their uncle Mervin in his construction business. So Daed let him live in Lancaster with Mervin's family, and a driver brought Jacob home on weekends and holidays. But it seemed to Samuel that his brother grew more restless with each passing year.

When Jacob turned nineteen, he quit working for their uncle and began traveling, picking up jobs as a carpenter and, as Jacob put it, seeing the world. He lived on his own for two years, calling home from time to time or sending occasional letters about his latest adventures snow skiing, scuba diving, or deep-sea fishing. The whole family worried if he'd ever come back home to live. But one day he showed up—with bruises, stitches, and a cast on his leg. He said he'd been in a little accident, and that's all he'd say. But something had changed him. Some of it good, like the fact that *restless* didn't describe him much anymore. Some of it not good, like the secrets he held on to so tightly.

Samuel got up. "Denki, Leah. My favorite cookie or not, that hit the spot and will certainly make it easier to work through lunch."

She picked up Hope and put the pup in the cart. "I'm going to ride out farther to see if I can spot Eli. As early as you guys started today, he'd surely like a snack."

Jacob winked at her. "You're a keeper."

"Denki."

They drank the last of the liquid in their cups and put them in the cart. Jacob covered the plate of cookies and set them out of Hope's reach, then sent Leah on her way.

While watching the wagon slowly meander farther into the orchard, Samuel said, "If we didn't need Rhoda to become a partner, you might find yourself attracted to her."

Jacob stretched. "What makes you think that?"

"What's your number one complaint about most girls?"

"They're boring."

"She's quirky and difficult but not boring. What's your second complaint?"

"They're either overconfident about their looks or filled with self-doubt. Both are enough to drive a sane man off a cliff."

"I think she's too focused on her berry patch and her family to worry much about her appearance."

Jacob didn't ask what she looked like. No surprise there. He had a long list of picky things about women, but how they looked wasn't on it.

"What about my third complaint—that most girls cycle through more emotions in a day than a man does in a year. I can't take that."

"She's no peaceful dove, but other than that I don't know. I hope I never have to find out. I do know she's been the cause of a lot of hearsay on the chat line lately."

Jacob started for his mower. "What made her the source of rumors?"

"She broke into a woman's home to help her."

"Hmm. So she doesn't scare easily." He nodded. "I think I'm looking forward to meeting her."

"You can't start anything romantic, Jacob. We can't afford emotional messiness ruining what we could build as partners. Besides, after a few dates what are the chances of you actually liking her?"

Jacob sighed. "True. Wish it wasn't, but it is. I just turned twenty-three and not an interesting girl in sight."

Samuel climbed on the mower, standing behind the horses, and took the reins in hand. "It'll happen. And when it does, the mystery woman will knock those stinky socks right off your feet."

TWENTY-THREE

Rhoda wiped the sweat from her forehead. "Landon." She tried choking back the sheer annoyance of the moment. "How did you miss the fact that you needed gas?"

Landon tapped the clear plastic of the dash. "The stupid gauge on this thing is broke. It registers as full all the time, and sometimes I forget how long it's been since I pulled into a station." He moved the gearshift. "Just get in the driver's seat and steer. I'll push it to the shoulder of the road."

"I can't do that." She got out of the truck. "I'll push. You steer."

Landon stepped out of the truck and slammed the door. "Now is not the time to try to make me go insane. I have to be back at work in less than thirty minutes."

"Maybe you should've thought of that before you began a sixty-minute trip with twenty-five minutes worth of gas." Sweat dripped down her back.

"I'm trying to do you a favor. Could you do things my way this time?"

"I can't afford to do anything else that will add to the crazy rumors about me, and someone seeing me behind the wheel of your truck while you push it down the road will definitely add fuel to the fire."

"It'll only take a few minutes, and we're stuck on a deserted back road. No one will see us. Certainly no one who knows who we are."

"Someone calls up the chat line, mentions that Englisch man who works for Rhoda Byler, and pretty soon folks put the info together. It's not like your Englisch world. We're a much smaller population, and it isn't hard to figure out who was seen where." A car went down the road on the opposite side, a driver with an Amish passenger. "See?"

"Fine. We'll do it your way." Landon started to get in behind the wheel, but then he stopped and slammed the door again. "No. You'll hurt yourself trying to push this heavy thing."

She mimicked his sigh, then slammed her door even harder. "You can't fool me. You just like slamming doors. Or is this how the Englisch pump gasoline?"

Landon opened his door and slammed it so hard the truck rocked.

She followed suit. "Seems an odd way to get gasoline, but okay."

The familiar sound of a bridled horse shaking its head caught her attention. She turned to see the silhouette of an Amish man riding a horse in the field next to the road.

"Duh net schtobbe." He motioned at Landon, who had no way of knowing the man had just told him not to stop.

Rhoda tried to swallow. She couldn't tell if the man was teasing or disappointed in her behavior. She peered up at him, unable to see his face under the shadow of his straw hat.

It seemed the man didn't understand what she and Landon were doing— that they were letting off steam. *"Du duh net verschteh."* You do not understand.

He shifted on the horse, and she caught a better glimpse of his face. He was young, early twenties probably. That meant he was less likely to be offended at her cutting up with a non-Amish man and probably too busy for the chat line.

He got off his horse and leaped over the fence with ease, then looked at Rhoda. "If you'll steer, the two of us will push it off the road."

Having an Amish man with them helped solve the problem of her steering while Landon pushed. The three of them, if seen, would get a few chuckles, but it wouldn't be considered inappropriate.

She slid behind the wheel, hoping to goodness she didn't embarrass herself. How did one steer a vehicle anyway?

"Put it in neutral, Rhodes, and pull the handle to the parking brake."

What was he talking about? "Neutral? Parking brake?"

"Here." Landon slid in next to her and pushed and pulled things before hopping out again.

Her hands trembled a bit. What a way to spend her first time behind the wheel of a vehicle! Sitting in the middle of a road while two men pushed it.

The Amish man eased up to the side of the truck. "If you want to go right, turn the wheel to the right." He spoke softly, as if he understood how frazzled she felt right now. "It's similar to tugging on the reins of a horse. But don't turn the wheel too far. That'll cause too much friction, and we won't be able to make the vehicle budge. Just a gentle tug in the direction you want to go."

"Okay."

"You ready?"

She gave him a grin. "No."

He paused as if he were willing to wait right there until she said yes.

"Ya." She nodded. "Please, let's do this."

He went to the back of the truck and joined Landon as they pushed, but the truck went nowhere. The Amish man ambled to the open driver's window again and peered inside. "You have your feet on the brake."

"What?" She glanced down. Ya, she had both of them pressing that pedal. "Oh. Sorry."

He rubbed his fingers over his mouth, and she wondered if he was trying to hide a smile.

"Not a problem." He returned to the back of the truck, and this time when he and Landon pushed, the truck rolled to the side of the road—and kept going!

The Amish man ran up to the window. "The brake! Now!"

"Oh, ya." She jammed her feet onto the pedal, and the truck jerked to a stop.

"Gut. Pull the gearshift toward you and then to the left until the red line is on the *P* instead of the *N*."

She followed his instructions. "So that's how that works."

He rubbed his mouth again. "Ya."

"Hey, Rhodes." Landon stepped forward. "Are you chatting about the weather or asking where the closest gas station is?"

The man gestured in the opposite direction from the way they were headed. "It's about ten miles back."

Rhoda followed his gesture, then looked at him. "And how far to Kings' Orchard?"

"By paved road, about two miles in the direction you're headed."

"Great job, Landon." Rhoda got out of the truck, trying to suppress a chuckle. "You just *had* to run out of gas right before you dropped me off."

"Keep it up, Rhodes, and I'll let you hitchhike there."

The man cleared his throat. "Do you have a phone with you?"

Landon pulled a cell phone out of his pocket and handed it to him. The man called someone and gave instructions to bring five gallons of gas to Kings' Road behind the back tierce, and then he passed the phone back to Landon. "Someone will be here in about fifteen minutes." He tipped his hat, climbed back over the fence, got on his horse, and rode off.

Rhoda turned to Landon, hoping she didn't look as bewildered as she felt. "Strange he didn't introduce himself."

"He's one of your people. I thought the whole purpose of living as you do is to be peculiar. Although some of you are more strange than others," he said with a wry smile. "Besides, we didn't introduce ourselves."

Still trembling a bit, she opened the tailgate of the truck. "Oh, ya, like you Englisch are not strange."

"Of course we are." Landon stared after the man, who was disappearing over the horizon. "But I think he might take the cake. Speaking of dessert, I'm hungry."

"You should've eaten." Rhoda plopped down on the tailgate.

Landon sat next to her. "My boss at my second job asked me to use my lunch break from my first job to take her to a place I don't think she should go. Maybe this is a sign."

"Oh, it's a sign all right. It's a sign that you forgot to feed your car."

"Seriously. Maybe you're not supposed to even consider going into business with the Kings." Landon adjusted his ball cap. "You've built Rhode Side Stands through your own hard work. You don't need them. If you want to make apple products, buy their fruit and sell what you make under your own brand."

It made sense, she had to admit. Still… "I haven't decided what I really think of the idea. I'm simply going to listen to what Samuel has to say."

"Like I told you, there's plenty of land in Maine. And I'd help your family move."

"It's all you can do to take off for a lunch break. How are you going to help us move to another state?"

He lowered his head. "The mail store cut my hours again. Starting next week. And I'm the only employee now who isn't a family member. My grandmother owns a small store, and maybe she could use some more help."

"She has plenty of help. You've said so yourself."

"I have to do something, Rhodes. She'd put me to work, and I could live with her."

He sounded so downhearted. Maybe there was a benefit to Samuel's offer that she hadn't considered. "Then perhaps the answer is for me to have more work for you to do. If I like the Kings' setup, it may be the answer for everyone."

"They would want me as part of the deal?"

"I made sure of it. And if I do this, I'll need more work hours from you. Lots of them. And no one is moving, not you or me."

"You haven't been exactly excited about coming here today."

"I've had mixed feelings. I'll admit that. But you know how I can have a one-track mind-set concerning business."

"Maybe your lack of enthusiasm is a gut feeling about the whole proposition. I have the stuff my granny sent me in the glove compartment." Landon wiggled his eyebrows at her. "We could look at it now if you want. Got nothing better to do while we wait."

"Not interested, thank you."

"Fine." Landon checked his watch. "Think he really phoned for help, or will we still be standing here at sunset?"

"He called."

Their conversation meandered, but finally a man in a shiny red truck pulled up behind them. He got out and smiled at them. "I heard you need some gas." He grabbed a red jug from the bed of his truck.

A nervous chill went through her. Was it excitement? Or reluctance? She had no clue. And she should.

But part of her wanted to return home, not keep going.

TWENTY-FOUR

Catherine stood next to her Mamm at the back of the full-sized van as the driver opened the tailgate doors. She placed her heavy package inside. "I'm so glad Samuel came up with this idea. I've been keeping my eye out for a great canister set for years. I love the one we found."

"I've never seen better. Perfect size for holding powdered baking items, and they're stackable."

Catherine heard a familiar laugh, and her mother's voice faded. She climbed the two concrete steps to the sidewalk and searched for the source of the laughter. About half a block away, Arlan was walking with a group of Englisch kids, chatting freely and carrying a guitar case.

What was he doing? And why?

"Catherine dear?"

Catherine blinked and pulled her eyes from watching her brother. "Ya?"

"The driver was talking to you. We've been to every store we were interested in around this area. Do you want Mrs. Parker to drive us across town to the fabric store?"

"Maybe." She wanted to follow Arlan to see where he was going. But how could she without her mother finding out?

Her mother's hand clutched her wrist. "I thought he was working today."

Catherine turned to her Mamm. She'd followed Catherine's gaze and spotted Arlan. "I did too." Catherine didn't dare take off on foot. What if the group hopped into someone's vehicle?

She looked to the driver. "Mrs. Parker, could you turn the vehicle around and trail that group of teens?" She pointed, but they had gone around a corner.

"I guess so."

Her Mamm shook her head. "I'm not sure this is a good idea. What if we find answers that we don't want to know?"

"Then wait here, and I'll be back shortly."

Mamm hesitated. "No. If you think it's a good idea, I'll go with you."

By the time they got in and were headed in the right direction, they barely caught sight of the group before getting stopped by a red light. They moved forward a block and were stopped again, but they could see where the group was going.

Arlan appeared to be having a grand old time, laughing and cutting up as he walked with three girls and two guys, most of them wearing jeans and T-shirts. One girl had on shorts. The group turned, and it was hard to see around the vehicles to tell exactly where they'd gone. It looked as if they'd left the main sidewalk and headed up a walkway.

"There." Catherine pointed. "Drive to that spot and pull over."

As the van approached, Catherine saw two buildings near the area where they had lost sight of Arlan: a church with a white steeple and double-wide doors, one of which was propped open, and a brick warehouse that had signs in the windows advertising secondhand clothing. Had the teens gone into the church on a Friday? Or had they gone into the other place? Mrs. Parker stopped the van, and Catherine opened the door.

Mamm grabbed her arm, disappointment mirrored on her face. "Let's go shopping or go home."

"You don't want to know what he's doing here when he's supposed to be working?"

"Sometimes what keeps a relationship from shattering is minding your own business and enjoying what does exist between the two of you."

"Then stay here." Catherine got out, but she wasn't surprised when Mamm followed her. They went to the open door of the church and peered inside. The teens were rowdy, laughing and talking loudly as they messed with music equipment. "Testing, testing." One young girl spoke into a microphone and tapped it. "It's dead."

One of the boys cursed and bounded onto the stage. "I put new batteries in that last night."

A spotlight came on and centered on Arlan. He chuckled and strummed the guitar loudly.

If Catherine had the guts, she'd walk down the center of the red carpet aisle and give Arlan a piece of her mind. What was he doing with a group who cursed in church? And wore shorts and practiced to be in the spotlight on center stage? She believed these youth were rebelling just as much as Leah, only their self-indulgent parties took place in church. Surely their parents didn't know how disrespectful they were being. And where was the preacher or any adult? Did they even have permission to be here?

Her mother sniffled, and Catherine turned to look at her. Fear of what was happening with her only son etched itself on Mamm's face. Catherine put an arm around her shoulders and walked her back to the van, wishing she'd handled the last few minutes differently.

"Kumm, let's go home." Catherine did what she could to comfort her Mamm on the ride back.

"This is worse than his going to a few parties or playing instruments at bars or what have you with his friends." Mamm stared out the window. "After those things our youth return to us with a renewed commitment to our ways, but attending a church, going to a place where he feels that it's right to play his music and that God accepts him? We could lose him this way."

"He told me himself he's confused about everything, Mamm. He'll be fine." Catherine didn't know if she was lying to her mother or if she was simply hoping and saying it out loud.

But after they arrived home and she got her mother calmed, she was going to see Samuel. From now until the end of October, his attention would be fully consumed with the apple orchard, as it always was. But he had to heed her this time and talk to Arlan.

Rhoda waited beside Landon's truck. After the stranger poured the gas into the tank, he refused to take any money, saying he was paying back a favor he owed.

She and Landon got into the truck and continued down the road. In mere minutes they pulled into a gravel driveway. The mailbox read "King."

Landon stopped the truck, and they got out. A woman and three girls came outside. Rhoda recognized Leah, but she stayed back. Did she think Rhoda would say something that might get her in trouble?

"You must be Rhoda," the woman said.

Leah stepped forward. "Ya, that's right. And, Rhoda, this is Mamm."

The woman held out her hand. "Elizabeth."

As they exchanged niceties, Rhoda saw Samuel coming out of the barn.

"Rhodes, I hate to run, but I gotta get back to work."

She turned to Landon. "Thanks for the ride."

"I'll pick you up after work, around four thirty." He got into his truck and left.

"Rhoda. So glad you could make it." Samuel held out his hand, and she shook it. "Would you care to come inside for a minute? Maybe freshen up or get a glass of water?"

"No, I'm good. I'd like to see your operation."

"So what's first—the office or the orchard?"

"Orchard."

"I figured as much. I already have two fresh horses saddled and waiting." He blinked and glanced at the barn. "Unless you'd rather not ride a horse."

"It's been a while, but I don't mind."

"Then right this way." He turned to Leah. "Care to go with us?"

Shock covered Leah's face, and then she smiled. "Not this time." She rubbed her stomach.

"Not a problem," Samuel said.

As Rhoda followed Samuel toward the barn, she glanced back at Leah. "Is she not feeling well?"

"She's been sick at her stomach a lot lately, even up at night with it. Jacob thinks it's nerves. I wonder if she damaged her health, drinking like she was."

"Maybe it's a combination of things. I gave her some licorice tea when she was at my place, and it soothed her bellyache. Would you mind if I fixed some different kinds of herbal teas and gave them to her? That way she could discover which one works best for her."

Samuel untied the horses. "I know all of us would appreciate your effort or suggestions."

Appreciate her effort? Why was he talking in such formal terms?

He handed her a rein and then held the cheek pieces of the bridle on each side of the horse's face, encouraging the creature to remain in place while Rhoda struggled to mount it. He climbed on his horse with ease and rode ahead of her out of the barn.

"Mark the house in your mind, and remember it sits due east."

"Okay." She hoped this next venture was easier than steering a vehicle while men pushed it.

Once on the path leading to what she assumed would be the orchard, they rode side by side. As they came to a knoll, she saw apple trees spreading out in all directions. They stopped their horses.

Samuel gestured across the land. "The orchard, with about eight hundred trees, takes up thirty acres."

Her heart pounded at the breathtaking sight. "When does picking season begin?"

"We have several varieties of apples, and the earliest ones will be ready in about three weeks."

Looking out at the sea of trees laden with fruit, she understood why he was pushing so hard to find answers. "I never thought about apples needing to be picked in mid-August. I always visualized them as a fall harvest."

"The bulk will ripen from mid-September to the end of October."

"I bet this place is crawling with pickers during that time."

"It's busy, kind of stressful, but it's what the other nine months of the year are all about."

"The view is magnificent."

"It is, isn't it?"

She drew a deep breath. "The air carries the sweetness of the apples."

"That's because we don't use mulch."

She turned to see his face, and he was grinning. She laughed. "Are you making fun of my composting methods?"

"Definitely." After a moment he grew serious again. "I believe this plan can be profitable for everyone, and we'll do anything we can to make the start-up as smooth as possible."

The horses meandered, and all she could see in every direction were perfectly placed trees. In fact, everything looked the same. No landmarks, nothing standing out as distinctive. She tugged on the horse's right rein and made a full circle. "There's no sense of direction from here."

"Not at first. After a little time you'd learn where certain types of trees are located. That helps. Do you know about what time of day it is?"

"Around two, I think."

"Ya, that's right. Now glance at the sun."

She followed his direction. "Oh, I get it. The sun is heading west, and it's past noon, so that way is west." She turned the horse. "And that's east."

"Ya."

"Now I understand why you told me to mark your home as due east."

"Very good."

She appreciated his foresight to know she'd get disoriented and that he had planned ahead of time to address it. "What kinds of apples do you grow?"

"Mostly Gala, McIntosh, Red and Golden Delicious, and Baldwin. They ripen in that order."

She stopped below a tree that was heavy with medium-sized fruit. "This is spectacular. You must get fifteen bushels from one tree."

"Good estimate. Most people have no idea. When a tree is healthy, nearly half of those fifteen to twenty bushels will be cider apples."

"That seems like a lot."

"Ya, maybe so, but it's always been that way. We may get hit a little harder on that than most orchards since we don't combat the pests with chemicals."

"And what you call cider apples can be used for canning?"

"Ya."

Did he really think her small setup could deal with that much produce?

They rode farther out, and she saw two men, mere specks on the horizon, riding east. "Workers?"

"Ya."

She hadn't imagined how overwhelming the trees and fruit would feel. The acreage seemed to go on forever. "Samuel, this is a huge operation. I can't keep up with anything close to what you need. I could can the produce from two, maybe three trees in a day. That's less than two hundred trees in a two-month period. And I'd need full-time help to pull that off."

"I'm surprised you think you can do that much."

"How's that amount going to help?"

"We don't know that it will, not yet. That'll take sitting down and plugging in all the figures—cost of making the product and such. But the difference between what we make when selling cider apples outright and what we can make per jar of canned goods should be enough to do all I'm hoping, for you and for us. Maybe we could expand next year."

"You're expecting a lot, more than you realize, I think. And there is so little time to prepare for the massive amount of work."

"Most of the trees on the back tierce are Baldwin. Those ripen last. You would start out canning the Gala. Use those weeks as your practice runs for working out the kinks." He studied her, and the shadow under his broad-brimmed hat couldn't hide the determination in his eyes.

"I'm not sure I *can* do what you're asking. Or that I want to try."

"There must be something you'd like to do or to purchase that would make the extra work worth it for you."

Actually, being able to hire Landon full-time would mean a lot to her, but her cellar was simply too small. The unexpected longing to be a part of Kings' Orchard surprised her, but how could she keep up in her cellar?

"Well, let's go to your office and make lists of needed supplies and talk overhead. I don't think this will work, but we should look at the numbers."

They returned to the barn and tended to the horses, chatting about their businesses.

"This way." Samuel went ahead of her and opened a door to what looked like a tack room but was a small, rustic office.

A man sat behind the lone desk, making notes in a book. The top of his straw hat was all she could make out.

"Jacob."

He looked up, and she recognized him as the man who'd helped her and Landon on the side of the road. He grinned and stood. "Did you arrive at your appointment on time?"

"I did, denki. And without the need to hitchhike."

"Gut. Very gut. I'd say I've met my good-deed quota for the year, then."

"Was that the first and last?" Her thoughts were moving swiftly to keep up with Jacob—but no faster than her heart.

"Yup." The way he said it reminded her of the way Landon imitated some actor named John Wayne.

"Glad you hadn't filled your good-deed quota before today."

"You should be. Otherwise you'd still be in the middle of the road, possibly holding a detached truck door."

"Uh." Samuel motioned. "This is my brother Jacob, but it sounds as if you've met."

"Not officially." Jacob held out his hand. "But I believe you're Rhodes."

She shook his hand. "Most call me Rhoda, but ya. It's nice to meet you, Jacob. Denki for helping a stranded pair."

Jacob moved out from behind the desk. "You are quite the team. That bit of entertainment will last me at least a week or so." He removed his hat, revealing a thick head of wavy honey-brown hair.

Samuel went behind the desk and took a seat. "What are you two talking about?"

"Nothing." Jacob waved his brother's question away. "I kept it all business. Right?"

"Very much so."

Jacob put his hat on a nearby filing cabinet. "I would have introduced myself proper-like if I hadn't realized who you were. I knew there'd be time for all that later today."

Samuel motioned for her to take a seat beside the desk. "You'll have to excuse my brother. He insists on challenging women when he meets them, wanting to see if anyone can, well, keep up. Which explains why women don't tend to talk to him more than once."

Rhoda took a seat. "Ah, that's why your rescue was so brief. If you were going to have one conversation with me, you wanted to hold out for a longer one."

Jacob stared at the floor before he angled his head, his eyes peering at her through thick lashes. He smiled. "Actually, you have it all wrong."

"I do?"

"I was hoping to avoid any conversations with you."

"Jacob," Samuel chided.

Rhoda laughed. "You lost that one. And now that I realize it's your goal, I'll convince every woman I know to take turns chasing you around this orchard, making you talk to us."

Jacob grinned. "I have strong convictions about not *talking* to single women. You'll keep that in mind while picking out who to bring here, right?"

"Absolutely. I'll bring elderly, married women only."

Jacob pursed his lips and rolled his eyes. "Women never hear a man right."

Samuel cleared his throat and began talking about the possibilities of her partnering with them. After several minutes they determined she couldn't do more than twelve bushels a day, and having more than one assistant wasn't possible, not inside her tiny kitchen.

Jacob rocked back in his chair. "Then, if you're not opposed to the idea, the answer is to find a bigger workspace."

Rhoda considered his words. "Two problems with that. One, it's a tall order to fill between now and the beginning of the harvest. Two, I still have my own fruits to tend for at least another month. I have to remain close to home."

Samuel propped his cheek on his fist. "We seem to be getting the cart ahead of the horse. If we found a solution for each issue you've mentioned, and we paid you enough for the work to be worth your while, are you willing to partner with us?"

Rhoda picked a pencil off the desk and fidgeted with it. "Part of me would like to be associated with a business as unique as Kings' Orchard, to have at least one season of working with you to see what we can accomplish. But—"

Leah came to the office door. "Catherine's here."

Leah's body language made Rhoda think she was warning them more than announcing a visitor. Rhoda glanced from one man to the other, trying to get an idea of who Catherine was.

The lines on Samuel's face drew tight. "What?"

Jacob rolled his eyes again, but despite his smile he looked less amused. "Girlfriends tend to come over unannounced."

Was the woman Samuel's or Jacob's girlfriend? Neither man gave her any clues.

"Excuse me." Samuel stood. "I'll be back."

So Catherine was Samuel's girlfriend. Rhoda's eyes met Jacob's, and she hoped he couldn't see any traces of disappointment. She knew now that the sparks she'd felt while with Samuel had ignited only in her, not him.

Samuel worked his way around the tight fit between the office furniture—

the desk and file cabinets—and Jacob and Rhoda. But before he was halfway
to the door, a young woman with light brown eyes and hair stepped into the
office. She caught a glimpse of Rhoda and froze.

Samuel went to her. "Catherine, come in and meet Rhoda."

Catherine looked at Samuel, clearly surprised by Rhoda's presence, perhaps as much so as Rhoda was to learn Samuel had a girlfriend.

Samuel put his hand on Catherine's back. "Rhoda is considering partnering with Kings' Orchard to help us increase our profit for this year's crop."

Rhoda stood, and Jacob got up to shift out of the way. Rhoda went toward
Catherine and held out her hand.

Catherine's face flushed. "It's nice to meet you." But the tension radiating
from her told Rhoda otherwise.

After they shook hands, Rhoda returned to her chair.

Catherine ducked her head toward Samuel's arm. "A paid trip to Lancaster
and money to spend? Really, Samuel?" she whispered.

"Let's step outside for a minute."

Without another word Catherine turned and walked out.

Samuel paused, then looked at Rhoda. "I won't be long."

Leah didn't budge, and the room was uncomfortably silent.

"You planned and schemed to get rid of me for the day?" Catherine's voice
echoed from elsewhere in the barn. Samuel said something, and then their
voices faded.

Jacob and Leah watched Rhoda, seemingly not knowing what to say any
more than she did.

A young man came into the room, brushing past Leah, then glanced out
the door behind him. "What's going on with those two?"

Jacob took Samuel's place behind the desk and nodded toward Rhoda.
"Rhoda, this is Eli, our youngest brother. Eli, this is Rhoda."

Eli's smile welcomed her. "You have no idea how glad I am to finally meet
you."

He was a charmer. "You have a lovely place. The orchard is a true sight to behold."

"You're right. It is. After growing up with seeing it every day, I forget that part sometimes."

Jacob motioned for Leah and Eli to sit. He looked at the blank piece of paper Samuel had pulled out. "Leah and Eli, let me fill you in on what we've been talking about and see if you have any ideas."

Their voices faded as Rhoda's attention drifted. Wasn't it natural for a person involved with someone else, be it a spouse or a steady, to mention them while talking?

So why hadn't Samuel said one word about his girlfriend?

TWENTY-FIVE

Samuel's emotions swung like a pendulum between agitation and understanding. He and Catherine stood in the pasture on the other side of the milking barn, a place far enough away from the horse barn and the office so no one could see or hear them.

Catherine shooed a fly away. "I came back early because Mamm witnessed something very upsetting in Lancaster—Arlan and his secret life. I was desperate for your advice. When I get here, I discover that my brother isn't the only one neck-deep in secrets."

"I was neck-deep in business." Samuel couldn't afford to get pulled into a long conversation about Arlan, but he had to verify his gut was right—he didn't need to head to Lancaster immediately. "What was Arlan doing?"

She explained, using the words "different religion" several times, and Samuel knew Arlan could wait. Catherine was more out of sorts than the situation called for, but that didn't surprise him. "He's not thinking of joining a different religion, only a different denomination."

"Only? There is no *only* about this, Samuel. You can fix this. I know you can."

His patience wore thin, and he tried not to scream the question that often banged around inside him when she wanted him to *fix* something. "How?"

"I don't know, but you always find solutions for whatever is important in your life. I've never seen you face a problem you didn't solve."

"That's what owners do for a business. I can't troubleshoot Arlan's life or change how he thinks or what he wants. I don't own him, and neither do you."

"You could at least try to talk him out of this, reason with him the way only you can do."

"I'm not leaving here to talk to Arlan, not right now. I have to get back inside with Rhoda."

Catherine's face registered an unfamiliar look, maybe insecurity. "Rhoda." She pointed at Samuel. "You didn't want me to know about her, did you?"

"I don't have time for this right now."

"Why don't you tell me the truth about her, Samuel? She's young and beautiful, and you knew I wouldn't agree to her becoming a partner with Kings' Orchard."

Samuel gritted his teeth. He couldn't remember ever longing to walk away from Catherine, but he *had* to get back to Rhoda. He hadn't thought for one moment that Catherine would accuse him of having a personal interest in Rhoda. "It's business, nothing more. I kept the details from you because I didn't want to upset you. The orchard isn't doing well, and I wanted to have something good to share before we talked about it."

"What's wrong with the orchard?"

He explained about the back tierce and then spent ten minutes trying to calm her back down.

Catherine's hands shook as she wiped tears off her cheeks. "So everyone, including Rhoda, knows about the problems, but you told me nothing?"

"I was going to. But first I wanted to have the good news that she'd agreed to work with us."

"Good news? There is none as far as I can see. You kept secrets from me while sharing them with another woman. If she doesn't work out, we'll have to wait years to be married. And if she *does* agree to this plan, you'll be working beside someone who is single, smart, and beautiful."

"She's the only chance we have."

"That's your defense?" Catherine scowled. "I tell you she's gorgeous, and you say she's the only chance we have of getting married while I'm still of child-bearing age?"

He wanted to scream. "Would you stop exaggerating? I have been focused day and night on solving the orchard problem while protecting you from the stress of it. And if I don't get back in there soon, Kings' Orchard may lose its best chance to stay profitable—and *that* will cause more problems than I have time to explain."

"We don't need to have our own place or to be financially secure to marry. We have each other."

Samuel set his jaw. "I've seen too many Amish couples say the same thing before they married, and years later they're still living with one set of parents. They have little ones who drain their finances, and the stress of sharing tight space with parents or in-laws makes them sorry they didn't wait. I won't do that to us, to you."

He shoved his hands into his pockets. "You should see how packed Rhoda's parents' home is with her two married brothers and their five children all under one roof. They should have had the foresight and self-control to wait until they could afford a place of their own."

His conscience stabbed him. If Rhoda heard him, she'd have several things to say, and then she'd leave without a second thought of partnering with them for a season.

"Okay." Catherine sniffed and lifted her chin—a good sign. "I hear you. Still, you shouldn't have kept your meeting with her a secret."

"Be reasonable, Catherine. You expect me to fix whatever is not working for you. I'm trying my best to do that. Did you want to know about the trouble on the back tierce?"

"I had a right to know about Rhoda."

"You have no cause to doubt my motives for talking with her. Rhoda could be someone's grandmother or grandfather for all I care. All I see in her is a woman who has the business savvy to redeem this year's crop and to keep my plans for building a home on track."

"Swear it?"

"No." He gazed at her, his anger melting under her innocent stare. "You don't like it when I do."

After seeing Arlan as she had in Lancaster and then discovering Samuel in the office with a woman she didn't know, she sort of had a reason to overreact.

She wrapped her arms around him. "I'm sorry, Samuel."

"Forgiven." Although this time he felt no peaceful release after he said the word. "But how am I going to explain to Rhoda your reaction or my abrupt departure?"

Catherine took him by the hand. "I have an idea."

He hoped her plan to redeem Kings' Orchard in Rhoda's eyes was a good one. "Okay, tell me."

While Jacob, Leah, and Eli talked about the issues with Rhoda's canning setup, Rhoda kept mulling over why Samuel hadn't told her that he had a girlfriend. He'd told her about the orchard, his siblings, his grandfather, and the problems they faced with cider apples. He'd talked about his hopes for a solution, where Rhoda fit in the picture, and more. But he'd never mentioned having a girlfriend. And why had he arranged for Catherine to be preoccupied while Rhoda was here? Whatever his excuse, she knew it'd be lame. What possible defense could he give?

Leah slapped the desk. "I think I know the answer."

Rhoda blinked, realizing she needed to pay attention. But the way Samuel had handled today left her doubtful that she wanted to partner with Kings' Orchard. Her first impression of him was his loyalty, but it seemed he also had a manipulative side.

"Jacob, the answer to a bigger canning facility is right here under your nose."

He frowned. "It is?"

"That old stone eyesore at the west edge of the orchard." Leah turned to Rhoda. "There used to be a farmhouse maybe six hundred feet from here. When my grandfather built the home we live in now, that place became the *Daadi Haus,* where his parents lived. It had a big detached summer kitchen—

you know, for women who do a lot of cooking and canning in the summer months. It was a way of keeping the rest of the house as cool as possible."

"That's a great idea!" Eli clapped his sister on the back.

Jacob's jaw set. "It's not usable."

"It could be with some carpentry work." Eli fixed Jacob with a look. "You could do it. It has a stone floor that's pretty solid even though it may need a little work. Some of the rock walls need rebuilding, and it's missing a roof. I've helped you fix the plumbing in our house lots of time. I bet we could do that too. The only thing we may not be able to do is run the gas line."

Leah moved to the edge of her chair. "It'd be perfect. And surely being so close to the orchard would be a plus."

Jacob didn't seem to be a fan of the idea—to say the least. "That's too much work, and we have too little time."

His response made Rhoda breathe a sigh of relief. Right now all she wanted to do was make her good-byes and wait for Landon. "That settles it then. It was thrilling to see your orchard, and Samuel's belief in my skills is flattering, to be sure. But we're not going to find a suitable solution."

"Jacob, what are you thinking?" Eli leaned on the desk. "Leah's come up with a solid answer, and you're going to shoot it down?"

Jacob smiled at his sister. "Your idea is a solid one, and I wouldn't have thought of it, but—"

Eli moved to the front of the desk and jabbed his index finger against it. "You're a topnotch carpenter. I'd help you, and we could do the masonry and remodeling fast and for minimal money. You *know* we can. How expensive could it be to hire someone to run a gas line from a tank to the stove?"

"It's not doable." Jacob stared at his brother, clearly aiming to get a message across.

Eli studied him. "But…" Realization flickered in his eyes. "Oh, ya." He backed away from the desk.

Leah's eyes said she understood Jacob's unspoken message too. "I guess we weren't thinking as clearly as we'd hoped. Sorry."

The tension in the room was exhausting, and Rhoda was tired of all the secrets surrounding the King siblings. The partnership wouldn't work. She glanced at the wall clock. "Landon will be here soon."

Jacob's green eyes bore into hers. "We lost our momentum when Samuel was interrupted. He'll be back. He could lead a group out of a swamp at night and never lose a person. My strong suit is adding levity while he works his miracles."

Rhoda relaxed a bit. "You admire him."

"If you tell him that, I'll have to call you a liar."

She laughed. Whatever else weighed on Jacob, he had a great sense of humor.

A vehicle door slammed, and she rose. "Landon's here."

Jacob stood. "Leah, would you tell Landon that Rhoda will be out in a minute?"

"Sure. Take your time. I'll show him around." Leah hurried out the door.

"Just stay right here." Eli pointed at Rhoda. "Mamm fixed lemonade and cookies. You can't go without having some, or we'll never hear the end of it."

With that he left, she presumed to get the refreshments.

Jacob rubbed the back of his neck. "Today was really important to all of us, much more than it appears. And I can't imagine how you must feel or what you're thinking, but could you stay for a bit longer?"

If she left now, Samuel would likely come to her house later tonight. She had to stay, for closure.

So she sat, hoping that he would return soon—and that he'd accept her decision to decline his offer.

TWENTY-SIX

Samuel walked into the barn with Catherine. After they were inside the building, she released his hand, tapped on the door to the office, and entered. "Rhoda,"— Catherine went to her, hand out—"I'm afraid I may have been less than welcoming. I can assure you that my response isn't a good indicator of how any of us feel. I was unaware of the problems in the orchard. It's my fault for not knowing. I don't ask questions, and Samuel tries not to worry me. He made plans to occupy my day, and when I surprised him, I was caught off guard. I was upset that he'd kept a secret." She fidgeted with her apron. "But he was justified because I'm a skilled worrier." She smiled, sincerity evident in her eyes. "I hope you'll understand."

"I understand." Rhoda looked at Samuel. "And for your family and business, I wish I could give you the answer you're looking for, but I can't. The logistical challenges are too great."

"The what?" Catherine turned to Samuel.

"She means the planning, fulfilling, and coordinating between her canning facility and Kings' Orchard is presenting too many issues to overcome." Samuel glanced at Jacob, hoping to get some idea of what had taken place during the thirty minutes he'd been gone. Jacob appeared as lost as Samuel felt. "But we'd just begun to brainstorm solutions before I left."

Rhoda offered a polite smile. "I'm sorry."

Eli came to the door of the office. "Rhoda, we set up snacks on the picnic table. Daed is washing up and said he'd be out in just a few minutes. Mamm and the younger girls are already there."

"That's very kind. Denki. I'd like to meet the whole family before Landon and I head home."

"Landon's here?" Samuel glanced at the clock. It was past four already?

"Leah took Landon on a tour of the place," Eli said.

Rhoda walked out of the room as if all had been said that could be said and it was time to part ways. With a sigh Samuel and the others followed her to the picnic table.

Could today have gone any worse?

She met his parents and youngest sisters, then she took a seat on a bench at the picnic table. The group chatted about how delicious the cookies were and how dry the weather had been lately. Samuel couldn't think of anything that might cause her to change her mind.

Kings' Orchard needed her.

Jacob stood a few feet away, an uneaten cookie in one hand and a full cup of lemonade in the other. Something had taken the wind out of his sails too, and he stared into the distance. Samuel followed his gaze but didn't see anything.

Catherine picked up little Hope and put the puppy in Rhoda's arms, doing everything she could to be welcoming and friendly.

Rhoda remained polite, but the excitement Samuel had seen in her eyes when they were in the orchard was gone. He'd had a window of opportunity to talk up the good things and discount the obstacles, but now all that momentum was lost.

If Landon and Leah had already returned from their walk, Rhoda would have said her good-byes and been gone.

Daed smiled at Rhoda. "What do you think of Kings' Orchard?"

She set the puppy on the ground. "It's the most lovely acreage I've ever seen."

Jacob tossed the contents of his cup on the ground. "Rhoda's been great, coming here today, but it's not practical or reasonable for her to consider canning for us."

Samuel cringed at Jacob telling his parents of Rhoda's decision. The finality of it all made him sick.

"Well, we appreciate your coming," Mamm said. "It's been so nice to meet you, and I'd like to see you again. We have a family gathering in Lancaster next Friday night."

"We do?" Eli asked.

"Remember?" Mamm said. "It's the King yearly gathering."

"Oh ya."

"Only family comes," Mamm said. "And the cousins who are seeing someone special often bring them. The youth always enjoy volleyball, a bonfire, a hayride, and lots of food."

Daed brushed cookie crumbs off his shirt. "We gather at my brother's house. It isn't too far from Morgansville, maybe twenty or so minutes by horse and buggy. Would you allow my boys to come by your place in a buggy and bring you over? It'd mean so much after you took the time to come here and talk business."

Rhoda wiped drops of condensation off her cup. "That's very nice, but—"

Mamm placed both hands on the table toward Rhoda, forestalling her refusal. "We'd love for your family to come too."

Samuel wasn't fooled. His parents weren't ready to accept Rhoda's answer, but Rhoda wouldn't even look at him.

"My parents won't be home next weekend. They're going away Friday morning to spend a few days with relatives while looking for houses for my brothers."

Mamm patted her apron. "You'd be all alone for dinner, and we'll have plenty. The boys could pick you up around seven and take you home a few hours later. You won't miss any work time, and if you enjoy it half as much as I think you will, you'll be ever so glad you came."

"Maybe. I guess. But I'm not good at gatherings."

Jacob walked to the table and shooed a fly away from the plate of cookies, and it seemed to Samuel that he'd shaken himself free of whatever was haunting him. "Which explains why you've never come to district-wide youth events or tri-county singings. I've been wondering about that."

"My presence has a way of stirring discomfort."

Jacob straddled the bench on the far end of the picnic table. "It's up to you, Rhodes. But there won't be a lot of youth there, mostly cousins. And I say that anyone who feels the least bit uncomfortable with you being there, whatever their reason, should get over it or go home."

"I know that tone and my brother," Eli chuckled. "If someone gets out of line, Jacob will escort them off the property, even if it's their own place."

Katie giggled. "But he'll tell them something humorous and be ever so polite while he's doing it."

The family laughed.

"Denki, I'll think about it." Rhoda looked at the driveway and saw Leah and Landon heading their way. "Landon's back, and we should be going."

A few minutes later she was in the truck, and Landon was backing out of the driveway as Samuel's family waved to her.

Catherine picked up Hope. "Rhoda's certainly good at saying no under pressure. I would've caved a dozen times and given the answer everyone was looking for."

Samuel slid his hands into his pockets. "She knows how to handle herself in awkward situations, and that's what she was in." He still didn't understand what had happened while he was out of the office. He'd thought she was on the verge of saying yes before he left.

He turned to Eli. "What happened while I was gone?"

His younger brother pointed at Jacob's retreating back. "Our ideas ran head-on into his past, whatever that black hole is."

Samuel went to the picnic table and dumped the ice and liquid out of plastic cups. The girls made quick work of taking all the items inside, leaving him at the table, engulfed by defeat. Should he search for Jacob or leave him alone? Could he find the key to unlock what had happened today if he asked Jacob the right questions? He sighed. Could talking to Jacob ever reveal anything?

Catherine came out of the house and sat beside him. "All Amish women know how to can goods. Why not find someone else?"

"It's not that simple. She's had years of practice, and she has contacts in place for selling the goods in numerous stores across several states, a reputation for excellence, an understanding of how to get permits, and a knowledge of marketing."

"I didn't think about all that." Catherine reached down and petted Hope. "Maybe she'll reconsider."

"I know what *I* did wrong. And you. Maybe after a few days, I can patch up the holes we caused. But I need to know what else happened." Samuel rose. "I'll be back in a bit." He went after Jacob, heading toward the area his brother had been staring at. Once Samuel rounded an island of underbrush, he spotted Jacob sitting on a fallen tree, staring at the summer kitchen.

Samuel moved in closer. "Mind if I join you?"

Jacob didn't answer, so Samuel sat beside him. Neither spoke. The loud chirp of cicadas and soft birdsong surrounded them as the sun dipped behind the trees. "What's your take on today?"

"Several missteps on our part. But it was a long shot with too many obstacles to overcome."

Despite the sense of defeat, Samuel wanted to find a new angle to work, one that would convince Rhoda that partnering with Kings' Orchard was as great as he believed it would be.

"She has to be confused about what took place." Jacob put his hands on each side of him on the log. "I know I am." He crossed his legs. "Did you tell her you had a girlfriend?"

"That had nothing to do with business." Samuel plucked a piece of bark from the log. "You think it mattered?"

"She seemed surprised."

"I came down pretty hard, asking her whether she had someone. Does she think I misrepresented who I am? Or that I have double standards for men and women?"

"Do you?"

"Maybe." Samuel tossed the piece of bark on the ground. "Probably. I've never considered working with a woman before, and being prejudiced seems a natural King trait. But it's one that can change with a little practice and hearing a woman's perspective. I'm willing to learn."

"Catherine caught her off guard."

"Unfortunately, the way Catherine pounced would have caused unease even if Rhoda had known about her. And I'm none too happy about that."

Samuel fought the irritation trying to build. Catherine should've trusted him and respected him enough to let him explain later. He had always known that she relied on him too much, but her fix-it-and-fix-it-*now* ways had to stop.

In the two years they'd been dating, their relationship had always been stressed during the harvest. The work absorbed his time and energy, and she usually accepted it. What they didn't need was for stress to start early, but with the issues on the back tierce, that's exactly what was happening.

He plucked another piece of bark from the log. "Do you think that's why she turned us down?"

"By itself, no. But it was a bad situation, and between that and my baggage, Rhoda never got a chance to see the benefits of working with us."

"Your baggage?"

Jacob's fingers trembled as he sat more upright and tapped them together. "Leah suggested we remodel the summer kitchen for Rhoda." Jacob used his thumb to wipe sweat from his forehead. "You should've seen Leah's confidence when she came up with a plan that could help us. And Eli jumped on board, volunteering to do all he could to assist me." His eyes glistened as if he were tearing up, but surely not. Not Jacob.

Samuel's heart pounded. He hadn't thought of remodeling the summer kitchen. It had been designed for canning and cooking for large families. "It's a solid idea. And since we can't afford to hire a carpenter, maybe—"

"I can't." Jacob got up, staring at the broken-down summer kitchen. "I just can't."

Samuel stayed seated. He gritted his teeth, fighting to keep from screaming, *Of course you can!*

Several minutes ticked by, and finally Samuel stood. "Then we'll find another way."

But he knew there might not be any other way. He had money put back for building a home, but he couldn't use that on a gamble they'd make enough profit to pay the property tax *and* replace his savings.

There were times in life when a man couldn't do certain things. And Samuel couldn't gamble with what savings he had.

And, clearly, Jacob couldn't pick up a hammer again.

How could he have let things get so off course today? Now Jacob felt responsible for letting down Kings' Orchard. Before then only Samuel and Eli carried that weight—Eli for not taking care of the back tierce and Samuel for not checking on Eli's work.

Years from now when they looked back on this time, would they be able to accept that they had buckled under their shortcomings rather than battled against them?

TWENTY-SEVEN

"Leah!"

Leah moaned. Mamm was calling. But it was late on a Sunday afternoon, for Pete's sake. Who wanted something done now? If she hadn't needed to stay close to a bathroom because of her nausea, she'd have gone to the hayloft to read. She tucked her newest thriller under her pillow and went to the landing.

"Ya, Mamm?"

"Arlan's here to see you."

She probably should have brushed her hair and pinned it up afresh, but she hurried down the stairs. He stood in the kitchen, talking to her parents. His black hair was disheveled, and his clothes were crumpled. This was Arlan, all heart and passion and not the least bit interested in appearances.

They were good friends, and she regretted how little they'd seen of each other lately. He boosted her self-esteem, and unlike his sister he respected her opinion.

He smiled, showing a row of white and slightly crooked teeth. "Thought maybe you'd care to go for a ride."

"You thought right."

Mamm considered them. "Are you attending the singing?"

"I wasn't planning on it." Arlan glanced at Leah as if trying to read her thoughts.

"So what's the plan?" Daed asked.

Leah hated when her parents did this. If she walked out the door on her own, they'd let her go without asking much of anything. But when a guy came to pick her up, they wanted answers.

Arlan didn't seem the least bit bothered. "No exact plans. But there are several possibilities. My aunts have been making different kinds of ice cream for weeks and storing it in the freezer. They're pulling all of it out this evening for a taste test to determine which one is everyone's favorite. We might go by there or meet up with some friends and go wading in the creek. Or we may just go for a long ride. Whatever we do, I'll have her home by ten, if that's okay with you."

Daed motioned for them to head out the door. "Go and have fun."

She grabbed Arlan's wrist. "Well, come on, then."

He said a quick good-bye to her parents.

"Such a gentleman, always making sure my folks approve." She climbed into his buggy.

He went around to his side and got in. "I've missed your sass, Leah. How are you?"

"Okay, I guess. Not up for eating ice cream."

"You're not feeling good?"

"No, I've been puking my guts out for weeks, but I'm losing weight."

"Sounds like a bad diet plan."

"Tell me about it. Maybe the problem is I've been missing you. What've you been up to?"

He drove the carriage onto the road, glancing at her more than where he was going. "Working a lot, moving from farm to farm, cutting and hauling hay. I've been waiting on the music store to get a new shipment of guitars. It should happen this week. And I've been going to a protestant church on our between Sundays. I'm still thinking about leaving the Amish."

"So basically nothing new."

"Not a thing, except Catherine's discovered all my secrets."

"Oh poor Samuel."

"Your brother?" Arlan made a face. "Excuse me?"

"You heard me, and you understand why I said it too."

"True. You got me on that one. So what book are you reading now?"

They talked fast about everything. The odd but nice thing about him was he didn't have to agree with her to like who she was.

"So that's it?" Arlan studied her face. "You and Michael are done?"

"Ya, I guess so."

"You're not sure?"

"I'm positive. It's just hard to say it out loud with any oomph. My heart keeps holding on, which is annoying, but it's where I am. I believed he was who I wanted him to be, not who he was."

"What'd you want from him?"

"A stupid fairy tale, I guess. I longed for him to be unable to live without me, for him to make me feel good about myself, and for him to take me away from here. Well, he can easily and gladly live without me. I've never felt worse about myself in my life. And I'm stuck right here in Harvest Mills for the rest of my days."

He pulled onto the gravel parking lot of a little white church and parked the rig to the side. "I'll take you away if you need it."

"Oh, you're so sweet to me. It's a shame we didn't fall in love." She elbowed him.

"I don't have to buy a guitar, and I can use that money to help support you."

She chuckled. "Why would you do that?"

"Because you'll need help with the baby."

Her heart lurched, and a wave of nausea hit. She bolted out of the rig and walked toward the creek. Arlan followed her.

Thunder rumbled in the distance, and the muggy breeze made the lush trees rustle.

"I'm *not* pregnant!"

"But Catherine said—"

"Catherine?" Leah was sure Michael wouldn't spread that rumor. Jacob was the only other person to know about her scare, and he wouldn't tell. If the accusation had come from someone she'd attended parties with, she might be able to understand it, but Catherine? Anger burned through her. "Your sister is a liar. She probably said it just to make me look bad."

"Don't get mad at me. I'm on your side."

"Where are Samuel and Catherine tonight?"

"My house, last I saw them. Samuel talked with me about music and attending non-Amish churches. I'm sure Catherine put him up to that."

Leah marched back to the carriage. "Come on. She's got some explaining to do."

Arlan got in. "You sure you want to make a scene? Catherine's not used to being confronted."

"Of course not. She's used to crying her way through an argument, and everyone around her gives in to whatever she wants. Well, not this time."

It didn't matter to Leah that she could've been pregnant. Catherine's jumping to conclusions and telling lies had her fuming. If Catherine were as much of a saint as she pretended to be, she would've kept her mouth shut.

"Like I said, I've been sick a lot lately." She watched the scenery through the open window as the horse trotted down the road. "Mamm made an appointment for me to see a specialist in about three weeks. So here's the good news: I may be dying of some illness. But your sister is a liar."

Arlan faced her. "Leah, what you're going through is scary."

"You bet it is. But Jacob is convinced it's a bad case of nerves or some such, so I prefer his diagnosis."

"You should have told me. Is there anything I can do?"

"Yeah, back me up when I confront your sister for saying I'm pregnant."

"Okay. I mean, she did say it, and it's not true, so she deserves what she gets, right?"

"Right."

The horse clipped along, seemingly taking forever, and Leah's stomach hurt worse by the minute. Jacob had to be right; the pain, nausea, and vomiting had to be a nervous stomach. That understanding brought her a lot of relief, but she wished she knew what to do for it.

Arlan pulled in front of his home, and she hopped out of the buggy.

He came around from the other side. "My guess is they're in the sitting room, talking with my parents."

"I'll wait out here. No sense in getting your folks involved."

"All right. I'll be back in a minute with both of them."

Leah went to the side yard and paced. Who did Catherine think she was, saying something like that?

Just then, Samuel and Catherine rounded the side of the house.

"Leah." Catherine came to her, looking worried. But was it for Leah or for herself?

"You okay?" Samuel angled his head.

"No, I'm not. My stomach hurts all the time. I'm not sleeping for being sick,"—she glared at Samuel—"and your girlfriend is telling people I'm pregnant."

Samuel frowned and turned to Catherine.

She looked panicked, as if she needed a way out of this mess. "I shouldn't have shared my concerns with Arlan. But are you?"

Had she prepared for this moment? Leah gritted her teeth and doubled her fists. "Am—"

"Catherine." Samuel's eyes blazed.

"I…I don't mean to be unkind. But she went out dressed like a tramp, got drunk, and has spent weeks being sick."

Samuel grew still and quiet. Leah wasn't sure who he'd turn to—her or Catherine—but one of them was about to get an earful.

"It's nice to know"—his voice was like ice—"that my girlfriend cares so little about my sister that she can't control her tongue." Samuel's eyes bored a hole in Catherine. "Daed listens to the chat line regularly, and clearly Rhoda said nothing about Leah's night at her house, but *you* start rumors?"

"Rhoda?" Catherine stared at Samuel, and her ever-present tears began flowing. "Are you going to compare me with *her* from now on?"

"Do not shift this argument to something it's not. This is about you and what you said about my sister—that's all."

Catherine wiped at her tears. "I only said it to Arlan."

Leah could not care less about Catherine's tears. The woman cried over a wrinkle in her dress. "Why?" Her stomach roiled with nausea. "Why did you do this? To embarrass me? To make Arlan hate me the way you do?"

Nausea got the better of her, and she hurried to the edge of the cow pasture. She gagged several times, but she had nothing on her stomach to lose.

"I'll get her a drink and a washrag." Arlan left and returned a few moments later.

After sipping on the drink and wiping her mouth, Leah dumped the rest of the liquid onto the lawn. "Denki." She gave him back the rag and glass. "I'm going home." She never should have come here.

Samuel nodded. "Sure." He walked beside her as they crossed the side yard, leaving Catherine and Arlan behind. Her brother motioned for her to go toward his rig instead of Arlan's.

He was taking her home? She'd expected him to be a little frustrated with Catherine, correct her, and make her promise not to tell that lie to anyone else, but had he sided with Leah to the point of ending his evening with Catherine?

"Samuel!" Catherine ran to him.

"Not now." He wouldn't look at her. "My sister is sick, and we don't know what's going on. I told you she had an appointment with a specialist, and if you'd brought up this topic with me privately, I'd have respected that." He finally met Catherine's eyes. "To say I'm disappointed doesn't begin to cover it."

Samuel went to the passenger's side of the rig and opened the door for Leah. Catherine followed him to his side of the rig. "I'm sorry. I wasn't thinking."

"We'll talk about this later, but you *were* thinking. You said you were concerned, you wanted Arlan to stay away from her, and you said something you shouldn't have to accomplish that."

Samuel got in, and they began the drive home.

Guilt hounded Leah, and she had to speak her mind. "She was a little justified to think what she did."

Samuel glanced at her. "And I was a little justified to react as I did."

Leah stared out the window. She didn't like Catherine, and clearly the feeling was mutual.

TWENTY-EIGHT

Samuel opened his eyes as if an alarm clock had gone off. Early morning darkness surrounded him. Humid air hung thick. Not even a slight breeze floated in through the open windows, only the constant buzz of cicadas drowning out all other insects. He pushed the thin sheet off and sat up. He didn't need a clock to tell him it was time to begin his day. It'd be another scorcher. But for the first time in his life, he wasn't looking forward to the cooler weather that would accompany the harvesting of apples.

It'd been only three days since Rhoda came to the farm, and he'd spent every minute hoping she'd change her mind and call, even to say she was reconsidering her stance. He wanted to call to see if he could persuade her, but a botched conversation would only set her decision in concrete—if it wasn't there already.

He was confident about what he wanted—had been since the idea of her canning their cider apples first came to him. He'd gone over her visit in his mind dozens of times since she left, and his frustrations with himself and Catherine had only grown. He should've told Catherine about Rhoda and vice versa. If he had, Friday would've gone so much smoother.

Catherine. He loved her, but his patience with her was wearing thin of late. What would possess her to tell Arlan that Leah was pregnant? Leah had a right to be upset. As a future member of the King family, Catherine should protect the family, not lie or gossip about them. If rumors that Leah was pregnant spread through the community, regardless of the source, Leah would blame Catherine.

The faint smell of coffee and frying sausage drifted into his room from under the closed door. Having showered and shaved before bedtime last night, he slid into his clothes and headed downstairs for the coffee pot, aided only by the dim light from the gas pole lamp in the kitchen.

The floorboards under him groaned, and his Mamm turned to face him.

"Marye." She slid a pan of biscuits into the oven.

Samuel rubbed his eyes before grabbing a coffee mug. "Good morning to you, too, Mamm."

"It just finished perking." She turned off the stove eye under the percolator.

He poured the steaming liquid into his cup, plunked a spoon into it, and then sat in a chair near the oven.

A set of footsteps coming down the stairs, too light to be Jacob, Eli, or Daed, surprised him. Who else would be up while it was still dark outside?

"Leah?" Samuel blinked. "You're up early."

"I was too restless to sleep." She went to the sink and ran water over a washrag.

Mamm put her hand on Leah's back. "Your appointment with that specialist can't get here soon enough for me."

Leah hugged Mamm, which struck Samuel as odd. A few weeks ago she would've pulled away, silently blaming and punishing Mamm for everything that wasn't going her way.

"Denki." She squeezed the excess water from the cloth and pressed it to her lips.

Mamm returned to the stove, where a pan of sausage sizzled.

Leah sat across from Samuel. "I have the answer."

"I'm glad somebody does." He smiled at his sister. "I hope this isn't about getting revenge on Catherine."

Mamm turned to face them, the spatula in her hand dripping grease from the sausage. "Why would she want that?"

"He's kidding, Mamm."

Mamm went back to her cooking.

Samuel lowered his voice. "You didn't tell?"

"I most certainly did. I made sure Catherine knew that I knew and that you knew what she'd said about me. That's enough."

"I appreciate your not saying more than that."

Eli thudded down the stairs like a stiff old man. He rubbed his eyes. "We need rain, not just for the crops, but so I can get a day to sleep in." He went to the refrigerator and poured a glass of orange juice before sitting next to Samuel.

The back door opened, and Jacob strolled into the room, looking as if he'd spent the evening in a brawl—and lost. His shirt was untucked and unbuttoned, bunched oddly around his suspenders.

Leah leaned toward her brothers. "Where's *he* been?"

"My guess is he's been staring at the summer kitchen." Eli stifled a yawn. "That's where I saw him late last night."

At the summer kitchen? "Was he there all night?" Leah asked.

Eli shrugged.

Jacob got closer, and they hushed. He yawned while Mamm passed him a cup of coffee.

"What's all the whispering for?" Jacob took a seat.

"I told Samuel that I have the answer." Leah propped her elbows on the table.

"About the orchard?"

"Ya. Samuel, call Rhoda. Tell her I'm sick. The girl has a so-called cure for everything."

"That's right." Samuel had forgotten about his conversation with Rhoda concerning Leah. "I talked to her about your symptoms, and she wanted to mix up some teas."

"I seem to be the topic of a lot of conversations." Leah brushed granules of sugar off the table. "Anyway, set a time, and let's go visit her—you, Jacob, Eli, and me."

Samuel considered his sister. "All of us?"

"Us four, ya."

Without any doubt Leah didn't want Catherine to be part of it. Well, neither did Samuel, not on this mission and not until she rethought some of her ways.

"Leah may be onto something." Jacob stirred his coffee. "Rhoda has a short history with each of us, except Eli. And she has chemistry with each of us. I saw it."

"Ya." Leah arched her back, stretching it. "Everyone but Catherine."

"Let it go, Leah." Jacob stirred his coffee. "Samuel and Catherine have enough chemistry for everyone combined."

"Yuck." Leah faked a gag.

Samuel dipped two fingers into his coffee and flicked the liquid at her. "What does our chemistry with Rhoda have to do with the business deal?"

Leah wiped the drops off her face. "When people like you, they're much more willing to do business with you."

Jacob took a sip of his coffee. "Leah's absolutely right. I saw that happen time and again when working away from the farm."

Eli stretched. "Could we do this with a call, maybe use the speaker phone?"

Samuel set his mug on the table. "I thought of that idea when I woke, but we need a chance to break the ice, and a call may not do that. If Rhoda closes the door in our face one more time, we can't approach her again."

"But once we're there," Jacob said, "we ask nothing of her concerning Kings' Orchard. Just let the visit be an icebreaker, ask for suggestions concerning Leah, and invite her to Friday night's cookout again."

Samuel looked down at the dark coffee in his cup. "She's still likely to turn down working with us."

"Maybe." Leah pushed a string to her prayer Kapp behind her shoulder. "We're not trying to make her do something she doesn't want to do, are we?"

Jacob removed the mug from his lips. "Leah, don't ask Samuel that question."

"Jacob's right," Eli chuckled.

"You know, Leah, you should join the orchard crew for breakfast more often." Samuel lifted his mug to toast her. "You're good at thinking things through."

"Good, I'll be the brains of the outfit, and as long as no one needs any real work from me, we'll get along fine."

Jacob grinned. "That's what Samuel says. *All* the time."

"Great," Samuel said. "Two jokesters to contend with. We'll have to rename our orchard from Kings' Orchard to, uh, something else."

"That was brilliant, Samuel." Jacob took a sip of his coffee.

"Somebody give me a break." Samuel rubbed his face with both hands. "It's been an exhausting few days, and no one has solved the issue of Rhoda needing a bigger kitchen to provide the kind of help we require."

"I've been thinking about that too." Leah looked from Samuel to the others. "It'd mean asking favors and owing money we're not sure we can pay back, but, hey, what is family for?"

Samuel shook his head. "No. We're not going to tax Uncle Mervin's construction business by asking him to do us a favor. This economy has them struggling too."

"Let's take this one step at a time." Jacob set his mug on the table.

Leah nodded. "If Rhoda agrees to partner with us, we'll figure out everything else."

Samuel didn't know what had changed Leah of late, but he liked what he saw. Over the years he'd worked with his grandfather, Daed, and brothers to operate the family business, but with Leah joining in the efforts, she made them feel like a team.

Now if they could get Rhoda on board, they'd become a powerful alliance.

TWENTY-NINE

From inside her cellar, Rhoda heard a car door slam shut. It couldn't be Landon at ten o'clock in the morning. She let the blueberries in her hand fall back into the sink of cool, clear water. After grabbing a hand towel, she went outside, pausing on the concrete pad at the foot of the cellar stairs. The early-morning downpour that had chased her inside had turned to a gentle mist.

She went to the top of the steps. An unfamiliar driver remained in his extended-cab truck, and Samuel King was standing on her driveway, looking at her garden. Two passenger doors on the vehicle were open, but she could only see who was on this side: Jacob and Leah.

Both of them were studying her fruit patch.

Thoughts and emotions swirled. She wanted to be left alone, sort of, but she couldn't deny that she hungered for a new adventure. Besides, how long had it been since her peers did anything but avoid her?

When she'd ridden through the apple orchard, she'd felt like a kite sailing high on a March wind. But she'd had a crash landing, although even now she wasn't sure what had caused it. One moment a steady wind kept her soaring, and the next she was plummeting. She knew one reason was based on a solid business fact: she and her cellar kitchen were no match for what the Kings needed. And then there was the discovery that Samuel had a girlfriend. On one hand, that was no more than a simple disappointment. On the other, it was ridiculous that he hadn't given any hint he had someone. And she didn't like the idea of working with someone who manipulated his girlfriend so she'd be gone for the day.

Samuel went to the gate and peered inside, trying to see past the trellises hanging thick with raspberry vines. "Rhoda?"

She drew a breath. "Over here."

The four of them turned from the garden toward her home.

"Hi." Samuel crossed the driveway. "I started to call first, but then, well… I hope you don't mind."

"To what do I owe this surprise?"

"Our driver ran out of gas." Jacob grinned.

They were so welcoming, and being pursued by successful business owners stirred something within her. Something new.

A sense of camaraderie between peers.

She held up her index finger and thumb, indicating an inch of space. "That story would hold a tiny bit more clout if your driver hadn't left his engine running."

"Your dog ate my homework." Jacob looked at his siblings, all of who were blank faced and yet somewhat amused. "Ya, that's it."

Rhoda put the towel on her shoulder. "I don't own a dog."

Jacob nodded at Samuel. "He has one I'll pay you to take."

Rhoda broke into laughter, and some of her disappointment from Friday faded. She liked Jacob's sense of humor.

Samuel stepped forward. "We were hoping, among other things, you'd have some advice or maybe something on hand to help with Leah's stomach ailments."

"I put a box of licorice tea bags in the mail to her Saturday morning, along with instructions. They'll probably arrive today. I also ordered licorice root when I got home on Friday. I expect it to arrive tomorrow or Thursday. Even so, it'll take me a few days to turn it into something she can steep and drink. The fresher the ingredients and the more natural state they're in when I begin grinding them, the better they'll be for her. I have a few tea bags on hand if she'd like me to fix her a cup now."

"You don't waste any time when you set your mind to something," Samuel said.

Jacob removed his hat and slapped Samuel in the chest with it. "What he meant to say was, that was very thoughtful, and we appreciate that you went out of your way like that. As a punishment for Samuel's poor people skills, I think you should take his dog. I'll help by bringing her to you."

"Samuel,"—Rhoda removed the towel from her shoulder—"I'd guard that dog if I were you."

"Ya," Jacob said, "because there is no way that mutt will guard you."

Rhoda chuckled. "Leah, would you like some tea right now to see if it'll help?"

"If it's not too much bother."

"It's not. The last of the tea bags are in my cellar, and you're all welcome to come, but it'll be a tight squeeze."

"I'll wait out here"—Eli pointed to the vehicle—"with the driver."

The rest of them went into Rhoda's cellar. She put a kettle of water on the gas stove to boil.

Jacob glanced around. "This is where you do all your canning?"

"It's not much to look at, but it's functional."

"It is that, I suppose." Jacob peered into the pot that Landon described as looking like a cauldron as it hovered over the fire. "I guess that makes it much more functional than an Amish girl behind the wheel of a truck with her foot on the brake while two men *try* to push it."

"Just what are you saying about my driving skills, Jacob King?"

He grinned. "All I'm going to."

She suppressed a smile. He was far more charming than she was comfortable with.

Her cellar was primitive, to say the least, and it still surprised her that Samuel believed she could be of help to him and his family's business.

The tea bag needed to steep fifteen minutes, and between Jacob's wit, Samuel's keen interest in her business, and Leah's gratitude, the time flew. By the time Leah took one sip of her tea, most of the awkwardness between them had melted.

Leah rubbed her stomach. "It sort of numbs it, doesn't it?"

"Licorice is one of the most versatile herbs in the world." Rhoda got a washrag off the sink and wiped down the work station. "It has an emollient effect, soothing mucous membranes, such as the throat and stom—" Oh dear. She was prattling. When she looked up, every pair of eyes was on her. "Sorry. It's my passion."

"Why don't you grow it yourself?" Samuel leaned against a counter.

"As far as I know, licorice can't be grown in the US, although if I had a greenhouse, I'd be tempted to give it and lots of other herbs a try."

"Didn't you once have herbs?" Leah set the mug on the work station in front of her. "Lots of them in raised beds? I was sure I saw them several times when I was at a neighbor's place."

Rhoda went to the sink and grabbed two handfuls of blueberries from the water. "I did until last May, actually." She dropped the berries into a colander. "Which reminds me, if word gets out that I've given Leah herbal *anything*, I'll get in trouble."

Leah frowned. "Why?"

Rhoda's eyes locked on Samuel's. He understood plenty. She hadn't explained her whole life story while they were on the phone discussing his invite to Kings' Orchard, but she'd shared enough. And he'd been kind about it.

"It doesn't matter." Samuel straightened. "And what you're doing for Leah won't be mentioned. But if you'd like a place to grow herbs, one that won't be seen by passersby or questioned by anyone, we can provide that for you."

Jacob pulled his billfold out of his pocket. "How much do we owe you for what you've ordered and anything else?"

Rhoda shooed him away. "Put your money up."

Samuel got a jar of fruit off a shelf. "If you're going to treat us like friends, would you let us do the same by coming Friday night?"

"That's nice, but it's for family, and I'm not family."

"These harvest kickoffs aren't a youth function," Leah said. "And they aren't open to everyone, just like Mamm said, but to family and invited friends."

Rhoda looked at Jacob. "You're very quiet. Why's that?"

His green eyes were focused on her. "Du duh net verschteh." He repeated the first line she'd ever spoken to him. *You do not understand.*

She could see that he wasn't joking around, not even a little. What didn't she understand? It was obvious to her that she couldn't provide the kind of help Kings' Orchard needed, but apparently this group did not feel the same way or they wouldn't be here, would they?

"Rueben," Lydia called to someone outside. "Can I help you?"

"Rueben?" Rhoda turned and ran out of the cellar and up the stairs. She heard the others following her. Rueben stood beside Eli, leaning against the driver's truck, so involved in a conversation that he hadn't even heard Lydia. Either that or he was ignoring her.

Rhoda went over to him, and he looked up. Rhoda's Mamm and both sisters-in-law were outside now, ready to defend Rhoda if need be since all the menfolk were at work. No one in her family trusted Rueben Glick.

Rueben said good-bye to Eli, tipped his hat to Rhoda, and left.

Rhoda looked from one person to another. "What was that about?"

"What, with Rueben?" Eli pushed away from the truck. "He was out for a walk, and when he saw me, he stopped to chat. I probably haven't seen him in two years. Didn't realize he lived near here." Eli turned to Samuel. "He's the guy who hits a homer nearly every time he's up at bat during the annual auction to support the schools. It's a shame we see him only once a year."

Rhoda glanced at the women in her family, but they didn't say anything. If Eli wanted to believe Rueben was a superstar of some sort, they wouldn't say otherwise.

Lydia put her hand on her lower back, making her protruding stomach look even larger.

Mamm stepped closer. "You have company, Rhoda?"

"Mamm, you remember Samuel? And these are three of his siblings." After she made the introductions, her Mamm invited them to go inside for a drink and fresh fruit.

Surprisingly, Samuel accepted. Did he not have any work to do today? Rhoda lagged behind, letting them go in ahead of her.

Jacob dropped back too. "I hope this isn't a sore subject with you, but I enjoyed your visit last week."

Rhoda nodded. "Denki. It was thrilling to see the orchard, to ride among the trees and feel swept away in its splendor." People ate every day, and oftentimes they didn't pause when standing in the fresh produce section of the grocery store to realize the magnitude of God's earth that feeds them. Her reaction was just the opposite. Every seed and bud and piece of fruit she saw made pleasure sprout anew within her.

Had she been too hasty in turning down their proposition?

"About this Friday." Jacob seemed relaxed and confident as he interacted with her. "Our driver will pick us up at our house and take us to Lancaster right before he gets off for the weekend. We'll help set up whatever the women need, and later we'll drive a rig here and pick you up, say around seven?"

She wasn't one to attend a gathering, and accepting might make them believe they stood a chance of her saying yes to their business offer. If she felt a little more sure about at least canning for them this fall, she'd accept.

The sound of a vehicle drew her attention. Landon pulled his truck in behind the other one. What was he doing here this time of day? When he got out of the truck, he looked as if he'd been sucker-punched. She knew that look. He'd been given more bad news about his job; maybe he'd been let go or they'd given him notice which day would be his last.

Rhoda turned back to Jacob. "I'll be ready and waiting."

THIRTY

Rhoda lifted the rack of Mason jars out of the steaming water in the bath canner, but her mind was on the Kings and their visit here two days ago. She needed confirmation to help her decide what to do—a gut feeling or a sign of some kind. Something. But all she felt was what she'd felt the day Samuel first asked her: that things would end badly.

After placing the rack on the counter, she used a thick cloth to lift and set each jar on a shelf to cool for the next twenty-four hours. She hurried out of the cellar and into her house. Late for dinner again.

Her family had begun eating without her. Daed sat at the head of the ten-foot table. He stopped eating and folded his hands as he watched her. Five adults and five children followed suit. Rhoda hurried to the table. Four of her nieces and nephews were in their highchairs. Her eldest nephew, Enos, sat in a booster chair.

"Sorry I'm late." Rhoda took her regular seat near her Daed. "Lydia came to me and said dinner would be ready in an hour, and I needed to find a stopping point and come upstairs. Then I totally forgot until John came to the cellar and yelled."

Her brother John sat stone faced, irritated. "We said our prayers and began without you."

That was obvious, but apparently he needed to vent. Daed winked at her before he bowed his head. It was a second prayer, and the other adults tried to keep the children hushed during it.

Rhoda closed her eyes. The aroma of fresh baked bread and chicken spaghetti filled her nose and mind, reminding her of all she had to be grateful for.

Denki, Father. Denki for Your love, for my family, for food and clothing, for my business. She paused, unsure whether to ask Him again about this proposition Samuel had made. Goodness knows the man himself sparked her interest, but he had someone. So what was the right thing to do? Break all ties, or take on enough work that she could hire Landon full-time?

Poor Landon. He'd never been in love with his job, but not having one at all was so much worse. His last day would be in a week or so.

Daed shifted his flatware, letting her know prayer time was over. She chided herself for not praying throughout that time. What had begun as a prayer had ended with her pondering questions. She hadn't given God or her family the respect due them.

She put the cloth napkin in her lap. "I really am sorry for being late. I know it's annoying."

John cut some long noodles into manageable pieces for his four-year-old. "You need to wear a buzzer around your neck that vibrates a little stronger for every five minutes you're late."

Her brother Steven choked on the water he was drinking. "Chicken feathers, John." Steven coughed into his napkin while others chuckled. "If it keeps increasing every few minutes, it'll end up shocking her to the point of pain or death."

John passed her the pan of chicken spaghetti. "I think the fact that you know she'll continue ignoring it until she's in pain or unconscious is all the justification I need for being annoyed."

"You want me to list all you do that annoys the rest of us?" Steven shot back. "How about if we start with the number of times you've woken me up this week? You just have to keep your own hours, banging around at midnight. The babies being up and crying is one thing, but your nonsense is flat-out ridiculous."

"I'm not going to bed at nine or ten to suit you."

"Fine. But stop pulling out pans to pop popcorn or heat up leftovers after everyone's settled for the night."

John passed his wife the salt and pepper. "At least I don't leave a trail of destruction in my path as I go through the house. You're worse than all the children combined. And everyone knows when you've brushed your teeth because the toothbrush is left out, and there's toothpaste all over the sink and counter."

Lydia stayed focused on her two-year-old daughter, and Phoebe didn't lift her eyes from her plate. The two young women did their best to keep peace and to reduce the tension between Rhoda's brothers, but John and Steven were as opposite in nature as a cat and a dog. Rhoda's ability to get lost in her work and tune out the rest of the household made her oblivious some of the time, maybe most of the time.

Daed picked up his knife and clinked it on his glass. When the room grew quiet, he put the knife on his plate. "We have blueberry cheesecake for dessert with my favorite, a graham cracker crust."

Mamm grinned. "Drizzled with chocolate sauce."

Daed lifted his glass toward his lips and paused. "So what did you young men get done at the Potter place today?"

Steven and John locked eyes. Clearly, the work hadn't gone well. Considering they spent twenty-four hours under the same roof most days, it was surprising they got along as well as they did. But she hadn't seen this level of tension in a long time. Maybe it was the news of two more babies joining the ranks in a couple of months. Or maybe her eyes were now open to the stress because God was trying to tell her something.

She looked down at her plate. "While you're gone over the weekend, I'm going to a King family function in Lancaster."

The frustration dropped from her brothers' faces. They hoped that if she agreed to can for Kings' Orchard, she would give up her oversized berry patch. But she couldn't do that. Those plants were gifts from her Daed because he believed in her dream. And with her profits she helped the family make ends meet, and she put money away so she could one day build a kitchen that wasn't in a cellar.

"All weekend?" Concern creased Steven's brow.

"No, just Friday evening. They have relatives in Lancaster, and that's where it'll be held. 'The boys,' as their Mamm calls them, will pick me up and bring me home."

"Tomorrow?" Mamm studied her.

"Ya. I guess I should've mentioned it sooner, but I only agreed on Tuesday to go."

"You don't look excited about it at all."

Rhoda turned to Phoebe. "I wish I knew what to do. Part of me wants to help the Kings. Part of me needs to do so for Landon's sake. But I keep wavering, like wheat in an open field."

Lydia jumped up and left the table. "Ach, I meant to tell you!" She jerked open a kitchen drawer and pulled out a small faded-blue book. "Look what I found." She handed the book to Rhoda.

Rhoda eased open the delicate book, and her heart began pounding like crazy. Mammi Byler's recipes! The yellowed pages filled with faded ink had never looked so wonderful, and even with the extra wear and tear the book had been through since she'd last seen it, her great-great-grandmother's handwriting was still readable. These pages held apple recipe after apple recipe.

Could this be the sign she'd been asking for?

"You found them!" Rhoda pulled them to her chest, feeling so many things. A few moments later she studied them again. "Look, she's got recipes for apple butter, applesauce, jelly, jam, and pie filling. None of these are like the ones we use."

Lydia's eyes brimmed with tears. "Phoebe and I have been ransacking the attic almost every day since Samuel ate supper with us."

The thought of her sisters-in-law, especially Lydia at seven months' pregnant, working in that attic for more than a week during the dog days of summer melted Rhoda's heart. "You two." She got up and gave them each a hug.

"And what about me?" Mamm said. "I did their chores while they searched."

Tears fell from Rhoda's eyes. "Denki." She squeezed her Mamm tight.

John sighed. "I cleaned the supper dishes one evening, and Grump over here moved the heavy stuff for them." He pointed at Steven.

She rolled her eyes and sat down. "Then I'll hug your wives twice. Once for their hard work, and once for making you pitch in."

Drawing the book close to her once again, she knew she'd never chance losing this treasure for a second time. She'd copy each recipe onto loose-leaf paper and tuck the original book away for safekeeping in a place her brothers would never dare to move a stick of furniture—her bedroom.

Steven rubbed his wife's back. "Our little sister has a point, Brother."

Little sister. How those words stung. Her brothers should have two little sisters, not one.

Rhoda studied the recipes again. If only Emma were here to enjoy this gift.

Daed smacked the table. "Ach, Rhoda, I forgot something too. I went by the hospital this morning to check on Mrs. Walker. Someone from her church was there and gave me an update. Her hip is broken, and she's in what's called a medically induced coma to help her body cope with the trauma."

Rhoda found it hard to swallow. Would the woman be angry with her anew, wishing she'd died rather than go through what lay ahead for her? Should Rhoda have minded her own business? Or when she received inklings and insights, did that make it her business? She never knew for sure. She only hoped she'd made the right decision this time.

"That's terrible." Lydia voiced what everyone seemed to be feeling.

"Could be a lot worse." Daed slowly twirled his fork, wrapping spaghetti around its tines. "The doctor said if she'd been in that house much longer, maybe as little as a few hours, she would've died. By the time her two grown children checked on her, it would have been too late."

Rhoda knew what he was saying—that by following her intuition, she'd saved Mrs. Walker's life. Would the woman or her children come to see it that way?

And what—she wondered for the umpteenth time—might have happened if she'd been quicker to follow her intuition two years ago?

Rhoda turned her attention to the apple recipes again. "These are such a huge blessing. But there's no way I can be of any real benefit to Kings' Orchard." She ran her fingers over a worn page. "I'm not the answer Samuel seeks."

"Well, perhaps not when it comes to canning apples." John pulled on his left earlobe, a habit of his when he dared to say something he shouldn't.

Rhoda's cheeks warmed. "He has someone."

Lydia put a few more noodles on her two-year-old daughter's plate. "If you're not the answer and he has someone, why are you going Friday night?"

Rhoda looked through the recipes again, imagining her great-great-grandmother planting, tending, and harvesting apples. In her mind's eye she could see her Mammi Byler as a young woman with little ones around her as she concocted her recipes, changing them as needed until they were perfect. "I'm not completely sure, but the orchard captured a part of me, and it won't let go. And if I did this, I could hire Landon full-time, and he really needs the work." She paused. "Jacob King's sense of humor mends something in me, something so torn and forgotten I hadn't realized it was still there." She shrugged. "I know that sounds silly at best."

Mamm grinned. "Is *he* seeing anyone?"

"I don't think so, unless he was simply teasing, but it doesn't really matter. I guess it took Samuel having a girlfriend for me to realize that the Kings' proposition is purely business."

"Knock, knock," Landon called through the screen door.

"Kumm." Mamm motioned for him.

Lydia and Phoebe got up. One took out dessert plates, and the other pulled a cheesecake out of the fridge. As Steven and Jacob cleared the dinner plates off the table, Landon grabbed a barstool from the kitchen island and moved it to his usual place, next to Rhoda.

Steven put the dirty plates in the sink. "When you went out to the King place, did you see any land or farms for sale?"

"I didn't. Landon, did you?"

"No, but my grandmother lives in Unity, Maine, and it's beautiful, with great soil and affordable farms."

"Good grief, Landon." Rhoda crossed her arms. "Let it go already."

John tilted his head. "How affordable?"

Landon intertwined his fingers and stretched, popping his knuckles. "My granny's always sending me information about homes and acreage for sale because she keeps hoping I'll move up there near her. There are several houses sitting empty right now because of the economy. The other day I got an envelope full of ads from her. One old place with three greenhouses, an orchard, and eighty acres is selling for not much more than a hundred thousand dollars."

"What?" John's eyes went wide as he looked from Daed to Landon.

"That's more sad than it is interesting." Lydia put the blueberry cheesecake on the table in front of her husband. "An empty house means some family lost their home. An abandoned orchard means they probably lost a place that's been in the family for generations."

Lydia's observation tugged at Rhoda's heart. Isn't that what Samuel was doing his best to prevent? Kings' Orchard wasn't to that point, not even close. But clearly the pressure was on, and Samuel was working hard to find solutions. It gave her a different view of his not telling her he had a girlfriend and his not sharing the circumstances with Catherine. He wasn't trying to manipulate either of them for selfish interests. He was simply trying to hold on to what he had.

John helped himself to a slice of cheesecake. "I know plenty of Amish families who'd jump on the idea of starting a new community somewhere affordable if a church leader was willing to spearhead the move."

"John,"—Daed made a downward motion with his hand, as if gesturing for a dog to calm itself—"you can't imagine the work involved in establishing a self-sufficient, separate culture while cultivating good ties with the local community. It's a nightmare. Trust me."

Steven dug his fork into the dessert his wife had put in front of him. "I'm so sick of this downturn I can't stand it. No wonder the Kings are willing to branch out and try something new. Crops always take the blows, what with the weather, insects, and such, but when the economy forces the costs of farming up and keeps the price of selling low…" He shook his head. "I don't know how any farmer is holding on to his land these days."

"Most aren't," John added.

Between the recipes in her hand and her brothers' conversation, Rhoda wondered if it wasn't merely Samuel and his family—and, for that matter, her family—trying to encourage her to work with them.

Was God directing her toward Kings' Orchard?

THIRTY-ONE

Jacob added more wood to one of two bonfires he'd started. He stoked it, making sure the embers caught the new wood on fire. People filled his uncle's yard. Tables had been set up outdoors on one side of the house, and volleyball nets were on the other. Some of the women were cooking in the kitchen. Others covered tables with snacks. Men performed their own task: preparing to grill the meat. Most of the youth spread out here and there, enjoying another preharvest kickoff.

It was about time for Samuel and him to drive a rig to Rhoda's place. Eli wouldn't be going with them. He was in the middle of playing baseball, and no one loved the game more than Eli.

Jacob went in search of Samuel. When he spotted Catherine, he knew Samuel wasn't far away. She tossed a ball for Hope, but the only one fetching was Samuel.

Jacob laughed out loud. "Did it take you long to train Samuel to do that?"

His brother picked up the ball and slung it at Jacob. He ducked before it smacked him in the shoulder, making him laugh. Hope started barking.

"Tell your girl bye and meet me at the barn." Jacob picked up the ball and tossed it toward the dog. Hope saw it coming, yelped as if she'd been injured, and ran back to Catherine for safety. The ball landed on the ground and rolled, untouched.

That dog was useless.

Jacob went to the barn and hitched a horse to a rig. About the time he was done, Samuel arrived and headed for the driver's seat.

"Uh,"—Jacob stepped in front of him—"you're in the passenger's seat tonight. Up front on the way. In back once Rhoda's in the carriage."

"We're keeping this all business, Jacob. I'll drive. You ride in back once she joins us."

"That 'all business' plan hasn't worked in our favor. Time for a new plan."

His brother stared at him, saying plenty without opening his mouth.

"Come on, Samuel. You've gotta cut me some slack about Rhoda. She's fascinating and beautiful and not seeing anyone."

Samuel went to the passenger's side and got in. "We can't afford for anything to get us off track."

Jacob climbed in the driver's side and took the reins in hand. "I hate to burst your balloon, but we're not *on track* where she's concerned. There is no track right now. Relax. Stop trying so hard and see what happens."

"Do you intend to make your interest known?"

"No, of course not. It's way too early for that, whether the business deal is on the table or not. I just want to enjoy one evening with her and see if we might be right for courting. If she goes into business with us, we're only talking about one harvesting season. I'll keep a respectable, business-focused distance until it's over."

"I've only talked to her about one season, but if she accepts and it goes well, I'd like to work together for as many years as she is willing."

Jacob propped his elbow on the open window. "And maybe, if she and I did grow to care for each other, our involvement would make her *more* likely to hear you out, not less."

"You're just coming up with arguments to do this your way."

"Maybe. Or maybe you believe that if you work hard enough to do things well enough, you can fix every situation. You can't. No one can. Relax a little. Let this thing with Rhoda take its own course."

Samuel sighed. "Life is not that simple."

Jacob shook his head and fell silent. Nothing else he could say on the topic would change Samuel's mind. Soon they were pulling into Rhoda's driveway.

Samuel and Jacob got out of the rig. He went toward the garden, and Samuel started for the front door of the house, but then he followed Jacob.

Before Jacob opened the gate, he spotted Rhoda crouched in front of a black-berry bush, picking berries and whispering to herself. Maybe she was praying. He cleared his throat, but she didn't notice him. Instead she looked to the back of her garden as if seeing someone, and she spoke aloud. "Of course I should go tonight."

Jacob glanced at his brother.

Samuel shrugged. "There's a fair amount about her you don't know, and this is just one aspect."

Jacob opened the gate. "Rhoda?"

She startled and quickly rose to her feet. "Is it already that late?" She picked up the gallon pail and came out of the garden.

Jacob pulled out his pocket watch, wishing he'd arrived to find her primp-ing rather than talking to herself…or to someone in her imagination. "Five minutes 'til seven." He took the container from her, and she peeled out of her gloves.

"Kumm." She went inside, and they followed her. After she took the con-tainer from Jacob, she washed her hands. "Samuel, you'll never guess what my sisters-in-law found."

"Do I get a hint?"

"My great-great-Mammi Byler."

Jacob watched Samuel and saw recollection flash in his eyes.

"You found her recipes?"

"We did!"

Rhoda sounded so giddy that Jacob almost smiled. The surprise of seeing her talk to herself began to wear off. It was bound to be a simple habit.

"I made several batches of items from her recipes today." She went to the table and put her hand on a cardboard box. "You can get them tonight when you bring me home."

Samuel walked to the box. "I say we take them now and let everyone who's interested have a taste."

"The recipes yielded absolutely scrumptious items." She went to the refrigerator and pulled out a plastic bowl with a lid. "I had to use store-bought apples, and I made only a few of the items she has recipes for—apple butter, cider, jam, jelly, and pie filling."

She grabbed two forks from a drawer, passed one to each of them, and pulled the lid off the bowl. "Try this."

Jacob peered inside. "Pie filling?"

"Similar, but this is for apple dumplings. The consistency is a little different, and the apple slices are smaller."

He and Samuel eagerly dug their forks in.

Jacob's mouth watered. "Wow," he mumbled around the delicious bite.

Samuel took longer, savoring the concoction. "That's incredible, Rhoda." He wiped his mouth with the back of his hand. "Are you reconsidering canning goods for us?"

"I am. But my tiny cellar can't handle a lot, and I'm wondering if the answer you need is found elsewhere and maybe I'm supposed to help with that. Either way, I'm willing to do what I can for this season. Maybe I'll be able to help you find a more permanent solution between now and next year."

Jacob almost let out a whoop. He loved this plan. It was the best of both worlds. Her commitment to help this year would keep the two of them connected for the next few months. As for finding someone else to take on the canning in the following years? They had plenty of time to figure that out.

Samuel's deep sigh showed his relief at her words. "Let's share this news with the family and celebrate."

Rhoda grabbed a sweater off a nearby chair. "I'm ready."

"A sweater in August?" Jacob asked. "The first week in August, no less."

"I might need it later tonight. I can leave it here if you prefer, and if I get cool, you can return for it."

"Now that I think about it, your plan's a good one." Jacob picked up the box of canned goods from the kitchen table. "And we'd better enjoy tonight because we've got more work to do than we can even imagine if we're going to get your business ready for the onslaught of apple season."

THIRTY-TWO

Rhoda stood on one side of the volleyball net, giggling at the many conversations and quips making the rounds during the game. Samuel was on her team, but to her right Catherine sat in a lawn chair on the sidelines because she didn't play volleyball. Instead, she kept Hope from getting tangled up in the players' feet. This game wasn't Rhoda's specialty either, and she'd told Jacob and Samuel that. But they wouldn't believe her, so she was proving it to them the hard way, which had been more fun than she'd had in years.

Rhoda had pulled Leah onto their team, and despite her initial reluctance to play, she seemed to be having a good time. The rest of the two teams were made up of Kings galore whose names she didn't remember, except Eli.

"Rhoda, heads up!"

At Jacob's warning she looked up to see a whir of white hurtling toward her. She backed up a foot or two and swiped at it with her clutched hands. To her surprise she made contact with the ball, sending it ricocheting to the side, and she expected to have earned another point for the opposing team. Instead, Samuel spun around backward, got under the ball, and knocked it over the net behind him to score a point. A round of cheers went up from her team.

The players all shifted over one spot, and she ended up facing Jacob. "Denki for the warning."

"This isn't her sport." Samuel repeated what she'd said earlier.

Jacob made a face at his brother. "Hey, she hit the ball."

"Ya, Samuel, what's your problem?" Rhoda pointed at Jacob. "I'm the best player *he* has."

Samuel chuckled. "He's not on our team."

She couldn't have imagined how different, how lighthearted and funny

Samuel was when the pressure of Kings' Orchard wasn't pulling on him.

Jacob grinned. "I knew I wanted you at this gathering for some reason."

She stretched the net toward herself a tad and let it go. It smacked him in the face, and he went to his knees, holding his left eye. "Ouch."

Rhoda hurried to his side. "Jacob, I'm sorry."

He fell over and rolled on the ground, hollering. When she realized he was playing, she stood and pretended to kick him although she barely touched her shoe to his side. He writhed as if her light tap had put him in agony.

"Kick him again." Samuel's grin was as infectious as it was unexpected.

Rhoda had enjoyed every minute since arriving here hours ago. Samuel's family had tasted the canned goods she'd made earlier today. They'd oohed and aahed over how delicious the food was, and they welcomed the idea of her joining Kings' Orchard as a partner.

She spun away from the laughing brothers. "Hope!" The dog in Catherine's arms sat up, yelping in response. "Get Samuel. Go on, *get* him."

Jacob jumped up, clapping his hands as he'd done in the van, urging the puppy into a frenzy. The little puppy broke free of Catherine's hold and ran to Samuel, barking like crazy.

"Did you teach that dog to fetch me?"

"Ya," Jacob said. "Like anyone could train that dog to do anything except bark."

"Ready to serve," Leah yelled.

Samuel scooped up Hope and took her back to Catherine before returning to his spot. Rhoda hurried to hers, trying to curb her laughter. When her eyes met Jacob's, he winked. A friendly gesture, nothing more, but a hint of attraction flickered in his eyes.

In the last four hours, the awkwardness of getting to know each other had disappeared completely between her, Jacob, and Samuel, as had all professional politeness. She'd made sure these brothers realized she didn't mind being teased as long as they didn't mind her dishing it back to them.

The two men were different in many ways, but both seemed to have good hearts. And she had to admit that Jacob had a bit of unwelcome power over her. How could she go twenty-two years and not feel pulled to one man and then feel it from two men in a matter of weeks?

But she was over her crush on Samuel. He had someone. Perhaps what she'd been feeling for Samuel wasn't romantic attraction after all. Maybe what she'd felt was simply the beginnings of a budding friendship, like what she enjoyed with Landon.

And maybe what she'd thought she felt for Samuel was God's way of getting her to Kings' Orchard so she could meet Jacob. And what a wonderfully surprising man he was.

Leah's serve bounded over the net, and the two teams managed a few volleys before Jacob sideswiped the ball, making it skim the net and fall to the ground directly in front of Rhoda. A few moans escaped along with applause, assuring her it was a good game despite the last play that cost her team the win.

"Denki, Jacob." She gave him a cheeky grin.

He held up his hands, shrugging. "Sorry. I didn't mean to, really."

"Ya," Samuel chuckled. "I believe him. He had no reason to do that. You needed no help in losing the game."

"You two are awful." She pointed at each one. "I can see now how it will be working together this fall."

Jacob came under the net and pushed Samuel. "I told you not to invite her to this unless we were on our good behavior."

"This *is* our good behavior, Brother."

Jacob made an apologetic face. "I'm afraid he may be telling the truth."

Rhoda wagged a finger at him before ducking under the net and going to Leah. She looped her arm through Leah's. "I refuse to help lose another game. Let's do something I'm good at—roasting marshmallows."

"You do know you helped us win a couple of games, right?" Leah smiled at her.

"My winning streak is clearly over. Let's soothe our disappointment with junk food."

They went around to the side of the house where two open fires were blazing. Near them, picnic tables were set up with sticks and all the fixings for s'mores. About fifteen young people, ranging from the midteens to the mid-twenties, sat in lawn chairs or stood around talking and roasting marshmallows.

Rhoda and Leah each grabbed a stick, put a marshmallow on it, and held it over the fire. After they'd eaten it and started roasting a second, Jacob joined them.

He skewered a marshmallow with a stick. "I've never done this."

Rhoda stared at him. "You're kidding."

He shrugged. "Always seemed like an odd custom. And I don't like marshmallows."

"Then why are you holding one over the fire?"

"Figured it was time I got the hang of something new—sort of like you and volleyball."

She raised her stick away from the fire and pointed it at him. "Maybe we should practice volleyball with warm marshmallows."

"Maybe." He tried to pluck the gooey treat off her stick.

Rhoda jerked it away from him before returning it to the heat.

"Jacob," Leah chuckled, "yours is on fire."

He pulled it out of the flame. "No, it's not."

But it was, and he couldn't see the side that was burning. He turned it one way and then another, finally spotting the small row of flames. "Ach, it is on fire." He swung the stick back and forth, causing the fire to grow, and the marshmallow flew off and hit his shirt—still flaming.

He looked around. "Where'd it go?"

Rhoda chortled, pointing at his chest.

He looked down and knocked it off his shirt, flinging it toward Rhoda. She jumped back.

"Sorry." Jacob's green eyes were large with surprise and an apology.

With good wrist action, she whipped her stick, and the perfectly toasted marshmallow hit him in almost the same spot as the first one.

"Rhodes, what are you doing?" He removed the stringy mess and held it out to her, stepping closer.

She pointed at him with her stick. "Don't you dare come near me with that."

"It's a little adornment for your hair. Might sit nicely on top of your prayer Kapp." He moved in closer, and she could smell his aftershave.

She refused to run. He might chase her, and that would seem too flirtatious. She grabbed Leah, pulling her between them and using her as a shield. Leah laughed and spun the other way, breaking Rhoda's grip. When he had the gummy white ball mere inches from her face, he popped it into his mouth.

"Good decision," Rhoda told him.

He studied her, a lopsided, pursed-lip smile on his face. Her heart raced.

Leah grabbed her by the hand. "Kumm. The hayride's about to begin." They rushed that way, and Leah turned back. "Jacob. Kumm."

Although keeping some space seemed wise, Rhoda's heart leaped when Jacob did as his sister demanded.

❦

Samuel watched from a distance as Rhoda and Jacob cut up and played in a way he and Catherine never had. He hoped Jacob knew what he was doing.

Since Samuel had left Catherine on Sunday night to take Leah home, he'd had minimal contact with her. He'd called her on Monday and said he'd see her tonight but not before. He'd needed time away from her to cool off, and she needed to do some serious thinking about her motivation behind lying to Arlan.

Loyalty meant so much to him, and she knew that. Nonetheless, she had chosen to behave in a disloyal way. It wasn't about how she felt toward Leah. True loyalty held a person firm despite ever-changing emotions, like holding on to a tree in a windstorm.

Leah, Jacob, and Rhoda climbed onto an already-moving hay wagon. Their laughter filled the air, and Samuel couldn't help but laugh too.

Rhoda's decision to work for them relieved and thrilled him. And maybe the new friendship Leah had with Rhoda and the good time they were having would help scrub away his sister's frustration with Amish life. Maybe Rhoda could use Leah's help with the canning. If she did and Leah was agreeable, it might benefit both of them.

Catherine walked up to him, leading Hope on a leash. "Samuel, I need to tell you something."

"Sure. Go ahead." He kept his eyes on the wagon as it moved farther into the darkness of night, trying to understand the multitude of emotions within him.

"Samuel,"—Catherine took his arm—"I know you're just now getting over being upset with me, and I don't want to cause any problems. But we need to talk."

He looked at her. "Of course. What's up?"

"You think I'm wrong to keep asking you to talk to my brother, don't you?"

"Ya. I've talked to him some. You know that, but I'm not even sure what I should say to him. He's playing music about God and attending a church, not selling drugs or stealing cars. Maybe it's not our place to say anything."

Catherine crouched to stroke the pup a few times, then stood. "If Arlan was one of your siblings, wouldn't you do something? You did for Leah."

Samuel hoped this wasn't going to turn into an argument, not tonight. "I got involved in Leah's mess because she's seventeen and was wrong—both morally and legally. It's not so clear with Arlan. Who are we to decide where God wants him?" He heard Leah and Rhoda laughing and peered into the woods to see if he could spot them.

Catherine half shrugged and gave a weak nod. "Just one more thing, on a different topic. You won't like it, but it needs to be said. Okay?"

He appreciated the way she accepted what he'd said about Arlan. Maybe a week apart from each other had done them both some good.

"I know you're not aware of this, but you've been flirting with Rhoda all night."

Samuel's blood instantly pumped hot. "Don't be ridiculous. We've been having fun, nothing more."

"If you asked some of the others who are here tonight, I think they'd agree with me."

"If I wanted to flirt with Rhoda, which I don't, I wouldn't do it in front of you and family."

"I realize that. It's why I said you didn't know you were doing it."

He studied her, unsure of her motivation.

She crouched to pet Hope again. "Amish tradition dictates that men and women stay separate from one another in all ways possible, even at church and certainly in the workplace. All of us know to steer clear of temptation. But you went in search of a *woman* to work beside. And, ya, I'm having a few problems with it."

His confidence in her reasoning had been undermined, and he didn't like where that left him. "Rhoda isn't a temptation. Now ask me if losing patience with you is one."

"Don't yell at me."

Samuel drew a deep breath. "Oh, that wasn't yelling. Trust me."

"I'm not a child. I know what I saw between you and her."

Samuel removed his straw hat and raked his hand through his hair. "We've talked about this, Catherine. You can't take this attitude with Rhoda. We need her."

Her face reddened. "And you can't tell me what I can and can't feel. We're not married, you know. We aren't even engaged."

Hope ran back and forth, barking at them. How had their discussion taken *this* turn? "I've told you, Catherine, that I need to wait until—"

"Save your breath." Catherine yanked the pup's leash. "Come on, Hope." She looked at Samuel, her eyes brimming with tears. "It's not my fault you can't see the truth staring you in the face."

As he watched her storm back to the house, he leaned against a tree. Why hadn't he gone with Jacob, Leah, and Rhoda on the hayride? It would have been fun.

But even if it hadn't been, it would have been better than another argument with Catherine.

THIRTY-THREE

Rhoda sat in the front of the Kings' buggy, watching the battery-powered headlights cut dim white beams into the dark night. At almost 2:00 a.m., the roads from Lancaster to Morgansville were nearly empty.

Cool air blew into the carriage from the front windows, and Rhoda put on her sweater. But there was tension in the rig for some reason, and no outer garment could protect against that.

Jacob drove the carriage in silence, one hand managing the reins and one holding a bottle of water he was sipping. Samuel was in the back with Leah. Rhoda glanced at Leah, who dozed with her head on Samuel's shoulder. Loud music boomed from somewhere, the bass vibrating the air. Rhoda guessed it came from the place where Leah had gone to that party weeks ago.

Rhoda's family and other Amish didn't turn in complaints against noisy neighbors, but why didn't the Englisch nearby call the police? A neighbor once told her Daed that they wore earplugs and kept a fan on high right beside them. Maybe most of her neighbors had their own way of tuning out—windows closed and air conditioners, fans, and televisions running.

A young Amish woman stood on a street corner, covering her face with her hands as if she were crying.

Rhoda touched Jacob's arm. "Stop."

He did as she asked. "Why?"

"That woman." She pointed.

"Where?" Jacob looked where Rhoda had directed.

The woman lowered her hands, staring at Rhoda.

Emma.

"Sorry," Rhoda mumbled. "I guess my eyes were playing tricks on me."

Jacob seemed confused, but he got the rig moving again and soon pulled onto her road. The headlights illuminated the fence around her berry patch. Something about the familiar sight seemed odd. She studied the place, focusing on a strange shadow in the fence. Her eyes adjusted, and she realized the dark shadow was a ten-foot hole. She gasped. Jagged wood poked out from the smooth white fencing strewn over the ground. Broken slats. Rhoda couldn't catch her breath.

What—or who—could have done this?

"Stop here. Please."

Though they were only a few yards from her driveway, Jacob pulled the rig next to the curb. "What's wrong?"

Rhoda got out and ran to her garden. Under the glow of the moonlight and street lamps, she saw wide, deep-treaded tire tracks running from the road through the broken fence and into her berry patch. She couldn't tell how far they went. "Can you point the headlights this way?"

As if he'd anticipated her need, Jacob came to her side with a kerosene lantern. She took it from him and walked into the shadowy field. Her heart sank as the light revealed row after row of blueberry bushes, all pulled up or flattened to the ground.

A loud moan escaped her. "No."

"Oh, Rhoda." Leah stood next to her, gazing at the destruction.

Samuel joined them, carrying a second lantern. Together, the four of them walked from the blueberry patch to the strawberries. The tire tracks continued—not in perfectly straight lines, but weaving in a way that indicated this was done purposefully. And the driver was either drunk or having fun.

Probably both.

They continued to the raspberry and blackberry patches and discovered equal damage there. Her enemy—or enemies—had certainly been thorough. She couldn't tell in the dim light whether one or more trucks, maybe even a tractor, had invaded her property.

And ruined her life.

Rhoda held her breath as she headed toward the grapevines. She'd already finished picking most of the berries for the season, but her grapes hadn't quite ripened yet. She'd anticipated a bumper crop this year. Just that morning she'd been delighted how the vines were heavy with almost-ripe fruit.

But the intruders hadn't left her even that. The trellises had been mowed down.

She almost sank to her knees, but she remained upright, looking down the length of the field. What had been vibrant with promise when she left the house hours ago was now rubbish.

"Seems like neighbors would have heard the racket it'd take to do this kind of damage and would have called the police." Jacob's tone was grim.

"Seems like." Numbness was her friend right now. She wouldn't collapse. That's what the intruders wanted, wasn't it? She fought the desire to run crying into the house.

Music vibrated the air around her, coming from down the block.

"I can't believe it. All the years I spent tending this berry patch, and now it's…ruined." She couldn't catch a full breath.

"Who would've done such a thing?" Samuel's question trembled with outrage.

Who indeed? Rhoda's shock gave way to speculation. The tire tracks were big. As though they came from a tractor. Or a monster-sized truck. Did Rueben Glick hate her this much? How could he accomplish such destruction? No Amish owned a truck large enough to make those tracks. Rueben had Englisch friends. Did one own such a vehicle?

Dizziness got the better of her, and she sat on a pile of upturned dirt and stems from broken plants. Jacob crouched beside her and held out the bottle of water he'd brought with him.

Between sips of the tepid water, she gazed at her land. Would she wake to find this was a bad dream?

She looked at the concerned faces of her new friends. No, this was no dream.

Eventually her ragged breathing and her pounding heart calmed a bit. But she still didn't have the strength to stand. She scooped up a handful of soil. "I started this garden when I was a little girl. Daed bought each of his daughters a blueberry bush and helped us plant them."

She ran her thumb through the dirt in her palm, remembering the excitement she'd felt at putting that first tiny bush in the ground. Images of her brothers trying to snatch fruit ran through her mind, and she chuckled. "The hardest part of keeping my harvest safe was stopping my brothers from eating the fruit straight from the vine. Daed shooed them away time and again, making sure everyone in the family knew the berry patch was mine to handle as I saw fit. Daed's bought me at least one new plant for every birthday and Christmas since. And when I graduated, he helped me expand into an entire vineyard."

She longed to call him and tell him what was going on, to feel the comfort of his arms. But he'd take this news hard. He'd paid a high price over the years to protect this land for her. His heart would break as much as hers when he saw what had happened to their precious field. She spread out her fingers and watched the soil run through them.

Samuel looked around at the moonlit field. "I saw a few plants that weren't uprooted. And you can replant the ones that were only partly damaged. With your skill at cultivation, I imagine most will survive. At least some will."

"Ya." Leah's face brightened. "You started out with one blueberry bush, and you created all of this. Surely you can make a fresh start with whatever we can save."

Jacob stood beside his brother, and Rhoda felt his gaze on her face. "Where do you keep your shovels?"

She stared up at them. Didn't they understand the severity of the devastation? She couldn't start over with just a few bushes, even if some were left. "I appreciate that you want to help me, but—"

"They're probably in the shed." Samuel headed to the small wooden building like a man with a plan. Leah and Jacob followed him.

Their desire to do something to salvage the situation touched Rhoda's heart, but it was hopeless. She looked at the house, the windows dark. Everyone in her family was gone for the night. She'd been away all evening. How did the vandals know no one would be home?

The way the property sat, Mrs. Walker would have heard and seen whoever did this. Even though the woman didn't want anything to do with Rhoda, she'd have called the police had she been home, but she was still in the hospital.

Rhoda looked at the other homes. She imagined the households were so used to tuning out the parties, revving engines, and nonsense that not one of them thought to look out the window.

In less than four hours, the sun would rise, and the destruction would be visible to everyone.

She'd have to call her Daed in the morning to tell him what had happened. They'd return from the relatives, where they'd hoped to find a home for one of her brothers. Her house, so quiet and peaceful now, would be filled again with the noise and stress of numerous family members all squeezed into one home. What would they say about her ruined fields?

Although her brothers would grieve along with her and would work beside her as much as possible to reestablish her plants and get them yielding a healthy crop again, they would long to use the plot for their own families. If she didn't replant, her family could build a house on that land, maybe two. Her brothers would try to hide their thoughts for her sake, and they would feel bad for her, knowing how much she loved her berry patches. But in the place where dreams and hopes grow without encouragement, they'd imagine how great it'd be to build their homes on this land.

She listened to Samuel, Jacob, and Leah rummaging through the shed and rubbed her weary eyes. Was keeping the land selfish? Was God showing her that she needed to let her brothers have her property? Even if the business plan with Kings' Orchard didn't work out, she had other options. There were fields she could rent to grow her berries. Her brothers had no other alternatives.

She rose, feeling the weight of the grief that had just begun.

The King siblings came back, armed with gardening implements and wearing gloves and sympathetic faces.

She steeled herself. "We're going to clear the land and burn all the uprooted plants."

They stared at her as if she were crazy.

Samuel's brow furrowed. "Rhoda…are you sure?"

How could she be sure of anything? "I won't let the neighbors see my plants uprooted like a white flag waving on a pole. I refuse to give the vandals that kind of satisfaction."

Jacob leaned against the handle of the shovel sticking in the dirt. "Maybe you need some time to cool off a bit and think this over. You don't want to make any rash decisions that you'll regret later."

"My mind's made up. In time my heart will follow." Rhoda clutched the handle of the shovel in Jacob's hand. "Whatever time I have for canning this fall now belongs to Kings' Orchard. And at least one of my brothers will have a piece of land to build on. Maybe both of them."

She'd met Samuel, Leah, and Jacob only three weeks ago, but they were willing to give their time, energy, and hard work to help her try to save her dream.

She closed her eyes, seeing the sprawling vines and tendrils of her garden sparkling with dew in the early morning sun.

Some wondrous things grow in the heart, not the ground.

THIRTY-FOUR

Samuel lit a kerosene lamp in the phone shanty. Rhoda stood near him, quiet but going through all the right steps. He looked up the number for where her Daed was staying, dialed it, passed her the receiver, and stepped to the side.

Rhoda shifted it closer to her mouth. "Uncle James, this is Rhoda. I'm fine, but I need to talk to my Daed."

James said something Samuel couldn't make out.

"Ya, I'll wait." She jerked air into her lungs, her fingers trembling when she rested them on her lips.

"Rhodes." Her father came on the line. "What's wrong?"

"Daed…" Rhoda's voice cracked for the first time, and she thrust the phone at Samuel, shaking her head.

He eased the phone from her hand. "Karl, this is Samuel King. When we brought Rhoda home tonight, we discovered that vandals had destroyed her garden and vineyard, and I think she'd like you to come home." Samuel assured Karl several times that Rhoda wasn't harmed, not physically. They said good-bye, and he hung up.

"Denki." Rhoda's voice was barely a whisper. "I need to call Landon."

Samuel couldn't imagine why she had to notify her assistant when it was nearly three in the morning, but he handed her the phone.

In a few minutes, when she was done, he'd have to call his uncle Mervin. He hated to disturb them at this time of the morning, but he had to tell him what had happened. It was the only way to head off a panic when the sun came up and his family realized Jacob, Leah, and he were still gone.

"Landon, it's me."

Samuel could hear Landon's response. He had no complaint that Rhoda was waking him at three in the morning.

"Someone's…destroyed my garden, uprooted nearly every plant and plowed down the trellises we built."

Landon's words were laced with concern. "What can I do for you, Rhodes?"

Their conversation gave Samuel a better understanding of their relationship and a greater appreciation for Landon.

"I need you and your dad's Bobcat."

Rhoda's flat words almost broke Samuel's heart. Apparently, Landon didn't like them, either.

"Rhodes, no. We can replant and reestablish. File charges this time, and put a stop to it."

"The decision is made, Landon. I need the Bobcat and its headlights. Are you going to help me or not?"

Silence hung in the air. It was odd how overcome with emotion she was with her Daed and how in control she was with Landon.

"Okay." Landon's voice had become a hoarse whisper, but Samuel heard him clearly. "I'll be there as quick as I can."

"Thanks. See you soon." She pressed the Disconnect button and handed the receiver to Samuel. The sadness on her face stirred him. He'd like to get hold of the people who did this and march them to the police station. Because the Amish were nonresistant and believed in always turning the other cheek, they avoided involving the police as much as possible, but this needed someone with legal authority to step in.

Rhoda walked away, and he dialed his uncle's number, wondering who— if anybody—would answer at this time of night. Had everyone gone to bed, assuming that he and his siblings would slip in when they returned? Or was Catherine waiting up for him, maybe sitting in the barn with Hope—either feeling sorry about their argument or coming up with more accusations to hurl at him?

To Samuel's relief, his uncle answered. "I've been worried about you. Everything okay?"

He explained the devastation of Rhoda's berry patch. "We're going to stay and help her clear the land. I doubt we'll finish in time to get back to your place before the driver picks up everyone in the morning."

"You want to tell Catherine, or should I pass on the message for you?"

Taking the easy way out was tempting. "I should probably talk to her myself. Is she awake?"

"She wanted to watch for you, but your aunt convinced her to get some sleep. She's in Dorothy's room with the rest of the girls. I can have your aunt go in and get her."

"No. I don't want to disturb everyone." Especially since he had no idea how Catherine would react. "When she wakes up, tell her that we're all right and that I'll call her as soon as I can."

As Samuel left the phone shanty, he noticed Rhoda giving instructions to Jacob and Leah. "We'll drag or haul everything to the back side of the property. Landon will dig a hole there when he gets here. City ordinances allow for fires as long as they're in a pit and we bury the ashes when we're done."

Her strength made him want to be stronger, more patient with disappointments, more determined in the face of battles. He'd been impatient with Catherine of late, hiding situations as he saw fit and then being frustrated when she reacted like a woman caught off guard. He joined the group, and they worked in silence for quite a while before the rumble of a motor started out low and grew louder as Landon pulled up in his truck, towing the Bobcat.

He got out, surveying the destruction. Rhoda went to him, and after a moment of talking quietly, he nodded and returned to the trailer to get the Bobcat.

A van pulled up to the curb more than an hour later, and Rhoda's family poured out. Her sisters-in-law and brothers unloaded sleeping children and headed for the house.

Her Daed walked toward her. "Rhodes, I'm so sorry."

She went to him and fell into his arms, sobbing. Samuel wasn't sure which surprised him more, that she was crying or that his own eyes stung with tears.

Rhoda's Daed held her tight, whispering words Samuel couldn't hear. Rhoda's Mamm put one hand on her husband's shoulder and the other on her daughter's. Rhoda's brothers and sisters-in-law came outside, their children probably tucked back in bed. The two brothers and their wives repeatedly expressed how shocked and appalled they were at this senseless destruction.

"We'll help you replant," John insisted.

Rhoda shook her head. "No, and I don't want to discuss it."

"But—," Steven began.

"No." Rhoda pulled away from her father's embrace and explained her plan to continue clearing the field so it appeared to have been intentionally plowed instead of destroyed by vandals.

Rhoda's Daed rubbed her shoulders. "That berry patch means everything to you."

"I'm doing the right thing, and we all know it. I'll pour my time and energy into canning for Kings' Orchard." She looked both of her brothers in the eye. "This is your land now." Her voice trembled, and she had to take a few deep breaths before she continued. But her face showed tender resolve.

Samuel watched this close-knit family embrace one another, heard their heartfelt assurances of support and encouragement. What he'd seen as weakness in her brothers—marrying before they owned their own homes and had their financials in good order—was in reality a strength. Both had sacrificed certain comforts to form unions they did not regret. And whatever stress it caused, they obviously dealt with it while learning patience and growing in love. This was the kind of family he hoped to build with Catherine. But his lack of patience was undermining them.

Rhoda wanted the property to look as if what had been done was her doing. Since most of the fence was intact, he and Jacob needed to repair the damaged part. He motioned to Jacob. While the others worked in the berry patch, Samuel and Jacob went to the shed and found a couple of hammers, a box of nails, some long boards, a can of white paint, and paintbrushes. Samuel gathered several boards about the right size while Jacob loaded the smaller items into a wheelbarrow. They took everything to the fence and worked in silence. As Samuel hammered boards into place, he tried to figure out how to help Rhoda make enough money canning for them that she'd gain in profit rather than lose because of the vandals.

He heard a loud *whoosh,* and he and Jacob turned to see a blaze go up in the middle of the field. Rhoda, her brothers, and Landon stood silhouetted against the bonfire, staring into the flames.

Samuel's heart went out to Rhoda. He couldn't imagine how devastated he'd feel if he were watching Kings' Orchard go up in smoke.

Jacob picked up a paint can. "Guess that's good enough for now."

Samuel turned and saw Jacob examining the new fence. "Reckon we'd best get everything back to the shed then."

"You go on ahead," Jacob said. "I want to clean up a little here first. I'll catch up in a minute."

"Suit yourself." Samuel filled the wheelbarrow and pushed it to the spigot. After cleaning the paintbrushes, he took everything into the shed. By the time he'd put it all away, the dark night was beginning to lighten, although there was no sign yet of the sun. He closed the shed door behind him.

Rhoda's Mamm came out the front door. "Breakfast!"

John, Steven, and Landon went to the house. They appeared to want Rhoda to go with them, but she declined and lingered by the fire.

As Samuel walked toward her, Jacob came from the other direction, carrying a bush with its roots wrapped in old cloths he'd gotten from somewhere.

"Samuel and I repaired the broken fence."

Her face looked as barren as her land. "Denki, Jacob. I didn't even think about that. I'm glad you did."

He set the bundle at her feet. "I found this near the fence line."

She knelt. "Jacob." His name was barely a whisper on her lips. "You found an undamaged blueberry bush."

"I guess it was close enough to the fence to be protected."

Even from a few feet away, Samuel could see that his brother cared how Rhoda felt.

"I'll see you inside." As Jacob headed to the house, Rhoda cradled the blueberry bush like a sleeping infant.

Samuel walked up to her and cleared his throat. "Aren't you going inside?"

"I can't. Not yet." She watched the remains of her plants smoldering in the large hole.

Despite his hunger Samuel sat beside her. "It probably doesn't feel like it, but you've handled this mess well, shown a lot of courage."

"I'm pretty sure who did this." The sadness on her face gave way to hardness. "Rueben Glick." Her lips curled as if saying his name brought a bad taste to her mouth.

Samuel waited for her to explain.

"Remember the man Eli talked to when you were here a few days ago?"

"Ya."

"He's Rueben Glick, and he may be quite a baseball player, but he's the reason I had to get rid of my herb garden. He convinced Mrs. Walker and others that I used the herbs for some sort of black magic."

Samuel looked around the barren field. "And you think he's responsible for this?"

"Ya, I do."

He stood. "Even though it's not the Amish way to call the police, I think you should this time."

"No."

He held out his hand. She moved the blueberry bush to one arm and put her other hand in his, letting him help her up.

She gazed into his eyes. "I believe in our ways, Samuel, even when there's little evidence to indicate our nonresistance works."

"It's perfectly acceptable to involve the authorities when destruction of this magnitude takes place."

She cradled her blueberry bush, staring into the fire, reflections of the flames dancing in her eyes. "Maybe God is letting me get what I deserve, or some small part of it. If I hadn't been so driven by tending and harvesting my strawberries, I would've taken my sister to the store earlier in the day, and she'd still be alive."

Samuel shook his head. "I'm sorry about your sister, and I can't begin to know the pain and guilt of what you've been through. But, Rhodes, this isn't God showing you His will. This is what godless men do while trying to show their might."

"My decision stands. Now all I need to do is figure out how to forgive Rueben."

Rueben being forgiven wasn't high on Samuel's list. He was more interested in Rhoda thinking about what he'd said and finding a way to let go of her guilt concerning Emma.

And he didn't agree with Rhoda letting Rueben off the hook so easily. God used civil authority to confront the lawlessness in people just as He used doctors to confront the sickness in people. But he'd leave this topic alone—for now.

THIRTY-FIVE

With two freshly baked blueberry pies on the seat beside her, Catherine held the reins firmly, guiding the carriage toward Samuel's house. She'd seen him early that morning, when he, Jacob, and Leah finally arrived back at their uncle's home. Immediately after they got there, everyone piled into the van, Craig drove them to Harvest Mills, and he dropped Catherine off at her place. During the trip home, the three explained what had taken place at Rhoda's, but Catherine didn't get a moment to speak to Samuel alone. In part because he was exhausted, but something else was on his mind too.

And she had to know what it was.

A multitude of butterflies had taken up residence in her stomach, but her nervousness over seeing Samuel was about the only emotion she had that made sense. It was awful—a tragedy, really—that Rhoda's fruit garden had been destroyed. But Catherine wasn't as sad as she was threatened by it. Besides, it couldn't have happened at a worse time. Catherine had been ugly and petty about Rhoda, and Samuel had seen it. To make matters worse, he was still disappointed in her for telling Arlan that Leah might be pregnant. It was a careless remark, and she shouldn't have given in to the temptation to say it. She just wanted Arlan to wake up and realize who Leah really was. Now Catherine looked like a whiny, gossipy, green-eyed monster.

She pulled up in front of the house and stopped. Truth was, she had to get her thinking straight, her mouth under control, and her attitude right before she wrecked her future. Everything Samuel told her about Rhoda made sense, and maybe he hadn't been flirting with her. All Catherine knew for sure was that she disliked and distrusted Rhoda.

And it made no difference that she had no basis for those feelings.

Trying to shake off her self-loathing, she got out of the carriage and managed to pick up a pie in each hand. When she reached the house, she used her foot to knock on the screen door. Hope immediately started yapping and came running from the kitchen.

Leah stood at the sink, washing dishes, and glanced through the screen door. "Kumm."

That's all the welcome Catherine got and maybe was more than she deserved.

"Hi, Leah." Catherine held up the pies, indicating she couldn't open the door on her own.

Leah pulled her hands out of the sudsy water, grabbed a dishtowel, and headed her way.

Catherine's heart remained on Samuel. He was a good man who hadn't been in a hurry to find a girl. He attended singings, but only because he liked social gatherings. Catherine had set her sights on him from the start and had done all manner of attention-getting tricks before he gave her a second glance— not that he knew that. And now, when their relationship wasn't progressing the way she wanted, she blamed him.

That was just wrong.

Leah opened the door, but she didn't offer to take one of the pies. She simply returned to the sink.

Samuel's mother, Elizabeth, walked into the kitchen. "Hope, hush!" She pointed outside. "Betsy, come take this dog out before she has an accident." She turned to Catherine and took one of the pies. "Welcome. It's always so nice to see you, and you're always bringing us such delicious blessings."

Catherine glanced at Leah. Apparently she hadn't informed her mother about what Catherine had said about her. "Denki." She set the pie on the counter next to where Elizabeth had put the other one. "Is Samuel around?"

"He's not inside. That's about all I know. Probably in the orchard or the office."

Catherine waited, hoping Leah would volunteer to help her find him as she had always done before. Samuel's sister seemed able to walk the farm for a few minutes and just know where Samuel was.

Catherine remained at the island. If she had a few minutes with Leah, she could apologize again and get Leah to warm up a bit. She bet Leah hadn't given Rhoda the cold shoulder as they worked side by side throughout the night to get her acre in good order. And no doubt, neither had Jacob or Samuel—

No. Stop it. Catherine shook those thoughts away. She *had* to get a better attitude before she really messed up how Samuel felt about her. "Did you get some sleep when you got home?"

"Ya," Leah rinsed a plate. "I slept most of the day, but I think Jacob and Samuel only took naps."

"That's good to know. He'll be irritable, and I'd better tread lightly. Or maybe just leave." She meant it as teasing, but Leah flashed her a nasty look.

"Good idea. Go home."

"Leah," Mamm scolded.

Catherine felt caught in a snare. But what really upset her was that it was one of her own making.

Jacob walked to the open door of the barn office. He needed to call Sandra, and he'd expected the office to be empty at this time of day. But Samuel and Eli were there, apparently in the middle of a serious discussion about Rhoda's ruined fruit patch. Jacob would call Sandra later.

Rhoda needed help, and he had the ability to provide it. If only he could.

Feeling numb and overwhelmed, he walked to the summer kitchen. The gaps in two dilapidated walls and the missing roof mocked him. He had the skills to remodel this place, to make it better than it'd ever been. It could be perfect for what Rhoda needed.

He went to the fallen tree and sat. His palms were sweating, and his heart raced at the thought of doing carpentry work. But he wanted to do this for Rhoda, to give her a roomy, spacious kitchen with lots of windows.

The scenery around him faded, and he saw himself on the roof of a two-story home. Men were crawling all over the place—inside the house, on the roof, in the yard. They'd worked long, hard days, and he'd known every number associated with the job—from the amount of roofing nails they'd need, to how many cubic yards of concrete were in the foundation, to the exact taxes each man would owe, whether he worked forty hours or overtime.

Jacob had enjoyed the work. It felt right and good. And he never had to hide his talents. If he wanted to try his hand at something brand-new, Blaine, the construction foreman, was glad for him to do it. Moreover, Skeet Jones, the developer, groomed Jacob to be the lead carpenter of his company. It didn't take long for Jacob to prove himself in that position. He'd been doing carpentry work full-time for his uncle since he was fourteen. In less than a year, Jacob had worked his way up from lead carpenter to superintendent. He wore an expensive leather tool belt that jangled as he walked, and he kept it filled with tools and hardware. It was hard to believe now, but at the time he believed that job had freed him.

Then the lies began falling like droplets all around him.

In one way his realization began the day Blaine climbed the ladder to the roof, carrying a heavy load of shingles.

"Help." Blaine's red face dripped with sweat.

Jacob hurried across the roof to him. "You don't do manual labor. What are you thinking?" He pulled the weight off him and tossed the shingles on the roof.

"Sandra." Blaine spoke barely over a whisper, trying to catch his breath. Jacob looked below, spotting Sandra, his wife, standing near her Ford Explorer, her hand shielding her eyes as she watched Blaine.

"You're going to kill yourself trying to impress your wife." Jacob picked up the bundle of shingles and tossed them higher onto the roof where the workers were.

Blaine finished climbing the ladder. "You'll understand someday."

"Some things are too stupid to understand."

When he looked back, Blaine was losing his balance.

Before Jacob could get to the man, he fell. Jacob lunged, grabbing Blaine's hand. Jacob landed on the roof with a thud, but he held onto Blaine, whose arms gripped the roof while the rest of his body dangled—

"Jacob?"

Jacob nearly jumped out of his skin. He turned from staring at the summer kitchen to find Samuel beside him, his hand on Jacob's shoulder. Jacob blinked, a cold shudder running through him.

His brother sat on the log beside him. "I always saw this old place as nothing but an eyesore. Now when I look at it, I wonder what our ancestors' lives were really like. Did our great-great-grandfather argue with his girl like I've been doing with Catherine?"

"No comment." Jacob drew a deep breath, trying to release the memories he'd just recalled. Samuel never asked questions, not because he didn't care, but because he did. "It sounds so simple—pick up a hammer and get to work."

"Jacob, I've made a decision, and I don't mean it to corner you in any way."

"Concerning…"

"I'm going to dip into my savings and use it to help Rhoda find some new land to rent or buy. Maybe use some of it to help her get a better setup."

"You haven't pulled out money in ten years or more. It's been the hammer you couldn't make yourself pick up, so why now?"

"I believe she's the answer we need, and now that she doesn't have to tend to her own garden, she has the time and energy to pour into Kings' Orchard. All we need to do is create a kitchen where she can get the maximum done in a day. I know that sounds selfish, but I believe she needs to be busy."

"Ya, I agree with that."

"About her destroyed garden, remember the man Eli talked to while we were at Rhoda's?"

"Of course. Neither Rhoda nor her family seemed comfortable with him dropping by."

"I spoke with Eli about it. He didn't mean to do anything wrong, but he told Rueben that Rhoda and her family would be gone last night." Samuel studied him. "I can't begin to understand someone like Rueben, and I'll see to it that charges against him are brought to his church leaders."

Jacob knew he should mind his own business, but he had to make sure Samuel had thought to involve Catherine in this decision. "Have you talked to Catherine about pulling money from your savings to invest in the partnership with Rhoda?"

"Not yet. She won't take it well, but this venture could be the real future for Kings' Orchard. She doesn't have to understand that right now."

Jacob stared at the summer kitchen, shaking his head. "I'm wrestling with the idea of remodeling this place."

"I know."

"Since Rhoda has no reason now to stay near that cramped cellar, this place would be ideal for canning our apples. Between your money and my skill, we could make this the best canning kitchen ever."

Samuel broke off a piece of bark. "And if you can't do it, we'll use my money to hire the remodeling job and still manage to make it better than what she has now."

Jacob swallowed despite how dry his mouth felt. "I want a chance to get past my hang-ups."

"I think you should."

"Ya, mostly because if I don't, you'll look like a hero, and I'll look like something the cat dragged in."

"She doesn't know you were a skilled carpenter, and she won't know where the money came from, other than Kings' Orchard."

"I loved it out there, Samuel. Not just the ocean or my job, but the people. When my world fell apart, you'll never believe what I missed most of all."

"Leah's challenging ways?"

Jacob chuckled. "Us. Just you and me, as different as night and day, talking until we figured out what to do about whatever mountain stood before us, whether dealing with the orchard or my construction jobs."

"Don't forget we also skirt around the ones we don't want to climb."

"Until now."

Samuel nodded. "Until now."

Jacob wanted to tell his brother why he couldn't pick up a hammer. At least, about some pieces of those missing years. "I actually saved his life."

Samuel focused on him, surprise reflected in his eyes, but he didn't ask whose life. He waited, and Jacob knew his brother was ready to listen all day if Jacob wanted it.

"Blaine McAlister, carpenter foreman. We were on a roof, and he's a big man who almost fell off. I held on, though most of his body was dangling from the roof. I couldn't pull him up, but there was no way I was going to let go. Because of the angle—we were at the corner of the building—no one else on the roof could help me. I could hear Blaine's wife screaming. The three of us were good friends, or so I thought." Jacob swallowed hard. "While holding on to him, battling to keep a grip until someone could get a ladder moved or something, I thought that once he was safe, things would be right again. I believed saving his life was the only acceptable outcome. But that was the beginning of the end of hundreds of lives."

Samuel's brown eyes reflected the respect and compassion Jacob needed to go on with his story. But he'd no sooner opened his mouth than they heard Catherine calling to Samuel.

Samuel moaned. "Hold that thought. I'll be right back." He jumped up and headed toward the sound of her voice.

But after a few minutes, Jacob knew Samuel couldn't get away, and if he did, the mood between them wouldn't be the same. He got up and waved to Samuel from a distance. "I'll catch you later, okay?"

THIRTY-SIX

Unbelievable.

Samuel watched Jacob leave, and it was all he could do to restrain his anger. After years of waiting for Jacob to open up to him, he had to be interrupted by Catherine. And then, when he asked her to go away quietly and let him and Jacob talk, what did she do?

Refuse.

"Why is everything that's going on in your life more important than what's going on in *mine*?" Catherine's cheeks flushed in frustration. "It's like I need to take a number and wait in line, the way I do at that bakery I hate going to."

Samuel was weary of her demands. "It's not more important. But if we had a date and I arrived to discover you and Arlan in the middle of a serious talk, I'd leave you two alone."

"If Arlan were actually *talking* to me and you showed up, I'd invite you to join us and be thrilled you had finally found the time to have a conversation with him!"

"And I'd stay because it's what you want, but I asked you to give Jacob and me time. Instead of going to the house and waiting, you started complaining."

"So everything I do lately is wrong, is that it?"

"Pretty much, ya." Samuel wasn't backing down, and at this moment he didn't care where it led. "Look in the mirror, Catherine. Figure out what's going on with *you*, because I can't keep doing this."

"What are you saying?"

Her wide brown eyes bore into his, and he knew he should find the words to ease the tension, to calm their emotions. Several sentences came to mind that would bring perspective for both of them, but he couldn't make himself say any of them. "I'm tired. I was up all night, and this heat is wearing on everyone. I think we should go our separate ways today before we burn a bridge."

"It was *your* choice to work all through the night to help Rhoda, and now you're too tired to talk to me? I don't like who she's become in your life, Samuel. I don't like it at all."

"I came up with this plan for us, for you in particular, and it's not good enough? I expected that saving the orchard from financial ruin would make you happy, but that seems impossible."

"You should've talked to me about it first."

Samuel stared at the woman before him. "Okay, maybe I should have. If you feel this strongly about it, I guess I was wrong."

"I don't want Rhoda to be a part of our lives. Period."

He put his hands on her shoulders. "My plan is a solid one, and the King family needs her expertise. If she'll accept my help, it'll be good for all of us."

She backed away from him. "What kind of help are you talking about giving her?"

"Time, energy, and money for starters."

"Money from where?" She looked at him quizzically, and after a moment understanding registered on her face.

Samuel took her hand into his. "I know how this must sound. I really do."

She pulled free. "No, I don't think you do. I can't stand by and allow this."

Was she giving him an ultimatum? Something hard and immovable took up residence inside him. "I'll do what I think is right. I'd hoped you'd see that and appreciate it, but I'm not altering the plans I've made."

Her eyes filled with disbelief, and without another word she hurried toward the house.

When they'd last spent time apart, it seemed to do both of them some good. So he let her go.

Rhoda took the sole remaining jar of blackberry jam off the shelf and placed it in the box at her feet, the last of her garden's produce, canned and ready to ship. She looked around her beloved cellar, now void of fresh fruit and delicious aromas. It had been four days since she'd found her garden destroyed.

As Tuesday wound to a close, her cookstove was lifeless. The fireplace was filled with cold ashes. The counters and shelves were empty. She couldn't stand the look of the place, but going outside hurt worse. The barren space that once held her garden reminded her of a desert.

"Knock. Knock."

She turned at the sound of Samuel's voice. When she peered through the screen door, she saw him and Jacob standing at the entryway. She hadn't heard them arrive or come down the steps.

"Kumm." She closed the box of goods.

Samuel's eyes moved about the desolate room. "We've brought you another proposition. One we think you'll like."

Jacob stepped forward. "At some point he'll remember to say something personal before he begins talking business. Like maybe, 'Hello, how are you?'" He bowed slightly.

"Hi, Jacob." She returned his gesture with the slightest of curtseys. "I'm as well as can be expected. And you?"

"I'm much the same. Thank you." Jacob turned to Samuel. "Take notes, man."

Samuel studied her, his eyes serious and unhappy. "You don't look so good."

Jacob shook his head. "He's like trying to train a cocker spaniel."

Rhoda smiled, and it felt a bit odd. She hadn't smiled in what felt like forever, but it'd been mere days since she'd had such a wonderful time at the King family gathering.

Right now she felt as empty as her room, and she needed something to do with her hands. She should invite them upstairs, but instead she leaned back against a counter. "You took time out of a workday to come here instead of calling? Why?"

"That's what I said." Samuel put his hands in his pockets, looking a little antsy. "But Jacob felt it was important to check on you in person."

Her eyes met Jacob's. "Ah." The more she knew of Jacob, the more she liked him. And he seemed interested in her too. She pulled her attention back to Samuel. "So what's your new proposition?"

"Before we talk about that, we need to tell you that it's our fault Rueben knew you and your family would be gone last Friday night."

"*Ours* or Eli's?"

Samuel's eyes widened. "You know?"

"When some of the shock wore off, it dawned on me. Eli meant no harm, and I take no offense. Ungodly meanness was in Rueben's heart, and he'd have discovered a perfect opportunity to do what he wanted without anyone telling him when we'd all be gone."

Samuel nodded. "Ya, well, here's what we were thinking—"

Jacob removed his hat and smacked his brother with it. "We appreciate your attitude, Rhodes. And we have some ideas we'd like to present. If you don't like them, we'll understand. But we're hoping you'll at least consider them."

Samuel crossed his arms, looking more relaxed by the minute. "May I share the plan now, Jacob?" Samuel's teasing made her smile.

"Would you like to go upstairs and sit at the kitchen table?"

Samuel turned to Jacob. "If I say yes, is that too businesslike for you?"

"If *I* say yes, would you stay in the cellar while Rhodes and I go upstairs?"

Rhoda chuckled. Whatever they had in mind, she wanted to say yes. She needed to be a part of something bigger and stronger than she was on her own. Kings' Orchard and the men who ran it fit the bill to perfection.

"Kumm." Rhoda went up the stairs.

Her father and brothers were standing in what used to be her blackberry patch, talking to a couple of land surveyors about parceling up the property. Her family was wasting no time in getting the proper construction permits. Soon they'd know whether they could get building permits for one home or two. Before winter set in, at least one house would stand where her berry bushes once grew, and children would play in the grass that would be planted in place of her garden.

Her mother stood on the driveway and turned toward Rhoda. "This will be best for everyone in the long run."

"I know, Mamm. I know."

Although her heart ached at the thought of making her last deliveries to customers, it hurt even more being here, staring at the cemetery where her life-long dream had died.

She headed for the house, unable to remember a time when she didn't have canning to do—not since she was a little girl, anyway. Now there was nothing left to can. Once the last box was delivered, Rhode Side Stands products would cease to exist.

She went inside, hearing her sisters-in-law and their children moving about upstairs. She looked over her shoulder at the brothers. "May I get you some lemonade or water?"

"Water. Denki," Jacob said.

"I'm good, but thanks." Samuel pulled out a chair from the kitchen table and sat.

Rhoda put ice and water in two glasses. She passed one to Jacob and took a seat on the opposite side of the table from the brothers. "So what's on your mind, Samuel King?"

She listened as he shared their plans for the summer kitchen and how they wanted her to stay on their property anytime she had a mind to.

"We'll hire Landon as a farmhand."

"*You'll* hire him? You don't even like him."

Samuel squinted. "I have vision problems."

Rhoda raised an eyebrow. "Meaning?"

"It seems I can't see anything right the first few times I look at it. You won't hold that against a man, will you?"

"Depends. Are you willing to trust what I say the object looks like?"

"Probably not every time. I mean, nobody's right all the time."

"I am." Jacob plunked his hand against his chest.

Samuel rolled his eyes. "With the exception of my brother."

Rhoda realized she did a lot of laughing when she was around these two. She took a sip of her drink. "Are you really thinking of hiring Landon full-time?"

"We'd like to talk to him about it and make an offer, but we'll limit it to six months for now. Then we'll reassess. He's never done this type of work and may hate it. I know you find him valuable, but I'm not sure we will once the canning season is over. If he accepts, he'll work wherever we need him most—with you or us. And he'll be available to drive you back and forth between our place and your home whenever you want."

She liked the sound of that. "He'll be good at taking the products to different buyers and getting them on board to order from us. And he has a Rhode Side Stands website set up for orders as well. He'll contact all those customers about the new apple line."

"Excellent." Samuel drummed his fingers on the table.

Rhoda played with a drop of condensation on her glass. "The summer kitchen is a building that sits off by itself, right?"

"Ya." Jacob nodded. "I'll start remodeling it soon and get it operational as quickly as possible."

He ended his sentence there, but Rhoda heard his thoughts: *if I can make myself.* But why would a carpenter think that?

Jacob motioned. "When the remodeling is done, the kitchen will be bright and airy, unlike your cellar."

"How big a space is it?"

"Eight times the size of your cellar." Jacob smiled. "And laid out with canning in mind."

"Really?" She glanced from one to the other. "I like how this is sounding."

Samuel leaned back in his chair. "It's nothing grand, and I don't want this offer to sound like more than it is, Rhoda. It's a practical space, and the size of it will enable you to can more goods."

She frowned, looking to Jacob for backup. "Explain"—she waved her hand up and down, motioning at Samuel—"this."

Jacob laughed. "Not sure we have that much time, but here goes. He's offering full disclosure so you don't enter the agreement thinking it's one thing only to discover it's another. He does that a lot, and once a person agrees to the raw, ugly view he gives, he feels he's been extremely honest, so the deal, in his mind, is binding."

"Ah." Rhoda ran her fingers over the wooden tabletop. "Glad to finally understand that about him, and I appreciate his honesty."

"As I was saying,"—Samuel straightened the front of his shirt collar—"there's much to do and not much time to get organized, so we've been looking at ways to use the space in the summer kitchen for every possible contingency. One of which is if you wanted to sleep there, you could."

"I accept."

"You can't say that yet." Samuel frowned at her. "I haven't finished explaining, and you haven't seen the setup."

She focused on Jacob. "I accept."

Jacob raised his glass in the air. "I accept your acceptance."

She touched her glass to his.

"Although the first of the apples will be ready soon,"—Samuel continued as though they hadn't said a word—"the bulk of the crop won't be ripe for five weeks yet, and then we'll harvest from sunup to sundown until the end of October. Our aim is to have that kitchen operational in three weeks."

"Sounds perfect. I have a lot to do to wrap up here and customers to contact, to let them know I can't fill the orders and such."

Samuel looked at her. "Have you called anyone yet?"

"No, and I know what you're thinking. When I call to tell them about Rhode Side Stands not being able to fill the orders, I should let them know about the new line of apple products I'll be making."

"You're quick." Samuel grinned. "We've been brainstorming labeling ideas. And since you're giving Kings' Orchard your recipes and helping us through at least one season to get us started, we wondered if you might like a label we came up with. Kings' Orchard is well known for its apples, so we want to use that. We'll keep our usual logo, the one stamped on the apple crates and such. It's a silhouette of a horse and buggy under an apple tree with a full bushelbasket next to it. And we'd keep the name 'Kings' Orchard' at the top. But for the labels on the canned goods, we thought we'd put 'by Rhode Side Stands' at the bottom."

She knew his aim was to be generous, but he'd missed the mark. "You'd like to make me feel as if I still have my business. Is that right?"

"Ya. You haven't lost it. It's just facing a lot of changes." Jacob smiled. "Like Samuel and his poor vision."

"The problem is that the layout for the label is wrong. I don't want to be listed at the bottom, as if my recipes and canning products aren't worthy to share the top of the label with Kings' Orchard."

Samuel took a sideways glance at Jacob before responding to her. "I thought you'd consider it a generous offer."

"You thought wrong. It isn't all that surprising, is it?"

Jacob watched, like a calm spectator unwilling to get between the two of them, at least at this point.

Samuel's jaws tightened. "I suppose it's not surprising that you think I'm wrong." He paused. "Well, go on."

"My recipes. My work. My reputation. My established buyers will be purchasing my canned goods. Maybe you should put 'Kings' Orchard' at the bottom of the label and 'Rhode Side Stands' at the top."

Samuel splayed his fingers, palms up. "That's not happening. We approached you to partner with us—not the other way around, remember?"

"And I'll not be an underling at Kings' Orchard. If I'm a partner as you say, then treat me as one."

Samuel gestured from the top of her head downward. "This is the Rhoda Byler I met the first day I came here and the one I argued with in front of her family while we shared a meal. She sees nothing the way I see it."

She reached over and tapped the table in front of him. "The names of both businesses at the top of the label. Since my products carry the most in-store recognition, I suggest 'Rhode Side Stands' go first, but I may be negotiable on that."

Samuel blinked once and opened his eyes wide. "May?"

"Ya." She leaned back in her chair. "Keep being stubborn, and I'll change it from *may be negotiable* to *won't be*. Any questions?"

"I have one." Jacob raised his hand. "Do you two know that you're like oil and water?"

A car horn tooted, and Samuel stood. "That's our driver returning for us. If we need more time, I'll ask him to wait."

"No, we've covered plenty."

Samuel moved toward the door. "You have a lot to do, and we don't want to pressure you, but the sooner you can come to the farm, the better. And please tell Landon we'd like to speak to him as soon as he can find the time in his schedule."

"Denki." She followed them outside. As she waved good-bye, she saw that Mrs. Walker's curtains were drawn to the side and the windows were open. A medical transport service had brought her home from the hospital this morning. Rhoda hadn't seen her children visit her yet. Maybe work kept them from being able to fly in. But if that was so, who was taking care of her elderly neighbor?

Rhoda went to her cellar, opened a partially full box of raspberry preserves, and pulled out a jar. Her father had told her that Mrs. Walker no longer held any ill will toward her. But would she mind if Rhoda made contact with a peace offering in hand?

She went down the sidewalk, turned the corner, and walked up the woman's porch steps, her palm sweating against the glass jar she held. She knocked.

A young woman in a pale-blue uniform answered the door. "May I help you?"

"My name's Rhoda. I live down the block." She pointed toward her house.

"I'm Maggie, Mrs. Walker's nurse for the next couple of months."

"I brought something for her." She raised the jar of preserves. "Perhaps you could give it to her?"

"Let her in." Mrs. Walker's voice was barely audible, but she sounded cranky.

The nurse stepped aside so Rhoda could enter.

She found Mrs. Walker lying on a bed in the middle of the living room, her face pale.

"You can leave now."

Rhoda handed the preserves to Maggie and turned to go.

"Not you, child." Mrs. Walker shooed away the nurse, who nodded and then disappeared into the kitchen. "Come here, dear." She gestured Rhoda forward with shaky hands.

Rhoda approached the bed. "I thought you might like some of my preserves. They're from my last batch."

Mrs. Walker reached out and took Rhoda's hand. Her fingers looked frail, but they had a firm grip. "That's so thoughtful of you. Thank you."

The woman seemed genuinely grateful.

She picked up a pad of stationery that was beside her on the bed. "I was going to write you a note. But what needs saying is best done in person." She looked toward the kitchen. "My mother was one of the most superstitious people I ever knew. Every shadow and every speck of light meant something threatening, a warning of bad things to come." She grimaced. "I promised myself I'd never believe the nonsense she did. But I've been much, much worse without even knowing it. When you fell in front of my home while trying to get to your sister—when you said that she was going to be killed before it happened—it scared me. And I was convinced you must be a witch." She took a drink of her water. "But that's not at all who you are, is it?"

Rhoda shook her head. "I sense things sometimes, mostly just an intuition as an event is unfolding. Unfortunately, I usually pick up on what's happening when it's too late to do anything about it."

The nurse came in with a plate of toast covered in preserves. "Would you like a taste now, ma'am?"

"Of course I would."

The nurse pushed a button on the bed and helped Mrs. Walker to a semi-upright position. Then she set the plate on a wheeled tray and positioned it over the woman's lap.

Mrs. Walker took a tiny bite of the toast. Her eyes closed for a moment. "Mmm." She took a slightly bigger bite. "Oh my. This is delicious."

"I'm glad you like it."

The nurse returned to the kitchen, and Mrs. Walker swallowed another bite. "You knew I was in trouble, and you acted on those feelings before it was too late. You saved my life. I'm glad, because I want to be here for my teenage grandchildren, to see them marry and have their own children. I don't get to see them often, but when I do, it's wonderful. They tell me I make a positive difference in their lives, and I want to be here for them."

Mrs. Walker gazed at the barren field between their properties. "But now I need to say something I wish weren't true." Her quivering lips curled up.

Rhoda waited, unsure what to say to comfort the elderly woman.

"I know you didn't plow your fields on purpose. And I know I have to accept some of the blame for what happened."

"But you weren't even out of the hospital."

"Neighbors are saying you plowed the fields down yourself to make room for your brothers to build. But I've seen you. For years I've watched you tend your berries with more love and affection than a lot of folks give their own kids. You wouldn't give them up voluntarily. And I know your father wouldn't ask it of you."

Rhoda moved to the window, looking at her barren land. "You had something to do with what happened?"

"Not directly. But in my fear, thinking I was protecting others who might come into contact with you, I helped spread the rumors that you practiced witchcraft. I backed up that Amish man who came by here, asking how I felt about you and those herbs—because he thought you were using them in incantations, and I said I thought so too." She pushed the wheeled tray away from her.

"An Amish man?"

"Gluck or Glack."

"Glick. Rueben Glick."

"Anytime he came looking for support or information to take back to your people, I gave it to him. I don't even know why. None of what I thought makes any sense now. But my gossip and influence probably helped people get it in their minds that ruining your gardens was the right thing to do." She looked into Rhoda's eyes. "I'm ashamed of myself."

Part of Rhoda wanted to lecture the woman and walk out, but she moved to the chair beside the bed and took Mrs. Walker by the hand. "It wasn't just you. But I forgive you."

"Good." Mrs. Walker patted her hand. "Thank you." She held her hand tight, fighting to get control of her voice again.

How sad that misunderstandings between them had stolen so much, and now that they were finally resolved, Rhoda wouldn't be across the fence working in her garden where they could've spoken regularly, taking away loneliness for both of them. She moved to the window, and with her garden uprooted, she could see her home clearly now. Landon's truck sat in her driveway, reminding her that she had much to do to wrap up business. "I need to go."

"I'm glad you came to see me. You come back anytime. I'm going to be praying for you every day."

"Denki." Rhoda left, grateful for the truth Mrs. Walker now understood. She hurried toward her driveway, anxious to make the final deliveries and to get Landon to take her to Kings' Orchard. She wouldn't tell him about Samuel's idea of hiring him, but once he was on the property, Samuel would waste no time filling him in, and she'd get a chance to see the summer kitchen.

THIRTY-SEVEN

Dark enveloped the land as Jacob took a seat at the picnic table by himself. He'd given his word, but could he actually do the work? He'd told Rhodes he'd start on it, but since he'd arrived home from her place six hours ago, all he'd accomplished was pulling his tool belt out of its hiding place in his bedroom and placing it inside the summer kitchen. Then memories began suffocating him, and the next thing he knew, he'd walked out of the shabby building and gone to the barn office. He'd spent the rest of the day helping on the dairy side of the farm—feeding and milking cows, paying bills, and updating ledgers.

A vehicle pulled into the driveway, and he shielded his eyes from the bright headlights. The engine stopped running, and the lights disappeared. The passenger door opened, and Rhoda got out. Jacob couldn't make himself move. Landon eased from the driver's side, and Jacob watched the two of them head toward the house.

Rhoda glanced around, spotted Jacob, and redirected her path. "Hello."

"Hi." He motioned for them to join him.

Samuel stepped out of the house and spoke to Rhoda, and then he and Landon went toward the barn to talk business. Rhoda moved closer to the picnic table, where he now sat. The casual look on her face suddenly changed to one of concentration, and she looked around. "The air carries a wonderful aroma of the ocean. Do you smell that?"

"I don't, and whatever you're picking up, it's not ocean. We're too far."

She breathed deep. "I've only been to the beach once, when I was twelve, but I remember that fragrance clearly."

"What, dead fish?"

"No. Briny water and sunshine and salt air with hints of seaweed and surf."

This woman just might be as quirky as she was fascinating. "You like the ocean?"

"I was terrified of it." She took a seat across from him. "But I dipped my toes in the edge of the water, feeling the tickle of white bubbles. And I sat on the beach and enjoyed the magnitude of the ocean. I even spotted a few dolphins frolicking."

He lifted one eyebrow. "Frolicking?"

She looked at him, seemingly seeing right through him. "The aroma's not really here right now, is it?"

He chuckled. "Not at all."

Her expression changed, as if she finally understood. "You love the ocean." The authority in her statement was undeniable.

His heart jolted. She'd picked up on a part of who he was, or rather used to be. "This is a weird conversation, Rhodes."

"Sorry. I shouldn't…" She shrugged. "So where is the summer kitchen from here?"

"It's a little over a thousand feet that direction, just beyond the dip on the other side of the office barn."

"A thousand feet. Can you put a concrete visual to that?"

"There's a little more than five thousand feet in a mile, so basically it's a fifth of a mile from here."

"Well, why didn't you say so? That I can wrap my mind around."

"I can show you if you're willing to walk across a rough path in the dark."

"I really want to get a glimpse of the place—whatever I can make out in the dark."

"I'll get a lantern. Do you want to step inside the house and say hello?"

"No, I'll wait here. If I'm going to be coming and going all the time, I'd rather everyone get used to me not stopping in for a chat."

"You and Samuel are more alike than you probably realize." He rose. "I'll be right back."

He found the lantern and lit it, then returned to where Rhoda stood at the edge of the apple orchard, looking out across it. He walked to her and gazed at the view—acre after acre of rolling hills and lush trees shrouded under the beauty of night.

"This may be the most gorgeous view I've ever seen."

"Hold that thought, because the building you're about to see is hideous." He held out his arm. "It's a rough path between here and there."

She took his arm, and he led her down a narrow, bumpy path, dodging rocks, potholes, and clumps of brush, until the summer kitchen came into sight.

She paused. "You have your work cut out for you." She released his arm and walked ahead to enter the open doorway. He came in behind her, casting the light in whichever direction held her interest. "It has lots of potential, but you must be quite the carpenter."

"That's the hope."

She turned to him, came close, and took the lantern. Holding it up, she studied his face. "You don't want to do this, do you?"

He knew she saw things and picked up on the unspoken, but this was eerie. He wasn't sure he liked this side of her. What else might she pick up on? "It's challenging me, but I want to do the work, very much so."

She set the lantern next to his tool belt on the beat-up, weathered block counter. "Tell me your plans."

Jacob walked from one wall and corner to another, describing what he hoped to do. She added her thoughts, and soon they were coming up with ideas he hadn't thought of before.

Rhoda smiled at him. "You have vision."

"Says the clairvoyant to the carpenter."

She laughed. "I see or know only what's given to me, and most of the time I botch what I am given. You can look at a broken structure, or even nothing, and see what it can become by your own hands. That's a truly powerful gift."

Her words encouraged him, and even though his apprehension didn't fade, his excitement at the prospect grew. She freed the hammer from its loop in the tool belt and held the rubber-gripped handle out to him.

Inside that run-down structure, with only a dim lantern giving light, he stared at her. It was as if she held out to him the right to own his past and use it to build a new beginning. He took the hammer from her, feeling freer than he had in years, and gazed into her gorgeous eyes, a color that was so brilliant the name blue didn't do it justice.

Was he looking at someone who'd unlock his secrets and maybe, just maybe, free him from them?

Samuel climbed the ladder and inspected a Gala apple. The first fruit of the season would be ready to pick in about a week. That gave them five working days, eight at the most, to get ready for the harvest. He plucked an apple and descended the ladder.

For the last few years, he'd given the first apple of the season to Catherine. His heart weighed as much as a bushel of apples of late. It had been eleven days since they had fought over his decision to help Rhoda, and they hadn't spoken since. He'd seen her at church on Sunday. Their eyes had met occasionally as he sat with the men and she with the women. She smiled, looking sad and lonely. He missed her. But he wasn't ready to try to fix what was wrong between them any more than she was.

Voices echoed against the hills, and he saw Rhoda riding bareback as she topped a hill. The Morgan broke up ground as she leaned low, spurring it onward. She looked behind her. Jacob crested the knoll on a mare, gaining on her fast.

Rhoda brought her horse to a natural gait and ambled to Samuel. "*Guder Marye,* Samuel."

"Good morning, Rhodes."

Catherine hadn't been here for nearly two weeks, but Rhoda had been a regular. In spite of their playing around this morning, Rhoda and Jacob both worked hard and stayed focused. The six of them—Jacob, Rhoda, Eli, Leah, Landon, and he—were making good progress toward having the summer kitchen fully operational by the time the first apples were ready to harvest.

Rhoda held out her hand. "The first apple of the season?"

He passed it to her. "It's not perfectly ripe, but it's close. I'll run an iodine test before we begin picking."

"Jacob said you have a team of pickers ready to flood the orchard when you need them."

"Everything seems to be going well." And part of it was because he'd stayed focused on his tasks rather than being distracted by helping Catherine with her latest crisis.

But how was she faring? The question stabbed deep, and he did the only thing he knew to do. Ignore it.

Jacob's mare thundered to a stop. "You do not play fair, Rhodes."

She glanced at him, mocking disgust. "Samuel, your brother refuses to speak honestly."

"How was that not straightforward?" Jacob gasped for air.

"What you mean is that I cheat." Rhoda raised an eyebrow. "Admit it, man."

Jacob chuckled but said nothing.

Rhoda pulled the apple to her face and breathed in deeply. "Delicious."

"Gala, actually," Jacob countered.

She mimicked throwing it at him before handing it back to Samuel. Maybe he should wrap it and mail it to Catherine.

Rhoda glanced behind her, and Samuel saw Landon coming toward them on a pony, its little legs going as fast as it could. "Jacob, did you stick him with the pony so you could try to catch up with me?"

"Hey, you're the one who stole my horse and took off before I had this one bridled. Landon said he was going to hang around the barn until you got back. He must've changed his mind."

She slid off the Morgan and passed the reins to Samuel. "I'll be back in a few." She walked toward Landon.

Samuel looked at his brother. "So you've completely tossed out the window any attempt to keep a professional distance?"

"Not at all." Jacob got off his horse. "If not for my agreement with you to keep everything professional until the harvest is over, I'd have made it clear to her that I'd like us to court." Jacob slapped the end of the reins against the palm of his hand. "Do you blame me?"

"No." Samuel clutched the apple in his hand. "I understand. And I'm glad you've finally found someone you're interested in."

Samuel watched Rhoda meet up with Landon. The young man slid off his pony, and the two of them began walking toward the brothers.

Jacob turned his back to them. "You've always respected my privacy and not asked questions, so if you want the same in return, just say so." Jacob looked Samuel in the eyes. "I've not seen Catherine in weeks, and you've not left to go see her."

"Ya." Samuel inspected the apple in his hand as if it might hold the answers he needed. "I haven't seen or talked to her in almost two weeks. The saddest part is that for every single thing I miss about her, I have an equal number of things I'm relieved not to have to deal with. And I fear I'll stop missing her before I'm ready to give up the breathing space."

"I hate it for you."

"I appreciate that. And if you ever want to talk again, like we were doing before she interrupted us, just let me know."

"Will do." He mounted his horse. "I have to get back. That quick dry concrete should be set by now."

Samuel motioned for Landon. They needed to work on mending ladders and apple crates. There'd be no time for such things once the harvest began and the pickers arrived.

THIRTY-EIGHT

Catherine pulled the carriage into Samuel's driveway. She'd been too demanding, and Samuel wasn't one to be pushed too far. Surely he was as ready for them to make up as she was. No sooner had she stopped the carriage than Hope came sprinting across the lawn toward her, yapping like crazy. Catherine got out and knelt in the grass, nuzzling her soft fur. "Did you miss me, sweetie?" She rubbed the pup's fluffy ears. "I sure missed you."

She hadn't allowed herself to come by for a visit but had spent two weeks mulling over her last argument with Samuel. *Look in the mirror, Catherine. Figure out what's going on with* you, *because I can't keep doing this.* The challenge had hurt, even though it was exactly what she needed to hear.

She'd pondered a thousand things during their time apart. And as she did, she began to appreciate that he gave her time to think on her own, neither breaking up with her nor insisting she immediately change.

Samuel was a wise man, and she looked forward to being in the circle of his guidance for the rest of her life. She'd worked through so many confusing thoughts, enough to drive a sane girl crazy. But now her mind was clear, and she had peace.

Grieving the loss of being the only young woman in Samuel's life had taken time, and it could easily be something she'd deal with for the rest of her life. She'd finally admitted to herself that it wasn't for Arlan's sake that she had told him Leah was pregnant. She'd done it out of spite. It had irked her to see how much Leah seemed to get away with. But Catherine had been petty and had betrayed Samuel's strong sense of loyalty when she lied about Leah. She'd done damage. But how much?

She sighed and gave Hope a final pat, then returned to the buggy and took out the insulated carrier she'd brought. Finding the front door of the house open, Catherine poked her head inside and sang out a greeting.

"In here," Samuel's Mamm called from the living room.

Catherine found her on the sofa, holding a copy of *Die Botschaft,* an Amish newspaper. She set the paper on an end table beside an empty water glass and stood. "I haven't seen you around much lately. Is everything all right between you and Samuel?"

"We hit a little rough patch." Catherine smiled. "But I think we're going to be fine now."

Elizabeth nodded at the insulated carrier. "Nothing a special blueberry pie can't fix, ya?"

"That's the hope."

Samuel's Mamm picked up her water glass and headed toward the kitchen. "He's out in the orchard, probably in the summer kitchen. Would you like something to drink?"

"Yes, please. Summer kitchen?"

"You know, that abandoned stone building." Samuel's mom opened the icebox and pulled out a pitcher of lemonade. "Used to belong to the Daadi Haus."

Catherine had seen the structure in passing and wondered about it. She'd always figured it was used as a tool or equipment shed. "What's he doing there?"

Samuel's mother filled two glasses. "He and Jacob have been remodeling it. Putting in appliances, hooking up the plumbing, even setting up a little bedroom."

Catherine's heart leaped. She could think of only one reason Samuel would do all that work, especially this close to apple harvest. He'd come to the same conclusion she had during their time apart: that they were meant to be together. And he'd figured out a way to build a home for them.

If she remembered correctly, the little stone building wouldn't exactly be spacious. But how much room did they really need? It'd be a fine starter home, a place for them to live while Samuel worked on a bigger house.

He had to be as excited as she was to start their married life.

Catherine took a few gulps of the lemonade, thanked Samuel's Mamm, and hurried out the back door, cradling the pie carrier in her arms. Her legs couldn't move fast enough. She could hardly wait to see Samuel, to tell him about her insights and the repentance she'd come to. In their time apart, Catherine had realized it wasn't Samuel's place to fix everything for her, not even Arlan. She had to rely on God and find peace within herself.

If Arlan ended up leaving the Amish, she'd miss her only sibling something fierce. But she wouldn't expect Samuel to stop Arlan. Soon they'd be married and raising children together, and that would be all she'd need.

The old stone building came into view. It had a roof now, and the missing walls had been rebuilt. Catherine picked up her pace, hoping the pie she carried would survive intact. Although Samuel cared more about the taste than the appearance, she wanted everything to be perfect when they saw each other and ended this time apart, never to separate again.

As she neared the summer kitchen, panting from exertion and excitement, she heard Samuel talking. Oh, how she'd missed his deep, rich voice. Almost as much as she'd missed his welcoming warm embrace. And his lips on hers as he said good night before he returned to his carriage.

The sound of a woman's voice stopped Catherine a few feet from the building. She slowed her breathing to listen more carefully. It was Rhoda Byler's voice. What was *she* doing here?

Perhaps Samuel wanted a female's opinion on how to fix up their little newlywed cottage. Scolding herself for being suspicious, Catherine moved a few steps closer.

Surely Samuel and Rhoda weren't in there alone. Samuel's Mamm said Jacob was helping with the remodeling, but Catherine didn't hear his voice.

A door with new wood and shiny hinges blocked the front entrance. Catherine went around to the side of the building and found an oversized window opening without glass in the frame.

Leaning against the brick cooling shelf that extended from the window, she peeked inside. Samuel stood next to Rhoda, each of them holding an edge of a large piece of paper with something drawn on it in pencil. Their shoulders were nearly touching.

"Jacob and I had this all plotted out, and I see what you're saying, maybe." Rhoda glided her fingers along the huge piece of paper. "But see this straight edge I penciled in?"

Samuel studied it, tracing right behind where her fingers went. "Ach, I do now. That explains why I changed the plan. I didn't see that." He tilted the paper. "So what is it you've drawn on the plans?" Samuel sounded so lighthearted.

"A line, silly."

Samuel laughed. "Well, duh, Rhodes."

Catherine's heart sank. This relationship was all business? Why was he calling her by her nickname?

"Remember my cellar?"

"How could I forget it? But there was no line drawn in your cellar. I know that much."

"Of course not." She poked Samuel's arm.

The friendly gesture stabbed Catherine's heart.

"I had a counter that ran right up to the edge of the sink. That made it easy for me to get my fruit from the colander into a bowl without dripping on the floor."

"Ah, yes." Samuel took a step away from her and gave her a formal bow. "Your wish is my command, Rhodes."

Rhoda giggled, and Catherine felt sick. What was going on?

Rhoda was supposed to be canning apple products for Kings' Orchard at *her* place. Not here. Especially not in the home she thought Samuel was fixing up for the two of them.

Samuel set the drawing on a brand-new cookstove that sat between a large, shiny icebox and a deep sink—all much bigger than necessary for a two-person home.

Or a twenty-person home for that matter.

Catherine stared at their backs as they bent over the plans. All right. So Samuel wasn't fixing up the place for them to live in. As disappointing as that was, she shouldn't have raised her expectations in the first place. And she certainly wasn't going to ask him to fix how she felt. She'd deal with it. She'd already decided Samuel was worth whatever she needed to do to keep his heart.

Such as not eavesdropping outside the window. Catherine set the insulated carrier on the ground and pulled out the pie. The top crust had shifted a bit during her race out here, and some of the blueberry filling had seeped over the edge of the pan. But no matter. She started for the front entrance, ready to knock on the door, surprise Samuel with the still-warm pie, make friendly conversation with his new coworker, and wait till they had a chance to renew their relationship in private.

"Now, about that bedroom…" Rhoda's words brought Catherine back to the window.

"Did I alter those plans too without realizing it?"

Catherine's knees felt weak. Rhoda was going to live here?

"Well, this wall…" Rhoda pointed to the paper, but then they left the plans on the stovetop and walked to a small entryway at the back of the room.

Samuel held back a curtain hanging from a rod at the top. Rhoda stepped inside, and Samuel waited at the door for her to pass through. A few moments later he entered too, leaving the curtain swaying and blocking Catherine's view. She couldn't hear anything else they said.

But their laughter made her stomach turn.

Catherine's fingers tightened around the pie pan. What had Samuel been doing the days they'd been apart? While she'd been soul-searching, crying into her pillow, and sorting through all her thoughts and feelings, he'd been making plans to move another woman onto his property.

Sure, Rhoda was here to work—to do canning that would help save Kings' Orchard. Supposedly so that Samuel would finally feel financially secure enough to ask Catherine to marry him. But he was clearly fine without her.

As a matter of fact, she had never seen him look and sound so happy.

Had he missed her at all while she was gone?

Look in the mirror, Catherine. Figure out what's going on with you.

Obviously while she'd been doing that, he'd discovered something new going on within his heart.

Catherine looked at the pie in her stiff-fingered hands. Part of her wanted to fling it at the stone house and let Samuel see the gooey mess when he opened the door. Instead she set it on the brick cooling shelf. When Samuel saw it, he'd know she'd been there. If he still wanted her, he'd come talk to her.

Her heart breaking, she picked up the insulated carrier and walked away.

She wouldn't question Samuel. Wouldn't force him to look her in the eye and give her an answer. She'd wait.

If he came back to her, she would accept him with open arms and an eager heart. If not…

She'd lose the only man she'd ever loved.

THIRTY-NINE

As soon as Leah finished her Saturday chore of sweeping all the floors, she headed for the old summer kitchen, eager to talk to Rhoda. She hoped to catch a few minutes with her.

Alone.

Although she'd spent a lot of time with Rhoda lately, helping to get the new kitchen set up, they were always in the company of others. It looked as if Rhoda's new canning kitchen would be fully operational by the time the harvest began next week.

The herbal teas were helping her a lot. She'd been to the specialist and told him that the herbs were causing her stomach to hurt less and that her bouts of throwing up had almost stopped. He did some blood work, but he felt that if she was doing better on the herbs, she should give that a try for a few more weeks before they ran any further tests. His office called a few days later to say her blood work had come back clean.

The doctor gave her some dietary guidelines, and she had to be careful what she ate. She was weary of drinking licorice tea so often, but how could she argue with the results?

What she wanted to talk to Rhoda about had nothing to do with her recent stomach issues, though. She wanted to earn money so she could make some real plans for leaving here. She could be a strong helper, every bit as good as Landon. But what would Rhoda think about it, especially after the horrible first impression Leah had made on her?

Sure, Rhoda had been nice to her, but trusting Leah to work next to her during grueling days was different. Leah was nice to her little sisters, but she didn't want them helping her bake cakes. They made the chore harder.

It'd be such a great feeling to know she was earning money that would help her leave one day. She appreciated that her family cared more about her than she'd realized. It made her feel better about herself. But she still wanted to be free of the Amish life. Parties hadn't been difficult to give up, but she longed to be free to listen to music. Maybe, in time, she could learn to play an instrument like Arlan. If Rhoda would hire her and she worked six days a week, she'd save every penny for her departure.

Leah went up the path to the stone building. Through the screen door she saw Samuel and Jacob installing a generator-powered, commercial-sized dishwasher. She went inside. "Hey, when can we get one of those for the house?"

Jacob chuckled. "Good question."

Samuel looked up from connecting a water hose, not a trace of a smile on his face. "When a government inspector requires it for a permit."

Jacob stood and stretched. "Once this is in, Rhode Side Assistance should be ready for inspection on Monday."

"What's Rhode Side Assistance?" Leah looked around.

Jacob grinned. "Since Rhoda's assisting us with our business, the nickname seemed to fit." He put a Phillips screwdriver on the thick butcher-block table. "It's also a reference to when I met her."

"Have to admit, Rhode Side Assistance is a catchy name." Samuel groaned as he twisted a wrench.

Leah had no idea what first encounter Jacob was talking about. "Is she around?"

Samuel fastened a clamp. "She and Landon had a long shopping list. Assuming this place passes inspection on Monday, we need to be operational on Tuesday. That'll be our first day of picking."

Leah just stood there, disappointed that she wouldn't be able to talk to Rhoda. Dogs growled and yapped from somewhere outside, so she went to check it out. A few steps to the side of the summer kitchen, she saw Hope and a few other dogs fighting over something. After shooing away the neighborhood dogs, Leah picked up Hope.

The poor thing had a few scratches on her face and ears. As Leah tried to assess the damage, Hope whimpered and tried to squirm out of her grasp. She set the pup down, and Hope immediately went for a mangled aluminum pie tin. "So that's what you were all fussing over." She picked it up. It smelled faintly of blueberry, but there wasn't a speck of filling or piecrust. The dogs had licked it clean. "Silly things."

Leah took the disposable tin to the Dumpster that Jacob had been using while remodeling the summer kitchen. Hope stayed on her heels, probably looking for more pie. "Where'd you get that anyway? Have you been digging in Mamm's trash near the house?" She picked up the puppy, whose stomach felt a little engorged. "Mamm won't be happy if you've made a big mess of the trash." She scuffed the fluffy ears as she went back toward the summer kitchen.

Samuel came up behind her. "Hey, would you mind helping me for a minute? I need to get a couple of loads of dirty dishes to test that thing out."

Leah had washed the breakfast dishes that morning, but with all the baking Mamm was doing for church tomorrow, there'd be more dishes by now. She fell into step with her brother. "Where's Catherine been lately?"

"Busy, I imagine. I haven't talked to her in a while." Sadness clouded his eyes, and Leah wished she hadn't asked.

The two of them went into the kitchen, and Mamm was more than happy to donate two large basins of dirty dishes for the trial run of Rhoda's new dishwasher. "Don't put them away when you bring them back, though. I want to inspect them first to make sure they're as clean as I'd get them."

They agreed and headed out the door with the basins.

Samuel nudged her with his elbow. "You know, Leah, I have to say, you've really changed in the last few weeks."

"Think so?" She shifted her basin from one hip to the other.

"When I brought you home from Rhoda's last month, I wasn't sure you'd keep your side of the bargain and stay away from the parties. Your restriction ended this weekend, starting last night, and you didn't even mention wanting to go anywhere."

At first she didn't want to go back to Brad's or anywhere else her friends hung out, because she was so embarrassed by Michael's treatment of her. But the longer she stayed away, the more she realized she hated those parties. Besides, she was busy helping the family get the summer kitchen set up.

"I'm really proud of you, Leah."

He didn't know about her pregnancy scare, and if he did, he'd probably feel different. But he was right. She had changed. She wasn't the same girl who'd been intoxicated and had passed out in Rhoda's berry patch. She'd learned a bit about life and herself, and even though she wouldn't remain Amish, she hoped she never acted like a fool again.

They went inside the summer kitchen. Mamm's two basins of dishes didn't fill half of the cavernous machine. Samuel turned on the generator, and Jacob ceremoniously closed the lid to the dishwasher and turned the dial, but nothing happened. "Are you sure you hooked it up?"

"Of course I hooked it up." Samuel checked the connections anyway.

Jacob studied the installation manual. "Says here there's a little green light on the front panel that's supposed to come on when it's running." He bent down and checked more closely. "I don't see anything." He looked up at Leah. "Do you?"

"What does this do?" She grasped a small black knob and turned it from left to right. It clicked into place. And a little green light came on.

"Well, what do you know?" Jacob slapped her back. "I had no idea we had an engineer in the family."

"Ya," Leah said. "Leave it to a manual dishwasher to figure out how to operate an automatic one."

She helped them for a while, but when Rhoda didn't show up, she walked back home in the waning light. She so wanted to help Rhoda with the very first canned goods made. This venture was the beginning of something huge and maybe lasting, and she wanted to be a part of the start-up.

FORTY

The summer kitchen smelled of cooked apples, sugar, cinnamon, cloves, and an array of other spices. Rhoda surveyed the mess inside the new canning house. Her first full day of work, and the room looked as if she'd thrown a tantrum.

Her favorite apple product to can was apple butter because of the pungent aromas that filled the room. So that's all she'd made today. She'd work on something else tomorrow...if she could get this disaster cleaned up by then.

Leah sank into the chair under the window, wiping her sweaty forehead with the edge of her apron. "I can't believe we canned thirty-six bushels on the first day of the harvesting season."

Landon leaned against the doorframe, apparently enjoying the slight breeze. "You've never done nearly that many, Rhodes. Then again, a bushel of blueberries is a lot more pieces of fruit than a bushel of apples." He brushed at spatters of apple butter on his shirt.

Rhoda didn't know how she would've gotten through the day without her two helpers, but they were exhausted. She had begun the day by walking the orchard with Samuel before sunup, going over procedures and plans. While they walked, he told her of the trouble between Catherine and him. He vacillated between going to see her and keeping the situation as it was, but he didn't know why he couldn't decide which direction to take.

He seemed rather lost without Catherine, and Rhoda hated that he was going through the heartache. But the news didn't cause her to think any differently about Samuel. Whether he was free or bound to someone didn't matter. Even as hidden as Jacob stayed, she liked what she saw in him.

Once the workday began, the King men and their hired help had used a trailer to haul apple crates to her front porch throughout the day. With the exception of a quick lunch break, she, Leah, and Landon had worked nonstop ever since.

"Why don't you two go home and call it a day, ya?"

"No way." Landon stood straight. "I'm not leaving you to clean up all this by yourself."

She swatted his arm. "I'm fine. You do as you're told, and no back talk."

He turned to Leah, who looked pale and exhausted. "Come on. My truck is parked to the side. I'll give you a lift to the house."

Leah's body looked as limp as a wet washrag. "I like that plan. Anything to spare me having to walk those thousand feet." Instead of getting up, she looked at Rhoda. "You know I'm happy to stay and help, right?"

Rhoda moved to take Leah by the hands and tug her off the chair. "Denki for offering to keep working. But as tired as you are, you'd probably break half my jars." She gave Leah's fingers a slight squeeze. "Besides, I'm actually looking forward to having a little quiet time after such a busy day."

"If you're sure…"

"I am."

Leah gave Rhoda a quick hug. "It was fun today, wasn't it?"

"Ya, it was. Now go." She raised an eyebrow. "You need some rest. It all starts again bright and early tomorrow."

Landon opened the screen door for Leah. "It was Rhoda's pleasure. Trust me."

They left, and Rhoda collapsed onto the chair Leah had just vacated. Her back, neck, and legs were stiff and sore. But contentment worked its way through her, imparting a sense of well-being she'd thought had been uprooted along with her demolished berry patch. She hadn't felt this happy since that youth gathering at Uncle Mervin's, before she knew her crops had been destroyed.

A whistle sounded from the doorway. Rhoda looked up and saw Jacob's cheeky smile.

"What a mess. Been keeping house long?"

She pulled the dishtowel off her shoulder and held it up. "If you'll come a little closer, I'll smack you with this."

"Too lazy to stand?" He moved in but not so far that she could reach him with the towel. If she knew Jacob, he'd probably done that to tease and torment her.

He leaned against the counter. "Mamm sent me to tell you that she's holding your dinner for you."

Rhoda rubbed the back of her neck. "She won't be too happy that I missed dinnertime and ignored the second call to come eat as well, will she?"

"You shouldn't ask questions you don't want the answers to. Besides, if you don't eat, you won't have the strength to do the work."

"I can't say I'm particularly hungry." She leaned her head back and closed her eyes. "I've been sampling my own products all day."

Jacob gave a mock gasp. "You thief! Stealing from your partners. You should be fired."

She opened one eye and peered at him.

He grabbed the towel out of her hand and twisted it in his fist. "Or maybe whipped."

She chuckled at his mischievous expression. "I couldn't help it. I had to make sure everything tasted right."

"Why don't you let me be the judge of that?" He flung the towel over his shoulder and walked up to the pan on the stove. After scraping a bit of apple butter off the edges with a wooden spoon, he stuck it in his mouth. "Mm-mm-mm." He licked his lips. "I've been eating this stuff since before I had teeth, but it never tasted like this."

Her face flushed from his exuberant praise. She got up, took the spoon and the pot from him, and carried them to the sink. "These dishes won't get clean by scraping a bit off the sides."

She flicked on the hot-water faucet. As she turned, she saw Jacob filling a pot with canning utensils. "You don't need to do that. You've had a long day too." Even as she said it, she knew she didn't really want him to leave.

"Aw, don't worry about me. I'm used to this. Matter of fact, I never have more energy than after the first day of apple picking." He set the pan in one of the sinks. "After months of preparation, it's exciting to see all those ladders set up against the trees with full buckets coming down, being emptied into crates, then taken back up again." His green eyes were bright, and she wondered how bloodshot and weary her eyes were at this point.

She tucked loose strands of hair behind her ears, fully aware she needed to comb and pin her hair.

Jacob's eyes met Rhoda's, and she finally admitted to herself that what she felt for him fascinated her.

Jacob winked. "Besides, if you don't let me help you out, you'll still be cleaning up come morning, when it's time to start again."

"You could be right about that."

After the sink was filled with hot, soapy water, Rhoda turned off the faucet and started washing.

"Hey, Rhodes." Jacob grabbed a fresh towel out of a drawer and began rinsing and drying. "Why are we washing dishes by hand?"

"The dishwasher is sterilizing Mason jars for tomorrow."

"Makes sense." He set a clean measuring cup on the shelf. "Did you use as many spices today as you expected?"

"No, and I'd like to know your secret. How do you always know figures and estimations? I was off by a case, and you had it down to the jar."

He swiped the towel over a spoon and tossed it into the drawer. "Good at guessing, I suppose."

"Hmm. You're far better at *guessing* than telling lies."

He stopped and looked at her.

"You're beyond good at numbers, Jacob King. You know it, and I know it. And if you're going to be bad at something, I'm glad it's lying."

He smiled. "The family knows I'm good, but they don't really know. Understand?"

"Ya." She wouldn't ask any questions. They made him uncomfortable, and it was nice discovering tidbits about him slowly.

She scrubbed a stubborn bit of cooked-on apple butter off the lip of a pot. "I have to be honest, if the rest of the season is anything like today, I'm not sure I can keep up the pace. Not unless I can figure out a way to streamline my efforts. Any chance we could go over how I've organized my day and see if you can uncover a better—"

A thwack on her arm made her whirl around. Jacob stood behind her with a huge grin, twirling the damp towel in his hands. "Can't say I didn't warn you." The mischievous glint was back in his eyes.

"Oh, now you're asking for it." She scooped a handful of suds and flung them at him.

He ducked just in time. The sudsy water hit the floor, and Jacob knelt to mop it up. "Towels make even better swatters when they're wet and soapy."

"Don't you even think about it, Jacob King."

He stretched the towel in front of him, tugging on each end with his fists. His impish grin nearly made her laugh out loud, but she held it in. After all, this was war.

Rhoda looked around for ammunition to use in her defense. Spying a stirring spoon with a good-sized dollop of apple butter in it, she lunged for it. As his arm reached back to prepare for a good swing, she snatched up the spoon and snapped it at him, aiming for his chest. Unlike the marshmallow incident, she smacked him right in the face this time.

"Ach! I've been hit!" He reeled as if mortally wounded.

She pressed her advantage and grabbed the towel from him. "Aha!"

He closed his eyes and turned his head, angling toward her the side of his face with the moist apple butter. "You win. Just smack that stuff off my face. I deserve it."

Instead she used the towel to gently wipe off the glob.

He faced her, his eyes soaking her in, making her feel as if he understood her. Accepted her. Wanted her. She'd never imagined experiencing the kind of attraction that ran between them. She'd spent so many years muddling through the long, dark tunnel of loneliness.

He remained stock-still as she removed the apple butter from his chin. She could feel his coarse whiskers through the cloth. The aroma of his aftershave still clung to him. Had he showered before coming here tonight? Her heart beat so hard she was certain he could hear it.

He cleared his throat and gently took the towel from her. "I…I think you probably got it all."

"Not quite." Noticing a bit more near the corner of his mouth, she dabbed at it with her forefinger.

He turned toward her hand and kissed her fingertip. Everything seemed to freeze, then move in slow motion. A dozen emotions flooded her every second that passed. He put his hand over hers, drawing all her fingers to his lips and kissing them. Rhoda's breathing constricted, and it was as though the world spun around her. She swallowed hard and eased her hand away.

But she could still feel his touch on her fingers and in her soul. She'd been alone for what felt like forever, avoided by most men in her community, never a date with anyone she admired. At twenty-two she'd begun to visualize herself as single forever. Right now she had no idea what she thought. Only what she felt.

Unable to stay near him, she went to the sink.

"I'm sorry." His voice was low and deep, right behind her. "I shouldn't have crossed the line."

She could feel his breath on the back of her neck. "It's just, well, I'm not sure I know you that well."

"What is there to know that you haven't seen over the last month? We've been together often. It probably equals a year of courting for some."

She turned to face him. The tender look in his eyes said she drew him the way he did her.

He swallowed, making the muscles in his throat constrict. "Clearly I should have kept things between us on a more professional level, like Samuel suggested."

"Maybe that's best for a while, give us more time to be sure of each step. Our lives are so entangled, and we need to be certain."

"Rhodes, look at me, please."

She did as he asked.

"What do you see?"

She gazed into his eyes and allowed herself to sense what she could. "A good man who carries blame I don't understand. But there is so much I can't see."

"Is the not knowing what causes you to shrink away?"

"I don't think so. But you keep a tight lid on part of your life."

He nodded, looking ready to walk away rather than tell her what he kept hidden.

She caressed his face, not as interested in his past as in his future. "Despite what I'm about to do, I believe it's best to tuck these few minutes away as a memory and begin anew the next time we see each other."

Confusion flickered through his eyes.

Trembling, she went up on her tiptoes and brought her lips to his.

FORTY-ONE

A kerosene lamp cast a dim, flickering glow across the old desk as Samuel jotted down figures in the appropriate columns. Thunderstorms rumbled in the distance, their dark clouds making the first rays of daylight slow in coming.

Apple-picking season had begun a week ago, and all of the Kings' property, even this rustic office inside the barn, carried the delicious scents of Rhoda's canning products.

Rhoda.

Her entry into life here in Kings' Orchard seemed destined. She made such a difference, and he didn't blame Jacob for feeling about Rhoda as he did. If she became his sister-in-law one day, well, he'd look forward to that.

His thoughts returned to Catherine. Her character weaknesses that caused her to rely too much on him to fix issues, to lie about Leah, and to resent Rhoda weren't what kept him from her. In his estimation she could overcome those faults easier than he could overcome his own. His lack of patience and hard-to-please ways seemed to be a part of his nature—issues she accepted. All in all, she had fewer faults than he did, so what separated them? It wasn't as though he'd given up hope for a future with her. He just couldn't make himself go to her, talk to her.

And he wasn't sure why.

Enough of that. He pushed aside thoughts of Catherine and filled in the last numbers from yesterday. The calculations for the orders coming in looked better than he would have dared to hope for after a month of harvesting and canning, and they'd only been at it a week.

Samuel closed the ledger, tucked it under his arm, and stood. Maybe he'd see light coming from the summer kitchen. He went to the side door of the barn and peered through the darkness and the few trees between the barn and Rhoda's kitchen. A tiny hint of light came through the windows, meaning she was up, but barely. She didn't bound out of bed in the mornings. Maybe that was just her way, or maybe she was too exhausted from the start-up of the canning season.

If the latter was the case, well, with figures like these, they could afford to hire more help for her.

Despite her certain drowsiness, he strode toward the summer kitchen, needing to get the final numbers on the applesauce she'd canned yesterday. Just as he raised his fist to knock, she opened the front door and gasped.

"Samuel King! Startle a body to death, why don't ya?"

"Rather not, at least until harvesting season is over."

"I appreciate that." She stretched while stepping outside. "I smell rain."

"Ya, it's been thundering for hours."

She faced him, frowning. "You've been up working all that time?"

"Ya. All I need now is a final count on yesterday's canning." He went inside, and she followed him. "That'd be the ones you did *after* you'd agreed to call it quits for the night."

She stifled a yawn. "The ones I didn't do are sitting right there." She pointed at a shelf that had been empty when he left last night and was now lined with jars of applesauce.

While he went to the shelf, she put on a pot of coffee to percolate. Before he finished counting, rain began to patter on the roof. She unloaded the dishwasher and set up the table for another day of assembly-line canning.

He closed the ledger. "Leah will probably open her eyes, realize it's storming, and go back to sleep."

Rhoda pulled two mugs from the cabinet. "There may not be any apple picking today, but there's no shortage of apples sitting in crates, waiting to be canned."

"I know. But I thought you might need a slower start to your day. I'll wake her when you're ready to begin."

She poured coffee into both cups and added the same amount of cream and sugar to each. A loud clap of thunder made her jump, and she spilled some of her coffee on her clean apron and dress.

He laughed before accepting a mug and taking a sip. "Didn't take you for one who'd be bothered by a little inclement weather."

"I never have been. Maybe I'm a bit jittery today." She set her mug on the counter and used a clean dishtowel to wipe off the liquid.

"Did you find the time to call your Daed last night?"

"Has a cat got a tail?"

He chuckled. "And nine lives, or so I've heard."

She went to the pantry and pulled out a loaf of his Mamm's homemade bread. "A day is not complete until I've talked to my Daed."

"Did you mention my idea about hiring another helper?"

"No." She put a slice of bread on a plate and passed it to him. "He'd side with you, and I don't. End of it, Samuel."

"Do you have to disagree with me on every topic before finally seeing that I'm right?"

She sliced herself a piece of bread. "You're annoying, Samuel King. Do you know that?"

Samuel sipped his coffee. "How should we go about finding your new help?"

"I said no."

He knew what needed to be done, as did Jacob. So Samuel chose to ignore her opposition. "I imagine you'll want to find someone who is careful to follow directions, doesn't dawdle, and can be a good fit with the three personalities already working here."

Her eyes met his, and he saw anger begin to mount. "I don't want another helper. Not yet. I just need to hone my routine. That's all."

"Trust me. You're wrong about this. The Sunday-evening singing is at our house this week. We could invite everyone to the summer kitchen for the snacks and fellowshipping time. We'll ask the girls to come early to help us get ready. Those who show themselves as interested, diligent workers and who take instruction well would make our best candidates."

As he explained his idea to Rhoda, he wondered if Catherine would come, perhaps out of curiosity. He wasn't sure how he felt about that. He should be ready to see her by now and to talk, but he didn't want to cross that bridge. Not yet.

His girlfriend and their troubles aside, his spirits felt lighter of late.

"No." Rhoda grabbed a filled jar and set it in front of him. "Do you need me to spell it out in apple butter across your forehead?"

Rain pounded on the roof. Thunder rumbled. The aroma of spices and coffee filled the air. This extension of Kings' Orchard felt homey and right.

"Just think about it today, okay?"

She nudged the jar of apple butter closer to him. "Your answer to everything I don't want to do is that *I* need to think about it."

"That's because when you disagree with me, you're always wrong."

She huffed. "We're not doing it your way. Not until I think it's the right thing to do."

Her opposing opinion irked him, but whether they agreed on this or not, they'd have a very profitable harvest. He knew that for sure now, and he wouldn't need to sell any land.

He set his mug in the sink and realized he hadn't checked that Eli had overseen the pickers putting away all the ladders and buckets last night. "I need to see if all the equipment is properly stored."

She raised her eyebrows. "Do you need an umbrella?"

"Hallo." Jacob swung open the screen door and stepped inside.

"Guder Marye, Jacob." Rhoda bowed her head, almost giving a curtsey, and Samuel saw her eyes welcome his brother.

Guilt nibbled at him. The feelings between Jacob and Rhoda appeared to be strong and growing stronger. But their relationship was on hold because he had asked his brother to keep a professional distance.

Were they doing that? If so, he needed to remove that barrier between them. Rhoda was not the type of woman who'd get out of sorts with Jacob and expect Samuel to fix things or she'd leave. That wasn't her way. She might ban Jacob from coming to the summer kitchen more than absolutely necessary, but that would be it. He'd talk to Jacob about it as soon as they were alone.

"I was just leaving to check the field." He pulled his hat tighter onto his head. "We don't want anything to get ruined by the rain."

He stepped onto the porch. After years of feeling pressure concerning the orchard and not knowing how to make the business more solvent, he now felt confident and hopeful. He'd finally found a solution for Kings' Orchard, but he wouldn't have if Leah hadn't gone to an Englisch party. He drew a deep breath.

God used the oddest situations to line people up and get them involved in each other's lives. He'd even used Leah's sinful ways to find an answer Samuel had been looking for. And from now on, he would be patient with the frustrating events, believing that God would use them to get His children to walk a new path.

FORTY-TWO

Rhoda opened the ledger Samuel had been writing in moments earlier and read the figures. "I'm trying not to argue with Samuel since he and Catherine aren't seeing each other, but he doesn't make it easy."

"About hiring another worker?" Jacob poured himself a cup of coffee.

"Ya."

"My vote is with Samuel on this one. Maybe then you'll have time for something besides work."

"You're both good men, but I'll be the one to make that decision."

Jacob studied her with his deep green eyes. But whatever came out of his mouth wouldn't necessarily be related to what he was thinking. "I know we're not supposed to be dating, but I'd really like to see you this weekend, even if it's at a group gathering."

She closed the ledger. "I'd think you would be tired of seeing me. I'm here from sunup Monday mornings to almost dinnertime on Saturday nights."

He rested his chin in the palm of his hand, his elbow on the table, and gazed up at her. "Nope. Not tired of seeing you yet."

"Gut." She playfully pinched his chin between her thumb and forefinger. "You're not so bad yourself." Truth was, she wanted time with him too. No matter how much they were together, she always wanted more. She got out the largest boiler and began filling it with water. "Actually, Samuel wants to have a gathering here Sunday evening." She explained the plan, aware of anxiety building in her stomach.

Jacob hauled in several crates of apples from the front porch. Wind whipped through the stone house, rattling the shutters. As she began setting empty jars on the table, goose bumps ran the length of her body, making all the tiny hairs on her arms, face, and neck stand on end. She swallowed hard, determined to settle down whatever was niggling at her.

Emma's innocent face flashed before her. *Save them.*

"Don't start this." Rhoda squeezed her eyes tight and braced herself against the counter.

"Start what?" Jacob's voice sounded distant.

She turned to face him, hoping to be drawn back to the workday in front of her.

He snapped his fingers in front of her face. "You okay?"

"Ya. Of course. Probably too much coffee and too little sleep." She walked back to the sink and turned off the water before moving clean jars to the work station.

A gunshot echoed inside her head, and she dropped a jar.

"I'll get that." Jacob grabbed a broom and dustpan.

What was happening? This was how she felt right before Emma was killed, but her intuition told her that more than one loved one hung in the balance this time.

She was just tired. That was it, and she had no desire to make herself a target of gossip again. Everyone in Harvest Mills seemed willing to give her a fresh start after the crazy rumors that had surrounded her in Morgansville.

Jacob swept the shards of glass into the pan, and suddenly she felt as if he were sweeping up the shattered remains of his life—as if it wasn't yet broken but soon would be.

"Rhodes?" Jacob clasped her arm, his voice muffled.

Chills upon chills layered her skin. This feeling was even stronger than when she'd sensed something wrong with Mrs. Walker. Acting on that had saved the old woman's life.

"Jacob, go to your house and get everyone in the cellar."

He led her to the doorway and pointed at the clearing in the distance. "The storm's over. The rain will be gone soon too."

She walked onto the lawn, studying the ever-brightening sky.

Jacob came alongside her, looking for evidence that couldn't be seen.

Was she wrong? Another shot rang out inside her, and she jumped. She grabbed him by the arms. "I *need* this from you. Please, Jacob."

He stared into her eyes, and she realized he loved her. Probably more than even he knew. He cupped her face in his hands and kissed her forehead. "Okay."

The earth rumbled under her feet. Was it real? Or a warning?

"Go!" She shoved him toward the house and ran in the opposite direction for the orchard. "Samuel!" She hurried farther into the orchard. "Samuel!" On she trudged, mud covering her skirts, rain drowning out her voice. "Samuel!"

A clap of thunder shook the ground, and the heavens opened. Rain fell harder, mixed with pea-sized hail. "Samuel!" Daylight disappeared as if someone had turned off the lights.

She spotted him at last. "Samuel!" *Please, God, let him hear me!*

He stopped and turned to face her—

The tree in front of him split, sending splinters of wood in every direction. Samuel fell, and she ran to him. Before she reached him, he got up and headed for her, limping and holding his leg. Lightning crackled across the sky, hitting a tree, exploding it. She screamed, covering her head with her arms.

When the sparks stopped flying, she ran for Samuel. A piece of something was sticking out of his leg and blood oozed through his trousers.

"Let's get out of here!" he yelled over the tumultuous sounds of rain, hail, and wind.

Rhoda put her arms around his waist, and he leaned into her. The wind ripped at their clothing and made it impossible to catch a full breath. The sound of wood twisting and moaning surrounded them. Seeing more than ten feet ahead was impossible, and Rhoda prayed they were going in the right direction.

The summer kitchen finally came into sight, and soon they staggered onto the porch and into the house. They went to the back room, which didn't have windows that could shatter and fill the air with glass. She eased him onto the bed, and he leaned his back against the wall. She settled beside him, closing her eyes and praying their families were safe.

Pans clattered. Glass broke. Roofing ripped off overhead.

Samuel wrapped her in his arms, assuring her they were safe.

The winds died, and the thunder became distant. Finally a deafening quiet settled over the place, leaving only the sound of a gentle rain.

She opened her eyes, tilting her head back to look into Samuel's face. "I sent Jacob to your house to get everyone to safety, but I didn't do it when I should have." Tears ran down her cheeks. "What if I waited too long?"

He hugged her tightly, saying nothing.

She eased from his warm embrace, and he released her. "I have to check on your family."

"I'll do that." He tried to get up and winced before collapsing.

"Stay off your leg." After helping him shift to a prone position, Rhoda covered him with a blanket, all except his leg.

Her knees threatened to buckle as she went through the roofless kitchen with glass, shingles, and cooking utensils strewn in her path. She whispered prayers as she headed down the path to the main house.

Her wet clothes clung to her, and water squished inside her black slip-on shoes. She saw a honey-brown patch of color through the underbrush and hoped she'd just caught a glimpse of Jacob's hair. "Jacob?" She ran.

He came around the blind, gaining speed. "Rhoda!"

She hurried to him, and he swallowed her in his arms, lifting her feet off the ground.

He put her down, embracing her tight. "Samuel?"

"Injured, but safe. Your family?"

"They're all fine. Katie has a gash on her forehead from some debris that hit her as everyone moved from the house to the cellar. A whole side of our house was ripped off, and the damage is horrendous, but everyone is alive." He touched the end of her nose. "Thanks to you. How bad is Samuel?"

"It looks like a piece of a tree lodged in his leg. But he's safe on my bed, with orders to stay there."

Jacob lowered his lips to hers and kissed her. "Forgive me for not being quicker to trust you?" He nuzzled her neck.

She backed away. "It's taken me most of my life to learn to trust myself. I even fought this time longer than you did. I'm just glad you were there to send for help."

"So am I."

She took him by the hand and started toward the office barn. "I need to check on my family. And Landon. Unless the weather kept him home, he was likely a few miles from here when the storm hit."

When the King house came into view, she couldn't believe her eyes. It looked like a dollhouse that had been dragged through the mud.

Jacob squeezed her shoulder. "The girls' room, where Leah, Katie, and Betsy were asleep, was hit the worst." His voice cracked. "But all of it can be replaced or repaired."

She wanted to stop for a moment so they could sympathize with and encourage each other, but she was desperate to hear her Daed's voice assuring her that everyone was okay.

They went to the barn. Other than the roof, most of the building wasn't damaged. The animals were skittish but unharmed. She'd always heard stories about tornadoes destroying one place and leaving its neighbor almost untouched. Rhoda grabbed the phone and pressed it to her ear but heard nothing. The lines were down.

Fear circled inside her as she replaced the receiver in its cradle. "It's not working. How are we going to get help for Samuel?"

"I'll hook up a horse to a wagon so he can lie in the back of it, then take him to the doctor."

"You think the roads are passable?"

"Not yet. I'll leave him here for now. Daed and Eli will help me get horses and ropes to drag the debris out of the road. And we'll bring saws to cut anything that's too large to move." He snapped his fingers. "By nightfall we'll have a path cleared between here and the main roads."

"Should I come too?"

"Stay with Samuel. Keep fluids in him, and keep him warm. He needs to get into dry clothes. I'll be back for him as soon as the roads are clear."

In all the chaos she hadn't thought about what Samuel needed, but Jacob was right. Back when she grew herbs, she'd read about people going into shock and how to prevent it. She hadn't realized that Jacob had been trained in first aid too.

"Got it."

He lifted her face upward. "Your family is fine. I'm sure of it. Can't you feel it?"

She closed her eyes, trying to sense peace about them. "I can't."

"Well, they are." He smiled before he tucked her head under his chin.

Even if he was simply trying to comfort her, she appreciated it and felt better for his saying it.

"Jacob, did you tell your family I sent you to get them into the cellar?"

His arms felt warm and strong as he held her. "By the time I arrived, the only thing on my mind was getting them to safety. And then my concern for you and Samuel took over every thought."

"Since the storm looked as if it was gone when I sent you to get them to the cellar, maybe we could keep that between us. People feel odd about certain things, you know?"

"Your secret is safe with me." His voice rumbled through his chest, vibrating against her ear, and she knew he'd protect her in every way possible. "We make a pretty good team, you know."

She took a deep breath, grateful to have his strength to draw from because today would be one of the longest, hardest days she'd faced since losing Emma.

FORTY-THREE

Leah shook like a newborn calf, unable to believe what'd happened. They couldn't stay inside the unstable home—Mamm wouldn't allow it—so Leah and her sisters walked the yard, picking up strewn clothing and bedding. Daed had set up a seventeen-gallon washtub, and the girls were washing clothes outside. Katie and Betsy wrung out the items by hand and put them on the clothesline, refusing to leave their parents' sight. The gash on Katie's forehead had stopped bleeding. It'd take months, maybe a year, to put their lives back together, but they milled about doing silly things like laundry, as if that was the beginning.

She wanted to run through their district and find out how the other families were doing, especially Michael. She shouldn't care, but she did. Still, Daed said she had to stay put, although he let her meander a bit into the orchard, looking for Hope. No one had seen her since the storm.

The sun shone bright, making it feel as if their disaster were somehow a charade. She'd like to thank God for protecting her and her family, but it'd been so long since she'd prayed. Did He even want to hear from her?

Jacob and Eli had left five hours ago to clear the roads to the nearest hospital or a doctor's place, and they hadn't been seen since. If Landon needed help, she hoped Jacob had come across him. Most of all, she wished they had a solution for Samuel. He lay in Rhoda's bed, shaking with pain, starting to lose consciousness.

Rhoda stayed by his side while Mamm made soup. Everyone prayed for a working phone line or some other way to get help.

Leah heard a yelping noise and started searching for the source. After circling the house, she came to a pile of clapboard siding in the front yard. She moved the wood piece by piece until Hope sprang free, barking excitedly. Leah picked her up and took her to Katie and Betsy. They rejoiced and held her close, but they didn't leave Mamm's side.

"Hallo!"

It was Jacob. Leah turned in the direction of his voice and saw him and Eli appear out of nowhere, riding bareback.

Jacob dismounted. "How's Samuel?"

Daed hurried across the yard. "He needs a doctor." He embraced Jacob. "I was getting worried. What kept you two?"

Jacob dropped the reins, letting the horse stand free. "It's a mess out there, but we got the last tree out of the road, and we can get him to the hospital now."

Daed shook his head. "A horse and rig can't get from here to the closest hospital no matter how clear the roads are. There's at least ten miles of highway."

Leah couldn't muster any anger at the Amish ways today. She was too grateful to be alive, but this was just another example of why she didn't want to hold on to the Old Ways. They should own a car. The minimum speed limit on a highway made using a rig illegal. A horse-drawn carriage went about ten miles per hour, and a horse couldn't maintain even that speed for long. A horse and buggy on a freeway was an accident, perhaps a car pileup, just waiting to happen.

Eli got off his horse "We've got the highway issue covered too."

"How?" Daed embraced him.

"We found Landon." Eli removed his work gloves. "He was on his way here when the storm hit, and he helped us clear the roads. But an intern who had a limb fall on his SUV needed a ride to the hospital, so Landon took him. Soon as Landon drops him off, he'll come here."

Jacob brushed bits of debris from his hands. "In the meantime the intern gave me instructions about moving Samuel. He said there wasn't much point trying to get an ambulance out here."

Daed picked up the reins of Jacob's horse. "What needs to be done?"

"I need to wash up. When Landon arrives, we need to get Samuel into his truck without putting any pressure on his leg or the wood that's embedded in it. And his leg needs to stay elevated. That means only Landon, Samuel, and two of us can go."

Mamm kept her hands on Betsy's and Katie's shoulders. "I'd better stay with the girls."

Daed passed the reins of the horse to Mamm. "The girls can help you take care of the horses."

Eli gave the reins of his horse to Katie and put his hand on her head. "Take good care of her. She worked hard this morning dragging fallen trees out of the way."

"I will." Katie beamed up at him.

Jacob started for the summer kitchen, and then he turned to Leah. "How about you?"

Tears pooled in her eyes. He hadn't lumped her in with the little girls, and he wasn't telling her what to do. He was *asking*. "I'm wherever you want me."

He motioned. "Kumm."

She hurried to his side, and the four of them—Daed, Jacob, Eli, and Leah—strode toward the summer kitchen. Most of the roof was missing from the old stone building, but the four walls appeared as solid as ever.

They entered the almost-unrecognizable room. Daed began picking up debris to clear a path. Despite the scattered and now dented canning equipment and the broken jars, the appliances appeared not to be damaged. Papers were strewn, but Leah knew Rhoda had the original recipes tucked safely away somewhere.

Jacob eased his way to the tiny bedroom, and Leah went with him. The bedroom was about two feet wider than the twin bed inside it and no longer. Leah guessed this area had once been a walk-in pantry.

She saw Rhoda kneeling on the floor beside Samuel, holding his hand, whispering.

"How's he doing, Rhodes?"

At Jacob's voice she jolted, then looked so relieved to see him. "I've decided he's a tough old bird."

"Ya." Samuel's voice was hoarse. "Let me lie around all day with a kind woman tending to my every whim, and I'm as tough as they come." Samuel held up one hand. "Anyone checked on Catherine's family yet?"

"Ya. Eli took a few minutes to ride over there while Landon and I were taking a breather. A tree fell in their yard, and the branches destroyed their front porch and broke some things in the kitchen, but no one was hurt."

"Es iss wunderbaar gut."

Samuel was right, it was wonderful good. But Leah couldn't restrain her anxiety. For no sooner had her brother muttered the words than he dozed off. Or had he lost consciousness?

Jacob motioned for Rhoda to come to him. They went into the main room.

Leah took her place beside Samuel. His chest rose and fell as if breathing were a job all its own.

Samuel opened his eyes. "Don't you worry, Leah. Daed's always said I had apple trees in my blood. This isn't anything new, not really."

Why did this have to happen? "I'm sorry, Samuel."

"Sorry? What for?"

She shook her head. He didn't need her to dump her guilt on him. "For not being a better sister, a better person."

"Me too." He waved his fingers. "I mean, I'm sorry I haven't been a better brother."

She kissed his cheek. "I knew what you meant. Rest."

She heard a car engine. That had to be Landon.

Jacob came to the doorway and gestured for Leah to come out of the room. She did, but she stayed nearby. Rhoda was at the sink, staring out a broken window. If only they had a way to reach her family.

Jacob moved to the side of the bed. "Landon's here. We have to move you to his truck without putting any pressure on your leg or the wood in it. I think the best way is if I carry you."

Landon walked inside, wearing muddy jeans and a soaked and torn T-shirt. Leah wanted to hug him, but she wiped her hands on her apron instead.

He looked past her. "Hey, Rhodes." His voice was barely a whisper.

Rhoda turned.

He went to her and held up his cell phone. "They're safe. I just now got through, and the block your family lives on sustained no damage at all."

She grabbed the phone. "Can I talk…"

"The call dropped, and the cell towers are too busy to get another call through right now, but I talked to your Daed after the storms passed. He said to give you a hug." Landon whispered something else that Leah couldn't hear, and Rhoda put her arms around his neck.

"Girls." Landon shook his head and released Rhoda, wiping his misty eyes. "Well, come here." He motioned to Leah.

She did, and he hugged her tightly, like an exuberant child clutching a teddy bear.

"I'm glad you're safe and here." Leah backed away and poked his shoulder.

"My truck didn't fare so well. It's pitiful, and I guess that's what happens when a guy doesn't have the sense to get out of a hailstorm."

"That bad?"

"Let's just say my vehicle won't be much to look at anymore."

Leah bit her lip. "I don't think we got much hail, but the wind did enough damage on its own." If the whole orchard was hit as hard as the part she'd seen, there wouldn't be any more apples to can.

Landon checked his cell phone and slid it back into his pocket. "About seven houses in the area are worse than this one. Several of them are Amish homes."

Leah's knees felt weak. "Whose?"

"I don't know any names. Jacob will."

"Anybody hurt?"

"Not in the Amish homes. News said five people have died across the state."

"I don't want to be around when Samuel fully understands the extent of the damage that's been done to the orchard."

Rhoda rubbed her chest. "It'll break his heart."

Leah dreaded when that day arrived. Clearly tornadoes and hard times hit no matter whether a person lived the Old Ways or the Englisch way. Her relationship with her family had changed a lot lately, and she was grateful, but it wasn't enough to make her want to stay living under the ways of the Amish. If she tried, surely she could find a way to leave peacefully when the time came. But that would be a while.

Throughout her whole life, she'd needed her family. Now they needed her. And she'd stay to see them through this upheaval, however long that took. But only until then.

FORTY-FOUR

Standing in a neighbor's home, Jacob's hands trembled a bit as he nailed another header fastener into place. He hated doing carpentry work. It turned him inside out, but he had no choice.

Eli passed him another bolt. "How come no matter what each support beam needs in the way of metal fasteners, we use triple that amount?"

Jacob ignored him and finished securing another joist. They'd spent day after day helping secure the underpinning and load-bearing walls in damaged homes.

Eli stepped back, admiring their work. "There is nothing pretty about it, but it sure does give new meaning to the term *support system*."

Jacob climbed down from the makeshift scaffolding. If he'd known eighteen months ago that coming home would lead to this type of work, would he have returned? He slid his hammer, ratchet wrench, and two sockets into his tool belt. "Let's wrap this up with a minimum of conversation. We need to go."

Rhoda, Leah, and Landon were at the summer kitchen, canning as many apples as could be plucked from fallen trees or scavenged off the ground. The ones that weren't any good for canning, Rhoda used to make mulch.

No one had time to eat or sleep properly, let alone talk. The critical needs were too great. Many of their Amish neighbors had suffered similar fates, needing work done so they could move back home or be safe in the homes they refused to leave.

Few Amish had homeowners' insurance. Most were uninsured, or they belonged to a co-op run by the Amish. The owners of the house Jacob and Eli were working on were from the same district as the Kings. They were good people who wanted the brothers to stay for dinner and spend the evening talking.

Jacob shook hands with the couple, assuring them they were safe. They thanked him over and over. "You're more than welcome. Glad to do it."

While they talked, he backed out the door, nodding for Eli to do the same. "Ya, it was quite the storm." He carried his toolbox to the rig, talking as the homeowners followed him. The idea of his Daed letting slip his newfound fear concerning Rhoda had weighed on Jacob all day.

The man put his hand on Jacob's shoulder, his eyes misting. "You sure you can't stay for dinner?"

Jacob had witnessed as many misty eyes and sobbing folks this week as he had when… He refused that thought, angered by the memories the tornado had unearthed. Everyone's emotions were raw, and the rebuilding had only begun.

"I sure do appreciate the invite." Jacob set his toolbox behind his seat and climbed in. "But we need to go."

"You tell Samuel we're praying for him."

"Sure thing." Jacob eyed Eli, who was taking entirely too long to get into the carriage. "Kumm," he muttered.

Eli removed his tool belt and laid it on the seat before getting in. He hadn't even closed his door when Jacob tapped the reins on the horse's back. He waved to the couple and smiled.

"In a hurry?" Eli closed the door as the rig picked up speed.

"I thought we'd be back home hours ago."

"You sound edgy and impatient, a lot like Samuel lately."

"Maybe if you wore his shoes, you'd sound like this too."

"I don't know what has you most out of sorts—having to do this type of construction work or worrying about what Daed might say while you're away from Rhoda."

Both had him edgy, but at least Daed had given his word that he'd keep his thoughts to himself. Jacob loved him, but his thinking that Rhoda had brought them bad luck was ridiculous.

Eli half shrugged. "It is a little eerie that we've witnessed two uprooted crops since we've known Rhoda, and she had a stake in both ventures."

"That's nonsense, Eli, and you know it."

"Ya, you're right, I guess."

He guessed? Jacob wished Daed would stop talking nonsense. He was tempted to tell Daed that Rhoda had saved their lives, but he'd promised to keep that between him and her.

Eli propped his elbow on the window. "You think Samuel felt up to going to the orchard today?"

Most of the trees were a twisted, mangled wreck. "I hope not. I think we have a few days left before he'll try that. But we've got to have another meeting and come to some decisions about what to do. Once he sees the destruction, I want to give him a concrete plan and some hope."

Rhoda needed that too. She was ready to throw in the towel. All she wanted to do was wrap up her work at Kings' Orchard and go home to be with her family. He didn't blame her. Losing two businesses in one summer was too much.

Oddly enough, Landon was the voice of reason. Jacob hadn't been able to say anything that made a speck of difference in Rhoda's mind, not yet anyway. But Landon wanted to take everyone to Maine to look at a farmhouse sitting on an abandoned apple orchard, complete with several greenhouses.

Jacob pulled onto their driveway. "Eli, what do you want?"

He shrugged. "To undo what the tornado did."

Jacob drove to the doorway of the barn and stopped. "And we can, but it'll take money and at least five years to replant all the trees and have apples bearing enough fruit to be profitable again."

"That's not what I meant." Eli got out.

Jacob wished he knew what to say to Eli. And Rhoda. And Samuel. And his parents. And himself. "It is what it is, Eli." Jacob went to the horse and began removing the harness. "And I understand how you feel." Jacob woke during the night in a cold sweat. The tornado damage was enough on its own, but it'd dredged up memories he struggled to cope with. "There's really only one question, Eli: what to do from this point forward."

"You're all for this idea of Landon's, aren't you?"

Jacob led the horse into a stall and put feed in the trough. "I've looked at the figures. This plan will work if we all do our share. Otherwise, we'll lose the farm and still not have a way to make a living."

Eli took a burlap sack and began wiping the horse down. "We don't have the money to buy it."

Jacob removed the wire from a bale of straw and spread it around in the stall. "It won't be easy, but I've been working the numbers. Through the co-op we get some compensation for the damage to our place. If we take that, plus pull every cent we can from the operating funds, what each of us has put back, and what we can borrow, we can make it work. Samuel knows trees like I know numbers. If anyone can get the orchard in Maine healthy enough to produce a decent crop next year, he can. It's the only way to cover the taxes on our place and keep food on the table during the years it'll take to replant and reestablish Kings' Orchard."

Eli laid the now wet burlap sack across the wall of a stall. "If you're that sure this is the only way to get on our feet again, count me in."

"Excellent." Jacob dusted off his hands. "Five down—Landon, Leah, Daed, you, and me. Two to go."

Eli came out of the stall and latched it. "Rhoda's been clear. She's not leaving her family."

They walked toward the barn door. Leaving Pennsylvania wasn't Rhoda's only obstacle. If only he knew what the real problem was.

Eli paused. "And you really think Samuel will consider establishing Kings' Orchard elsewhere?"

"When reality sinks in, he'll know we don't have a choice. But right now my goal is to get him and Rhoda to agree to go there and look." Jacob tucked his shirt in better. "I'm going to find Rhoda now. You see how Samuel's fared today."

Jacob went into the summer kitchen. Landon had a white apron tied around his waist as he peeled another apple. He had mounds of them peeled in a gigantic bowl in front of him. Leah stood next to him, slicing apples.

"Where's Rhodes?"

Leah looked up. "Orchard, gathering apples, but I think she'd like to be left alone."

"She go on foot or horseback?" Jacob would leave her alone if she indicated she needed that.

"On foot."

He figured she'd be near where Samuel was injured. That area seemed to draw her of late. He strode in that direction until he spotted her.

She had a burlap sack in one hand, and as she picked up each apple, she seemed to speak to it before putting it in the sack. Was she talking to herself or praying?

Regardless of her many ways that he didn't understand, he loved her. "Hey, Rhodes."

She looked up and smiled the lost, sad smile she'd been wearing since the tornado came through. He trotted up to her and took the heavy sack of apples from her. "We need to talk."

"Not again, Jacob. I'm too tired."

He took her by the hand, and they meandered to a nearby fallen tree and sat. She seemed distracted as he once again shared his thoughts about going to Maine, but he continued, explaining his reasoning.

"I can't."

"Why?"

"Because it'll end badly, just like this has. I knew it would." She placed her hand over her heart. "I knew it when Samuel first asked me, before I met you."

"First off, this isn't the end. Second off, you saved my whole family. How is that a bad ending?"

She didn't answer. It'd been like this between them for days, and he didn't know how to reach in and pull out the real Rhoda. Had she picked up on Daed's attitude?

He shifted the sack of apples and released it. "The destruction and aftermath have been hard, and you're not feeling like yourself. Maybe you never will. But what's really bothering you?"

After a long pause she folded one hand inside the other. "Ever since Emma died, I see her, sort of. I hear her inside my head, and she warns me of things."

Chills ran up his spine. He'd never believed in such things before, but he knew that Rhoda didn't exaggerate or lie. "What kind of warnings?"

"A word or two usually. The day of the storm, when I was unsure if my imagination was running wild or if my intuition was telling me what was about to happen, she screamed at me, *Save them!*"

Jacob knew the world they lived in, the bodies and minds that made up who they were, was more than any person could understand. How could he look at a garbled mess of numbers and untangle it with a glance? It wasn't him, not really. It was a gift that worked whether he wanted it to or not. "I think I like your sister."

Rhoda licked her lips, keeping them drawn in as tears filled her eyes. "Ya, me too. If I'd responded sooner the day she was shot, she'd be here."

"Tell me about that day."

She did, and he asked questions as she went along.

"A random robbery." Rhoda stared at the clouds. "All those two young men wanted was what was inside a cash register drawer—the lifeless nothing of cash. Someone said afterward that it was probably to buy drugs. Emma startled them by coming in when she did, and they shot her." Rhoda stared at the sky, and he waited, unwilling to rush her. "If I'd gone with her that morning any one of the numerous times she asked, she would've been safe at home before that burglary."

"That's hindsight. Of course it's clear *now* what you should've done. If you'd had any idea that waiting until later in the day would cause her harm, you'd have been at the store when it opened. You can't blame yourself for not knowing that before it was too late."

"Ya, I can. Not only did I put her off until she struck out on her own, but after she left, I began to sense what was going to happen, and I still ignored the warning and kept tending to my garden."

"How long beforehand did you know what was going to happen?"

She explained each detail, and finally he knew what she didn't.

"Rhodes, there wasn't time for you to get there. The distance from your place to the store, whether you ran, bridled a horse, or hitchhiked, was too much. There wasn't time."

"Then why would I pick up on it if I wasn't supposed to stop it?"

"I don't know. Sometimes when I'm at the bank or in a store and people around me are talking about their accounts, I know all sorts of information about their financial life that no one else would pick up on. Why? I'm not meant to counsel them, to walk up and start giving advice. I have a bizarre gift, and it operates at the oddest times."

"I've heard her voice so much since the storm, telling me, 'It's time.'"

"Time for what?"

"I never know for sure, but I think she's saying it's time to go home."

"The words aren't connected to anything specific?"

"Not that I've been able to figure out. She said it before Rueben found a way to pressure my Daed into removing my herb garden. And she's saying it now."

"As if it's a warning of some type."

She nodded.

"But it's an unknown variable. You'll never know what it means because there isn't enough information."

"What?"

"When Samuel began talking to you about the orchard, he mentioned how many acres we had and how many trees per acre and how many apples grew per tree in a season. Every piece of information had a number or an approximation to it. But he couldn't have shared any figures with you if he hadn't known how much land we had or how many trees or how many bushels of apples a tree produced."

He stood. "It's time to clean up the mess left by the tornado. It's time to punch Rueben Glick's lights out. It's time to stop worrying over what all you'll get wrong and just live. You see into people at times. Look into yourself and finish the statement: 'It's time…'"

She stared at him. Had he sounded like a madman? Her eyes scanned the orchard before she stood. A smile crossed her face. "I think I know."

"I'd love to hear it."

"It's time to stop."

His heart pounded. That's not the answer he wanted to hear. She looked so weary, much as he had when he finally stopped trying to fix his mess of a life among the Englisch and come home.

She bent and picked up an apple from the ground. "It's time to stop worrying what Emma means." She brought the apple to her nose and smelled it. "It's time to let go of my guilt and enjoy whatever small joys the day brings. It's time to do whatever it takes to live and love and help those around me when the opportunity comes."

"Is it time to at least look at the apple orchard and farm in Maine?"

She held out her hand. "It's time."

This is what Jacob wanted, a way to build hope in all of them, however small or however much work it would take. Hope for a better tomorrow is the only way he knew how to get through today.

And once Samuel saw his orchard, he'd need that too.

FORTY-FIVE

Samuel woke, groggy, as snapshots of memories floated through his brain. Lying on a twin bed in the summer kitchen. Rhoda beside him, promising him he'd be fine. And despite the pain and anguish, he'd believed her.

He remembered Jacob carrying him to the truck and then waking up in a hospital bed. He remembered being released days later. Various memories, disconnected segments, all giving him distorted images of his life. He was weary of floating in and out of some half-conscious, drug-induced state.

Enough was enough. He wouldn't take any more pain medicine. He needed to be fully awake and alert, and he'd find a way to cope with the pain.

He tried to pry open his eyes and place his surroundings. He managed to catch a glimpse of the room he was in and saw a young woman sitting on a couch nearby, but he couldn't make out her face. His mother towered over him.

Now he remembered. He was on a bed in the living room.

Mamm smiled down at him. "That's it. Time to wake up, take your medicine, and get some nourishment."

He opened his eyes. "No more meds." In a rush he bolted upright, searching for Rhoda. Was she safe? Samuel pushed the sheet off him and sat upright. His leg was covered in bandages.

"Whoa, easy, young man."

His head swam. The tornado was gone, long gone, but he couldn't lie back down. "Where is everyone—Rhoda, Leah, Jacob, Eli?"

"Not far. Everyone is helping around here."

Relief took the edge off his panic. "What day is it?"

"You ask the same question every time you wake up." Mamm smiled. "Wednesday, September seventh. The doctor cut your pain medication in half yesterday. He said you'd be more awake today, might even remember some of what has happened since you had surgery."

"Rhoda's family?"

"They're all fine. You've spoken to her several times this week. Their house wasn't touched."

He relaxed a bit. He did remember that. But his mind was playing tricks on him, blending his dreams with reality. "And Catherine?"

His mother looked across the room. He blinked several times, trying to focus.

"Hi, Samuel."

"Catherine." Bits of conversations he'd had with his siblings returned to him. "Jacob said your family fared well."

"We're good, much better than you've been."

Samuel glanced around. Large blue tarps covered the gaping holes in the house. "Is it safe to be in here?"

Mamm passed him a bowl of soup. "Ya. Jacob and your uncle Mervin's construction crew worked while you were in the hospital and put new support beams in." She pressed her hands down her apron. "Well, I'll leave you two alone."

He ate his soup, wishing the disorientation would go away.

Catherine moved an ottoman to the side of his bed and sat on it. "I've been so worried about you."

An ache the size of the gaping hole in the house opened within him. But it wasn't for her—or them. What was it? He set the soup on an end table. "I'll be fine." Why hadn't she come to see him before his injury? "But I'm not up to talking about anything right now."

She reached for his hand. "May I come back and see you again?"

He wasn't good at telling her no unless he was angry, and he had no strength to do so now. What had happened to them, to the connection from his heart to hers? "Ya. Maybe you should wait until next week, though. If I get my way, I'll be off the pain meds by that time and able to think."

Surprisingly, she nodded. "Okay, if that's what you want. Next week, then." Catherine squeezed his hand and walked out, leaving him alone in this muddled, weird place.

His home surrounded him, but it didn't. He'd expected the sight of Catherine to stir his heart, for her presence to remind him how much he'd missed her, but he barely felt the heartache over the chasm between them. Was that a side effect of the medicines too?

If she'd been impatient about marrying him when the orchard had a few issues, she'd never understand the length of wait they'd face now.

If he was interested in her waiting.

He lay down on the bed, staring at the flapping blue tarp.

Nothing resembled the life he'd once known. Nothing.

Catherine put on her best dress, feeling as nervous as she had on her first date night with Samuel. She ironed her prayer Kapp and combed her hair, repinning it half a dozen times before scurrying out the door to hitch the horse to the carriage.

Within fifteen minutes she was pulling into Samuel's driveway. Leah was in the yard, hanging clothes on the line.

Catherine wished she didn't need to speak to her, to apologize and be met with sarcasm and smart remarks, but she went to her. "How are you holding up?"

Leah clamped a clothespin onto a damp shirt and sighed. "As well as can be expected."

Catherine kept telling herself to apologize. Even though she knew she'd been wrong, saying so didn't come easy. "I'm sorry for what I said about you to Arlan. It was wrong."

Leah shrugged. "I was wrong too, about lots of stuff."

Wow. Catherine hadn't expected her to say that. "Is Samuel inside?"

"No. He got in the pony cart and drove to the orchard early this morning.

He's been there ever since, just staring at it. Rhoda and Jacob took him some lunch awhile ago. They're probably still with him. They aren't far. The orchard is too full of debris to get a cart past the edge of it. Want me to help you find them?"

"Nee, but denki."

Catherine walked to the orchard and easily spotted the horse and cart. She kept going and soon saw Samuel with Rhoda and Jacob, all three sitting on a fallen tree. Rhoda was on one side of Samuel, Jacob on the other. They were looking at a large piece of paper, maybe a map of some kind. A batch of small magazines sat stacked beside them.

They seemed to be making serious plans. Until July, Catherine had been the only woman Samuel cared anything about. Had she been replaced?

"Samuel?"

The three of them looked up. Samuel folded the map. Rhoda and Jacob stood, greeting her before they excused themselves.

"I hope I didn't interrupt something important."

"We can get back to it later."

"You look a lot better than last week."

"Got a ways to go, but I'm stronger."

She sat beside him, absorbing the ruin. This apple orchard had never meant more to her than a way for Samuel to make a living so he could marry her. Now she missed it. Missed seeing Samuel's eyes dance when he talked about the pruning or good news concerning the yield. It'd been a part of him, perhaps more than she ever had. "I don't understand what happened to us, Samuel."

"Wish I could say I did."

How could their two years of courtship turn into something that resembled the destroyed orchard around them? "I know I was wrong, and I'd like for us to start new." She weighed each word. If she'd done that all along, they wouldn't be in this mess. Or would they? "I came to tell you that weeks ago, but, well, I left a pie for you and hoped you'd at least come see me."

He shook his head. "I don't remember a pie."

What would have happened to it? Had Rhoda ruined it, as she had everything else between Catherine and Samuel? "I left it on the cooling shelf in the windowsill of the summer kitchen. I can't imagine what could've happened to it." She fought the temptation to ask if Rhoda might have tossed it away. It'd be best to tuck that green-eyed monster out of Samuel's view until she could free herself of it. Was that even possible?

She cleared her throat. "I'm sorry, Samuel. I should've spoken to you, not just left a pie." She fumbled with her fingers, wishing he'd say something. "I…I need to know. Do you care for Rhoda?"

He turned to her, frowning. "I imagine she'll be my sister-in-law one day."

"Really?" Catherine jumped to her feet. "Is that all it is between you and her?"

When he didn't answer, her excitement faded. Samuel reached beside him and grabbed a small magazine. He flipped the pages, folded the periodical in half, and passed it to her.

"An apple farm?" She turned the book over and back again. "Where is it?"

"Maine."

She melted to her knees. Could he seriously be thinking about moving? "I love you, Samuel. We've both been through too much recently, and I think the pressure and stress has caused us some problems. Maybe that's what has torn us apart, but it doesn't have to stay that way." She took his hands into hers. "Please."

He gazed into her eyes, and it gave her hope.

"We're going to Maine as soon as I'm strong enough, hopefully in a few days."

"We?"

"Jacob, Eli, Rhoda, my Daed and hers, Landon, and Leah. Our uncle Mervin will go as a church leader, to give his approval or disapproval of the plan. And one of Rhoda's brothers will go because he's considering moving there too."

Her heart broke. If they'd stayed strong the last couple of months, he'd speak of his love and his hope for their future. But he didn't seem to have an encouraging word for her.

Samuel picked at the bandage covering his injured leg. "If we like what we see and feel it's worthy of our time, we'll try to secure a lease-purchase option on a nearby farm while aiming to buy the farmhouse and orchard out of foreclosure. Depending on what we find out and the report we give, there are four other families who may want to move with us—establish a new Amish community. If we do this and can buy the orchard, I'd have to start living there as soon as I'm well enough."

"You've decided all this since I saw you last week?"

"Landon had the information. His grandmother lives there. He got Jacob on board, and once Jacob believes in a plan, no one is more persuasive. But everything is tentative at this point."

He talked without disappointment or anger, sounding much as he would've before they parted, except sadder. She longed for some crumb of hope.

She got off her knees and sat beside him. "If you get everything you hope to out of your visit to Maine, what will happen next?"

He picked up another book and flipped the pages back and forth. "Jacob will return here and do the construction work on our house until it's done, which may not be till spring. Rhoda has a few weeks of work to do here, canning all she's been harvesting from the fallen trees, the few remaining rooted ones, and what can be salvaged from the apples on the ground. Then she and one of her brothers will join me." He moved a bit and winced. "If the orchard in Maine is salvageable, it'll take a lot of work."

"But you won't have a harvest to can from for quite some time. Why would Rhoda move up there so soon?"

"There are three huge greenhouses on the property. She'll spend all winter creating mulch for the fields and maybe growing berry plants. We're not sure if the mulch will help as much as we need it to, but an orchard left unattended for two years needs every chance it can get."

"And what about me, Samuel? Is there any room in your life for me?"

He looked down, and her heart sank. "I don't know, Catherine."

She hated that tears were running down her cheeks, but she couldn't stop them. "We should at least try, shouldn't we?"

"I'm tired of trying, and I can't even give you a good reason why. I'm sorry."

Catherine rose. That was it then. She could say little else. "I've always loved you, Samuel. And if you decide I'm worth the rough patch we've been through, I'll be here in Harvest Mills, waiting."

FORTY-SIX

Rhoda stared out the side window of the van, amazed at the scenery that surrounded them. The road they traveled wove through long sections of tall trees, past large farms with barns and silos, and through small residential towns with modest homes, most boasting well-tended vegetable gardens. The largest sections had been plowed under and mulch added in preparation for next year's crop.

It struck her as odd that many homes had a garden and that they were well manicured. Aside from her fascination with the gardens, she was most thrilled by how familiar it all felt. Different from Pennsylvania, of course, but similar enough that it felt almost like home.

And after the devastation they'd left behind, the beauty of Unity, Maine, refreshed her.

Landon kept his eyes on the road most of the time except when he glanced at Rhoda in the rearview mirror, grinning at her delight. "I knew you'd like it here."

Hail had damaged Landon's truck beyond repair, so the insurance company had covered the cost of a rental vehicle until it could be replaced. He'd paid the difference to get an enormous van, big enough to carry ten people. They were a bit scrunched, but no one minded.

Rhoda's Daed sat up front with Landon. Samuel's father and uncle had a more limited view from the row behind her, but that's where they'd wanted to sit. Her brother Steven and Leah shared a bench seat with her. And Samuel, Jacob, and Eli were in the last row.

"Look." Rhoda pointed out her window at a sign. "Maine Organic Farmers and Gardeners Association."

Landon pressed the brakes, almost coming to a crawl. "It has a motto of some sort." He peered and then chuckled. "Listen to this: 'If the world were to end tomorrow, I would still plant an apple tree today.' It's a quote by Martin Luther."

Landon picked up speed again, and they all pointed out various items of interest. The anticipation in the van was tangible.

A light rain began to fall, and Landon turned on the windshield wipers. The mist made everything sparkle, giving the scenery a mystical quality.

Her family had been able to secure only one building permit for the land that was once her fruit garden. John was building a home there, but Steven wanted more than just a lot. He'd shared with Rhoda how he longed to find a place with enough land that he could divide it for his own children—and his grandchildren—when the time came. As Rhoda looked out the window, she couldn't help but feel he could find such a place here.

"That's it." Landon pointed and then pulled the van alongside the curb in front of a tiny yellow house with light-green shutters. Blue hydrangea bushes lined the sidewalk.

As the group piled out of the van, a short, white-haired woman in slacks and a blouse came out, rushed up to Landon, and gave him a hug.

"Granny, this is Rhoda."

She raised her arms toward Rhoda, her eyes sparkling. "Landon never told me you were beautiful. Come here."

As Rhoda bent over slightly to enjoy the woman's hug, she giggled at the blush that colored Landon's cheeks.

After introductions were made all around, Granny invited them inside to use the bathroom, stretch their legs, and get a quick bite to eat. After the ten-hour drive and eating only packed lunches along the way, they were all eager for a break.

Granny's house was small but cozy. She warmed a large pan of tuna noodle casserole in a microwave oven in a matter of minutes and made them all feel like family.

Once they'd double-checked the maps and expressed their gratitude for her food and generosity, they stuffed themselves back into the van for the last leg of their journey.

A few miles past a lovely lake, they rounded a corner and saw a plot of land with straggly trees, their branches thin and brown. "This must be the place," Landon called out to the backseats.

He eased the van down a long driveway of cracked concrete to a large, rather dilapidated farmhouse. Electric wires ran to the home. "The Realtor's a friend of my granny's. He said he'd leave the place unlocked for us so we could check it out. If we're interested, I can call him, and he'll meet us here to discuss the details."

As they got out of the vehicle, Rhoda watched Samuel gaze at the barren, sickly trees. His Daed, brothers, and uncle walked with him, as did her brother Steven.

The rest of the group followed Landon into the house.

"Phew!" Leah held her nose.

Rhoda sniffed. "It does smell a bit musty, doesn't it?"

Daed tried to open a few windows, although some were stuck so tight they wouldn't budge.

They went through the front room, living room, dining room, and bedrooms. "Four fireplaces." Leah made a face. "That'd take a lot of wood and work. It does have gas heating, right?"

"A home is only as warm as the people in it." Daed grinned as Rhoda quoted the old family saying. "But there's a large propane tank sitting out back." She pointed through a dingy window. "So I'm sure there's gas heat."

Leah wrinkled her nose. "The bedrooms are tiny."

Daed looked out the bedroom window. "It gets really cold here, and small rooms are easier to heat and only meant for sleeping."

They made their way back to the kitchen, a room Rhoda had barely glanced at earlier. But this time she realized it was the largest kitchen she had ever seen in a house. Bigger than the summer kitchen! It had a cooking fireplace, built forever ago, maybe refurbished at some point, and it had an old crane for hanging pots, and two tiny brick ovens with iron doors for baking bread.

"Look at all those cabinets." Leah came up beside her. "And tons of counter space." Leah flipped the electric light switch. Nothing happened. "Yep, that's about right for an Amish home."

Rhoda ran her hands along the brick of the fireplace. She didn't know why, but she felt connected to this home.

Leah sneezed. "Like the rest of the place, it could use a good cleaning."

"That stove would have to be replaced." The rickety-looking thing couldn't possibly cook anything properly. Rhoda opened the refrigerator. It stunk. And it was electric. A gas line would have to be run, but they wouldn't need to purchase new appliances. They could move all the ones from the summer kitchen.

She could see herself working here, doing whatever she could to help the orchard come back to life and then, in time, canning the harvest.

This plan meant so much to the Kings, especially Jacob and Samuel. But she was getting ahead of herself. She'd get a vote, but the decision wasn't up to her.

She looked out the dirt-crusted window and saw the King men walking the neglected orchard. Their opinions would carry far more weight than hers. If the trees were too far gone, nothing else mattered.

But now that she'd seen this place, she wanted to nurture every bit of it back to life.

A poke in her back made her jump and turn around. Landon stood there, a wide grin on his face. "Well, Rhodes, what do you think?"

"I think you're still pushing for the same thing you've been wanting for years." She spotted her father in the doorway, his back to her. "Landon, why don't you find something more useful to do than pestering me?"

He followed her gaze. Clearly getting her hint, he corralled Leah out the door.

Rhoda joined her Daed. He put his arm around her while continuing to stare across the yard. Rhoda followed his gaze.

Oh, he knew her so well.

"Greenhouses." Four round-roofed, glass-and-wood buildings stood in the distance. It was all she could do to keep from racing to them. But she remained at her father's side.

"Ten hours isn't so far." Emotion made his voice hoarse. "And Steven will be here with you."

"And Phoebe and their little ones." She nudged his side. "Landon will come get you and bring you and Mamm here whenever you want. Might be a nice getaway for you two."

He gazed down at her, his eyes misting. "I know you're itching to go check out those greenhouses."

"I am. You want to come with me?"

"You go on. I want a minute with Steven and with Samuel's Daed. I have questions."

She gave him a kiss on the cheek and then scurried toward the enclosures in the field.

The minute she walked into the first greenhouse, her heart soared. The place smelled of earth and fertilizer. And new life, despite the season. As she strolled down the aisle between rows of plant stands covered with broken clay pots, her mind's eye visualized a thriving indoor garden filled with starter plants. Berries. Grapes. Perhaps other fruits. Even—dare she imagine it?—herbs.

"I thought I'd find you here."

She turned and saw Jacob in the doorway.

He meandered inside, looking robust and hopeful. "The orchard looks promising enough. It'll take a lot of work." He caressed her hand.

She enjoyed how secure and treasured he made her feel. "So will the house."

"They're both in better shape than what that tornado left us back home."

Rhoda freed her hand and picked up a pot that had only a slight chip. "I can't help but wonder what kind of plants once grew here."

"And what kind of plants could grow here again."

She put the pot back on the shelf and stared at it. What else might grow if they relocated here? A new Amish community full of hope and potential. Friendships. Relationships. Families.

Love.

Jacob came up behind her and put his hands on her shoulders. "Are you in?"

His soft voice chased away years of loneliness. "Are you?"

"I am. It's the answer. I know it is."

She turned to face him. "I'm not as sure as you, but my vote is yea."

He put his finger under her chin and tilted her face upward. "You won't regret it." He kissed her, and she hoped he was right.

She smiled up at him. "I'm not regretting it so far." She brushed her fingertips over his lips. "Do you know who might vote nay?"

"Not yet. I'll talk to my brothers and Daed. But I wanted to know what you thought. You still have reservations?"

She shrugged. "I'm sure it's a lack of confidence from losing two businesses so close together."

He kissed her forehead. "I'm sure of it too." He winked and headed for the entry of the greenhouse. "Let's meet where the orchard abuts the backyard in about twenty minutes, okay?"

"I'll be there."

Samuel held on to the crutches while scanning the ragged orchard. These trees were in better shape than his tornado-damaged ones, but it'd take a lot of time, attention, and care this coming year and whatever nutrient-enriched mulch Rhoda could conjure up to make them bear fruit again. Eighty acres. Sixty of it planted with apple trees.

Wow.

But he wanted to talk to Rhoda before he gave his answer. He'd seen her go into the first greenhouse earlier. If he had his guess, she was in one of the others by now, inspecting, trying to get a *feel* for whether to move to Maine.

As awkward as a man on stilts, Samuel made his way across the rutty yard. He saw a shadow inside the third greenhouse and went that way. When he entered, he saw her kneeling, looking at some old pots and feeling the soil.

"You could play in the dirt year round in a place like this."

She glanced up. "I suppose that's the sort of stuff my dreams are made of."

He went closer and leaned down to catch her eye. "And I'm ready to try whatever crazy ideas you might have for mulch."

She grinned and rose. "So I take it you found what your dreams are made of?"

At her soft laugh, something resembling the power of a tornado rattled his insides, rearranging everything he'd once known as familiar. This was what he'd come in here for—to be alone with her, to be touched by their conversation. How had he not seen it before?

How had he missed what was happening inside him?

He turned away and put some distance between them, forcing himself to ignore the ridiculous feelings sprouting like apple blossoms in spring.

She dusted the dirt off her hands. "The kitchen is quite spacious. Plenty big to host a canning business. And these greenhouses have tremendous potential."

He swallowed, feeling his heart pound with every second that passed. Jacob would stay in Pennsylvania to rebuild the family home. Ten hours away. And Samuel would be here. With Rhoda.

He cleared his throat. "Are you willing to leave your family and your home? With no guarantees of what the future might hold?"

He wanted her to say no. Make it easy to end this now. Yet he also wanted...

What? What did he want? Why was this happening to him? His brother cared for this woman. If Jacob wasn't in love with Rhoda yet, he was well on his way.

But it seemed Samuel was already there. He should've seen it, felt it, but it wasn't how he worked. He seldom knew what he thought or felt until it just was. Like falling out of love with Catherine. He hadn't understood it. He'd only been aware that he'd grown unable to tolerate her tears and demands. And that he didn't want to go to her, to patch up whatever was wrong between them.

And now that he knew he was in love with Rhoda, he didn't know how to stop himself.

She waved her hand in front of him. "Hallo?"

He lowered his eyes, trying to recall what she'd said. "Uh, ya, that's true. Your folks can come here to visit when Jacob does. Are you sure you want to do this, Rhoda?"

Her eyes stayed glued to his face, and she frowned. Recognition flittered through her eyes. Did she know? Could she feel in him what had obviously been building for weeks?

"We should be getting back." She started toward the door.

"Rhoda." Why did he call to her? What could he say?

She turned. "I...I—"

Jacob knocked the door open. "Oops." He grabbed the door. "I didn't mean to do that. Kumm. It's voting time." He held out his hand to Rhoda.

She headed for him and glanced back at Samuel. He followed them out.

A light drizzle tapped on his clothes and face. The rest of the group stood in the yard, unfazed by the weather, and they crossed the yard to join them.

Jacob held Rhoda's hand, a huge grin on his face. "Well, Rhodes? What's your vote?"

She glanced at Samuel. "I already voiced it." Every face peered at her, and Samuel saw the hopeful expectation. Even her father seemed to silently encourage her to say yes. "If you feel this strongly, Jacob, I'm in."

Samuel's Daed looked at him. "Samuel?"

Samuel glanced at Rhoda and shook his head. "I don't know."

"Look." Leah pointed across the orchard, and the group turned. There, above the scraggly trees, hung two brilliant rainbows.

Two. He'd never seen a double rainbow.

The excited murmurs from the group weighed on him. How could he say yes when he was no longer sure this move was a good idea?

Landon shielded his eyes from the mist. "That's nice. Sort of cheesy, but nice."

Samuel could tell Landon didn't understand its significance. Rhoda looked at her hand inside of Jacob's. "For the Amish, a rainbow is a reminder of God's promises to His people. It's like God Himself is trying to give us a sign of what's to come, especially as there are two." She pulled her hand from Jacob's and crossed her arms. "But I don't feel that every rainbow is God giving hope for a specific decision any more than every storm is Him rearranging people's lives. Some things are simply nature."

Uncle Mervin beamed. "This town seems very promising to me. I'll be happy to make a positive report to the church and to the other families who've expressed interest in relocating here."

Samuel sighed. They had to try, for the future of Kings' Orchard and what could be in the future. He faced Rhoda.

She nodded. "We can do this."

"Attagirl." Jacob wrapped his arms around her, lifted her up, and twirled her around. He set her feet on the ground. "This will be a great adventure. One we'll all begin and end together." He took Rhoda by the hand and tugged her toward Samuel. "Let's pray."

Rhoda came to stand beside Samuel, taking his hand in hers. He tried not to look down, to see their hands linked together. But he couldn't help it. Any more than he could help noting how well her hand fit into his.

Shaking his head, he looked at the others. Leah took her Daed's hand, and one by one each person took the hand of the one next to them. Together, they bowed their heads in silence.

Samuel closed his eyes. Could he get this orchard producing again? Moreover, could all of them begin and end this journey together, as Jacob had said?

Or would this new adventure, this seemingly God-approved adventure, be the biggest mistake Samuel could possibly make? He didn't know. All he could do for now was move forward.

And pray he didn't get in the way of what God wanted to accomplish.

DUTCH APPLE PIE

Crumb Topping
2 cups quick oats
$2/3$ cup flour
1 cup brown sugar
1 teaspoon cinnamon
$1/2$ cup melted butter (no substitutions)
1 teaspoon salt

Mix all ingredients together and set aside.

Apple Pie Filling
6 cups apples, peeled, cored, and sliced (I use a variety
    including a few Granny Smith apples for best flavor.)
1 tablespoon lemon juice
$3/4$ cup water
$3/4$ cup sugar
1 tablespoon butter (no substitutions)
2 tablespoons cornstarch
1 teaspoon cinnamon
$1/4$ teaspoon nutmeg
pinch of cloves

Preheat oven to 350°. Prepare apples and place in large bowl.
Sprinkle with lemon juice to prevent discoloration. Set aside.
    Combine water, sugar, butter, and cornstarch in a medium
saucepan. Cook until thickened. Stir in apples, cinnamon,
nutmeg, and cloves. Pour into your favorite unbaked pie shell.

Sprinkle topping over apples. Bake for about 40 minutes. Remove and let cool a bit before serving. This pie is especially scrumptious when served warm with a scoop of vanilla ice cream.

Baking tip: You may use a pie crust shield or cover the rim of the pie crust with strips of foil for the first half of baking time to create a flaky crust without overbrowning.

APPLE DUMPLINGS

2 cups all-purpose flour
2 teaspoons baking powder
1 teaspoon salt
1 tablespoon shortening
$7/8$ cup milk (or 1 cup scant)
1 tablespoon butter
$2/3$ cup brown sugar
$1^1/2$ teaspoon cinnamon
3 chopped apples

Mix flour, baking powder, and salt. Work shortening into flour mixture. Add milk. Roll dough $1/4$ inch thick. Spread soft or melted butter on dough. Cover dough with brown sugar, cinnamon, and apples.

Sauce:
1 tablespoon flour
1 cup sugar

$^1/_2$ teaspoon salt

1 cup hot water

1$^1/_2$ teaspoons cinnamon

Mix flour, sugar, and salt. Add hot water and cinnamon, and boil 3 minutes. Pour over dumplings. Bake at 375° for 35–45 minutes. Serve with milk or whipped cream.

RECIPES PROVIDED BY SHERRY GORE

Sherry Gore is the author of *An Amish Bride's Kitchen*, the editor of *Cooking and Such* magazine and *The Pinecraft Pauper*, and a contributing writer for the national edition of *The Budget*. She is a member of a Beachy Amish Mennonite church and makes her home in Sarasota, Florida, with her family.

Sherry enjoys corresponding with reader friends everywhere. She can be contacted at www.SherryGoreBooks.com or via e-mail at TasteofPinecraft@gmail.com.

Acknowledgments

To our Woodsmall family of Massachusetts

Jack and Marion Woodsmall
Thank you for your hours of time and hearts of graciousness
as I sought to understand a subject you know so well—
the tending of apple orchards.

And to your wonderful brood of grown children and spouses—
Nancy and Tony, Brenda and Todd,
Susan and Steve, John and Maura—
thank you.
You opened your hearts to us.
You made room for us in your homes.
You laid tables of feasts.
You put on your walking shoes
and showed us the land, from rolling hillsides to rocky seasides.
You hurried with us to meet trains, buses, and shuttles.
You never hesitated to spend your energy and bless our time.
You showed us our Woodsmall heritage, which is rich indeed.
Moreover, you showed us your hearts, which are richer by far.
And we'll always remember…

And to my Old Order Amish friends,
who know my main character all too well
and wish to remain anonymous—
thank you for all your help!

To everyone at WaterBrook Multnomah,
from marketing to sales to production to editorial—
you are the BEST!

Glossary

Daadi—grandfather

Daadi Haus—grandfather's house. Generally this refers to a house that is attached to or is near the main house and belongs to a grandparent. Many times the main house belonged to the grandparents when they were raising their family. The main house is usually passed down to a son, who takes over the responsibilities his parents once had. The grandparents then move into the smaller place and usually have fewer responsibilities.

Daed—dad or father (pronounced "dat")

denki—thank you

Die Botschaft—An Amish newspaper, meaning "the message"

Englisch/Englischer—a non-Amish person

gut—good

hallo—hello

Kapp—a prayer covering or cap

kumm—come

Mamm—mom or mother

Mammi—grandmother

nee—no

Ordnung—means "order," and it was once the written and unwritten rules the Amish live by. The Ordnung is now often considered the unwritten rules.

Pennsylvania Dutch—Pennsylvania German. *Dutch* in this phrase has nothing to do with the Netherlands. The original word was *Deutsch,* which means "German." The Amish speak some High German (used in church services) and Pennsylvania German (Pennsylvania Dutch), and after a certain age, they are taught English.

Plain—refers to the Amish and certain sects of Mennonites

rumschpringe—running around. The true purpose of the rumschpringe is threefold: give freedom for an Amish young person to find an Amish mate; to give extra freedoms during the young adult years so each person can decide whether to join the faith; to provide a bridge between childhood and adulthood.

ya—yes

Pennsylvania Dutch phrases used
in *A Season for Tending*

Du duh net verschteh.—You do not understand.

Bischt allrecht?—Are you all right?

Duh net schtobbe.—Do not stop.

Du rei do?—You in here?

Es iss wunderbaar gut.—It is wonderful good.

Gern gschehne.—You're welcome.

Guder Marye.—Good morning.

In paar Minudde.—In a minute.

Wie bischt du Heit?—How are you today?

---

* Glossary taken from Eugene S. Stine, *Pennsylvania German Dictionary* (Birdsboro, PA: Pennsylvania German Society, 1996), and the usage confirmed by an instructor of the Pennsylvania Dutch language.

About the Author

CINDY WOODSMALL is a *New York Times* best-selling author with ten works of fiction and one of nonfiction. Her connection with the Amish community has been featured widely in national media, including *ABC Nightline,* the front page of the *Wall Street Journal,* and *National Geographic.* A mother of three sons, two daughters-in-law, and one granddaughter, Cindy lives outside Atlanta with her husband of thirty-five years.

Also from
CINDY WOODSMALL

Also available in
a 3-in-1 volume:

The Sisters of the Quilt series

The Ada's House series

Read an excerpt from these books and more on
WaterBrookMultnomah.com!

Coming Spring 2013!

Book Two
in the
Amish Vines and Orchards Series